EMLYN WILLIAMS

For Sarah and Elinor

EMLYN WILLIAMS
THE MAKING OF A DRAMATIST

John Russell Stephens

Border Lines Series Editor
John Powell Ward

seren

seren
is the book imprint of
Poetry Wales Press Ltd
Nolton Street, Bridgend, Wales

www.seren-books.com

© John Russell Stephens, 2000
Series Afterword © John Powell Ward, 2000

ISBN 1-85411-263-5 hardback
ISBN 1-85411-264-3 paperback

A CIP record for this title is available from
the British Library

The publisher works with the financial assistance of the
Arts Council of Wales

Printed in Palatino by
The Cromwell Press, Trowbridge, Britain

Contents

List of Illustrations

1. Emlyn Williams, Oxford freshman, aged 18
2. Mary Williams, aged 20
3. Richard Williams, aged 25
4. Emlyn Williams's birthplace, 1 Jones Terrace
5. White Lion, Glanrafon, with Emlyn, his father and aunt
6. Miss Cooke
7. Emlyn Williams and Sybil Thorndike in *The Corn is Green*
8. *The Druid's Rest*, St Martin's Theatre
9. *Night Must Fall* with Kathleen Harrison, Betty Jardine, Matthew Boulton
10. Emlyn and Molly Williams at home at 5 Lincoln Street in the *Sketch*
11. 15 Pelham Crescent
12. "Love to Miss Cooke from the Williams Family, 1946"
13. Cecil Beaton's publicity still for *The Wind of Heaven* at St James' Theatre (1945), Emlyn playing Ambrose Ellis

Introduction

Number 15 Pelham Crescent, on the borders between South Kensington and Chelsea, was the home of Emlyn Williams and his family between 1937 and 1962. Elegant, white-stuccoed and substantial, it is a four-storey Regency villa built by Nash and dated about 1830. On this particular summer's evening comes the buzz of conversation from the crystal-chandeliered drawing room. Its tall windows overlook a small garden and the ample shrubbery of the Crescent that insulates the house and creates an enclave of peace from the nearby congested thoroughfare of the Fulham Road. At the top of the steps leading up from the pavement and under the pillared portico are a young man and his girlfriend, awaiting a response at the brass-knockered front door. They barely conceal their surprise as an immaculately attired butler answers and shepherds the couple into the main reception-room on the right to join for pre-dinner cocktails several of the Williamses' friends who have already arrived, among them Richard Burton and Sybil, his Welsh-born first wife. The date is sometime in the early summer of 1956, a watershed year for the British theatre, a few weeks or so after the Royal Court Theatre's premiere on 8 May of John Osborne's third play and first success, *Look Back in Anger*.

What registered more than anything else with Osborne – indeed the only detail he chose to record about the dinner-party in his autobiography *Almost a Gentleman* (1991) – was the butler. Having just walked round from the poky terraced house off the King's Road he shared with the actress Mary Ure (soon to be his second wife), Osborne must have found this manifestation of upper middle-class domestic life amusingly pretentious. Williams had already made the theatrical big-time. The prime corner-site location and quality of the house (with neighbours such as Oliver Messel and Cecil Beaton), the rich but slightly understated furnishings, expensive motorcar, children educated at Stowe, said it all.

At first glance the affinities between the two men might seem to be rather limited. While both might be described as border men, the former from the northern borderland of the Dee estuary, and the latter from the southern end of the Wales-England border at Newport, Monmouthshire, their early lives were very different. Williams was the son of a labourer-cum-publican, Welsh-speaking, and catapulted via Holywell County School to Oxford University, while Osborne, who described himself as a 'Welsh-Fulham upstart' (having a Welsh father but brought up in his mother's territory of west London), not only had no university education but was expelled 'barely literate' from school at fifteen. Yet they did share a common interest in the theatre and both served apprenticeships as actors and stage-managers before becoming playwrights. At this date they even had the same agent, Margery Vosper, Osborne being one of her riskier new recruits and Williams one of her reliable 'bread and butter' clients. They also shared a supposed sexual ambiguousness. Williams had had at least two long-term homosexual relationships before his marriage and the occasional dalliance afterwards. On Osborne's side there were suspicions, widely held among those in the theatrical 'know', that he and the openly gay actor Anthony Creighton, with whom he had formerly shared a derelict houseboat on the Thames, had been lovers; but this Osborne categorically denied.

Emlyn Williams always liked to think of himself as in the vanguard of the theatrical world and was keen to keep in touch with new developments, even if they were not always to his taste, as by all reports *Look Back in Anger* was not. His teenage son Brook, who knew Mary Ure, had persuaded him to see it rather against his better judgement. Beside Osborne's as yet single success Williams could count several major achievements, but in truth Williams's days as a playwright were already over. The ideas refused to come and he was already written out. He was of the past as Osborne was of the future. Osborne's robust outspokenness, his rage against society and its false values had no parallel in Williams. He had none of Osborne's passion nor his politics and his plays – at least on the surface – seem to fall into the conventional moulds and patterns of their period. Yet they did bring some Celtic exuberance to British drama of the 1930s and 1940s, the period of his main achievement, and even in the earliest plays, like *Vigil* (1926) and *Full Moon* (1929), the cultural tensions in his background were compounded by the pressures of his sexuality, expression of which was certainly affected by Williams's awareness of the limitations imposed by censorship.

Williams's plays seem always to be in some sense about divided personalities: the drama is in the conflict. After the obsessive psychological thriller *Night Must Fall* (1935) came Williams's most accomplished play *The Corn is Green* (1938), which was in large measure the sublimation of the tensions in his own educational experience. Drawing on that rich Welsh vein in Williams's writing which inspired some of his best work, it vied with the finest of older contemporaries such as the Scots dramatist James Bridie (1888-1951) and J.B. Priestley (1894-1984) from the north of England, whose distinctiveness also derived at least in part from their regionalism. During the final months of the war came the sensitively crafted if eccentric Welsh Messianic drama *The Wind of Heaven* (1945), then the film *The Last Days of Dolwyn* (1949), written and directed by Williams, and in 1950 the untypical thesis-drama *Accolade*, which brought a significant dimension to the writing as yet another working through of distilled autobiography. Thereafter the only piece to achieve any popular success was another tense, psychologically acute crime drama in *Someone Waiting* (1953), effectively his last play. Most of Williams's work in the 1950s turned towards performance, at first as a reader of Dickens from 1951 and then of Dylan Thomas from 1955. At the time of his meeting with Osborne he was contracted to the Shakespeare Memorial Theatre for three major roles in the summer repertory at Stratford-on-Avon.

What, it may be wondered, did Britain's new 'angry young man', creator of Jimmy Porter, the scourge of the middle-classes, who was at the cutting-edge of the post-1955 dramatic renaissance in Britain, make of his actor-dramatist host? Twice Osborne's age, Williams was an establishment figure of some distinction. Slightly under average height, distinguished in appearance (and occasionally insufferably vain), he exhibited a shock of prematurely white hair and white bushy eyebrows and a resonant voice with an accent that hinted at his Welsh origins only when raised in passion or anger. Separated as they were by education and politics, Osborne and Williams did not develop into close friends, though they moved in several of the same circles. In addition to the link via Brook Williams, they had friends and acquaintances in common such as George Devine, Noël Coward, Terence Rattigan and Laurence Olivier. There were always moments, at least in Osborne's early success, for one whose entire theatrical experience up to 1956 was, as he put it, 'below-stairs', in which he felt less than comfortable with Oxford men such as Emlyn Williams. And Williams did have that incongruous butler, a relic of a now largely superseded pre-war social world. In a nearby mews garage – ready for the family drive down to the Berkshire farmhouse for weekend relaxation in tweeds and open-necked shirts – lurked the Williamses' Rolls-Royce, the kind of car beloved of duchesses and the like, but despised by Osborne for choking up Sloane Square on first-nights at the Royal Court. Osborne was then relatively impecunious (though soon to become what he termed 'preposterously rich'), while Williams could properly be described as an extremely wealthy man, his income secured not just by his work in the theatre but, since the mid 1930s, by bullet-proof shares in all the right public companies. In short, he represented those values encapsulated in an older culture that iconoclasts like Osborne dismissed as outmoded and irrelevant.

Except for a fairly brief appearance in a triple bill at the Arts Theatre in 1961 (followed by a short run at the Criterion) featuring three one-act plays – *Lunch Hour* (John Mortimer), *The Form* (N. F. Simpson) and *A Slight Ache* (Pinter) – Williams had no truck with the New Wave drama, the regenerative movement which swept so forcefully over British theatre after 1955-6. It was so different from his usual mode but he enjoyed the challenge, even though he was not alone in confessing himself bewildered by Pinteresque dialogue.

Yet, if Williams's playwriting career was effectively over before then – neither of the late plays, *Beth* (Apollo, 1958) and the rewritten version as *Cuckoo* (Guildford, 1986), merits even a footnote in the theatrical history of the period – there was not merely past reputation to reflect on but accomplishment and celebrity still to come in other fields. Osborne bravely challenged the taboo against homosexuality as a dramatic theme in *A Patriot for Me* (Royal Court, private club performance, 1965), yet Williams also stuck his head above the parapet and wrote with a fair degree of frankness about homosexuality and bisexuality in his autobiography in 1961. But for censorship, he might have been more articulate on the subject in the plays. His disclosure in *George* of his romantic male friendships at Oxford nearly forty years earlier was surprisingly revealing. In the late 1950s and early 1960s homosexuality was almost never discussed openly, though there were many – particularly in the world of the arts, theatre and film, including a number of Williams's closest friends – who were gay or bisexual. Understandably in a period when homosexuality was still illegal, few if any had made their orientation apparent to any outside their own close circles.

Stylistically much influenced by Dylan Thomas, whose writings helped put Williams back in touch with the early childhood he idealised in Flintshire, *George: an early autobiography* is one of the best examples of the genre published last century. Lucid, illuminating and imbued with a real sense of presence of the subject, it was compared by his publisher Hamish Hamilton with the foremost autobiographies of childhood, including L.E. Jones's *Victorian Childhood* and Laurie Lee's *Cider with Rosie*, and coupled with the poetic quality of Dylan Thomas (though 'too individual to be influenced by any of them') (L1/1). An immediate success in Britain, it rapidly achieved similar status in the USA, where its publishers Random House advised Molly Williams to buy herself a mink coat on the proceeds of an anticipated minimum sale of fifty thousand copies. This followed its unexpected selection as 'Book of the Month' in a country where autobiography – still less non-American autobiography – tended to get short shrift. On both sides of the Atlantic its appeal lay in its celebration of the glory and the dream of childhood and youth. But it is clear that its novelistic qualities sometimes take precedence over autobiographical truth. Daniel Owen – Williams's Flintshire compatriot and Wales's only significant nineteenth-century novelist – in *Rhys Lewis* (1885) has his eponymous hero exclaim at the point where he begins his life-story as a chapel minister:

> Rhys, what have you got to say for yourself? Remember to tell the truth [*Rhys, beth a ddywedi amdanat dy hun? Cofia ddweud y gwir*],

but he does not always do so. Nor does Williams, who was not above manipulating events or re-writing them to suit his agenda. To some extent this is in the nature of autobiography, but Williams's writing displays distortions or omissions sufficient to cast at least some doubt on the candour with which some larger issues are presented or addressed.

It is not hard to find specific discrepancies in the narrative; and it may be that in a more general sense too there is as much fiction and imaginative dramatisation in it as there is truth. In this respect Williams retains and refines the inventiveness of the character of Tommos in *The Druid's Rest* (1944), who represents his own some-times overactive childhood imagination. Apart from those matters that are verifiable by reference to extant correspondence (which sometimes of course has a strategy of its own) or external events, distinguishing between truth and fiction can sometimes range from difficult to impossible. This is perhaps most the case in the second autobiographical volume, *Emlyn: an early autobiography 1927-1935* (Bodley Head), published in September 1973. Williams took some persuading before agreeing to write it, in fear that after the triumph of *George* he could do nothing as good, and that it would simply degenerate into theatrical reminiscence.

Admittedly the sequel is inferior, but if the limpid lyricism of *George* is fled there are some compensations in terms of candour and the wisdom of experience. It also forced him into direct confronta-tion with his homosexuality. Some of the material for this he began assembling in 1968-9, and a few of the detailed memories of Bill Cronin-Wilson were recorded in a nostalgia mood – 'just a wave of affection' (L2/16) – directly after Williams had been to see *The Boys in the Band*, one of the first examples of gay drama to be staged in London after theatrical censorship was abolished in September 1968. Miss Cooke had died in 1964, and when Molly died in 1970 Williams had the chance to write his life in relative freedom without fear of upset or shock at some of the content. Up to a point he seems to do so, and his public acknowledgement of his sexuality was certainly brave for the time: a year before David Bowie's disclosure in *Melody Maker* in 1974 of a bisexual 'phase' became something of a *cause de scandale*. Yet there is also an element of self-censorship in

Williams's sexual history, and the presentation is occasionally disingenuous. The *TLS* (9 November 1973) was not unfair in suggesting that Williams had missed the 'opportunity to penetrate deeper into his own psyche' by presenting the conflict for him between his male lover (Fess) and his future wife (Molly O'Shann) through 'a descriptive technique more suited to romantic novels'. At any rate, it is almost certainly an incomplete narrative in this area, and it would be naïve to believe that Williams's complexly ambivalent sexual life was not subject to as much, if not more, shaping and re-ordering as some other elements in the life. A third autobiographical volume, not begun until the 1980s, exists only in a few fragments.

What Williams lacked in the psychological analysis of his own sexuality he tended to apply in other directions, to the psychoses of homicide and especially the sexual element involved, which fascinated him beyond all other interests outside the theatre. His visit to Hanover in 1931 in search of sites identified with a notorious serial killer was a prelude not only to the attempt at psychological drama in *Night Must Fall*, but to the way in which, for a period in 1966-7, every waking hour was filled with study of the Moors murderers Ian Brady and Myra Hindley, his account of whose serial crimes against children was published as *Beyond Belief: a chronicle of murder and its detection* (1967). Williams's immediate common ground with Brady was in the addiction to films, particularly those to do with crime, but there was no doubt too that the sexual constituents in Brady's and Hindley's relationship and in the crime itself engrossed him. In echo of his earlier excursion to Germany, Williams was chauffeured round the Brady-Hindley sites in the Pennines by his younger son Brook. His preparation and research was meticulous, even obsessive, an element which some of his friends and even family (Molly Williams appears to have threatened to leave him if he persisted in the venture) found really quite disturbing, as if in some hideous way Williams was, in searching out the origins of the evil, turning into an apologist for one of the most appalling crimes of the century. Somewhat controversially he argued that Brady's depravity was attributable to some defect in his genetic code. Commenting on Williams's constant presence in court throughout the trial at Chester Assizes in April - May 1966, Richard Burton could not disguise his incredulity:

Can your compassion extend to those monsters? I wonder about
it. I try to be calm and dispassionate but I'm afraid that given the
opportunity I would kill them with my bare hands.

(A8 14 May 1966)

Later, Williams's old friend Glen Byam Shaw took a larger perspective and concluded that it was

a terrible experience to read that book ... but an experience that
is 100% worthwhile because it teaches about life and human
beings (A8 9 July 1968).

Part documentary, part fictionalised, part surmise, part deduc-
tion, and dramatised where necessary in authentic Glaswegian and
Mancunian dialect, *Beyond Belief* is for all its sordidness a forceful, if
painful, narrative. It still retains its power to shock because it is so
carefully detailed, so involved with the minutiae of ordinary life and
the thinness of the barrier between it and the abyss: the stock-
control clerk and the typist become serial child-killers. For the *TLS*
reviewer there was the recognition that *Beyond Belief* was instructive
as well as an 'unsavoury exercise': that the real lesson of the book
was that

the peculiar horror of the Moors murders [was] due to our
abomination of the uninhibited expression of evil impulses
which we would recognize latent in ourselves, had we not been
browbeaten into thinking evil old-fashioned (8 June 1967).

Unlike the case of Dr Crippen – which has a kind of 'classic' status
in the annals of poisoners and which in late life also intrigued
Williams enough for him to publish a fictionalised account as *Dr
Crippen's Diary: an invention* (1987) – the Moors Murders still raises
more than thirty years after the crimes very powerful emotions and
passions because of the youth of the victims and the brutal sexual
torture to which they were subjected. Williams's analytical account
in *Beyond Belief* was a deeply serious exercise, even though perhaps
on occasion the dividing line between explanation and defence was
over-stepped. Indeed, Williams himself contacted Hindley in person
by writing to her in prison, but her reply is under embargo at the
National Library of Wales until 1 January 2017 (along with some

police photographs that he managed to obtain). Being responsible for the most detailed and evocative investigation into the psychology of two of the most pernicious killers of modern times is an epitaph that Williams might well have relished over and above his reputation in what he recognised as the ephemeral world of the theatre, certainly that of the actor.

Much of Williams's career was shadowed by the nagging suspicion that he might have been a greater writer than he was. At Dunedin, New Zealand, during an Antipodean tour in the late 1950s with his public readings of Dickens and Dylan Thomas, Williams was asked at a reception why he was not taken more seriously in critical writing on British drama. Put on the spot in this way he could reply only 'feebly' that it was probably because he was an actor as well (A8 17 March 1958). This was hardly the case; nor was it because he was Welsh and not English. After the Second World War and *The Wind of Heaven* expectations were still high; but the great play never came.

To the end of his life Williams was perfectly well aware of his failure to match others' expectations. Perhaps indeed he did not match his own, since in addition to tinkering late in life with long-completed scripts like *Night Must Fall*, there are examples in Williams's career of substantial rewriting over a number of years at an earlier period, as with *Port Said*, *Spring*, *1600* and *Beth*. He harboured a distinct sense that he could and should have done better. Yet perhaps the key limiting factor was not that Williams essentially wrote only what he thought he could sell to the commercial theatre, but that he was so deeply committed to the notion – passionately urged by his school-teacher mentor Sarah Grace Cooke – that a play should have no agendum other than a story to tell. In the manner of Victorian and Edwardian popular drama, plays should be fully crafted with a beginning, a middle and an end. Speaking to the Garrick Club less than six months before his death, Williams confessed that

> mostly, for me, it's been a series of – I have to face the deplorable fact – series of <u>well-made plays</u>' (K1/15).

This only confirmed what Williams had always accepted about his own limitations. To an interviewer for the *Sunday Express* (27 Sept 1953) he explained,

> I don't want to write serious plays ... if by 'serious' they mean plays which are supposed to put the world to right. I can't, anyway – I've never known what's wrong with it. I just enjoy telling a story. If I can move or excite an audience, or make them laugh – then I'm happy.

Williams was then only forty-eight years of age, and there was no suggestion of his dramatic stagnation. But that was essentially the case, though he went on acting and writing at intervals for the next thirty years (including a novel, *Headlong*, admittedly not very successful, published at age seventy-five, and a new play at nearly eighty-one) until his death in London from cancer in his flat at 123 Dovehouse Street, South Kensington, in September 1987.

From the perspective of the beginning of the twenty-first century, the position has not changed and no posthumous reappraisal is likely to uncover hidden genius. The *Collected Plays* (1961) – containing only the four plays written and performed between 1935 and 1940 – despite the intentions of Williams's publisher William Heinemann, never proceeded beyond the first volume owing to weak sales. Today, although the plays still retain a foothold in the amateur theatre and are still in print individually with Samuel French, the unfriendly responses to recent professional revivals, especially of *Night Must Fall* (1986, 1996), bear out the anachronistic quality of the writing: their status as dramas of their age rather than of all time.

Even the best of the plays is open to this criticism. *The Corn is Green*, if it works nowadays, tends to do so because it invokes the subliminal rags to riches myth and indeed it is the only play of Williams's to have been staged with reasonable, though by no means unequivocal, success in London in the last two decades of the last century. Unfortunately recent revivals have badly miscast the central figure of Miss Moffat – Deborah Kerr at the Old Vic revival for Williams's eightieth birthday and Patricia Routledge at Greenwich in 1991 – and in both cases reviewers also made accusations of clumsy stagecraft, creaking seams, sentimental melodrama and romanticised naturalism.

Perhaps Williams is too conventionally naturalistic to enjoy the present rank of some other leading 1930s contemporaries. Noël Coward's Wildean comedies of manners still have regularly successful exposure on the London stage, as has J.B. Priestley (who always denied he was a naturalist), particularly with *An Inspector Calls* (1945), which plays on naturalism only to reveal another reality. Having had a steady stage history in the amateur theatre, it was rediscovered in 1990s as ripe for Expressionist treatment in Stephen Daldry's remarkably successful, if controversial, revivals at the National Theatre and elsewhere. That a similar rebirth might overtake any of Williams's plays seems unlikely: his fate seems to be to be remembered principally in the theatre as a actor. Yet if Williams's plays are never of the very first order, they have a continuing interest both in themselves and because they are located in a life which in its broad sweep inheres the quality of myth. Its conflicting tensions, as conveyed through the autobiography and the parallel narrative of the letters, sometimes have an interest that shares at least equal billing with the works themselves. There is a strong sense in which Emlyn Williams writes his life through drama – not just in *The Corn is Green* – and there is at times as much of the life in the plays as in the dramatised scenes created for *George* and *Emlyn*. He straddles several significant boundaries: geographical, linguistic, cultural, class, sexual and professional. This attempt to explore such borderlines – from childhood to the early 1950s – focuses on the paradox implicit in a Welsh-speaking border Welshman who spent most of his life in England (including his entire professional career as actor and playwright) writing and performing in a foreign tongue.

One: Flintshire Childhood and Adolescence

Quicksands, shifting sandbanks and unpredictable tidal races make the Dee estuary a treacherous stretch of water. Milton's friend Edward King, the subject of his elegy *Lycidas*, drowned here in a shipwreck in 1637, and Mary, the heroine of Charles Kingsley's poem 'The Sands of the Dee', was lost in its 'cruel crawling foam'. Navigation is difficult and it was a melancholy graveyard for shipping even until recent times. From the Welsh side at low tide the exposed estuarial mudflats and sandbanks have a bleak beauty as fore and middle ground to the skyline occupied by the essentially featureless coastline of the Wirral peninsula. Nowadays, on the far north side of the peninsula the tower blocks of Birkenhead can be made out and, at greater distance on the opposite bank of the Mersey, the city of Liverpool.

To look across the estuary from the hills behind Ffynnongroyw, mid-way down the estuary, where his father was brought up, over the sands of Mostyn and Salisbury banks, is to appreciate that while topographically nothing has changed since Emlyn Williams's day, the distant view registers huge social and economic transformations. Not least, high-rise office and housing blocks have replaced the tall narrow red and black funnels of the Cunard trans-Atlantic steamers that once crowded the Mersey landing-stages and river. Perhaps on the *Lucania* (winner of the coveted Blue Riband for the fastest crossing between Liverpool and New York in 1893), but certainly on the *Britannic* and in the early days on more mundane ships which took him to Africa and South America, his father Richard worked until his late-twenties, generally shovelling coal in the searing heat below decks as a stoker. By contrast, his son was to sail in lavish comfort to New York as a first-class passenger, first on the *Carmania* and then on even larger and grander vessels like the *Berengaria* and *Majestic*, which conveyed him to increasing fame and fortune as an actor and playwright in North America.

The dull coastal plain on the left bank of the Dee as it flows seaward was, in Williams's childhood, much more industrialised than it is now. The novelist Emyr Humphreys (a more recent native of the area) labels Flintshire one of 'the four corners of Wales' (*A Toy Epic*), but it has perhaps always been the least glamorous of them. It used to possess considerable mineral resources, especially in coal and in lead (the extraction of which dates as far back as Roman times). At the turn of the century there was extensive coal mining at Point of Ayr and around Flint as well as iron works at Mostyn and a huge smelting complex at Bagillt, where lead from the whole of North Wales and adjoining regions ended up for processing. These industries, followed by the massive works at Shotton, were inscribed into an altogether darker and smokier landscape. From the narrow coastal margin occupied then as now by the road and the Euston-Holyhead railway-line the land rises abruptly, at first to no great height at about 130 metres, but elevated enough to see on a clear day the outline of Blackpool Tower thirty-six miles away. Behind it to the west, beyond the ridge where the remnants of the ancient borderline and earthwork of Offa's Dyke are occasionally visible, is a very different landscape. Halkyn Mountain belies its name, but together with the neighbouring Clwydian Hills it separates the estuary land of the border country from Denbighshire and the Vale of Clwyd, while further to the west lies upland Wales proper, extending to the grander mountains of Snowdonia.

Small though it is – smallest of the old counties of Wales apart from Radnor, another borderland – Flintshire contains two contrasting topographical and cultural landscapes: a hill country still rooted in the language and traditions of Wales's heartland and a coastal strip blending seamlessly into the more rural tracts of the Cheshire plain, a natural gateway into England. In Williams's time the beginnings were already apparent of the widening cultural and linguistic differences that formed part of his own experience. As borderland, Flintshire brought Welshness and Englishness into tension.

Writing the first volume of his autobiography, Williams knew something of his mother's origins in the hill country above Mold but confessed to little knowledge of his father's forebears. This was not surprising, as his father had had no contact with the rest of his 'curious family' (A1 2 Jan 1925) after they decamped without him to Lancashire in the 1870s. In fact, as Williams later discovered (mainly through the genealogical researches of his nephew David Emlyn Williams), his paternal ancestors were also firmly border people from the Flintshire hills, farming stock from Cilcain, near Mold, where the family is traceable in the records of the hammer-beam roofed church at least back to the 1690s. Further back a connection was proved, somewhat distantly through marriage, to Thomas Pennant, the eighteenth-century traveller and author of *A Tour in Wales*, to whom there is a memorial in the church at Whitford, a village Williams came to know well on his daily journeys to and from school at Holywell. The family however had come down in the world since Williams's great-grandfather Richard farmed eighty-eight acres at Cilcain and had the job of Overseer of the Poor within the parish. His son Robert Williams (1848-1907), Williams's grandfather, though born at Gors Farm, became a collier in Ffynnongroyw, where he developed a somewhat lawless reputation through an addiction to fighting and poaching. On his father's mother's side the large Griffith family could be traced back much further west to Llanrwst, the market town in the middle reaches of the Conwy valley, which Williams always considered an important part of his ancestry.

Like many families in north Wales, Emlyn Williams's family also had many connections through emigration in search of employment with Liverpool, Lancashire and elsewhere, but in his immediate history on both sides the links were exclusively with Flintshire. His parents were born within a year of each other and only fifteen miles apart. The birthplace of Richard Williams (1870-1943), Ffynnongroyw, was a grimy and occasionally unruly collier community just to the north of Mostyn. He was brought up at 1 Denbigh Row, a low-ceilinged terraced cottage on the main street backing on to the distant sea, by his paternal grandmother Catherine Griffith after his parents abandoned him on their sudden departure to Thatto Heath, near St Helens. Their escape over the border was occasioned (so it was alleged) by his father's having taken a pot shot at a Ffynnongroyw policeman or, according to other accounts, a gamekeeper. Emlyn Williams's mother Mary (1869-1944), youngest of the three children of Job and Elinor Williams, also born into a mining community, came from the hill village of Treuddyn, about halfway between Mold and Wrexham.

Richard Williams quarrelled with, or may have been ill-treated by, his grandparents and ran away from school in 1882 at the age of twelve to take a job as stoker on ships out of Liverpool. Only a year or so later, at fourteen years of age, Mary Williams left Flintshire to enter domestic service as a tweenie with a stockbroker's family in the Walton district of the same city. Liverpool, a magnet for wave upon wave of North Walians migrating eastwards, also attracted Mary Williams's brother's family, who settled respectably in Bootle and were later to provide their favourite nephew with a bed overnight and valuable opportunities for visits to theatres and museums. At Bootle's Trinity Road Wesleyan Chapel, where Mary's brother Jabez was a deacon, there was a well-established Welsh community, vigorously intent on preserving the religious and social traditions of home. Here, sometime in the summer of 1889, Richard Williams met his future wife. Though he spent long periods at sea, Richard proved an assiduous admirer. He was also good at his job: his Certificate of Discharge from the steamship *Britannic* (7 September 1894) after an eight-week long trans-Atlantic engagement bears 'VG' [Very Good] character stamps for both conduct and ability. Within three months, on 3 December 1894, he and Mary Williams (whom he always called 'Poll') were married at Trinity Road. On the marriage certificate Richard is rather grandly described as a 'Mariner'. He retained his job at sea and the pair commenced their somewhat fraught conjugal life at 39 Elwy Street, Toxteth Park, a cramped two-up-two-down terraced cottage whose only virtue was its convenient location on a direct tram-route to the docks.

With dense close-cropped hair and a moustache that grew more luxuriant as he got older, Richard Williams (except by his wife always known as 'Dic', the Welsh form of the diminutive) looked the tough and capable man he was. Among the several attributes he shared with his father was hard drinking, which confirmed his reputation as one of the lads. Only too aware from experience of many a spoilt dinner of Richard's fondness for alcohol, his wife was appalled at his passionate advocacy of their eventually running a public-house together back home in Wales. But following the death in 1900 of their first-born infant son in Liverpool, and as a first step to the realisation of Richard's dream, the couple returned to Deeside and a small cottage at Glasdir, overlooking Richard's birthplace of Ffynnongroyw. Through an uncle he found employment again as a stoker, land-based, at Point of Ayr colliery. By late spring 1901 Mary was pregnant again with their second child, but tragically Sarah Blodwen died within seven weeks of birth on 6 May 1902. Sometime within the following twelve months the couple moved half a mile further inland into the hills that rise steeply off the plain, still within easy sight of the sea, to the small settlement of Rhewl Fawr.

Little more than a string of cottages and barely distinguishable from the larger village of Pen-y-ffordd (now usually given as Williams's birthplace), Rhewl Fawr, part of the rural district of Llanasa, is shown as place of birth on the certificate registering Emlyn Williams's arrival on 26 November 1905 at 1 Jones Terrace. Like each of its neighbours, the four-roomed cottage at the end of the terrace was elevated from the road by a few steps; and in what was originally the tiny front parlour the Williamses contrived to run a greengrocer's shop. Evidently it was no great success and Richard Williams had no pretensions to the small businessman. For the civil record he appears under father's occupation on his son's birth certificate simply as 'General Labourer'. His eldest child's first name was chosen in honour of the future king, with Emlyn as an after-thought to give him something distinctively Welsh. Presently, at the newly opened Gwynfa Methodist Chapel (dated 1905), some hundred metres up the road on the opposite side, George Emlyn Williams headed the baptism register as first candidate.

Less than three months later the family was on the move again when Richard Williams finally achieved his long-term ambition and obtained the licence to run the White Lion, a 'free house' in the neighbouring village of Glanrafon. This was to be their home for the next nine and a half years. Glanrafon (shown on the modern Ordnance Survey map as Glan-yr-afon) lies a little over a mile inland of Rhewl Fawr, in a slight depression about one hundred metres above sea level, on the unclassified road to Llanasa. The White Lion was known locally as Pen-y-Maes and when the new landlord, proudly displaying the name Richard Williams on a large signboard above the entrance, took over in February 1906 he became known inevitably as 'Dic Pen-y-Maes'. Nowadays still licensed as a public-house and trading under its English name, it bears a plaque recording the association with Flintshire's famous son, who in his eighties became a Freeman of the Borough of Delyn. The pub stands apart from the village on the left of the road from Rhewl Fawr, near the top of the incline leading down into Glanrafon and the cross-roads. Changes have inevitably taken place (fairly considerable ones at the elevation fronting the village), but viewed from the side and rear its character has altered relatively little since the turn of the last century. Apart from the replacement of the original sashes with casements squashed tightly under the low eaves, it is in essentials the squat whitewashed homestead in which Williams spent his formative years.

Aside from the addition of a few modern houses grouped mainly around the cross-roads, Glanrafon is also largely unchanged nearly one hundred years later, and still retains the pleasing congruities of a typical estate village. Fourteen solidly built stone cottages once exclusively reserved for workers on the adjoining Gyrn estate still line the right-hand side of the road. Opposite is the old blacksmith's shop and the parallel-running Afon Garth (stream more than river), the proximity of which gives the village its name, which in English means 'by the side of the river'. At the cross-roads is a secondary entrance to the wooded estate of Gyrn Castle, then owned by Sir Percy Elly Bates, fourth baronet. Solid English gentry, the Bates family were not in year-round occupation as they had another established seat in Cheshire, but they were always in residence at least during the shooting season. Gaitered and moustachioed, Sir Percy (for whom as a small boy Williams once worked as a singularly unsuccessful beater) was a part model for Squire Treverby in *The Corn is Green*. Glanrafon's size afforded its inhabitants no taste of the kinds of activities larger villages enjoyed. There was neither chapel nor church within its boundaries and consequently, since they were almost inseparable from religion, no local institutions such as an eisteddfod to encourage inter-community rivalry or a branch of the temperance movement's vigorous social arm, the ubiquitous Band of Hope, which had cells in most villages and towns. This lack of organised social opportunity reinforced Williams's sense of his Glanrafon childhood as insulated from the outside world.

In this pastoral, undramatic, softly contoured upland territory Williams spent his early childhood. Its sheep-farming communities were a world away from the industrialised coastal plain a few miles below, to which he was to migrate as he approached adolescence. The upper fields at the rim of this 'warm bowl of peace that was Glanrafon' (G 24) gave a prospect of the vast expanse of the Cheshire plain. Nonetheless the sea was not far away. The lane over the hill towards Rhewl Fawr and on down to Ffynnongroyw and Mostyn afforded several glimpses across the estuary to the Wirral and Merseyside: there, his father insisted, lay 'another country, where Welsh was not spoken and the public-houses were open on Sundays'. Except for members of the local squirearchy, the village, 'humble, godly and isolated', spoke exclusively Welsh (the language it was understood that God spoke in the Bible). Even today few tourists tend to penetrate this area – they are mostly attracted to the northern coastal strip or further west – and pre-1914 Glanrafon was even more successful at generating a sense of apartness from the rest of the world. But although there was no post office and hence no telephone, it was not isolated since neighbouring communities were relatively accessible on foot through the lanes or fields. The nearest mail office, little more than a mile away, overlooked the village green at Llanasa, a spruce but rather stuffy village which retained a pontificatory air owing to the presence of its stately fifteenth-century parish church. The largest town within fairly easy reach was Prestatyn on the north coast, which at the turn of the century was a genteel resort for Edwardian visitors. It was the family's usual destination when shopping for larger items beyond everyday necessities that could be obtained over the hill in the few shops at Ffynnongroyw.

In the still innocent pre-war period, Glanrafon and its immediate surroundings was a rural backwater. In the quiet lanes strangers were almost never encountered and any form of motorised vehicle was greeted, especially by children, with intense curiosity. Until he went to secondary school almost all of Williams's travel was within a radius of no more than a few miles, mostly on foot, or occasionally in the cart that Richard Williams used to fetch beer supplies from Mostyn. Being chapel-goers, the family's spiritual home was Capel y Groes (a particularly severe example of late-nineteenth-century chapel architecture), about half way along the Glanrafon to Llanasa road. He and his mother (less often accompanied by his father) invariably walked there every Sunday. On weekdays Williams's first regular route was in a contrary direction via Gwespyr, through the fields and lanes, to the convent run by Benedictine nuns at Talacre, where he received his earliest formal education from the age of four. Later he attended for a short time the tin-shack schoolroom at Gwespyr (not mentioned in *George*) before transferring in 1914, when he was nearly nine, to the newly commissioned council school he described as 'bigger, more intimidating' (G 67) in the village of Picton. His horizons being essentially contracted to his immediate area made those occasional summer excursions to the beach at Llannerch-y-môr (adjacent to the lead works) or to the more health-ful air of the open sands at the tip of the Dee estuary in sight of the lighthouse at Point of Ayr, exhilarating high-spots in his childhood remembrance.

As with Dylan Thomas, with whose writings he later developed such an affinity and promoted in professional readings, Williams's childhood at Glanrafon was, in his recollection, almost always summer. Perhaps it was easy to romanticise: the autobiography conveys an impression of a life young and easy in the ferny coun-tryside. What is less evident is his sometimes despairing loneliness. Companions of his own age were few. His brothers Job and Tom, respectively three and seven years his junior, were on the whole too young to play with. There were some village children with whom he had contact in the fields or by the stream, but his relationship was never familiar enough to be invited into their homes. Most of those of school age in Glanrafon went to Llanasa, not Talacre. In one of the unused notes for *George* he describes himself as a

> [c]ompletely unnoticed little boy – completely alone ... – no friends at <u>all</u> (L1/1).

He took refuge in the interior life. What he fantasised about and craved more than anything else was an elder brother who would be his confidant and guardian. Hence his astonishment at discovery, on the authority of the family Bible, of Jabez (named after his mother's brother), born in Liverpool in September 1899, who died at the age of seven months. The sense that he had been deprived, cheated even, of the protection, companionship and opportunity for hero-worship that an elder brother would have provided goes some way to explaining Williams's patterns of early sexual behaviour.

By nature he was a solemn-faced, bookish and solitary child. In the absence of an elder brother his closest confidante was thirteen-year-old Annie Roberts from Rhewl Fawr, where she lived with her mother and her mother's soldier lover. She came to the household as a weekday live-in servant in 1908 and was soon cast in the role of Williams's 'mother-sister' (G 27). Mary Williams had no natural instinct for caressing and her signs of maternal affection grew ever fewer as she struggled to manage her often moody, sometimes drunken, husband and cope with the demands of the public-house.

As a mother substitute, Annie (whose real name was probably Agnes) was an important formative influence on Williams. So dependent was he that he dreaded her absence on Sundays, when she went home to Rhewl Fawr. He begged her not to allow Sundays to come. There were aspects of his life that he could not discuss even with Annie, such as his coveting of a doll belonging to one of his occasional companions; but in general he could talk with her on equal terms, shorn of the formality that still exists in the linguistic idiosyncrasy which Welsh preserves along with French: the distinction between the second singular and second plural personal pronouns (*ti* and *chwi*). Just like other parents, the Williamses, who at this stage within the confines of family spoke solely in the Welsh language, expected to be addressed with the more respectful *chwi* form of the verb. Between Annie and Williams their sibling-like equality was signalled by use of the *ti* form, which was more suitable to the insistent questionings of a small boy. Annie did her best to satisfy him with her limited supply of information; and what she lacked in knowledge and comprehension she made up for in her willingness to listen. Their intimacy lasted six years until Annie was a shapely nineteen-year-old, when an intoxicated Richard Williams apparently made a pass at her and she left soon afterwards in high dudgeon to work for an English family in Prestatyn.

Williams's environment at Glanrafon was almost exclusively

Welsh but in school at Talacre Convent he made his first contact with another 'consecutively spoken' (G 31) language. In his case, until about the age of eight, it was not so much the limited and stilted English uttered by the Benedictines to their charges but the French exchanged between themselves that was the only language other than Welsh which he heard in daily use. At this early period, apart from odd snatches overheard from customers in the bar of the White Lion or heavily accented expressions picked up from the nuns, English (which he assimilated only slowly over several years) tended to remain at a distance. English at school was a formidable challenge and also mysterious and intriguing. It was a language he learned first to write rather than speak by being required at Talacre to copy out in his neatest copperplate handwriting English proverbs, the meanings of which he could only guess.

Welsh was the language of the home and inevitably of the chapel. The unique sound of a hymn-singing chapel congregation in full voice or the *hwyl* of a preacher in full flight has the power to move. But for Williams, sitting stiffly in itchy knickerbocker suit and celluloid collar, repeatedly exposed to this Sunday onslaught in Groes Chapel's claustrophobic, unyielding, perpendicular-back pews, it had unexpectedly negative effects on his consciousness. He came to experience not so much the grandeur of his native language but the ordinariness: a disenchantment that was bound up with Williams's experience of Sunday. In Wales the Sabbath had a special oppressiveness, always more marked than in England, and there is no doubt that from a very early age the day was a trial to him. The boredom, loneliness and induced introspectiveness never fully left him either at Oxford or even in later life, when there was no expectation or desire to undergo the rigours of chapel attendance.

In common with other communities in Wales at the turn of the last century (and for that matter much later) Glanrafon came to a halt on Sundays. Normal life lapsed into a catatonic trance: no noise, no play, no laughter and (except for the thirsty ones who sometimes knocked nervously on the back door) no customers at the normally animated bar of the White Lion. The single recreation was reading, but only of the 'improving' kind; and the day was punctuated by meals and chapel regime. Chapel-going conferred respectability on a publican's wife and subconsciously this was how Williams viewed it as well. But afternoon Sunday School, the return home for tea, followed by attendance at evening service (which for Williams meant the additional ordeal of the sermon) was a dreary duty. What might have been magnificently theatrical, vibrant and engaging was nothing like and the linguistic grandeur of the hymns held no significance because it never connected for him with spiritual meaning. In chapel, Welsh as a pattern of sound and ultimately as a language lost its magic for a boy who learned to cope with sermons by retreating from the rhetoric into his own private thoughts. Welsh was Williams's first language – hardly could it be otherwise in this environment – and English was the foreign tongue; but as he discovered it was the latter which helped him defend and express the fragile inner world of the self.

Books were few in the Williams family, although of course Williams was familiar with the language of the household's *Beibl*, out of which he learned his verses for presentation at chapel services, his first experience of public performance. Participation in the service was expected from the Sunday School children and Williams complied without enthusiasm. Yet whatever it lacked as spiritual experience it was a first step in confidence-building, an opportunity for which Williams (and countless other biblical verse readers like him) had cause to be grateful. Although there was a view, especially amongst Calvinistic Methodists, that the drama was an evil to be resisted, the truth is that the Nonconformist chapel satisfied within its own confines, on an amateur basis, much of the appetite for theatre in Wales for at least a century. Inherently theatrical through the presence of a raised performing area (the *Sêt Fawr* [Big Seat] normally reserved for the minister and deacons), double-aisled and often galleried as well, the chapel introduced Williams not only to the general experience of performance in public but directly to one of the ways in which he himself was later to perform as a solo public reader. But perhaps because chapel rhetoric seemed to him so barren, he never appreciated the qualities of the stage in its rituals.

The alien setting of Anglicanism, to which Williams was occasionally seduced in search of a more distinctive experience, led him to respond more readily to its theatricalism in mood and ceremony.

An experience much later at Hawarden at what was evidently a 'high church' (that is, Anglo-Catholic) service revealed to him the sonorities of English. Although the sermon failed to impress (just 'platitudes on the joys of Easter', he observed), the reading of a biblical passage on the crossing of the Red Sea was a different matter: its magnificent inflections suggested that the reader

> might have been an actor on the stage, so different from the life-less renderings in a Welsh chapel (A1 21 April 1922).

Most of Williams's private reading was done in English. The books at Talacre were standard children's literature, such as *What Katy Did*, and numerous works of religious intent. On one memorable occasion Williams's father brought him as a present from Rhyl an abridged copy of Kingsley's *The Water Babies*. He also read a bowdlerised version of *Gulliver's Travels* and tried *Eugene Aram* (Bulwer-Lytton's novel about the schoolmaster who turns murderer). His attempt however to read a stray copy of *David Copperfield* left behind by a customer at the White Lion was suddenly terminated by his mother when, prompted by the opening paragraphs, he started asking awkward questions about childbirth. (He did not attempt to read it again until he was a pupil at Holywell, when the homo-erotic Steerforth-Copperfield episodes struck a special chord.)

Once after his return from chapel, his mother encouraged him to take up the *Sunday Companion*, which alongside other more directly pious attractions was running a serial by May Wynne entitled *'Neath Nero's Rule*, on the tribulations of the early Christians in Rome. Its blend of adventure, ritual and decadent magnificence immediately attracted him and he waited in fevered anticipation every Friday for the next instalment. The four-penny paperbound version of this serial, which he badgered his mother into sending for from the publishers, was one of Williams's earliest and most treasured possessions. Equally entrancing were its immediate successors in the same magazine on the persecution of the Israelites and, after the outbreak of war (which 'touched us scarcely at all' [G 73], mainly because at forty-four Richard Williams was too old to be conscripted), a jingoistic piece called *The Flag of Honour*. Less morally instructive but of equal value to Williams's imagination were the scraps which he gleaned from the *Liverpool Daily Post*, among which the horrific story on the Brides-in-the-Bath murder (to resurface thirty years later in *The Druid's Rest*) began to feed his embryonic interest in criminal psychology. But *Eugene Aram* was too wordy and he gave it up.

His first real book, he claimed, was Allen Raine's *A Welsh Singer*, which spoke of the romance he was starved of. This late Victorian novelette tells the story of fifteen-year-old shepherdess Mifanwy, whose elder foster-brother Ieuan takes the blame and a thrashing after she mislays a sheep. Ieuan and Mifanwy both seek their fortunes outside their native Wales. The latter (who becomes a circus performer, then an opera singer) falls in love with a simple Cockney lad, who in the climactic fire in a theatre rescues both Mifanwy and her brother but is fatally burned in the process, leaving Ieuan alone to care for Mifanwy's future. Williams lived the fantasy of identification as much with Mifanwy as the two men in the story, fascinated by her need for protection by the compounded figure of the elder brother and lover. The elided gender difference later became a subconscious feature of his sublimated emotional life in the plays, notably in *Full Moon, Night Must Fall* and, though less distinctly, in *The Light of Heart*.

Richard Williams's drinking became more serious. He eventually found himself in the invidious position of being banned from the public houses of his native Ffynnongroyw while still holding the licence for his own pub at Glanrafon. His alcoholism reached the point where his doctor warned of life-threatening consequences if he did not reform, and it was a sensible decision to give up the White Lion in July 1915 so as to be away from temptation. For a month the Williamses moved back to Rhewl Fawr to lodge, not without tensions, with relatives of his father's. With just one hundred pounds in their pockets from the sale of the residue of the lease on the White Lion, the family found new accommodation in late summer a mile or so away at 1 Mainstone Cottages, Berthengam. This plain, no-nonsense village lacked the enveloping charm of Glanrafon. It was draughty and unprotected from the south-westerlies blowing from the mountains; but it did share with Trelogan, its contiguous neighbour, a post office, two provision shops, at least two pubs and a newish council school, which Williams attended for a year. Their rented four-roomed cottage, one of a pair and several steps down in size and quality from the White Lion, drew water from a rain-butt and had a privy (which the Williamses always called the 'petty') in the overgrown back garden. It stood at the far edge of the village at the cross-roads on the route from Llanasa to Whitford two and a half miles south-east. One compensation for the relative poverty of their situation was that at the front the house enjoyed long, uninterrupted views over the Clwydian ridge as far as Snowdonia. At right-angles to the house, on the other side of the road, stood the Traveller's Rest (now a private dwelling), the presence of which was for Richard Williams the cottage's principal advantage, and it was there that he resumed drinking away the family's meagre means.

It was a difficult time for the Williamses. An unemployed father who enjoyed convivial company, stuck in a country outpost with little else to stimulate him except the pub on his very doorstep, had little chance of properly supporting a wife and three children. Mary Williams, though she made a few shillings a month on the quiet by renting out the side garden facing the Traveller's Rest to the school for allotments, rapidly came to the end of her financial and emotional tether. The rows became more frequent and public and after one serious altercation, she and the children lodged for two whole days with their understanding next-door neighbours. Williams's mother made an effort to provide a few extras, but they spent a miserable first Christmas at Berthengam.

In the spring of 1916 circumstances took a turn for the better. Richard Williams was taken on for war work in munitions at the Sandycroft factory up-river from Shotton. As it was too far for daily travel he took lodgings there and came home only on Sundays, walking up through the woods from Mostyn station. The experience of being a wage earner again made an enormous difference to Richard Williams's self-esteem. Although there were occasional lapses, regular employment seemed to curb his more upsetting tendencies and he recovered both his health and much of his native humour. He brought with him as much of his wage-packet as he thought proper to dispense to his wife and a pocket full of small treats for the family, including a copy of the *News of the World*. Yet there was no mistaking the sense of relief on Sunday nights, as the boys accompanied their father part way down the hill towards the station, that the household's patriarch was absent six days out of seven.

Two formative experiences took place while the family was settled at Berthengam: Williams's first visits to a play and to the cinema. The play was mounted by amateurs from Ffynnongroyw at the village of Newmarket (now Trelawnyd) on the top road between Holywell and Rhuddlan; but it made less impression on the young Williams than might be supposed since it was in his native Welsh. This was a major drawback for him because it made it too ordinary, too like everyday life. The cinema in English was different. On a visit with his mother and siblings to his father's lodgings in Shotton – also memorable as it was Williams's first ever train journey – they went as a group, leaving Thomas behind with the landlady, to the Connah's Quay Hippodrome to see the 'livin' pictiars' (G 98). The Saturday-night crowds pouring out of the 'first house' seemed intimidating as well as rough: indeed, films were still essentially a working-class recreation for industrial communities. Seated in the all-pervasive atmosphere of the 'smoke, gas, sweat, dust, and orange peel' (G 99) of the little corrugated iron picture-house, they saw their first silent movies: a clumsy Pathé newsreel, a jerky clip of George V walking in London and four reels of a sensational thriller called *The Juggernaut*, the climax of which was the spectacular plunge of a sabotaged train off a bridge into the watery depths below. It was a taste of what was to become for Williams a life-long fascination.

The medium of Williams's secular education was English, though casual communication was usually conducted in Welsh. But anything written down either at school or home was almost always in English. This oddity extended to Williams's parents, who wrote letters in halting English, and Williams's own first letter, written at the age of nine to Annie Roberts after she left them for Prestatyn, was also composed in his best English. Williams's headmaster at Trelogan School recognised his pupil's potential as a linguist and introduced him to the intriguing comparative exercise of reading the New Testament in French and Italian. However, it was

Williams's composition in English on the delights of town living (of which he had no experience whatever) which won special praise for its faultless punctuation and sense of the shape of the language. Williams suggests that as a direct result of this essay the decision was made to enter him, along with another pupil who seemed to show similar capabilities, for a scholarship to Ysgol Sir Treffynnon, five miles away. Better known as Holywell County School, it was part of a system peculiar to Wales but a more or less direct equivalent of the English grammar schools. Holywell charged six pounds a year, but the fees could be mitigated in part or whole by winning one of the scholarships on offer.

In the stratum of society from which Williams sprang, education was treated with considerable respect, even by those who did not have it. Yet it also problematised the issue of culture and language: the tendency to identify Welsh with homely rusticity and English with education and sophistication, a view first promulgated in the late 1840s by the notorious 'Blue Book' inspectors of scholastic provision in Wales. At the period of Williams's schooling the medium of instruction in village schools either church-based or where control was still exercised by the local squire was invariably English, even in chiefly Welsh-speaking areas. At County School level English again predominated; and at university level the natural instinct was to look outside Wales, even though Wales already had a well-established, federated university system comprising three colleges, to which a fourth was added in 1920 when Swansea acquired its charter.

In June 1916, at just over ten and a half years old, Williams was the youngest of all the scholarship candidates, but he came a very creditable thirteenth out of a total of twenty-one hopefuls, and was granted a four pounds annual award beginning the following September. In his immediate family his father, whatever his faults, was pleased and flattered at the prospect of his eldest son's making a scholastic career for himself at the County. But at school and later at university Williams harboured the suspicion that his mother was less supportive, cared less about his doing well, and would if truth be known have preferred his working for a living as soon as possible. Whatever the advantages, education also made him an outsider at home and over a period the cultural and linguistic divisions deepened.

Romantically named after the 'holy' well of St Winifred, Holywell had an undeserved reputation as the 'Lourdes of Wales'. Then a bustling though fairly drab hill-top town mainly given over to mining and industry, it was connected by a short branch to the main coastal line at Holywell Junction. As there was no possibility of the family's affording a bicycle, Williams walked every schoolday the five miles from Berthengam, through Whitford (close by the grave of Thomas Pennant, his yet undiscovered distant ancestor), along a route enlivened on a clear day by glimpses from time to time of the Dee estuary. It took an hour and a half each way and became almost as familiar as his own back garden. At Holywell County, because of the war, the teachers were mostly female, under the headship of J.M. Edwards (younger brother of the Welsh educationalist Sir O.M. Edwards), a Jesus man who despite his Oxford training remained in Williams's judgement 'imperviously Welsh' (G 123). Although Williams does not mention it, Edwards was author of a dramatic adaptation in Welsh, beloved by amateurs, of Daniel Owen's novel *Rhys Lewis*. A homely man, he was the kind of headmaster whose concern for pupils' well-being extended to the distribution of brown paper for stuffing down damp trouser legs when his charges arrived at school in bad weather. Yet even in this comforting environment, in some ways Williams did not quite fit. Initially he felt himself as much an alien presence here as he was later to be, at least for a time, at Oxford University.

There were clear distinctions at Holywell made by class and accent. Large movements of population in the area had taken place, with influxes of workers into the factories around Deeside, partly as a result of the war. Some pupils, particularly those of parents who worked for Courtauld's, came from essentially English backgrounds; others who came to school from Flint or areas further east, nearer the English border, spoke in hybridised Welsh-Liverpool, Welsh-Birmingham or Welsh-Irish accents. They were openly contemptuous of the Celts from the hills and made fun of their language. By confining his circle of acquaintance mostly to Welsh boys, Williams managed to keep a sufficiently low profile at school such that, mainly by saying very little at all, he made no enemies. He lived in fear however of being branded by nickname, but even Totty and his loud gang, whose arrival on the train from Flint coincided with Williams's own, tolerated him good-humouredly. Though he abhorred his accent he made a friend of Totty's second-in-command Wally and eventually even Totty himself. Ultimately Williams vowed to speak English with a purity of diction that was as far removed as possible from the abomination he heard daily from the Flint contingent.

At Holywell in 1916 Williams met the black-stockinged, pince-nezed Yorkshire-born teacher Sarah Grace Cooke, then aged thirty-three, who was to have such a profound and lasting influence on his school and university career and on his life as an actor and playwright. She began her professional life as an apprentice teacher in Leeds before becoming a student initially at Ripon and then at Rumilly teacher training colleges. To an external bachelor's degree in 1910 she added a London University M.A. in 1915. Her main subject was French but she also taught some Latin. Immediately upon her arrival at the County in 1912 from her previous post at Workington Grammar School, Cumberland, she began to make a formidable and distinctive contribution not only to the school's academic tradition but to its ethos. In her cool rationality and no-nonsense attitude to life and work she had the makings of a Suffragette – in the early days Williams's father, long before he even met her, often referred to her by this term – and her be-gowned presence in the school carried an air of authority to which not only pupils but every other teacher, including the headmaster, deferred. (She was regularly called upon to correct the head's grammar when he had to prepare a speech in English.) Under normal circumstances Williams would not have had such early contact with her, as in the younger forms Welsh was taught instead of French, but he learnt quickly, especially in languages. Form One Latin he found pitched at too low a level and he longed to recite the higher conjugations with Form Two; and in Welsh he was already so advanced that in the spring of his first term at Holywell Grace Cooke arranged for him to join her French class instead.

From the first, though their informal contact in the early years was minimal, there was something special about the relationship. Grace Cooke recognised Williams's potential and was keen to stretch him mentally. He was a willing pupil, intellectually curious and anxious to learn, who responded well to her discipline, organisation and rigour. And there is no doubt that he enjoyed the idea of being selected for special attention. For her part Miss Cooke meticulously preserved a proper distance between teacher and star pupil, but she could not wholly deny feelings which verged on the maternal. From quite early in their association she allowed herself to lessen the discomforts of his daily hikes to and from school: there was hot cocoa (supplied on arrival in Holywell in the landlady's front room at Miss Cooke's lodgings) and one morning in the dead of winter a parcel containing a new pair of stout Yorkshire leather boots awaited him. Later in his school career, following explicit instructions from Miss Cooke, Williams dosed himself every morning with a tablespoon of cod liver oil ('empty at one gulp and wash under the tap' [G 251]) from a bottle kept for his private use in a cupboard in the Mistresses' Room.

After glowing school reports during 1917 from Miss Cooke and other teachers about his exceptional progress, especially in English and the languages, Richard Williams was persuaded to fund the purchase of a second-hand bicycle. For the summer term Williams cycled exhilaratedly to school, lopping a full fifty minutes off the journey on foot. A bike gave him independence and a little more kudos amongst the other pupils, the boys especially. He was not a natural rider – there was a clumsiness in his style – but for the first time Williams felt he was 'one of the Boys' (G 141), though with none of the laddishness of his father. This was an important achievement in one who, though no weakling – his daily walks had quickly toughened him up, improved his lung capacity and given him a boxer's chest – was too uncoordinated to do well at football and who had to conceal as best he could from his schoolmates his shaming inability to whistle.

A major displacement in Williams's life took place in 1917, bigger than any so far in the course of his existence, when his father found a new and permanent job as a fireman on shift-work at the Summers' steelworks, on the opposite bank of the river to Shotton.

With a subsequent promotion to foreman, this was his father's job for the next fifteen years until retirement. It required a move from Berthengam fifteen miles down to the coastal plain. In early July the family's belongings were transferred (for a charge of three guineas by the Crosville Motor Co. as carriers) to Connah's Quay, in the crook of the Dee estuary. Williams met the prospect of his new life with unmitigated enthusiasm, first because of the area's affinity to the world of Arnold Bennett (whose novels he came increasingly to admire) and secondly because it meant moving closer to the border, closer to the English world of apparent sophistication and opportunity.

The main difference on the day of the move was that he became even more 'one of the Boys' than before. Leaving school he now joined Totty and Wally, along with the rest of the 'Flint lot', on the train to Holywell Junction, where they would change for the main line and trains going south-east to Flint and, fifteen minutes further down the line, the halt at Shotton-Connah's Quay. But other changes were more significant and long-lasting. In moving to Bennett's Cottages, Connah's Quay – the family home until 1932 – the Williamses left the greenness and tranquillity of the hills for a shabby industrialised township. Joined to its immediate next-door Shotton, it seemed a rough and ready sort of place, a hard-drinking, hard-working urban sprawl which lacked both civic niceties and any sense of community. The Williamses, especially Mary, made the best of it; but the move represented yet another drop in standards and quality of life, even though the four-roomed homestead itself was externally little different from Mainstone Cottages at Berthengam. The house no longer exists, but it is clear that except in respect of the water supply (which was piped to a tap in the backyard) it was markedly inferior to anything that they had previously lived in.

Urban life descended on the family with an almost suffocating vengeance. Given the right weather at Berthengam they could see Snowdon; here there was nothing but the railway embankment across their backyard or at the front the overbearing backs of the raised dwellings on the main road. Bennett's Cottages, 314a High Street, was huddled down a darkened alleyway flanked by the shops in the High Street. Out back was the usual earth closet and a shed that served as a wash-house, with a low wall separating the scrub patch of garden from 314b, its mirror-neighbour. In reconciling his wife to the move, Richard Williams had carefully avoided mentioning the presence of the London-Holyhead railway, but on the embankment goods wagons shuffled to and fro and express trains thundered immediately behind and above the cottage. Only Williams himself, thrilled on his first night at 314a by the hurtling passage at the level of his back-bedroom window of the London-bound 'Irish Mail', took unconfessed pleasure in the proximity of this escape route to the world outside.

For five people the house was sometimes unbearably cramped, but whatever its physical shortcomings – it was below high-tide level on the river and was often damp from flooding of the yard – it was made as comfortable as possible. The furniture from Berthengam fitted in, including the horsehair sofa, long-case clock, and family heirloom of the oak dresser, which Mary Williams had inherited from Treuddyn. In its cosy Welsh homeliness of the kind that Williams was to perpetuate in some of the settings of his plays there was no compromise; but culturally and linguistically it was a very different matter.

At Connah's Quay, literally on the threshold of England, the Welsh language was considered freakish and its use ridiculed. Soon after their arrival Williams's younger brother Thomas had a nasty experience in the local chip shop and came home in tears after being called a 'Taffy' by some youngsters of his own age who twitted him for speaking Welsh, the only language he knew. It has sometimes been supposed that this incident crystallised for Emlyn Williams his own distinctiveness as a Welshman and his feeling for and duty towards the language of his homeland. That is certainly the reading that Williams encouraged, since the significance of the incident was heightened in the retelling. By the time it appeared in *George* in 1961, Williams had cast himself as stalwart defender of his brother's honour and that of the language by swinging a bag of tinned salmon at Thomas's taunters, drawing blood and satisfaction at the same time. Yet from the original version of this episode made public eight years previously in a speech ('Yn ôl i Gatre' [Coming Home]) to an audience of Welsh exiles at the 1953 Royal National Eisteddfod, it is evident that Williams was not even present. As then told, the story was that Thomas just ran home and his mother dried his tears. The dramatising of the event through the invented detail of the tin of salmon (then an expensive luxury) and crucially his own role as conquering hero over the Philistine was a part of that process of image construction which Williams seems to have found necessary to assert his identity as a Welshman, given that he spent most of his life in England, writing in English.

Such as it was, the community at Connah's Quay was essentially urban in character: distant, alienating and undemonstrative. With the English border barely five miles away, the township looked naturally eastwards. Almost every influence was English, and within a few years the family lost a significant degree of its Welshness. The Williamses attended the local Wesleyan Chapel, which in contrast to chapel-focused rural communities, was engaged in a constant struggle to keep its traditions and threatened tongue from sinking under the relentless pressure of the everyday urban grind and the foreign language of English. While Richard Williams still occasionally over-indulged at the New Inn in Connah's Quay, his son stayed loyal to his chapel roots by becoming a member of the Wesleyan Methodist League of Abstainers. His brothers Job and Thomas went to the local school and came home speaking English; and within a year Williams found his parents beginning to substitute their habitual Welsh for English, not only to their children but in communication between themselves. Two years after his arrival in Connah's Quay the youngest in the family, Thomas, is said to have lost the language entirely. Common every-day experience was communicated in English and the Welsh 'brechdan' [bread and butter] became a north-west English 'butty'. Although the process of language loss was real, it was probably rather less dramatic than Williams made it sound and it needs to be said that neither Williams nor his parents actually lost the ability to speak Welsh. If later correspondence between parents and son was almost always in English, there was still room even twenty years on for the odd note or 'good luck' postcard in colloquial Welsh.

Williams always found it remarkable that during the whole of his association with Connah's Quay he could recall no one whom he could describe as a friend as opposed to mere acquaintance. On the whole there was nobody from school or chapel to accompany him in exploration and play. Indeed the immediate environs were neither inspiring nor inviting of adventure or inquiry, apart from the remains of the medieval castle at Ewloe, where Henry II defeated Owain Gwynedd in 1156. Exceptionally, in the school holidays he once or twice ventured with a companion to bathe in the character-building icy waters of Llyn Helyg in the hills behind Holywell, where they supposedly fantasised about girls; but for the most part he was confined to Connah's Quay and solitude.

As a township it showed only its backside to the river; but inevitably Williams turned to what was on his doorstep: the river estuary, where an occasional ship still tied up at the decaying wharf, though the port's coastal trade had been in steep decline since well before the war. The slip of land behind the houses, between the railway and the beginnings of estuary, was largely a dead land-scape, a cindery wasteland. There was no beach (in contrast to lower down the coast), not even a view, for the opposite bank was over-whelmed by the pallor of heavy industry in the great, smoking chimneys of the Summers steelworks. Moreover it was a dangerous spot; more than one child had been known to have drowned while playing and Williams and his brothers were under the strictest instructions never to bathe there. But swim he did, secretly when the tide was rising. And his exhilaration in his nakedness, combined with awareness of dangerous and forbidden experience as he struck out momentarily out of his depth, never failed to arouse him sexu-ally, no matter how cold the water.

The new circumstance of living in the shadow of a busy High Street and its plethora of shops soon palled. Although he usually made an effort to take a long walk at least once a week, sometimes the eight miles to Flint to borrow from the free lending library, but more often in the contrary direction of England as far as Queensferry (or exceptionally to Chester), his real need was to be driven from distraction by distraction. Williams's life at Connah's Quay was preoccupied by two principal activities: reading and the silent movies. In the daylight gloom or under the shadowy lamp in the front room of 314a – where he did most of his reading, evenings, weekends and in the holidays – he was closeted from the blighted world outside his small window.

The world of his imagination, mostly contrasted with (but occasionally complementary to) the immediate environment, was fuelled by the fiction of George Eliot, Scott, Wilkie Collins, Dickens, the Brontës, and Robert Louis Stevenson. Of contemporary novelists, after his brief infatuation with Allen Raine, he became keen on the romantic side of Rider Haggard but Arnold Bennett remained a favourite. His evocation of close northern communities seemed more and more to mirror aspects of Williams's own experience. Although Bennett was to an extent a model for his own writing, as he explained to Miss Cooke, Williams came to regard his critical observations in *The Craft of Fiction* as rather pretentious by

> trying to say perfectly obvious things in such a way they seem clever (A1 25 August 1922).

His teachers kept him on the right track in the established canon of English literature. Through Miss Cooke's generosity he came to possess a copy of the Irving edition of Shakespeare; and to house his growing collection of English literature Williams and his father built a crude but serviceable bookcase out of orange boxes to go in his favourite corner in the parlour. In truth however Williams was just as much at home with the pulp fiction represented in the shilling monthly magazines of Cassell, Nash and others, readily available on station bookstalls, as with any of the classics of English fiction.

Early in his life at Connah's Quay Williams developed his other major obsession: the cinema, which was wisely kept hidden from Miss Cooke. It was simply never broached as a subject since she had no interest in the new medium and regarded it, as did many like her, unworthy of the attention of educated people. Williams however was seriously addicted. During his first long summer holidays, at first with the family, but soon unaccompanied, he fell into a regular twice-weekly routine of picture-going. The early cinema made a mark on his imagination as deep as anything he read. He devoured everything possible at the Connah's Quay Hip. On offer was largely non-intellectual escapist entertainment drawing on and sometimes directly imitating the standard sensationalism and melodrama of the Victorian repertory. Williams fell utterly for its indulgent charm and romanticisation. As a kind of conscious anti-intellectual gesture, he began keeping a record of his film-going in a Holywell School exercise-book. Wednesday nights and Saturday mornings were continually occupied by films and even on the nights he did not go he still loitered around the building, enviously watching the mêlée of cinema patrons outside. He was fascinated by all the early stars like Edith Roberts, Eddie Lyons, Lee Moran, Ethel Clayton, Grace Cunard, Pearl White and, inevitably, Chaplin. His preferred diet was in romance and exotic thrillers such as *The House of Hate*, *The Web of Desire* and the lurid *Flames of Passion* (which he saw in about 1923). Some of these were shown as serials, so the incentive to return week after week was irresistible. His earliest experiences of film-going undoubtedly contributed very largely to his own desire to be a movie star and to the competition between his later activities in films and those of a playwright. Only at Christmas was the attraction of the latest film at the Hip subordinated to the magic of live theatre. Seated in the gallery at the gas-lit Chester Royalty, he saw *Dick Whittington* in 1917, thus beginning a tradition of pantomime-going which the Williamses as a family kept up for several years.

Ordinarily, the family's move to Connah's Quay would have meant a change of school to the neighbouring County School at Hawarden; but Holywell was keen to keep promising pupils and even paid Williams's season-ticket on the train. The journey, partly on the mainline and partly on the branch from Holywell Junction to Holywell Town, was itself an education. There was plenty of adolescent debagging horseplay, most of it fairly good-natured, but not until early 1918, from an older fellow pupil who at fifteen was alleged to have had some experience of women, did he learn the facts of life, told 'crudely but without prurience' (G 170). Even so Williams was unprepared for the elderly drunk ('grubby but expert' [G 188]) who tried unsuccessfully to molest him as he walked home on the river path from Shotton in the late spring of 1920. He craved more detailed sexual knowledge, but he had no idea where to obtain it, though a book on male adolescence found when browsing the shelves of the St Deiniol's Library at Hawarden gave him some of the answers in a puritanical sort of way. An elder brother would have been a real asset in this context. It was tempting fate, but only two weeks after the grabbing incident (either oblivious to or relishing the risk involved) Williams chanced upon an anonymous, rough-looking, young war veteran who was sheltering from the rain under Hawarden Bridge. Williams's prompting of the soldier to speak of the horrors of the trenches fed his inherent morbidity – he evinced a precocious interest in dead bodies – and, by further questioning, his curiosity on sexual feelings and sexuality in general. The frankness of the soldier's responses he saw as a kind of fraternal initiation rite.

Williams's advancement in the French language under Grace Cooke was rapid, partly through recognition of similarities in grammar and vocabulary with Welsh. In particular, the retention of the *tu* and *vous* forms in French mimicked precisely the same use of familiar and formal vocatives in his native language. Under Miss Cooke's tutelage he also made progress in Latin, and with his other teachers in English and History, with the result that at Christmas 1917 and 1918 he won prizes for being top of his form. In July 1919 he gained his Junior Certificate (Central Welsh Board) with distinctions in six subjects. Academic achievement came relatively easily to him and the prospect of study for the Senior excited him. To satisfy his voracious reading appetite, he obtained a reader's ticket for the Gladstone Library at St Deiniol's, where he became a regular visitor.

During 1918, in the period immediately following the Armistice, he completed his first piece of extended fiction, a sixty-eight-page romantic adventure story, set in the early 1600s, in locations ranging from Paris to Constantinople, which he titled 'Hearts of Youth'. Miss Cooke's crisp verdict that Williams had 'certainly given [his] imagination full play' (G 174) was capable of more than one interpretation. A longer piece called 'The Tombs of Terror', written at Easter 1919, was intended to be on the scale of *Bleak House* (which he had just finished reading) set in ancient Babylon. Its introduction, however, gives no hint of Dickens, only of Allen Raine:

> The sun sets! The great molten mass of fire is sinking o'er the rim
> of the deserts. Shadows creep across the sky, shadows deepen
> o'er the wastes, shadows darken the sluggish Nile – shadows
> come, silent and sinister, upon all. Night spreads her dark wings

over us, for the sun is going to its rest (C1).

The hero is a hermaphroditic street dancer named Pearla, who at the conclusion of Book One (where Williams abandoned the whole project) is brought to the brink of death, having being allowed two minutes to live.

Miss Cooke in later life argued that Williams's fascination with the theatre arose not out of his schooling at Holywell but from the innate feeling for drama in the Welsh peasantry, which was kept alive by the showmanship of the chapel sermon, despite Wales's 'so very very alien' obsession with Calvinism. 'H.C.S. never made you', she told him firmly when he was seeking information for his auto-biography, 'Wales did' (L1/1 10 November 1959). In some sense she was right in terms of the moulding of his Celtic imagination. Nonetheless, as far as the practicalities of theatre were concerned it is clear that Williams's fascination with performance began in earnest at Holywell. His instinct was to dramatise. A piece of run-of-the-mill dialogue from the French class textbook offered him an ideal opportunity to exercise this power during his first year. Playing out the piece before the class with his friend Willy, Williams responded to the revelation that he had just eaten *des grenouilles* [frogs] by repeating the noun with an amalgam of disgust and incredulity. Then clutching his stomach, he concluded the dialogue by mouthing the invented line '*Oh non, non, non*' as he ran off. As intended, it produced gales of laughter and a little temporary status amongst his fellow pupils. In retrospect Williams saw it as signalling an important victory over his self-consciousness under the protection of another language. Later, other possibilities offered themselves, including a first outing for Dickens (more than thirty years before he performed him professionally). For the St David's Day school eisteddfod in 1920, Williams chose the character of Mrs Nickleby, delivered in falsetto, for the recitation competition: a performance that won him first prize.

At sixteen Williams felt desperately guilty at not pulling his economic weight in the family household. Nevertheless after gaining several subject distinctions in the Senior School Certificate in 1920, he began work in the Sixth Form at Holywell for the Higher. His performance in French was enlivened by correspondence, under special arrangements made by Miss Cooke, with a native teacher in Haute Savoie (named Jeanne Tardy in the autobiography but whose real name was Hélène Daviet), who was empowered to set and correct his French essays. The intention was to refine his already highly competent linguistic skills. Except for occasional letters in early youth to Annie Roberts, Williams's response in French to Mlle Tardy's comments was his first piece of formal correspondence in any language. Soon Williams was allowed use of the school type-writer to initiate a regular correspondence with his new French teacher. Then Miss Cooke arranged for Williams, travelling at her expense, to spend the whole summer term of 1921 in Mlle Tardy's school at St Julien. The invoice from Thomas Cook for £8 9s. 4d. [about £8.45] included a night's accommodation in London, porter-age, and the services of a 'special representative' to accompany Williams through London and Paris. With this experience, which brought together so many formative elements – including not least his first absence from home and his first visits both to London and a foreign country – began the long correspondence which Williams maintained with Grace Cooke as his school-teacher patron for the rest of her life.

With a trunk on loan from Miss Cooke containing the latest fashion in night attire, a pair of pyjamas, which he insisted on packing, Williams set off wide-eyed and expectant on 7 April 1921 for the thrills of London and the continent. At Euston he was met by a Thomas Cook representative, who installed him in a hotel for the night, his first ever spent alone. Against the strictest instructions from Miss Cooke not to stray from the hotel, he ventured guiltily to see the revue at the Victoria Palace before continuing next day to Paris, where another Cook's guide escorted him from the Gare du Nord to the Gare de Lyon to catch his train bound for the Alps. His first extant letters to Miss Cooke, written partly in French on ruled exercise-book paper, are outwardly cool, self-confident and clearly intended to impress. Describing himself as *'déja tout français'*, he gives an account of his latest reading in Hugo, De Musset and Leconte de Lisle. To establish his independence, he pertly insists on his lack of homesickness ('and all that sort of rubbish'), adding that if anything was amiss he was perfectly capable of saying so: he was in no danger of

> pining away, getting visibly slenderer everyday, watering my
> pillow with hot tears every night, like a disappointed heroine.
> Please don't make troubles when there are none. I'll tell you
> immediately there's anything wrong (A1 28 April [1921]).

Under Mlle Tardy's schooling Williams clarified several tricky
aspects of French grammar and considerably improved his accent.
He even began to take lessons in Italian, a language with which he
fell in love straightaway and rapidly attained a degree of fluency. He
reported to Miss Cooke on being much taken by

> *la sibilance de la language. J'en suis très enthouiasé.*
> (A1 8 May [1921])

As will become clear, a number of the French experiences treated in
George were repackaged to provide what Williams evidently
believed would be a more compelling narrative. He describes for
instance his visit to Geneva, to the Chateau de Chillon and his sensitivity to the mesmeric and poetical grandeur of

> the grim Byronic fortress which on this lamb-gentle day soft-
> ened its reflection in the pellucid water (G 221).

Yet his letter to Miss Cooke (A1 28 April 1921) mentions nothing of
Chillon or Byron, only the 'wicked' experience of the Geneva
cinema, to see a spectacularly bloody Swiss film on Anne Boleyn.
Williams also claims that on one occasion he attempted to surprise
some tourists whom he thought were English with his command of
the French language, only to discover they were not English but
Swedish. In his letter in French to Miss Cooke this story is absent: he
writes instead of the Swedes being 'sour' and their language at a
distance sounding like English spoken by people who have no teeth,
which is also how he characterises

> *l'anglais de Londres, que j'ai entendu dans le train en venant ici.*
> (A1 6 June 1921)

Such small discrepancies matter little enough, though they do prefigure the more extensive re-fashioning and rewriting in the autobiography, especially perhaps in matters of Williams's sexuality, in which he was quite keen to show a balance in the division of attraction to male and female. As may be expected however, in reference to his emotional life in France there is a reticence in the correspondence with Miss Cooke. If we are to believe the account in *George*, he had a crush on thirty-four-year-old 'Tante Jeanne', as he liked to think of her. In private, they spoke to each other using the familiar form of address. Embryonic sexual stirrings are hinted at. When he is invited to spend a weekend at her family's farm, Mlle Tardy's thirty-year-old brother found Williams a disconcerting presence, somewhere halfway between nephew and fiancé. Yet because it was so very different a relationship from that between Miss Cooke and himself, perhaps Williams understood, through Jeanne Tardy, something of the closeness that might develop between teacher and pupil, but also how uncomfortable a sixteen-year-old adolescent might be in the presence of an older woman, whose very perfume only reinforced her sexual unattainability. Williams was aware that his knowledge of her was utterly superficial, but their parting at Annecy in late August at the end of the summer holidays is plainly represented as emotional on both sides. Later at home he said he poured out his feelings in a parody of a French tragedy.

In the letters to Miss Cooke there is equally no mention of Williams's feelings for the boy called Lambard, a seemingly inaccessible, almost visionary presence with black hair, green eyes and white jersey in the next class above. From a distance in the playground, he fitted the often reconstructed image of an older brother, even though he was actually much the same age. This relationship, after Williams shyly offered him a chocolate in the playground, eventually developed to the point where Lambard took notice of the slightly awkward Welsh boy and invited him to spend a couple of days on his parents' farm. But like other of Williams's relationships, it was so much better in the imagining than in the reality. The reality was that Lambard simply talked too much, and by his witless prattle talked himself out of Williams's affections, even though for a brief period he became that blood-brother – that 'forbidden hero' (G 235) – the fantasy companion of the adventure trail who seven hundred years earlier might have accompanied him to the Crusades.

Williams's return to Flintshire was punctuated by a brief stay in Paris, where he was joined by Miss Cooke (en route in the opposite direction to St Julien) and a couple of other Holywell teachers, one of whom was detailed to accompany him home. His first experience of French theatre gave him the opportunity to visit the Opéra to see *Faust* and the Comédie Française for Molière's *Les Femmes savantes*. But overall the visit was not a success. In his relationship with Miss Cooke, on so different a footing from that with Mlle Tardy, the former was regarded by comparison as having a French now too formal and precise; the trek through the compulsory tourist sites of Paris such as the Louvre and the Palais de Versailles was dutiful rather than illuminating. Miss Cooke was a great communicator and motivator in the classroom, but in the field she seemed to lapse into an irritating nag. Connah's Quay, reached after midnight and an hour's wait for a train connection back from Flint, was familiar and alien all at once. It was a kind of reverse exile. French was no longer intelligible there, and the accents of his fellow-countrymen sounded foreign; his mindset and emotions were still deep in France. Williams certainly cut a strange, not to say affected, figure next day as he accompanied his father to the station to recover his heavy trunk, still wearing his precious beret (which his mother, without conscious disparagement, insisted on calling his 'French hat' [G 247]). Ironically, that same day he learned that he had won first prize in his 'other' language for an essay in Welsh on the League of Nations at the 1921 National Eisteddfod in Caernarfon.

As school resumed at Holywell, Williams longed to show off his French but was crushed at Miss Cooke's insistence that his accent, especially the way he rolled the 'r' in the Parisian fashion, smacked too much of affectation. His mind was concentrated by the decision to put him through London Matriculation, which he was to sit at Liverpool in January 1922. In addition to the standard subjects of English and Maths, this involved examination in Latin, Italian and, for Williams, the entirely new subject of Greek, which (with the dedicated assistance of Miss Cooke, who was herself only a week or two ahead of her pupil) he worked at entirely by correspondence course in 'three and a half months, from scratch' (G 250).

Home was protective and engulfing, but the surprising discovery for Williams, when he went to stay with his mother's brother Jabez and his family in Bootle on the night before the examination, was how much more affectionate and demonstrative of feeling this Liverpool family was – now virtually completely Anglicised, except on Sundays when Trinity Road Chapel recalled them to their native tongue – over his own at Connah's Quay. By comparison, especially on his mother's side, emotions seemed overly restrained. Liverpool also provided a broad spectrum to interest him culturally, including the Walker Art Gallery (where he admired the powerful elder brother imagery of Poynter's 'Faithful unto Death' in the guise of a Roman centurion guarding Pompeii, as much as he did the seductive female nudes of Leighton and Alfred Moore), the latest silent films at the Apollo and, perhaps even more important, the offerings at the theatre. He was already familiar enough with pantomime, but during his last year at school he saw his first straight plays in English: Martin Harvey's production of *Oedipus Rex* at the Royal Court and J.M. Barrie's *Dear Brutus* at the Playhouse.

Once the tension of summer examinations was over, Williams attempted to write for the national newspapers and magazines but failed to stimulate any interest. Inevitably he chose to write in English, the language of commercial success; there was no thought of writing in his native tongue. This process of growing away from the Welsh language was of course reinforced at every turn during his school career. Although presided over by a Welsh head, the school's ethos was predominantly English. There was an annual eisteddfod, but while imitating the Welsh form it was an essentially English exercise. For that of March 1922 the school staged the trial scene from *The Merchant of Venice*, with Williams as Shylock: a performance much influenced by the illustrations of Irving and Beerbohm-Tree in Williams's trusty *Irving Shakespeare*. This was followed in May 1922 with the Casket Scene, with Williams playing Bassanio. From these Shakespearean fragments arose the opportunity of another staging, this time in the chapel attended by the pupil who played Portia. As a result of this and recognition of his facility as a reciter, Williams came into demand at social events, mostly chapel-based, for which he charged half a crown (£0.125) a time. In some weeks he managed to make three times that sum. Aware that

Miss Cooke did not really approve of his activities in this regard, he readily complied with her injunction to read as widely as possible, in French and English literature and in history. Outside school texts and associated works, one important weekly ritual concerned the *Observer*, a much-thumbed copy of which was handed to him every Monday afternoon with the instruction to read it from cover to cover and to assimilate its style, which his teacher promoted as a model of the best English. Most of all Williams devoured St John Ervine's theatrical column, through which he built up a secure understanding of the Georgian theatre of the early 1920s. But it was a sobering reflection that for all his experience of local theatre at Chester (for the pantomime), at Liverpool or even the cosmopolitan attractions of the theatre in Paris, he had yet to see his first West End play. Indeed Williams's sense of Welsh drama was no more varied – it was almost exclusively associated with chapel – but the experience of seeing a play (title unspecified) at Flint Town Hall, given by a chapel company from Rhyl, did for once make a special impact. It was as he reported to Miss Cooke 'simply splendid!', and 'full of Daniel Owen types', of the kind that brought to mind, in the English context, Hardy's Wessex peasants:

> Perhaps some day a time will come when a Welsh novelist will combine this faithfulness in depicting ordinary life with the Celtic mysticism and passion ... (A1 27 April 1922).

Despite Higher Certificate examinations looming threateningly in the background, Williams was preoccupied with two different but related artistic projects: the writing of a play for the Mold National Eisteddfod (for which the prize money was an unusually handsome one hundred guineas) and the staging at Prize Day, for the first time, of a complete play at school. The first entailed composition in English of an historical drama based on Owain Glyndwr ('*Drama Saesneg seiliedig ar hanes Owen* [sic] *Glyndwr*') – this was well before the institution insisted on strict obedience to a 'Welsh only' rule – which he began in the summer holidays of 1922 under the unhelpful influence of a newly discovered interest in the closet dramas of Stephen Phillips. During the new school year the theatre began to occupy more and more of his attention. In *She Stoops to Conquer*

Williams played a gauche and tongue-tied Marlow with such credibility that, despite the other limitations of the performance, a second staging looked to be possible, until the enterprise was vetoed by Miss Cooke on the grounds that it would interfere with academic work.

If Williams's growing relationship to the theatre was one of unequivocal enthusiasm, limited though his experience was, his attitudes to Wales and Welshness were distinctly ambivalent, a complex mixture of attraction and repulsion. Effectively he was split at least three ways. He was Welsh and Welsh-speaking, yet his normal language of communication was not Welsh but English and a strong emotional tie lay with a second 'foreign' language, French. In truth none and all of these languages were foreign. His school career and his border existence at Connah's Quay put him on the cusp of the cultural and linguistic divide. It diverted him resolutely away from his roots further to the west. As he put it in *George*, 'in Deeside [he] had felt an exile from rural Wales' (G 266); yet this was an exile who deep down had no passionate desire to return permanently, merely to keep open the romantic option for temporary refreshment.

From the start Williams's course of life brought him closer and closer to England, until he lived on its very doorstep. Williams's thoughts on this issue came to a head when it became clear that before long he would have to choose his future. Did his future lie, as with many bright pupils before him, along the path to one of the constituent colleges of the University of Wales (effectively Bangor or Aberystwyth)? Or did it lie further east? Emphatically, even at seventeen, the answer was England, ultimately London, just the same message as was announced to his subconscious by the Holyhead to London 'Irish Mail' on that first night spent in the back bedroom of 314a High Street, Connah's Quay. But unlike one of the two 'bad apples' at Holywell whose desire to go to London was connected solely with her ambition to go on the streets, Williams himself had as yet absolutely no idea what he would do there.

In the short term, Williams's ambitions for London – he gained his Matriculation Certificate in English, Greek, Latin and Maths for London University early in 1922 – were replaced by another quite different and challenging notion. Through the headmaster, Grace

Cooke put to him the idea of trying the competitive Open Scholarship in French offered by Christ Church, Oxford, worth eighty pounds per annum. As the competition was likely to be very stiff – he would be pitted against candidates from all over Britain, the best minds of his generation – all concerned at school, including at least on the surface Miss Cooke, agreed to regard the examination as being sat simply 'for the fun of it' (G 270). To the family the enterprise was '[j]ust an exercise' (G 271). Yet while at first Williams contemplated the hypothetical prospect of three years at one of the poshest Oxford colleges with none of his usual enthusiasm or exhilaration at intellectual adventure, the idea began to grow in his mind and over the next ten weeks he thought of little else except his work and the possibility of entering the 'rainbowed world' (G 272) round the corner.

It was the Long Vac in July 1923 when Williams (like a latter-day Jude Fawley challenging the citadels of the academic establishment) stepped off the train to begin the taxing series of scholarship examinations at Oxford University. After the nondescript railway station (just like Connah's Quay only bigger) Christ Church was a revelation. Tom Quad, dominated by Wren's tower, was humbling, as was the Gothic grandeur of the sitting-room temporarily vacated by the don whose rooms he occupied on Stair Two. He dined with three fellow candidates that first evening at the long refectory table, dimly lit by shaded candles. Under the richly decorated hammer-beam roof and oak-panelled walls of the largest medieval hall in Oxford, hung with probably the finest collection of portraits in any college, Williams sat spellbound by the sense of enshrined history.

In subdued conversation with the others he was fastidiously polite, anxious not to betray by word or gesture either the nature of his origins or his unease in the idioms and the ways of cultured English gentlemen, as he supposed his companions to be. All was so new, so unfamiliar, yet significantly Williams's instinct on his last two nights was to do what was second nature to him at home in Connah's Quay: he went to the cinema to see Gloria Swanson in *Her Husband's Trade-mark* and Viola Dana in *A Night of Romance*. Subconsciously it was as if he was already settling in to Oxford life: a necessary process of familiarisation, of preparing for the transition from visitor to native. Brief as was his introduction to Oxford, it was indeed a preface to the opening of another world, which was formally announced just as he was preparing for the train home. A small notice in the porter's lodge at Christ Church confirmed the election of Mr G. E. Williams to an Open Scholarship in French.

Preceded by a telegram to Grace Cooke containing the single word 'WON', he was in a matter of hours back in Flintshire and immediately re-immersed in examination preparations for the Higher. He gratefully received the plaudits of well-wishers: a restrained smile and firm handshake from Miss Cooke, a warm clasp of the arm from the head (who jubilantly decreed a half-holiday for the whole school), and from his father an almost visible glow of satisfaction. Even his mother was pleased enough to give him a special tea which included his favourite: jam roly-poly. A month later Williams's entry under the pseudonym 'Gwynfab' for the Mold eisteddfod on Owain Glyndwr, about which he had disclosed nothing to his parent or teachers, was short-listed with three others from a list of twenty-two entrants. On the pretext of going to listen to the music, Williams walked to Mold and sat in the stuffy overheated atmosphere of the eisteddfod pavilion to hear the verdict of the adjudicators, Dr W.J. Gruffydd and E. Vincent Evans. Increasing anticipation of success turned to disappointment as he learned that his entry was too old-fashioned, too grounded in the techniques of melodrama, and because none of the short-listed competitors had been judged to have achieved the expected stan-dard the prize-money was to be withheld for 1923. At different levels and in different ways, success at Oxford and failure at the National Eisteddfod marked out Williams's future course, as the siren call from beyond the Welsh border became more strident and insistent than anything at home attached to his native culture.

Two: Great Expectations

Oxford in the 1920s recovered its pre-war confidence as well as its student numbers and became noticeably less of a finishing school for the middle and upper classes. This is not to say that it had abandoned its class-orientation – it still bore resemblance to the Oxford of Evelyn Waugh's *Brideshead Revisited* – but the undergraduate who had come up merely to have a good time was much less in evidence. Some students returned to finish degrees begun at the outbreak of, or during, the war and constituted a small coterie mature in more ways than age. But most undergraduates were in the late teens and early twenties, of whom only a smallish number came from grammar rather than traditional public school backgrounds.

Christ Church, originally founded by Cardinal Wolsey in 1525 and re-founded twice more before the century was half over, was known to the cognoscenti as 'The House'. Not only the largest of the Oxford colleges, it was the richest and most prestigious, tending to attract more aristocratic students than any of the others. Being the seat of the bishop of Oxford, it was also very English in its deep commitment to the preservation of Anglican tradition. In Tom Tower, Wren's great masterpiece built over Wolsey's gateway, 'Great Tom' lorded over the whole of Oxford by tolling 101 times at precisely five minutes past nine to signal the closing of the gates and the beginning of the curfew on undergraduates. Among its past students were numbered thirteen prime-ministers, eleven governors-general of India, not to mention celebrities such as Richard Hakluyt, Sir Philip Sidney, John Locke, William Penn, John Ruskin, Edward Pusey and Charles Dodgson ('Lewis Carroll').

When in 1920 state scholarships and county awards came into existence for the first time, the complexion of the older universities slowly began to change. As an Open Scholar, Williams was an early beneficiary of the new system; but numbers overall were not large and he was marked out not only by his longer gown (the ordinary undergraduates wore the ruthlessly truncated variety) but his peasant origins, which even amongst students recruited from the grammar schools were unusual. During the summer immediately preceding his arrival at Oxford, as the pace of preparation increased, he became distinctly apprehensive about the impression he would make at Christ Church. His letters to Miss Cooke show him at this period – he was now in his eighteenth year – as a serious, rather prim, introverted and relatively unworldly young man, anxious about his response to the expectations of university society. A chance meeting in Shotton with a former student of Jesus (an episode excluded from the autobiography) confirmed all his worst fears and prejudices. Williams was troubled by his informant's diction and continual use of 'bloody' (coyly referred to as 'our Pygmalion adjective'), his impression being that such 'bad language' had been relegated to the back streets (A1 23 August 1923). He was fed the story (not entirely devoid of truth) that smoking, getting drunk, spending at least one night in gaol for inebriation and attending as few lectures as possible was *de rigueur* for any self-respecting undergraduate.

Williams was appalled not only at the apparent inanities of Oxford life, but at the news that wine was not 'flashy enough' for student consumption and that beer, the taste of which he loathed as a 'tott' [sic] from being playfully tempted by customers at the White Lion at Glanrafon, was the only really socially acceptable drink. Describing his feelings to Miss Cooke, Williams referred revealingly to 'when we [the family] kept a hotel', which provoked from her an impassioned letter taxing her former pupil with shame over his origin in what she well knew was not a hotel but a pub. Williams argued that his reference was merely in jest, but it did perhaps betray at some deeply subconscious level the desire to talk up his early history. (His father had something of the same social aspiration, which was seen by his workmates at Shotton as endearing rather than vainglorious: he was widely known by the nickname 'Lord Mostyn'.) Interestingly, the letters Williams wrote to Miss Cooke from Connah's Quay invariably omit the 'a' from the 314a High Street address. Williams was very much aware that the society he was to mix with at Oxford would regard the details of his past life and current home with a degree of incredulity.

Preparations for Oxford entry took up most of the rest of the summer. From their scanty resources Williams's parents did their best to supply all the requirements for their son's new life as an undergraduate, of which they could have little or no comprehension. His teachers too loaded him with going-away presents and Grace Cooke, in addition to providing several items of everyday use, went on the track of a second-hand dinner jacket. Owing to the dogged persistence of the headmaster, who continued to feel the greatest pride in Holywell's star pupil, Williams, in addition to his Open Scholarship and the County Exhibition worth £60 a year, was rewarded with a further grant of £40 a year from another source of educational benefaction in Caernarfon, making a grand total of £180. During his first year this was supplemented by a Goldsmith Exhibition, bringing in another £70 per annum.

Dressed in sports jacket and flannels but no hat – he insisted that hats were not worn at Oxford – and dragging off the train his heavy wooden sea-chest, iron-clamped, double-locked and felt-lined (obtained by his father through a dealer in Connah's Quay), Williams arrived to take up residence for his first term at Christ Church on 11 October 1923. To begin with he lived on Tom Quad, overlooking St Aldate's, on an adjacent staircase to rooms once occupied by 'Lewis Carroll'. Though well-worn, they were grand enough by comparison with Bennett's Cottages at Connah's Quay, and less of a drain on his comparatively meagre finances than were the studies on Peckwater Quad, where many of the wealthier, aristocratic students lived in classical Palladian style. With some trepidation and with no experience of the codes of conduct he was thrown straight into Oxford's rituals such as sipping tiny cups of coffee, going out to tea, to madrigal concerts, trials for sports and the rest of the unfamiliar social whirl of undergraduate life. But the cold reality was that it seemed like he was 'a guest in a great monastic hotel' (G 299).

The only other Scholar up at Christ Church at the same time (a year ahead of him) was A.L. Rowse, reading history, who came from a marginalised background in Cornwall not unlike Williams's own. His father was a clay-worker and Rowse was also a first generation university student. They never came to know each other well, but were on nodding terms at dinner and, with fellow undergraduate

Alan Lennox-Boyd, they once had breakfast with J.C. Masterman, the up-coming academic and polymath, then Junior Censor. No doubt there was reserve on both sides, but Rowse was quite formidable and not the easiest of individuals to get on with, even as an undergraduate. Indeed Rowse at the time disapproved of Williams and looked upon him as in some way betraying his own class: any student with his background he believed

> should be serious-minded and hard-working, if possible, members of the Labour Club (Rowse, 215).

Mixing with sons of peers and bishops as much as with lesser individuals, Williams tended to be impressed, even overawed, by rank. Politically conservative, he was a passionate monarchist and kept press cuttings of the activities of the royal family. What was particularly gratifying to him at Oxford was the relative ease with which he found himself in company with the sons of English gentlemen. The very earliest of these contacts were made through sporting activities, though Williams quickly discovered that this area was not his strength. He was no good at rowing nor even rugby, at which as a Welshman he was expected to excel. That rugby was (and is) essentially a south Walian sport was not readily appreciated. Williams had in fact never even seen a game. At an abortive rugby session (or it might have been football as this is how the story appears in his letter to Miss Cooke) he first met M. Drake-Brockman, from Westminster, whose father was in the upper echelons of the Indian Civil Service. He could scarcely conceal his pride in reporting to Miss Cooke on knowing him 'quite well': what was more, he was 'as rich as anything' and 'really nice though superior' (A1 ?6 November 1923). Despite Williams's failure to impress at team sports, Drake-Brockman befriended him for a while until his tragic death in a motor accident. It was in Drake-Brockman's open-top that Williams took his first trip in a motorcar, part way through the first term. They went to London, there and back in a rather hectic day, visiting a few key tourist sites but mainly, under Drake-Brockman's direction, the bars of Regent Street and Old Compton Street in a vain forage for female company. In truth, Williams was more fascinated by the posters outside the theatres off Trafalgar Square.

During that first term at Oxford, Williams – at least on the surface – began to blend with relative contentment into the routines and reflexes of university life. Having savoured the simple pleasures of book buying in the High one frosty day in December, on his return to 'a nice cosy fire' in his sitting room he wrote delightedly to Miss Cooke of his 'real second-hand "trouvailles", cheap and attractive', among which were two of Jane Austen's novels (A1 3 December 1923). Then as now a bicycle was a necessity for any Oxford under-graduate, and Williams acquired a spanking new Raleigh as an eighteenth birthday present from his benefactor. He derived consid-erable satisfaction from his first extended ride out to Blenheim and Woodstock, where he stopped for a drink at the village pub. His tongue-in-cheek claim to 'feel like a real Oxonian at last' however issued mainly from the sartorial statement of his long scarf and

> most beautiful light blue jumper combining discretion with great artistic perfection (A1 27 January 1924).

Such self-parody was not characteristic. Williams's consciousness of image derived from that strain of vanity in his make-up which was to be such a useful ingredient in the life of an actor. Yet for all the outward activity and the friendships, even from the start of his undergraduate career, there were moods black with unarticulated despair, a blankness which flowed from a feeling of essential isola-tion in the intellectual milieu of Oxford, an overwhelming sense – less of homesickness than of purposelessness.

Rather like Evelyn Waugh, Emlyn Williams came to terms with Oxford on the basis that it was to be enjoyed in itself rather than as a prelude to or preparation for somewhere or something else. If it was finally to mean anything for Williams, Oxford came to mean the theatre and the bohemian life that tended to be attached to it. Membership of the OUDS, the University's most prestigious dramatic society, was out of the question for a freshman in his first term. Thus the arrival of a hastily scrawled note from the French Club inviting him to read for a part in its forthcoming production of Labiche's comedy *La Poudre aux yeux* at Lady Margaret Hall – even if it was only to replace a last-minute pull-out – was very welcome. In December 1923 George E. Williams (Christ Church), as he is listed in the programme, made his first appearance on an Oxford stage. This entirely new departure he felt he had to explain to Miss Cooke, arguing not on the grounds that it would be invaluable for improving his French (as asserted in *George*) but that

> it would be mean to refuse (and I thought how very enjoyable it would be) (C1 25 November 1923).

In fact, though the *Isis* did report his Maître d'Hôtel as 'an astoundingly exact study' the experience was more social than theatrical: a means of drawing on the value of his linguistic experience in Haute Savoie and, at the cast party, introducing himself to the wicked pleasure of his first glass of champagne. Even so, he did not yet feel properly integrated into Oxford society, and by the end of the first term was looking forward to Christmas at Connah's Quay. 'Alas, I was never born to be an aristocrat', he wrote to Miss Cooke, 'so the sooner I come home the better!' (C1 25 November 1923). Netherheless, he was to prove that he could not only mix on apparently level terms, but convincingly play the aristocratic part on stage and in film.

By Hilary Term, Williams had been elected as librarian and secretary of the French Club. Through it he made other contacts and before the end of his second term at Christ Church he was admitted into membership of OUDS, which opened up the prospect of a huge social fillip to his career as an undergraduate. He was slow to take advantage of his opportunities as his account for 1924, detailing just one supper, one glass of beer and one telephone call, readily demonstrates. But more importantly the society was in the business of serious theatre. A new production of *Hamlet* was already being prepared for performance 12-16 February 1924, to which the London papers devoted some attention, mainly because of the unusual number of aristocrats to be found in the cast. It utilised the simplest form of production, which Williams much admired:

> beautifully staged with nothing but curtains, and arch and light.
> (A1 17 February 1924)

More than anything, it was a much-to-be-desired opportunity to associate not merely with the most prominent actors in the university but a professional producer in the person of J. B. Fagan and professional London actresses. Though Williams was only prompter for the second matinee (under strict instructions not to prompt except in the very direst of emergencies), he was utterly overwhelmed by the experience of sharing space with amateur and professional stars alike. It also brought his first contact with the 'young and passionate' Hamlet played by Gyles Isham (son of the eleventh baronet Sir Vere Isham of Lamport Hall in Northamptonshire), a student at Magdalen. Romantically good-looking and two years older than Williams, Isham soon soared to higher planes, first as president of OUDS and then of the Oxford Union. There is no doubt that Williams was much flattered by this acquaintance – the Ishams traced their family history back to the thirteenth century – and at the gradual development of acquaintance into friendship. After Oxford their paths crossed again in Fagan's production of *And So to Bed* at the start of their respective professional careers in the theatre.

As prompter for *Hamlet*, what Williams saw as special to his experience was that, despite the proximity of the actors to his corner of the stage, his having never attended a single rehearsal nor seen any of them out of costume sustained for him the magic of theatrical illusion, an illusion in which he himself played a part. It was, as he put it, like being at a play and in it both at the same time. He lived, ate and slept theatre, though with no immediate intention or even thought of making it a career. Nevertheless, from this date onwards Williams's passion for the theatre and all its works never faltered. Eagerly anticipating the next OUDS production, *Love's Labour's Lost* in Wadham College gardens, he vowed finally to lose all traces of his Welsh accent. In the event Williams was chosen to play not Biron (the part everyone seemed to covet) but Dull the constable, in whom a King's English accent was the last thing needed. An additional interest was the play-reading circle run by his friend Roy Newlands at Oriel. Supposedly, it was through Newlands that Williams met a young Canadian who on hearing that Williams was interested in writing for the theatre suggested that Emlyn might be a more memorable stage name than George. In *George* he dates the decision to make the change for stage purposes to Emlyn from this moment. The story however may have been a fabrication, as the notes for *George* suggest that the intention to change his name coincided with his first arrival at Oxford, when in anticipation of a bohemian life he carefully altered his books from George Williams to G. Emlyn Williams. In the programme for *Peter Passes Very Much By the Way* (March 1925) he appears as a split personality: Emlyn Williams for his main part as Trunchonia, a police-woman, and G.E. Williams for one of a group of lunatics. And it is clear that he went on using G.E. Williams for the main OUDS productions right up to 1926.

The most exciting and distinguished venture in the Oxford professional theatre during Williams's student days was James B. Fagan's Oxford Players. Run as a summer repertory in the newly converted Playhouse in the Woodstock Road, it was effectively an out-of-town branch of the London theatre. Though keen to be a regular playgoer, Williams questioned whether he could really afford the expense, but desire conquered caution when he convinced himself of the value of the theatre as an integral part of an Oxford education. He became more or less a fixture on Monday nights, when Fagan's company fed him an eclectic diet. At the Playhouse he had his first sight of John Gielgud in Congreve's *Love for Love* and was also exposed to a varied selection of modern and contemporary drama; but the work of Shaw, along with some of Ibsen and much of Strindberg, Williams found unpalatable or simply too difficult. During the spring of 1924 he frequented both the Playhouse and its rival the New Theatre, witnessing productions of Maeterlinck's *Monna Vanna* ('never saw a worse'); *Oedipus Rex* ('very interesting to compare it with the Martin Harvey version'); and Pinero's *Dandy Dick* ('very amusing as a skit on Victorianism' but not really worthy of the Playhouse) (A1 2 March, 10 March, 3 May 1924). Sutton Vane's intriguing fantasy drama *Outward Bound* he described as a thrilling thing 'marred here and there by foolish jokes that destroyed the whole illusion', and Ibsen's *Lady from the Sea* as 'more intelligible' than *The Master Builder* (A1 11 May 1924). On the whole Williams was less than impressed with contemporary offerings: 'so very few modern plays', he wrote to Miss Cooke, 'seem any use at all' (A1 26 May 1924).

Apart from occasional dramatic criticism for Oxford's student papers, Williams's creative talents were initially confined to poems rather than plays. Poetry he had written ever since Holywell, and it was poetry that first brought him into contact in May 1924 with Harold Acton, the most flamboyant aesthete in Oxford, whom Evelyn Waugh caricatured so brilliantly and with relatively little invention as Anthony Blanche in *Brideshead Revisited*. Oxford in the 1920s was crudely divided into hearties (the sporty, flannel-trouser types, who drove fast cars, such as Drake-Brockman) and the high-neck-jumpered aesthetes led by Acton, supported by such as Waugh, Richard Pares and Robert Byron. Most of the latter were members of several sets or clubs, including the Hypocrites, dedicated in its brief life to 'uninhibited revelry' (Waugh, 180) or the outlandish Oxford Railway Club, which held its first meeting in a specially hired restaurant-car attached to the Penzance-Aberdeen express. By contrast Williams led a much more downbeat existence, but he could claim acquaintance with Acton, among whose several trademarks were his side-whiskers, a gait somewhere between a limp and a waddle, a fastidiously rolled umbrella and an accent which made English sound more like Italian. As Acton was editor of *Oxford Poetry* for 1924, Williams submitted a few Holywell poems for his consideration, but all were politely declined. Anxious to discover the reasons for their being refused, Williams sought an interview with Acton in his lemon-painted Meadow rooms, , from the windows of which he had the habit of declaiming poetry through a megaphone. Tactfully, yet with characteristic candour, Acton explained that his poems were too conventional: 'very polished, finished and natural' but not what he was looking for, which was

> not pretty pictures but the soul gropings of the undergraduate.
> (A1 3 June 1924)

Such was the elegance of Acton's rejection that Williams 'left glowing with satisfaction' (G 336).

Whatever face Williams put on it, Acton's decision may in some measure have contributed to the incipient depression that he began to suffer from during the first half of 1924. Temperamentally, he was ill-suited to the heady mixture of solitariness and romantic gloom.

He found his rooms in Tom Quad too dark, especially in the rain. Craving the lighter, if damper, atmosphere of the accommodation overlooking Christ Church Meadow, he resolved to request a move for the summer term. But the room issue was not the root of the matter. As he neared the end of his first year at Oxford he was unsettled socially, intellectually and probably sexually. For the most part he was surrounded by males, some of whom he was certainly attracted to, though as yet probably in no sexually explicit way, but he was also a reluctant virgin and the desire to affirm his manhood by bedding a woman was strong. These general uncertainties tended to endorse his sense that Oxford and the prospect of the glittering prizes of academic life had for him more limitations than attractions. There was the prospect of his reading not only for double honours in French and Italian but Classical Mods as well (though this eventually proved impossible under University Statutes); but in reality his heart was not in such a difficult and all-consuming exercise. Mixing with top-fliers like the Rhodes Scholars convinced him only of his own inferiority: that he was not really cut out to be an intellectual.

The theatre instead dominated his consciousness. It was in late spring of 1924 that for the first time on paper his thoughts turned to the alternative career prospects of the stage. At first he suggested facetiously how preferable life might be as 'a penurious author or actor' to emulating his Oxford tutor in French, whose cosseted existence made him fatter and fatter, physically and mentally, everyday (A1 3 May 1924). Then, albeit tentatively, he began to debate in letters to Miss Cooke the possibility of a career in the theatre. Predictably she was unsympathetic and regaled him with stories about the insecurity of the stage. His argument was that his parents could not oppose such a course since they were entirely ignorant of the theatre; and that even if they did object he would be prepared to disobey them 'gently but firmly' (A1 26 May 1924). A different version of events, on a different time-frame, and excluding the comments on his parents, appears in the autobiography. This asserts merely that Grace Cooke 'guessed' his 'ambition' close to a year later, in the spring term of 1925 (G 358).

During those vacations which he spent at Connah's Quay

Williams valued the security and the familiarity of the cottage hearth; but, as when he paid his first revisit to Holywell School, there was a sense of alienation in meeting old acquaintances or school friends who had gone elsewhere within Wales to further their education. Whatever formerly they had had in common was now lost, and he felt he was viewing them remotely through glass. Anxious to escape the charge of having developed at Oxford the 'side' he so much despised in others, he was careful to pass the time of day with even the most distant of acquaintances encountered in the streets. But in truth he saw few people outside the family circle, except on Sundays, when everyone met at chapel

> to rub off the week's edges with a few narcotic platitudes.
> (A1 2 January 1925)

The independence of Oxford had released him from the weekly drudgery of chapel, though he did once venture to the Wesleyan Prayer Meeting for undergraduates: an occasion that did not impress him since

> everybody ... looked very much concerned with the higher things but weren't a bit really (A1 18 November 1923).

Yet at home he was perfectly happy to re-immerse himself in the social life of chapel, taking an almost child-like delight in Sunday School excursions to Rhyl or Llangollen. Charabanc trips he confessed to liking best, as there was more chance of something going wrong. Vacation life at Connah's Quay was generally uneventful and isolating, serving only to underline the distance between Oxford and his Welsh hinterland past. The only possible compensation for the exoticism of his friends holidaying in foreign parts lay in his escape route to the provincial theatre. His first Christmas vacation was partly spent with his Uncle Jabez and family in Bootle, desperately hoping for the opportunity to go to see the Liverpool pantomime or some other entertainment. The Shakespeare was a special favourite, where he loved to sit in the crowed gallery

> amidst the smell of orange peel and eat a bun, though of course when I say that my gentlemen friends at Christ Church think I'm

making a heavy attempt at humour (A1 22 December 1923).

During the interwar years Baedeker-guided continental travelling, alone, with a friend or in reading parties – one of the dons at Balliol for instance regularly took small groups of favoured male undergraduates to the French Alps during the long vacation – was hugely popular at Oxford, more so than at Cambridge. Vacation travelling virtually became an institution. But until Williams discovered a source of finance in the competitive travel scholarships on offer he was forced to stay at home. Some consolation however was to be had in the way that so many of his fellow students ('the grand people'), whether skiing in Switzerland or climbing in the Alps, returned to Oxford 'as bored as when they went' (A1 21 January 1924).

Williams joined the travelling set himself in Easter 1924, when he was awarded a Heath Harrison Travelling Scholarship, which financed an extended excursion to Paris. He was accompanied by a fellow undergraduate award-winner from suburban Epsom, described as

> a stodgy Saxon with pale blue eyes, a permanent flush of uneasiness and a tooth-brush moustache (G 329)

who proved a not altogether congenial companion. They stayed at a small *pension* in the Place des Vosges and their sole interest in common it seems was their desire to lose their virginities. In the event, they succeeded only in losing a substantial amount of cash at the hands of a pair of tarts they picked up at the Folies Bergère. To Miss Cooke he admitted only that he had paid the briefest of visits to 'a night club', just for the experience:

> very interesting but, on the whole, incorrect ... still I only stopped 5 minutes which cannot be very wicked can it?
> (A1 16 April 1924)

Paris improved his accent but did little else; and his companion was a hindrance to his enjoyment, which revolved almost solely around the theatre. Even en route in London he had been to the latest revue (Noël Coward's *London Calling*) and to his first West End play, Somerset Maugham's farce *The Camel's Back*, at the Playhouse.

Williams says nothing about the experience, but it must have disappointed as it was one of Maugham's thinner plays. Foreclosed in New York and never published, it was hardly any better received in London.

Although Williams acquired a taste for vacation excursions, they were invariably much more ordinary in terms of destination than those enjoyed by the wealthier undergraduates. For the summer of 1924 he disinterred his French beret and shipped his new bike across the Channel, a copy of Homer in his pocket 'to complete the picture of the Scholar Gipsy on wheels' (G 341). He intended to cycle as far as Haute Savoie to renew his friendship with Jeanne Tardy (Mlle Daviet), with whom he had kept in correspondence, though at increasing intervals. This second French vacation of the year contained an episode treated in Flaubertian detail in the autobiography, the milestone of his sexual history when he lost his virginity to a girl arranged for him by a fellow-drinker at a café-bar in Rouen. This was, as Williams recalled, the city of Madame Bovary and it was still resonant for him with her sexual frustration and adventure. Appropriately it stirred his own sexual feelings also. In chance conversation with a Breton sailor four or five years older than himself, the talk spread to women and in the heady mixture of music, beer and the balmy summer night Williams confessed his virginal condition. For a few brief hours the seaman became yet another version of the fantasy elder brother and mentor. It was perhaps inevitable that Williams's sexual initiation with a prostitute in one of Rouen's back-street *chambres à louer* should be, as it were, under the stage management of the 'elder brother' – an experience that, while predominantly heterosexual, was not unambiguously so. Williams records in *George*, while negotiations were being completed, how his Breton companion addressed him as '*mon petit frère*' (G 345) and the night's sexual adventure ended with Françoise, having satisfied both men privately, inviting them into the bed to sleep either side of her.

Williams's treatment in the autobiography of his heterosexual history – still more that of homosexual experience – was fairly frank for 1961, before the so-called sexual revolution of that decade had taken off. But as the preliminary notes for *George* reveal he had absolutely no doubt about the central importance of the sexual in his life. One of his early ideas, later dropped, was to enclose sexual details within asterisks so that readers of the maiden aunt persuasion could avoid reading them if they so wished. Indeed Miss Cooke when she read the first draft of *George* confessed that she was bored by the amount of sexual detail that Williams insisted so fascinated him: 'I don't say cut out', she wrote, 'but I wld certainly cut down'. Even Miss Cooke however conceded on the Rouen episode: it

> struck me as beautiful. It is a very fitting climax, adolescence over, adult life begun (L1/1 October-November 1960).

The following night he repeated the experience with another prostitute and although Yves was downstairs sipping his beer, it was accomplished independently to show he was capable of doing without his 'elder brother' companion. The second girl, Rosine, Williams recalled, was 'like a plump doll that says Mama' (L1/2). She made more of an impression, despite her apparent distraction noted in *George*, and he even wrote to her afterwards. Cycling on south to Haute Savoie, he kissed 'Tante Jeanne' on arrival and speculated momentarily whether the mark of his sexual initiation with not one but two women might somehow be visible.

Back at Oxford his new rooms in the Meadow (formerly occupied by his friend Angus Rae) suited him no better than his old ones in Tom Quad. Still subject to periodic bouts of melancholy, Williams whiled away the early weeks of the Michaelmas Term of 1924 typing up on a rented machine the new play he had begun at Dijon, while attending some lectures at the university. A fantastical version of the Cinderella story, harking back to his memories of Christmas visits to Chester Royalty, it incorporated some bizarre new twists to the familiar plot, such as Prince Charming's being discovered to have had a previous relationship with and jilted one of the Ugly Sisters. Miss Cooke sent him her none-too-enthusiastic reaction in October, and shortly afterwards the agent to whom Williams had entrusted the typescript returned a polite refusal. Perhaps the best practical result that came out of the episode was Miss Cooke's realisation that her protégé, now a writer in earnest, needed a typewriter of his own. A portable Remington, long coveted in a Broad Street shop window and which precisely fitted requirements, became his as a nineteenth birthday present. This machine became his indispensable companion.

During the winter Williams became more involved with OUDS, though the social process was fairly slow and he was ever fearful of overstepping the bounds of familiarity through ignorance of public school manners. He had no desire to repeat the *gaucherie* of the previous year, when his unwarranted use of members' first-names had been brought gently but firmly to his attention. His social integration was helped by the dinner party given in his Meadow rooms on his nineteenth birthday, 'wildly expensive' (G 353) though it turned out to be. Indeed, paying his battels early in the new year, he had to turn to Miss Cooke for a loan until the following summer. At much the same time, he began rehearsals for the next major OUDS production, under Reginald Denham's direction with Robert Speaight in the title role, for Ibsen's *Peer Gynt* in the William Archer translation. Scheduled for performance on 10 February 1925, it was to be even more prestigious than *Hamlet*, notably in bringing Greig's music and the play into conjunction probably for the first time in Britain, where, apart from an obscure London performance in 1911 and an Old Vic production in 1922, *Peer Gynt* was hardly known. Several performers were co-opted into the cast from outside, including Clare Greet, Joan Maude (daughter of Cyril Maude) and Mary Casson (Sybil Thorndike's daughter). Williams was to play the Lean One, for which, in order to lose surplus weight, he started a daily regime of running round Christ Church meadow at the crack of dawn. Notwithstanding, the *Isis* pronounced that 'Mr Williams was a diabolical, if not very lean, Lean Person' (quoted G 362); but the *Times*' review failed to mention him and even contrived to omit his college affiliation from his name at the bottom of cast listing. However, directly after *Peer Gynt* Williams got elected to the OUDS Committee. His continued attendance at the Playhouse through 1925 produced at least one memorable experience – later to bear fruit in the images of Welsh life in Williams's own writing – when he went to see *The Comedy of Good and Evil* by fellow Welshman and recent graduate Richard Hughes, who had been up at Oriel three years earlier.

Emlyn Williams's friends at Oxford, in and out of OUDS, were predominantly bisexual or homosexual, mostly the latter. Given the circles he tended to mix in, this was not in the least surprising since Oxford acquired quite a reputation in this respect in the 1920s. Despite the presence of women (whose admission to full degrees, except in theology, dated from 1920), association was not encouraged and the university remained still very much a male preserve, an extension of the public school system. Oxford homosexuality could mean anything from what Evelyn Waugh called 'deep friendships' (Waugh, 168) to more sexually commited relationships. Such as Acton and Tom Driberg were homosexual in varying degrees – Williams does not appear to have known the latter – and there was Angus Rae, who one day announced to a shocked Williams (suddenly surprised by his own naiveté) that he was having trouble with his male lover at another college. Acton was responsible later for what was regarded as a scandalous number of the *Cherwell*, which defended Oxford's monopoly (over Cambridge) in what were described as 'girl-men'; mischievously Acton suggested that a schoolboy edition of Wilde's 1890s novella *The Picture of Dorian Gray*, already a gay icon, should be commissioned small enough to fit into a schoolboy's blazer pocket.

Williams undoubtedly cultivated several male relationships of a quasi-homosexual nature more or less from the beginning of his career at Christ Church, though he would have almost certainly regarded none of them in the explicit terms of Rae's. Rae himself was probably just a friend, but since his family lived in Wimbledon he was a useful London contact for the vacations. They were both attracted to the theatre, keen to see the latest London hits, and both developed a crush on the American actor Tom Douglas. From late 1924 to early 1925 he starred at the Criterion in *Fata Morgana*, an adaptation of a Hungarian play and the raging success of the London season. Douglas, with his deliciously velvety Louisville accent, was a sensation as the vulnerable twenty-one-year-old seduced by an older woman who never takes him seriously. His creation of a fully sexualised being whose potency seemed to cross the footlights provoked complaints from the public to the Lord Chamberlain, who in consequence requested the toning down of the seduction scene on pain of withdrawal of the play's licence. As

Williams recalled, not only women fell under Douglas's spell. Rae and he were seriously infatuated and lay in wait for him to emerge from the theatre, once contemplating contacting him by telephone to express their admiration. Williams eventually wrote him a short note of appreciation, which elicited from Douglas a casual invitation to look him up when next in London. The signature Williams endlessly tried to imitate and by his own admission (in a preliminary note for *George*, but never used) cried out his name like a love-sick Olivia in *Twelfth Night*. He never actually met him, but certainly Douglas expressed something of Williams's dreams of the theatre as a profession intermingled with his own deepest feelings of sexual ambiguity. Only two years older – another elder brother figure – it was Williams's fantasy to be his professional understudy. Douglas's stage performance he witnessed at least three times.

Emlyn Williams's Easter vacation of 1925 was shared between London, Connah's Quay and, during the last week, the home of a friend Herbert Rees, whose parents had a farm on the Welsh border in Radnorshire. Geography was not a strong point –

I am rather anxious to see a little of South Wales e'er I die
(A1 26 February 1925)

he told Miss Cooke – but it was the furthest south he had ever been in the country of his birth. Williams's mind however was elsewhere: he was continually drawn to London and the London theatre, which he regarded as the heart of things, and where he saw Coward's *The Vortex*, as well as further performances of *Fata Morgana* after its transfer to the Vaudeville Theatre. The prevailing image is of his disconsolate, aimless progress through the streets of the West End, vaguely anticipating another Rouen yet knowing that a repeat performance was probably impossible. The theatre however was still as intoxicating as ever. Tom Douglas's presence in it was an inspiration and to emulate him as an actor was Williams's constant aspiration.

Ironically, Williams's next direct experience of theatre was back home in Flintshire, where he agreed to take part in his chapel's production of *Y Bobl Fach Ddu*, the Welsh translation by the London-Welsh playwright J. O. Francis of his own play *The Dark Little People*, originally staged at the Aldwych Theatre in February 1924.

According to the account delivered to Miss Cooke, the Welsh version was premiered at Bagillt, where its 'riotous' audience received it 'very vociferously'. Although all the players knew their lines, they tended to muddle up exits and entrances so that while they appeared on stage at the right time it was 'more often than not through the wrong door' as there were three to choose from (A1 18 April 1925). Williams as the shepherd-boy hero consciously imitated Tom Douglas, but no one noticed. A few days later on 23 April the play went on to be performed at Wepre Presbyterian Church Hall, Connah's Quay, and during the early summer Williams had special permission to play in a postponed performance at Flint. Separated from the earlier stagings by almost six weeks and having had no subsequent rehearsal, it was 'an appalling production' (A1 30 May 1925). Williams recalled in the autobiography that the whole experience of being abstracted from Oxford and OUDS in the middle of term to play in Welsh in a remote chapel was both disorientating and disturbing.

The Welsh experience of theatre seemed alien and impenetrable compared with the siren call of Oxford. There so many glittering theatrical and other activities competed for attention amidst the drudgery of academic work, which continually failed to receive its proper share. Although he sweated over his (unsuccessful) entry for the Newdigate Prize, he neglected his formal studies in favour of more seductive exploits such as taking a walk-on part in a gloriously sunny and entrancing performance of the *Medea*, given on the steps of the Library in Peckwater Quad at Christ Church with Sybil Thorndike and Lewis Casson in aid of the League of Nations, or playing in a production of Chekov's *The Bear* at Banbury with Robert Speaight. He also managed an OUDS revue touring Berkshire and Surrey, and embarked on rehearsals for the OUDS double-bill of Rostand's *The Two Pierrots* and *The Fantasticks* scheduled for 19 June 1925 under William Armstrong of the Liverpool Repertory Theatre.

It was a dangerously crowded summer term, and the omens from his academic tutors were not good. At the examinations in early June 1925 he ploughed at Divvers, the first paper, being unable (according to the account in *George*) to answer a single question. It was almost a matter of honour to fail in Divinity at least once, but twice was pushing it, and this was actually Williams's third attempt. He quitted the examination room claiming to feel faint. His request for an *aegrotat* was refused as there was no medical evidence. It was a couple of weeks or more before he could bring himself to tell Miss Cooke the bad news and when he did so his account was thoroughly dramatised. He professed to be 'just recovering from a nervous breakdown' (A1 24 June 1925), the result of a panic attack a week before the examinations brought on by the threat of being 'sent down'. As a result he gave up all his OUDS commitments, 'swore off *The Fantasticks* and everything else and worked and worked'. But the night preceding the examination, he had a nightmare '(literally) on the subject'; then in the midst of the examination, 'which I was finding not too difficult', he felt queasy and fainted like a tragic heroine on the steps of the Examination Schools. In the unembellished autobiography none of these excuses appears and Williams seems content to put it all down to having done no work; there is no talk of depression, nightmares, or nervous breakdowns. This may or may not have been the accurate version of events but in terms of the autobiographical narrative it is evident that the deliberate underplaying allows the emphasis in *George* to fall on the more serious emotional and mental collapse of the following year, for which the experience of the summer of 1925 was but a rehearsal.

Miss Cooke had no time for failure. She minced no words: in her mind her star pupil had ploughed simply because he was a slacker. In truth the theatre had consumed virtually all of Williams's energies, not just the formal OUDS productions but the 'smokers', or revues, which invariably struck that bohemian note so much to Williams's taste. On advice from his tutor he rejoined *The Fantasticks*, but having won a second Heath Harrison Travelling Scholarship, Williams looked forward to respite from some of the pressures of life (in return for a promise to work on his divinity for the autumn resit) in a lengthy summer vacation to be spent in a solo tour of Italy. Florence, Assisi, Venice, Rome, Pompeii, Sorrento, all beckoned invitingly. There was no Rouen experience for him this time; and only one recorded homo-erotic experience, when he glimpsed a bronzed, bare-chested youth, apparently Venetian, who turned out to be a distant acquaintance from Oxford. From Italy he wrote to Miss Cooke, extolling the extraordinary beauties of the landscape he had passed through. But even in Venice, which he adored and where he had a back room overlooking a nunnery, he suggested that his

> convent garden might be at Holywell, [as] its beauty is universal. (A1 6 September 1925)

Back at Oxford in October, Williams began his third year. It was marked by two or three highly fashionable outfits of new clothes, including Oxford bags and the latest craze for high-necked jumpers, which were worn by all those who considered themselves up with the latest trends. His clothes, perhaps because they were a little daring, helped to compensate for the renewed gloom which descended on him in his rooms in the Meadow. In their winter prospect they became even more uninviting than those in Tom Quad. At the OUDS, fresh-faced new members made the society somehow less intimidating and Williams had his first glimpse of three particular newcomers, all younger than he, who in their different ways were to be increasingly important to him that year: pipe-smoking John Fernald, cherubic, plus-foured Martin Rellender (who soon startled Williams by claiming he was bisexual), and most of all Rellender's former schoolmate, a handsome but slightly diffident young man who reminded Williams of the head-boy type at school. He appears in *George* unidentified beyond a supposed membership of Worcester College and the pseudonym of 'Charles Garvenal'.

All three individuals were involved in the next big OUDS production of *2 Henry IV* for Hilary Term 1926, and Williams cultivated his new friends avidly. But his immediate preoccupation was to enter the society's informal competition to write a one-act play. The result was *Vigil*, written quickly and without apparent effort ('so easily that it was hard to believe ... that it was any good' [G 379]). Contrary to the detached context implied in *George*, it is quite clear that the play was conceived in the immediate heat of Williams's profoundest sexual feeling to date, for the fellow undergraduate whom many years afterwards he described as looking 'sexy even in bowler hat, his att[ittude] unmistakeable' [*sic*] (L1/2). He is represented in the autobiography as outwardly straight, indeed a hearty, sporty type; but Williams went to some length to disguise the portrait. The only clue is that throughout the preliminary notes for *George* he is referred to not as Charles or Garvenal but as Martin, which may or may not have been his actual name. Even if it was his real name, given Williams's desire to conceal his identity, the probability is that he is not to be identified, at least in no direct sense, with the Martin Rellender of the autobiography, though Rellender's confessed bisexuality certainly fits. What is certain is that the main product of this period – Williams's first staged play *Vigil* – is a work which has a morbid kind of obsession at its heart. And there is no doubt whatsoever that it reflects elements of Williams's obsessive emotional involvement with Martin, from whom in return he had little more than casual friendship. Referring back to the summer of 1926 he wrote: 'I resent being in his power, like *Vigil*' (L1/2).

Profoundly atmospheric and set in a remote manor house on the Welsh border, *Vigil* concerns the arrival of a disorientated English traveller (Atherton, the Stranger), who is intrigued to find Issaiah, an inarticulate farmer's boy, on guard outside his master's bedroom. Joined by another Englishman (Richman, the Permanent Guest), whose enchantment to the place has already lasted four years, the traveller discovers that he too is obliged to stay, spellbound by the hypnotic power of the sleeper in the inner room. They express a wish to murder their unseen host-gaoler, but this plan is abandoned as it becomes clear that the 'vigil' – which is essentially the boy's as he waits implacably for the death of the sleeper, whom he has been systematically poisoning over the past four weeks – is about to come to its grotesque climax. When death finally occurs in the small hours of the morning the two travellers become free to leave and the terrified Issaiah, after pleading in vain to go with them, in the now deep silence of the house, advances slowly along the passageway towards the room containing the corpse. The OUDS Committee accepted it as one of three pieces for their members' nights at the Oxford Playhouse from 24 to 26 November 1925. As director Williams recruited his friend Fernald, with Martin probably as an assistant stage-manager. Williams himself took the part of the mysterious farmer's boy and assembled a strong cast for the other two parts in Leslie Nye and Robert Speaight.

The final play in the triple-bill, *Vigil* won the honours as undoubtedly the best. It was dependent upon an atmosphere of accumulating apprehension, suggestive of the intimidatory mood of Maeterlinck's *L'Intruse* (1890). The reviewer for the *Cherwell* (28 November 1925) was especially impressed by 'its brooding horror and almost factitious suspense', which was attributed to the Grand Guignol manner. Williams's 'magnificent acting' as Issaiah allowed him

> to remain immobile at the back of the stage throughout the action, where inspired lighting threw his eyes into mysterious Rembrantian shadow.

After the play was published in the *Oxford Outlook* in early 1926, it had a second performance by OUDS at Cambridge Playhouse on 26 March 1926 for the NUS Universities Congress, when it shared the billing with a student group from Aberystwyth performing J. O. Francis's *The Poachers*. (Williams recalled that neither group made any effort to mix with the other.) The outcome of Williams's first public exposure as a dramatist was that J. B. Fagan of the Oxford Playhouse was so impressed that he wanted *Vigil* to be seen in London.

On the back of Williams's first stage success came emotional dejection with the loss of Martin from Oxford in 1926. According to the account in *George*, Martin (alias 'Charles') disclosed that he was to be sent down by his college for lack of work. His prospective absence was such a shock that Williams was able to cope only because the two of them vowed to spend one or both upcoming vacations in each other's company: Martin's plan was Easter in Paris and perhaps cycling to Spain during the summer. In Hilary Term the image of his exiled friend constantly recurred to Williams's mind, but he resolved to work as hard as possible for his forthcoming finals, while still keeping contact with OUDS for *2 Henry IV*, and with the aesthetic set.

He did not realise it, but things were beginning to fall seriously apart. Now more strapped for cash this term than any time previously in his undergraduate career, he also found his academic work deteriorating and he failed in Spanish when he tried for a third

Heath Harrison travel award. In addition the weekly bottle parties in his rooms at Christ Church were debilitating both because they interfered with his academic work and had a negative psychological impact. The steamy atmosphere of drinking and animated conversation amongst a large group of Oxford's aesthetes was merely an artificial shield from his increasing melancholia. The only upbeat news was on the professional front: James Agate in the *Sunday Times* noticed Williams's cameos in *2 Henry IV* ('I think I spy an actor in Mr G.E. Williams' [*Contemporary Theatre*, 36]) and (even more ego-flattering) J.B. Fagan had been as good as his word and arranged for *Vigil* to be played privately in front of some important theatrical contacts, including the redoubtable Sybil Thorndike and Lewis Casson, at the Fortune Theatre in London.

At Easter, the intention was for Williams and Martin to go off together to Paris after the one-off staging of *Vigil*, squeezed in between the scheduled matinee and evening performances of *Juno and the Paycock*. But the vacation started off on the wrong foot from the moment of Williams's arrival in London when, owing to a misunderstanding, he was stood up at a Lisle Street restaurant where he was to dine with Martin tête-à-tête. When he met him later at his mother's residence, Williams described him in a cancelled section of *George* as possessing

> the authentic sheen of sex-appeal. I felt years older than him, a twenty-year-old Socrates to his Alcibiades, for as he sat in that dim London tea-time, he was incandescent with youth. (L1/2)

Shortly after this Williams was moved to confess his feelings to him, despite awareness that it would cause Martin the profoundest embarrassment and be likely even to endanger their friendship. Martin took the declaration in his stride, but was privately disturbed by Williams's proprietary instinct. Having at school been something of a heart-throb and become fully aware of his charm and power over men as he matured, Martin was careless of the effects he had on others. Williams sensed his lack of feeling, having already been disconcerted by Martin's nonchalant account at Oxford, to the accompaniment on the gramophone of Gershwin's *Rhapsody in Blue*, of one boy having got 'a bit difficult' (G 389) and attempted suicide over his seeming indifference to him.

Even before they left for France, Williams had tied himself into an emotional knot. Knowing that Martin encouraged his attentions but apparently slept only with women provoked in Williams the deepest jealousy and torment. Though convinced that Martin was never going to be his in the way he wanted, he could not rid himself of the desire. All the commitment and the obsession came from Williams and, like the characters in *Vigil*, he felt fatally trapped. In the shortened published account of the Paris trip in *George*, Williams does not say exactly what went wrong. The extended version discarded from the published text shows that for the Paris trip they were accompanied by a third person, a long-standing friend of Martin's, en route for an independent continental tour. In apparent amicability the trio visited the Louvre and went to see a performance of *Phèdre*; but all the time Martin was planning the break. Finally the friend took Williams aside:

> I must tell you, for you own good, that Martin finds it all a bit – sort of cloying ... he likes you and admires your brain and so on, but he feels you are developing a sort of proprietary – (L1/2).

A discomfited and embarrassed Martin then brought the awkward situation to an end by an abrupt departure for home.

The break was neither as absolute nor bitter as recounted in *George*. Indeed Martin actually tried to remain friends, and it was Williams who decided that he could not have him on those terms. His sense of desolation was very strong when in late April 1926 he arrived at the gates of Tom Quad to begin the summer term. As things turned out it was to be his last at Oxford. Quite apart from his emotional turmoil, which he tended to keep hidden from his friends at the OUDS, there was the usual financial crisis; but this time it was more acute than before, largely because of the bills accruing from his weekly bottle parties during the previous term. Again Miss Cooke bailed him out with a loan of £35.

At a different level and from a totally unexpected direction came an even bigger distraction from the problems of his emotional life: the General Strike. University life at Oxford was totally suspended for the duration, and undergraduates were despatched to the docks at London, Bristol, Hull and elsewhere in order to keep essential services moving. Williams found himself at Paddington station with scores of fellow undergraduates, including Angus Rae (whom he noted was without his lover from St Edmund Hall). Everyone was given a slab of bread and mug of beer before being ferried 'stealthily across London in vans marked "Food Only"' to Hay's Wharf, where they were billeted six to a cabin on a 'nice passenger ship that plies between London and Denmark' (A1 20 May 1926). For the majority of undergraduates it was a kind of *Boys' Own* adventure; there was titillation through their jobs loading consignments of food stuffs and other duties, which associated them temporarily with an entirely different class. For a weekly wage of three pounds twelve shillings [£3.60] Williams unloaded 'pigs swathed in sacks that come gory from Denmark' (A1 10 May 1926). The camaraderie was satisfying. Williams grew a beard and evidently enjoyed the temporary diversion from Oxford preoccupations. In the autobiography he relates how the others went 'Up West' on Saturday night (G 402), seeking relief after the labours of the day, while he stayed behind to enjoy the peace and quiet and, on one occasion, a man-to-man conversation with a weather-beaten old salt to whom Williams lamented his thirty-month post-Rouen celibacy. This confessional moment seems designed to reinforce a quiet mood and renewal of the heterosexual impulse as part of the narrative strategy of the autobiography. It was probably invented, since the letters tell a different story. He wrote back to Flintshire of his attendance, along with most of the rest of the crowd from the ship, at 'a night party' in Bayswater, evidently mainly homosexual in character since it was overrun by a large group of chorus boys ('a curious feature of the stage') from the musicals *Lady Be Good* and *No, No, Nanette*. These were the authentic 'girl-men' that Oxford merely made a pretence at and put its aesthetes 'immediately and completely in the shade!'. From such as these, Williams observed to Miss Cooke in studied detachment,

> the mothers of the chorus girls need fear no harm, absolutely none (A1 20 May 1926).

Back at Christ Church later in the month the summer term

resumed its relatively tranquil course, except that Schools loomed in the near distance. Life seemed flat and tame by comparison with the animation generated by the General Strike. Thoughts of his shattered relationship with Martin still tortured his mind, perhaps prompted by strains of Gershwin (which Williams ever continued to associate with him). Occasionally he was glimpsed in the distance, when all the old desires came flooding back. It was, he realised, time to take stock. All he felt was a sense of uncontrollable drift, and yet within less than a month with examinations over he would have to make his choice of life and career. In probably his last letter to Miss Cooke before his breakdown, he struck a pessimistic note: after the examinations, he observed,

> I shall be faced with life: it is a dreadful thought.
>
> (A1 20 May 1926)

Half jokingly, he wondered what her reaction would be to receiving from him a letter from across the Atlantic, where he had gone 'to try [his] luck in the golden whirlpool of Holywood[sic]'.

Williams always found loneliness difficult and now, as finals approached, he found it unbearable. Unable to work in isolation, he set up a daily routine of revision with Reggie Colby, a friend made at the OUDS, who was at Wadham. But the breaking-point was not much delayed. Miss Cooke was given only the vaguest of hints of his troubled state of mind and could have had no inkling of the imminent serious turn of events. In his emotional predicament as a frustrated playwright and actor who was also a thwarted and jealous lover, he was unable to sleep properly and his depressive mood became ever gloomier as the interval to the examinations gradually lessened. One black day merged into the next as he tried to come to terms with his obsessions. In the notes for *George*, Williams observes that

> Martin's only crime was that like the sun, he shone on the boys and girls and bade them come out to play (L1/2).

But then came a reported sighting of Martin on the river. In *George* he is punting with unspecified individuals, but in the preliminary notes Williams identified them as a group of known homosexuals. With this further mockery, it was as if Williams had reincarnated as that unheeded schoolboy from Martin's past about whom the latter had been so *insouciant*. It was now Williams's turn to contemplate suicide, which, it is implied in the autobiography, would have been a real possibility had the means been readily available. Instead Williams found himself consulting the aptly named but ineffectual Dr Counsell (usually known in Oxford circles as 'Doggins'), whom Williams had originally succeeded at the OUDS as prompter. Disclosing half-truths, Williams could confess lamely not emotional desperation but simply an inability to work.

With the collapse of Williams's great expectations his mental breakdown followed immediately. His father, summoned from Connah's Quay by telegram, arrived literally overnight. Like a Joe Gargery ministering to a traumatised Pip, he bedded down in his son's rooms and took care of him until he was well enough to travel back to Flintshire. The trouble was that nobody could be apprised of the true cause of his mental predicament. Not his parents and not Miss Cooke, who was informed of events verbally by a pupil at Holywell, the son of one of his father's friends. Richard Williams was bitterly disappointed at being deprived of the opportunity to celebrate with his workmates his son's achievement of an Oxford degree. His mother blamed the theatricals, while Miss Cooke (not given on the whole to be especially understanding on issues of mental illness) urged him, as did his Oxford tutors, to return and attempt his examinations. Gossip in his home community tended to the view that Williams had 'coom a cropper poor lad' (G 411).

On the face of it he was merely suffering from the consequences of severe overwork, a more serious version of the panic that afflicted him in the previous year. There is a short gap in the weekly letters to Miss Cooke after 20 May (from Christ Church) until 2 June 1926 (from Connah's Quay). The May letter is from a student worried about what the future holds, while the June letter, in which the writing is noticeably weaker and more spindly, is from a convalescent who has been advised to take things easy while the damage to the mind is repaired: 'brain fever', they said (G 411), but quite what this meant clinically, if anything, is hard to know. His recreation was mainly listening to the wireless (a crystal set with headphones), which broadcast programmes from London under the 2LO call-sign, but the prescription also included light reading, golfing (with Miss Cooke's clubs) and country walks. Miss Cooke, though she barely understood what was going on since Williams gave her only cryptic clues ('I have realised the awful appropriateness of the metaphor "to prey on the mind"'), came to visit a few times, her first opportunity to see her protégé on his home territory. He made her feel as though she helped, especially in the excursions they made together by bus around Flintshire. This immersion in the things of everyday was part of a necessary coming to terms with ordinary life again after the distortions of Oxford. They even went as far as Liverpool, where Miss Cooke cannily had her charge examined by a psychiatrist, who could find nothing wrong that Williams did not already know about.

That summer, Williams's Oxford baggage literally came home in the sea-chest, a return of what Williams now saw as his Oxford coffin. Rehabilitation was a long process, which took nearly three months of the summer of 1926. Martin even ventured to inquire by letter about his health, but Williams was not in the mood for correspondence. During August he wrote almost no letters at all. He eventually divulged to Miss Cooke that his mood had been too dark, that what he felt was not 'real unhappiness', but rather depression,

> which it would have been boring to have enlarged upon, – a fact which the Romantic poets would have done well to digest, don't you think?' (A1 29 August 1926).

Overall it was by no means a wasted month, since the recovery therapies had begun to have the desired effect. Much of the time was spent in the company of John Stephen Roberts, another of Miss Cooke's protégés, who went up to Jesus from Holywell the year after Williams. They picnicked together, played golf, took bicycle rides into the county and, eventually after a three months' abstention on Williams's part, went to the cinema. Williams described him to Miss Cooke as 'a very pleasant companion, very sensitive and intelligent beneath his defensive surface' (A1 29 August 1926). It was about this time also that Williams returned to writing with his second serious play, the piece originally entitled *The Singing Pool*, a title rejected as 'too conventionally Celtic' (G 417) in favour of *Full Moon*, as it is now known. Like *Glamour* it has never been published. Williams typed the script and made several carbon copies, which were sent off to people he thought might be interested, including one to J. B. Fagan and another to a literary agent in London.

Oxford was now far away, though he had every intention of re-sitting Schools in June 1927. In the meantime, Williams decided that he would need to get a job. Teaching seemed the obvious answer. His first paid employment was to coach in French the fourteen-year old son (and in Italian two young neighbours) of William George, a Porthmadoc solicitor and brother of Richard Williams's political hero David Lloyd George. They lived at the small seaside resort of Criccieth, on the southern coast of the Lleyn peninsular facing Cardigan Bay. Thither he went in September to take up his duties, travelling by train. It was his first penetration deep into the heart of north-west Wales (never having previously been further west than Rhyl) and it made a great impression. All along the northern coastal strip, backed by the majesty of the mountains of Snowdonia, he was reminded of his inland ancestors, the Griffith family who came from Llanrwst. Most of all, at the string of country stations along the route, from the conversations amongst the passengers who got on or off, his journey brought him back into contact with his native language after a complete absence of Welsh at Oxford and a minimal exposure to it at home at Connah's Quay, totalling nearly a decade.

Emlyn Williams's destination was a substantial Victorian villa –

> a lovely mansion that dominates sky, mountain and sea on every
> side (A1 12 September 1926)

– called Garth Celyn that took him into the heartland of Welsh-speaking Wales. His employer's household at Criccieth proved to be a microcosm of all of what Williams valued as best in Welsh domestic life, an image that he kept returning to later as a playwright. It was he reported 'a very simple and charming family' in which Welsh was the preferred language of communication. His pupil William George junior, 'a precocious child in horn-rimmed specta-cles', indeed had had something of a similar experience to Williams himself in having been educated for a period outside Wales. He had been at prep-school in Kent for three years yet in returning had lost nothing of his Welsh, which he used as constantly and enthusiastically as everyone around him. This was a remarkable feat, and Williams gave it due recognition. In the autobiography the Garth Celyn establishment is described more patronisingly than in the Cooke letters – William George for instance is 'the picture of a right-living Welsh deacon' (G 419) – but Williams in fact could hardly have been more impressed by their unpretentious dignity. He even accepted with perfect equanimity their Sunday regime of chapel-going:

> just been to chapel . . . for the first time in years, and have the prospect of returning thither twice today,

he reported to Miss Cooke. They were for Williams a middle-class icon,

> a model of how a family should behave when it has acquired a little more money than its neighbours (A1 12 September 1926).

Though he never met David Lloyd George – he only pretended to his father that he had – he was much impressed by his wife, to whom he was introduced early in his stay at Criccieth. Mixing with the great and the good in London had given her no artificiality in manners. But perhaps the greatest impact was made by Lloyd George's daughter Megan, then aged twenty-four, to whom Williams taught Italian at seven shillings a lesson. In a sense, what she represented was not so much the perfect picture of animated young womanhood (though she was certainly that), but the perfectly balanced individual with feet in two cultures: urbane, intellectual, sophisticated, socially poised, very much a London girl, yet in contrast she could be equally as down-to-earth, as rustic as any of her Welsh neighbours. What made her especially interesting was her acquaintance not only with politicians but playwrights such as J. M. Barrie, John Galsworthy, Somerset Maugham and Noël Coward. Her Welsh was as fluent and as idiomatic as anything spoken by Williams's parents; but in English her beautifully modulated vowels betrayed no trace of Welshness. She was an inspiration in effortlessly combining the best of both cultures, being at home in either. There were moments, he claims in the autobiography, when he actually fantasised about marrying her. Amidst the daily tutoring work, the invigorating sea bathing ('glorious here' [A1 12 Sept 1926]), and the country walks which occupied his time, only once did Williams's thoughts revert to his failed Oxford love-life and the emotional cavity which succeeded it when, as he strode the hills above Criccieth, he was confronted by a distant figure, momentarily familiar, who was in fact just a farmer's boy sitting on a five-bar gate. Nonetheless it was a route he took care not to repeat.

At Criccieth two competing cultures lived side by side. Aside from the native Welsh there was a decided English presence in those who had retired there from north-west England or the Midlands, as well as a working population of English and an inevitable branch of the Women's Institute. Williams gradually became involved in both sides: tutoring in French daughters of English immigrants ready for 'coming out' and a mixed English-Welsh evening class. But in the main Criccieth was a decisive re-education in things Welsh. After about a month Williams found lodgings with a couple in their eighties. Their home called Ty Newydd he described as

> a delightful house facing the sea and the heather-clad mountains
> (A1 19 October 1926)

with distant views of Harlech Castle across the bay. He bought his own food but lived as one of the family. It was an experience totally Welsh in spirit and language, almost a reconstruction of his early life before Connah's Quay. Speaking English only with extreme difficulty, his hosts were effectively monoglot Welsh: Williams estimated that the old man did not know more than ten words of English. Indeed the Welsh atmosphere was so predominant that Williams found a certain alienating quality in writing to Miss Cooke in English.

Even here in the tiny protected enclave of Ty Newydd, the outside world continually impinged. To Williams's surprise, he discovered that the couple had a university-educated son with a DSc., living in London, though he never met him. Daily visits to Criccieth's lending library to scan the columns of *The Times* kept

Williams in touch with events across the border. His abiding interest was in the theatrical news, from which he learned of J.B. Fagan's newest comedy *And So to Bed*, opening at the Queen's Theatre in September and based on Pepys's *Diary*. Fagan seemed to have forgotten about *Full Moon*, but eventually a letter forwarded from Connah's Quay arrived with a proposal to include the play in his repertory programme for the Oxford Playhouse early in 1927. It took Williams a while to convince his parents that this was not merely another production for the OUDS, but the real thing: a foothold in the professional theatre. Grace Cooke, for her part, trying with a little difficulty not to be over-impressed, did her duty by emphasising the importance of his re-sitting his examinations and gaining an Oxford degree. That was something, she insisted with her usual forthrightness, that would 'outwear a week at any old Playhouse' (G 426).

Three: Debut

At Christmas 1926 Emlyn Williams left the restorative Welsh climate of Criccieth to return temporarily to Connah's Quay and await the call to Oxford. It was a difficult limbo period, his last extended stay in Flintshire, not helped by the fact that Fagan was forced to delay production of *Full Moon* a month over the originally scheduled date until 28 February 1927. Uncharacteristically, Williams filled in the time by going to local dances with old school friends, including Ena Hughes, who was a convenient, if otherwise undervalued, companion. Returning home one night from supper with the Hughes family he met a lone cyclist, who it turned out was a juvenile actor en route for Liverpool to play in the touring production of *No, No, Nanette*. To his enquiry whether he was 'from round here' Williams replied revealingly that he was from London, and 'in the theatre' (G 430).

These early months of 1927 helped resolve Williams's identity crisis by marking out the direction of his future life as playwright and actor. After much soul-searching he declined Fagan's invitation to play the lead in his production of *Androcles and the Lion*, which was to precede *Full Moon* at the Oxford Playhouse. It was as well that he did, since most of February was taken up with nursing two invalids at home in Connah's Quay. First his mother, then his fourteen-year-old brother Tom, succumbed to pneumonia, an especially serious and life-threatening condition in a pre-antibiotic age. Williams was thrown into the role of nursemaid and housekeeper, though he knew nothing of cooking beyond the ability to boil an egg. The only compensation for these dark days of illness and delirium was that Williams felt closer to his mother than at any time before or afterwards. A couple of days after the opening of *Full Moon*, he was released from sick-room duty as his patients were much improved and allowed to take a long weekend at Oxford. Reggie Colby had already telegraphed news of the play's favourable reception and writing to Miss Cooke on the train Williams reported it was 'exquisitely mounted and very admirably played'. Fagan was said to be 'very pleased'. Yet Williams was understandably apprehensive at returning to Oxford not now as student but as playwright. There was a conflict still between on one hand his guilt at his breakdown and the aborted examinations and on the other his new role as playwright, even though this was what he most desired. But he put a brave face on it:

> [t]omorrow I burst upon Oxford, and as you said it couldn't be a better entry.

On the Sunday night there was to be

> an aesthetic party ... in my honour, and <u>all</u> Oxford will be there
> (A1 3 March 1927).

If they were, Williams makes no reference to them or to anything resembling an aesthetic party in *George*. Instead following his last night attendance at his play he details only a theatrical supper of kippers, chips, tea, beer and shoptalk with some of the cast, prominent among whom were Alan Webb and Glen Byam Shaw. Perhaps the latter version better fitted the image of the playwright integrating himself into the world of the theatre, rather than revisiting the past glories of Oxford aestheticism. The press took a special interest too. This was less because of the relatively unusual circumstance of a student making a debut as professional playwright than of the gossip concerning Megan Lloyd George's enthusiasm for the play and the hints of a developing friendship (intellectual rather than emotional it seems) with its young author. Under the headline 'Miss Lloyd George and the Stage' a newspaper reported her eagerness to appear in a Williams play and Williams's comment in an interview (C1, unidentified newsclipping) that

> [w]e talk Welsh together sometimes ... but usually talk Italian, at which she is remarkably fluent, almost as fluent, in fact, as she is in French.

Emlyn Williams knew he was not the first Oxford undergraduate to have a play performed professionally – his compatriot Richard

Hughes, for example, had done so with *The Sisters' Tragedy* at the Adelphi, London, in 1924 – but the special nature of the experience took some getting used to. The huge red and black advertising poster outside the theatre convinced Williams of the actuality of his play, yet to sit front-of-house at the Oxford Playhouse as an observer of his own work was unsettling. He was in no way involved in its production, had not attended even a single rehearsal. It stimulated a curious alienation: a process in him of detached criticism, even down to the typography of the programme, over which he had equally no control. The one feature that seemed to give him a grip on reality was that the key roles, as played by Alan Napier and Byam Shaw, were exactly how they had been envisaged in the writing. Yet so were the others (Roy Malcolm, Alan Webb, Margaret Webster), whom he had not known. Indeed, this perhaps rather old-fashioned way of working by writing roles with particular actors in view (though it has a provenance as far back as Shakespeare and was almost a universal practice in the nineteenth century) did give him a kind of security as a playwright. Williams continued in this way through most of his professional career and it accounts for the presence of certain stereotypes in the plays. At Oxford Alan Webb not unkindly (and perhaps with some justice) referred to him as 'the Welsh Pinero' (G 437).

Full Moon had been begun before Williams's breakdown in June 1926 and the play was finished as part of his self-regulated therapy at the end of his convalescence in the late summer of the same year. This context goes some way to account for its strange intangibility and the depth of its passion and conviction. It is an emotional pressure-cooker of a play, set in a lone villa on a rocky island in the middle of a small lake in the Italian Alps. The inhabitants are an expatriate Englishman, his wife (whom he has ceased to love), their twenty-year-old son and a servant (their sole connection with the outside world), who periodically rows across the lake to buy provisions. Superimposed upon this unlikely but atmospherically disturbing setting is the old Welsh legend of '*Cantre Gwaelod*', telling of the drowned city under the waves of Cardigan Bay. Its church bells can be heard at certain times of crisis or, as in this case, at full moon when love is in the air. The arrival of another Englishman (played by Alan Webb) and his half-Italian daughter sets in train the

emotional drama as the intensity of the relationship between the girl
and boy (Glen Byam Shaw) causes the bells to sound in recognition
of their love. But their felicity is cut short, cruelly subverted by the
possessiveness of the boy's father, who wants to hold on to the only
relationship in his life that still has meaning. The subtext of the play
shows it to be a reading of Williams's own recent emotional trauma,
though he was aware of it only in retrospect. As he recognised in
George, his own psychological and sexual tensions are present both
in the father and in the girl. Like her creator, she is recovering with
difficulty from a failed love affair.

The play was over-long, partly owing to being burdened with
'atmosphere' in Act 1; but it had a certain intellectual appeal –
'thoughtful and clever', said the *Oxford Chorus* (4 March 1927) –
working through the emotional crises of the characters and there
were, as some of the other reviewers noticed, occasional touches of
Chekov, even of Strindberg. As in the boy-sentry in the lonely
border manor in *Vigil*, the theme of obsession is just as strong here
and as unresolved, for Williams was not betrayed into constructing
a false conclusion. The mood changes are sometimes under-
prepared for, but the overall effect of the writing combines
mysticism with Celtic lyricism (which may have been the cause of
Fagan's attraction to it as an Irishman). It was a technique that
(except in *Pen Don*) Williams did not go on to develop. In the *Oxford
University Review* the drama was described as presenting

> a small group of men and women each of whose desires mani-
> fest themselves in mutual conflict, but whose emotions
> nevertheless form one whole and move upon one course. The
> play exists as a curve of group emotion (3 March 1927).

It was in stark contrast to the other play being premiered at Oxford
on the same night, Edgar Wallace's latest thriller *The Terror* at the
New Theatre. Williams's association with Wallace came to be quite
close, and the subsequent direction of his playwriting talent inclined
somewhat more towards Wallace than it did to Chekov.

Fagan was impressed enough by the play and its relative success
at Oxford to suggest that after the examinations he might be able to
help Williams begin a career on the stage. In the meantime his

newest playwright (who had now received his very first royalties of five pounds from the performances of *Full Moon*) was invited to London as guest of the Fagans in order to broaden his experience of West End plays. From Oxford he went directly to London and was put up for four nights at the Kenilworth Hotel, adjacent to the Fagans' flat in Great Russell Street. He went to see Fagan's own production of *And So to Bed*, to *Juno and the Paycock* and the musical comedy *Sunny* at the Hippodrome (an odd choice Fagan thought for 'an intellectual Oxford playwright' [G 440]). However, it was not Oxford but London that was Williams's focus now. Still less was it Flintshire. Some days later, as his train steamed out of Chester for the remaining homeward leg towards Connah's Quay, Williams felt a sense of exhilaration rather than his usual claustrophobia: that he was now on the brink of fulfilment of his greatest aspiration, a career in the London theatre. From this point there would be no going back to the homestead at 314a High Street, except as a visitor.

The thought was partner to the deed. But the more or less immediate break with the family household was as unexpected as it was dramatic. Although Williams had earned a modest fee out of his first play, he was not a wage earner like his brothers Job and Tom, and there had always been in the background a certain resentment, mostly on his mother's side, that for the last six years he could have been earning a living rather than indulging himself at university. According to the scripted scene in *George*, the trigger incidents were absurdly trivial (over a crystal wireless set and a displaced armchair) but they were perhaps symptomatic of larger resentments built up over time. A cryptic note scribbled to Miss Cooke on the train indicated serious trouble:

> It is impossible for me to stay at home any longer, so I am looking for a job, anything, anywhere. I shall explain more fully when I write (C1 28 March 1927).

His report, among other matters, of the break with Connah's Quay was written up about a month later 'in the immense hush of the British Museum' (A1 26/27 April 1927), where he was waiting for a book delivery under the great gilded dome in the Round Reading Room. (He described himself as 'surrounded by dirty old ladies writing in little notebooks ... and lots and lots of unshaven bespectacled German philosophers'.) Implicating both his parents, Williams gave the immediate scenario for the row a more personalised cast. His father he asserted

> has never forgiven me for my precious 'nervous breakdown'

and 'lost confidence completely' in him as a result; and his mother fared worse:

> I don't get on with Mother, she doesn't really like me as much as [Job] my middle brother.

His story was that his father

> burst out and said I was good for nothing and was in the way.

Williams had planned, it seems, to live on his father's and brothers' earnings until October, when he might have found an opening in the theatre; but the row precipitated events and, in a mixture of anger and lofty pride, he walked out on the family early next day to catch the first train for Euston.

It was probably something of an exaggeration (perhaps to enlist Miss Cooke's sympathies) to describe himself as 'with no money and no prospects' (A1 26/27 April 1927) for, according to the autobiography, he had most of his Playhouse royalties still intact. At the Savoy, Fagan was as good as his word and, after a delay of about three weeks, slotted him into a six-line part as Pelling's 'Prentice in his comedy *And So to Bed*, at nine pounds a month. The only condition was that he 'had a shot at schools', for which Fagan even offered to pay his Oxford expenses. As Williams confided to Miss Cooke,

> [a]nything less like the conventional hard and rapacious West End Manager could hardly be imagined.

At Easter 1927, on Monday 18 April (not 4 April 1927 as given in successive editions of *Who's Who in the Theatre* and elsewhere), he was eased at a special holiday matinée into a play which had already been running in London for more than seven months. This appearance in *And So to Bed* at the Savoy – the play was transferred to the Globe Theatre two weeks later on 2 May – marks Emlyn Williams's debut as a professional actor. It also signals the division between the two autobiographical volumes: at this point *George* comes to an end and *Emlyn* begins.

*

Williams awaited with some trepidation Miss Cooke's registration of his career change now that an academic or teaching position had been rejected in favour of the theatre, at least for the time being. The intention was to combine acting with continuing work, mostly on a daily basis, in the Round Reading Room at the British Museum (as his digs were far too cramped for work) in preparation for re-taking Schools at Oxford in June. By now aware that the idea of obtaining a First was not in question, he was keen to assure Miss Cooke that although his spare time was limited

> I'm doing as much [work] as I can as I want a degree of some sort (A1 26/27 April 1927).

By July, four days before his viva, despite his confession to Miss Cooke of how little he knew, this resolve had crystallised into thoughts of a 'meritorious' Second, which was possible 'with luck' (A1 5 July 1927).

After the emotional upheaval of his recent Oxford experience and the abrupt termination of the romantic friendship with Martin (alias 'Charles Garvenal') – 'the self-appointed victim of a blameless passion' (E 13) as, with forty-six years' hindsight, he described his former state – Williams's avowed intention in London was to eschew emotional involvement with anyone. But this was difficult since he was temperamentally not suited to the solitary life and his sexual impulses at twenty-one were not easy to control. The London that he so much craved for professionally proved less inviting on a personal level. When not playing in the theatre or engrossed reading in the British Museum, Williams suffered a rather restless early summer before going up to Oxford for his Finals. A favourite occupation was lazing with his books in Hyde Park or on Hampstead Heath (even then a notorious gay pick-up point), where he implies that the occasional 'casual fraternization' on the grass (E 13) provided necessary companionship and discharge for his emotions. The busy metaphors in the writing at this point in the autobiography dissolve into euphemism, but the subtext implies a racy thrill in these transient, anonymous encounters behind negligently arranged newspapers. Instinctively he was drawn to these 'fleeting Edens', forbidden yet desired, as much by the sense of curiosity at the unknown as by the physical release. Their value lay in their uncommitted nature, now that he was free of the binding passion of his unsatisfied sexual life at Oxford. At the same time, in an attempt to keep the balance, there is the suggestion that he would have been just as happy at the prospect of another Rouen experience, but was much more wary of London as opposed to French prostitutes.

A chance meeting with a newly liberated Angus Rae (who proved to be better company now that he had sloughed off his Oxford lover) channelled him more directly into the homosexual scene: the Tea Kettle in Wardour Street and the Chalice bar in Coventry Street came well recommended. Williams sampled both alone and found them rather distasteful; but the 'men only' Long Bar at the Trocadero, just off Piccadilly Circus, in Shaftesbury Avenue, with its easy mix of gay and straight clientele, Williams found less intimidating and it eventually became a favourite. With Angus as chaperone, Williams was also introduced to the basement restaurant at the Criterion, in Lower Regent Street. After the 'respectable' diners had left at about 10 pm the place underwent a dramatic transformation as a celebrated meeting-place, variously known as the 'Witches' Cauldron' or the 'Bargain Basement'.

It was at the Criterion, according to the version in *Emlyn*, that Williams met the wispy, monocled individual he calls 'Pierre', who invited him to stay at his Chelsea studio. Williams, lodging with friends in north London, jumped at the chance. The relationship was perhaps fairly brief and may have been unimportant but the fact that his treatment of the episode is hedged by fabrications might suggest otherwise. Some discrepancies emerge between the story as he says it happened (as outlined in *Emlyn*), the version which he there claims to have told Miss Cooke, and the version actually delivered to her in the letters. Within a week of his debut at the Savoy Theatre he had written to Miss Cooke to say that he was

> living with a French Corsican friend [un-named] whom I met in Paris, in a lovely studio in Chelsea (A1 26/27 April 1927).

This individual is certainly to be identified with the figure in *Emlyn* whom he claims to have fictionalised for Miss Cooke as 'an old Oxford friend, Comte Pierre de Rilly' (E 17).

Williams did lie to Miss Cooke, but on completely different terms from the 'four untruths' he identifies in *Emlyn*. The only constant in the various versions is the address at Wentworth, Manresa Road, Chelsea. It is difficult to be sure which other details were true – some were almost certainly authentic – but he indicated to Miss Cooke that the studio was above a girls' school, in which 'Pierre' did some teaching in French and Spanish. It was supposedly a rather spacious *atelier* 'with rafters and orange curtains' and two beds, rent fifteen shillings a week. His friend, he went on,

> cooks beautifully and we are going to keep house.
> (A1 26/27 April 1927)

Given its intended recipient, this description clearly does not betoken a sexual relationship. Indeed this interpretation is also strongly resisted in the autobiography. Williams is keen to record the admission by 'Pierre' – who it is suggested is really Peter O'Reilly and Irish-American not French, though this may be a further piece of disinformation in that probably neither name is authentic – that he was 'not his type' (E 18). Yet the camouflage for readers of *Emlyn* and the deceits he says he engineered for Miss Cooke (a fiction imposed upon another fiction) might be seen as overdone if that was indeed the case. All that Williams admits to is that he and 'Pierre' did discuss sexual matters together very frankly; and that he was initiated, in another of his disingenuous poses claiming to have led a sheltered life, into a new range of gay jargon (in which his companion was as 'fluent as thieves' slang' [E 18]). What in *Emlyn* is referred to as only a very temporary arrangement over about three days – no more indeed than a 'brief wallow in la boue' (E 19) – actually lasted almost four months. Now with money to live on independently he soon found himself a cheerless furnished room near Kings Cross station; but he regarded the Manresa Road studio as his home until he went to Oxford for his viva in July. He also returned there afterwards while rehearsing in London for Fagan's forthcoming Oxford repertory during August and before going on tour with *And So to Bed*.

Williams revelled in the louche, bohemian style and the link with gay life. As he reports in *Emlyn* there were definite attractions about the Chelsea alleys, for occasionally 'on a midnight impulse' he would be drawn there 'for a quick dip in the murky briny' (E 28). These mysterious excursions, which invigorated him to work on the script for his latest project, often from the small hours until dawn, were possibly night-time equivalents of the pick-ups in the park. Perhaps most importantly they serve to illustrate how much Williams was intrigued by and indulged in the double life of the city: the coincidence of common everyday activity and the under-world of sexual assignation, a border-line between the respectable and the seamy that he enjoyed transgressing whenever his mood dictated.

London was often oppressive and, as Sundays still retained something of their old depressing chapel-like quality even in absence of religious imperatives, he was glad to have the occasional company of such as Ena Hughes. Once in May they went out to Epping Forest to read under the trees. But it is clear that Ena, though she never knew it, was just a doormat: Williams had no respect for her qualities of conversation and to Miss Cooke sneered at her lack of sophistication. As he explained, she was pleasant enough and

> above all a link with Holywell, Flint, and Connah's Quay, though I don't suppose she'd care to be labelled so.
>
> (A1 19 May 1927)

But later, after taking her to the theatre, he was more explicit in his criticism: that she was 'very ordinary', had a 'bourgeois' mind 'in the real damning spiritual meaning of the word', lacked conversation and humour, and was 'very undeveloped, without the charm of unsophistication' (A1 5 July 1927). Nevertheless, Williams persisted with her friendship, less out of a sense of the border links she represented (though that was evidently still of some importance) than in an attempt to retain some heterosexual impetus, though entirely platonic, in an emotional life that seemed for the most part inclined in the contrary direction.

Oxford loomed again for the final hurdle. Nevertheless, Williams found time to work on his third play. It was written partly to impress Miss Cooke, who had frequently extolled the virtues and the difficulties of writing dramas which observed the Aristotelian Unities, such as Racine had been impelled to do. This play was to out-Racine Racine, though at a distinctly more popular level, by making the Time the actual time and date when the play is being performed and Place the actual stage of the theatre in which the performance happens to be located. Nor was it in any way an emulation of his earlier plays: it was not Chekovian, nor even poetic but (as the subtitle denoted) 'a Ghost Story in Three Acts'. Conscious of the fact that *Full Moon* was in no sense a play for the popular market, Williams was firmly committed to the notion that *A Murder has been Arranged* was to be very different. As he announced to Miss Cooke, for the first time 'I'm going to write now, a frankly commercial thriller' (A1 5 July 1927).

Two days after the closure of *And So to Bed* on 18 June, he went up to Oxford for the examinations beginning on the following day. Tempting fate and testing his nerve, he stayed at Christ Church in Tom Quad, vainly trying to ignore the familiar sonorities of the great bell. Even here the theatre eventually intervened. In between his last examination and his viva, he was recalled to London for a walk-on part at three pounds a week in Fagan's Strand Theatre production of Strindberg's *The Spook Sonata*, running for one week only from 27 June. Several of his friends were in it, including Alan Napier as the Colonel, Byam Shaw as Arkenholtz, and Gyles Isham as Baron Skanskorg. Williams's report on it to Miss Cooke was to dismiss it as much too highbrow:

> a quite incomprehensible play by the Swedish writer 'Strind-bergh', all about a house where a dead man walks about in his winding sheet and an old woman has lived for 20 years in a

cupboard because she thinks she is a parrot.

Yet, he concluded, the theatre was unaccountably packed to over-flowing:

> [t]he ways of the theatrical public – the pit especially – are incalculable (A1 5 July 1927).

Williams's philistine attitude to a play he described as 'too obscurely symbolic' (E 23) is a little surprising, given the presence of a Strindbergian element in his own early work. But it actually says something rather important about the direction Williams chose to take in his career as a playwright. Professionally, he was on a completely different tack. His newest play *A Murder has been Arranged*, which he more or less finished in July 1927 (while staying in a rented room at 3 Council Houses, Radley, five miles outside Oxford, awaiting his viva), was unashamed popular entertainment. Williams craved such success, less for the money it might bring (welcome though it was) than for full acceptance into the area of theatre that he had come to know so well. In a theatre that tended to measure success on the length of run, his belief was that he could make a name for himself only in the commercial area. Nothing written to date had fitted such a specification. Although *Full Moon* was doing the rounds with the theatre managers, he had severe doubts that it would ever find a theatrical home

> as it is definitely not a commercial play, —quite apart from the question of merits and demerits (A1 5 July 1927).

After a week's intensive work, Williams announced in a triumphant flourish to his letter to Miss Cooke the completion of *A Murder has been Arranged*:

> 36,000 words on my little typewriter! 120 pages of a printed book! I think it's rather a feat of endurance! It's a complete thriller and if I don't sell it I'll eat every one of the 120 pages.
> (A1 [July 1927])

There was some delay but it was taken up for submission to the managers by Curtis Brown, 'the foremost dramatic and publishing agents in the world', who were, he told Miss Cooke, 'very keen' (A1 13 September 1927).

Williams's fractured relations with his family were amicably re-established by the summer. His mother regularly sent him homemade cakes and in the autumn a new muffler. Miss Cooke too became reconciled to the career choice of her brightest former pupil. She liked *Full Moon* and was pleased at the attention it was begin-ning to attract. Ivan Kyrle Fletcher paid two guineas to perform it at a play-reading circle in Newport and in mid-July it was the subject of a talk on new Welsh writing on the wireless, broadcast from Cardiff. Aware too how precarious Williams finances still were, especially during those weeks of rehearsal for the August repertory at Oxford when there would be no pay at all, she sent him thirty pounds. She was well prepared for the news of her protégé's degree classification, even though Williams himself nurtured a secret hope that somehow he might have pulled off a First. His first meeting with Miss Cooke after news of his Second took place at her home in Leeds, where he stayed while on his pre-New York tour with *And So To Bed*, in which he had graduated from Apprentice to Pepys's Boy, A.S.M. and Byam Shaw's understudy. It was less intimidating than expected; she seemed to have accepted the result with equanimity, though, like Williams himself, was aware that the degree class was no true reflection of his ability. It was in some way to be the story of his life as a professional playwright.

It is sometimes argued that Emlyn Williams learned (like Shakespeare or W.S. Gilbert or Pinero) how to be a dramatist by first learning how to be an actor, and that this was the key to his mastery of dramatic technique. Playwrights who know the theatre from inside do have an advantage, though it is by no means a prerequi-site of success. The truth is that in Williams's case at the time of his modest commercial success in London in 1930 with *A Murder has been Arranged,* his acting experience was actually still rather limited. He had played no major role in anything, either at Oxford or in London. Admittedly he had a reasonably varied experience, but all his London parts before that date were 'bit parts' or walk-ons. It sounded grand to be able to say that he had a free first class passage across the Atlantic on a Cunard liner and twelve pounds (or sixty dollars) a week for the New York tour of *And So to Bed*. But in raw theatrical experience he did not advance beyond what he had achieved in London or Oxford. In the early stages of his professional career, he learned more from listening and watching other people act than from interpreting his own roles.

Indeed, the American episode was altogether less invigorating than Williams anticipated. On passage to New York on the *Carmania* the ship was buffeted by an abnormally fierce Atlantic storm and, like most of the passengers, he was acutely seasick. In a quiet interlude, merely to pass the time, his companions agreed to a private read-through of his latest script. It was a salutary experience for its author, who had to recognise the truth of what the others fell over themselves to point out: that the play was 'most promising' but 'wants cutting' (E 40).

Altogether, Williams's first visit to North America was no great success at a personal level either. Desperately lonely, he realised for the first time the critical importance of letters as the links with everything he valued most in life. They were his security in a rather alien world. The arrival of the post was the big event of the day, even though in most cases it actually brought him nothing at all. From Toronto in late October he confessed to being

> seriously ill with homesickness, and it recurs in waves.
> (A1 28 October 1927)

Letters, or rather the lack of them, continued to be a main cause of concern throughout his eight months' stay and 205 performances of *And So to Bed*. Noting arrivals of British liners at the quayside in New York, he berated Miss Cooke for not mailing letters for conveyance on the faster ships: choosing liners like the *Majestic*, *Bremen,* or *Europa* meant that a letter arrived in five days, whereas most of the others took twice as long. As in Britain, Sundays were the worst days: there was no theatre to occupy his time and the mood of depression which he had first felt at Oxford began to cloud his consciousness once again.

In Montreal his loneliness found temporary relief when, by an uncharacteristic mistake in his French in asking for lodgings, he found himself in a brothel. He left hurriedly, only to return the following night to enjoy 'refreshing and natural' sex (E 46) after three and a half years' abstinence, his first re-run of the Rouen experience and significantly without the 'elder brother' presence. Back in New York, gloom began to settle: there was work but no social compensations or outlets. The play opened at the Shubert Theatre on 9 November, after which the others went on to first-night parties. Williams was not invited; miserable and alone, he dined at a drug-store counter in Times Square – drug-store attendants became his only source of conversation outside the theatre – and walked home to his solitary room on East 23rd Street.

In periods of enforced solitude Williams's sexual impulses were at their strongest. The pattern of relationships during his twenties follows a fairly regular alternating homosexual-heterosexual course. They seem remarkably evenly matched, designedly so perhaps for the purposes of the autobiography, yet it is evident that all the more affecting experiences were homosexual in kind. By far the most explicit from this period occurred in late December 1927 or very early 1928 when, recalling a recommendation made in London by his Chelsea friend 'Pierre', he visited on impulse the male-only Everard Turkish Baths, off 28th Street. Apart from the actual bathing facilities, this dingy institution, as large as a warehouse, comprised rows of 'private rooms' more accurately described as cells, with doors opening into a corridor along which men, draped ghost-like in their white towels, slowly paraded in the hope of sexual encounter. Williams sat in his cubicle, he implies, as a detached listener and observer, yet at the same time he seems part of the game as he awaits a discreet tap upon the door. Most clients appeared otherwise respectable middle-class city types, stopping off en route to their suburban homes and their wives. The autobiographical narrative is silent on the matter of a partner, if indeed he had one, but Williams evokes a powerful, homo-erotic atmosphere, a strange mixture of Kafkaesque insecurity and the sterile sexuality of *The Waste Land*, which he observes and dramatises. And the experience, with its implications of deceit and sexual betrayal, lodged deep in his memory.

Back in England about a year later during the uninspiring try-out for his new play *Glamour* at Aldershot, Williams began to realise the importance of writing only about what he knew from firsthand. In this regard, the possibility of using aspects of the Everard episode as the material for a play flitted crudely and unformed through his mind, only to be dismissed in the awareness that homosexuality, however circumspectly treated, was almost invariably a proscribed subject at the Lord Chamberlain's Office. The idea, however, continued to intrigue him because it was part of his own story. Some measure of encouragement might have been derived from the surprise licensing of Mordaunt Shairp's *The Green Bay Tree* (1932), which portrayed the anguish of a wife locked into marriage with a husband of homosexual tendencies. But the inference amongst several newspaper columnists and reviewers that the restrictions on homosexual subject-matter had been lifted was hopelessly premature. The Examiner of Plays noted for the official records at the time that some critics seemed

> influenced by a desire to appear knowing or by the unfortunate fact that homosexuality is in the air very much at present or at least in the theatrical air (Johnson, 173).

Unlikely as it might seem on the surface, Williams's career hints at some of the hidden effects of censorship. As a playwright, though evidently tempted to write about homosexuality and indeed to express his own divided sexuality (already detectable in veiled form in *Vigil* and *Full Moon*), he was forced into artistic compromise by the certainty of the censor's veto. And when Williams ventured more than twenty years later – as he did in *Accolade* – to write of the experience of the double life and sexual cheating he had to accept that very little had changed since 1930. For the purposes of satisfying censors (and to a large extent critics and audiences), his theme had to be rendered in exclusively heterosexual rather than homosexual or bisexual terms. What might have been his most daring and revealing play – 'Fess', based directly on his bisexual experience in the mid-1930s – came late, probably too late, when his dramatic talent had fallen into decline. It was perhaps an indulgence and never proceeded beyond manuscript. Significantly however it was conceived of and written only after the abolition of censorship in 1968.

Just before Christmas 1927 there was a welcome disruption to the routine. Out of the blue Williams received an invitation from a High School teacher, Olive Ely Hart, who had written to him earlier in London, to visit her sister and herself in Philadelphia. A mature age graduate student at the University of Pennsylvania, she was writing a doctoral thesis on modern Welsh drama. The theatre was her passion. On a day trip to New York she had managed to see no fewer than four shows, one of which was *And So to Bed*. Williams was impressed by the quiet air of luxury in their 'lovely old colonial home', complete with black maid, who brought him breakfast in bed on the first morning. The sisters' situation resembled that of Grace Cooke and her own sister, with whom she lived in Leeds during the school holidays. Olive Hart was, he wrote to Miss Cooke,

> a delightful woman, you'd like her immensely; she's very intel-
> ligent, with great charm and humour (A1 28 December 1927).

Williams's claim in the autobiography that he represented Hart to Sarah Cooke as writer rather than teacher (because he did not want to be labelled as a 'Teacher's Pet' [E 51]) is not true: on the contrary he was scrupulously open about her profession. But perhaps the discrepancy makes a point about Williams's subconscious abashment. They talked animatedly on teaching, race issues and the theatre. He enjoyed his status as a tame Welsh playwright, and his success in the social circles of Philadelphia led to his being invited back at approximately three-weekly intervals. The two spinster sisters were soon christened 'Aunt Olive' and 'Aunt Ada'. Williams felt safe with mature, de-sexualised women like them because they so much resembled Miss Cooke.

Olive Hart's thesis was privately published as a short monograph entitled *The Modern Drama in Wales from 1905 to the present-day* (Philadelphia, 1928). In the body of the book, Williams is represented within a small group of new generation Welsh playwrights which includes Richard Hughes, A.O. Roberts and 'Shirland Quin' (Enid Guest), balanced by several established writers such as J.O. Francis, Caradoc Evans and D.T. Davies. In her discussion of Williams, Hart offers a brief (slightly inaccurate) outline of his education followed by plot summaries of *Full Moon* and *Glamour*. Of the former, she argues that the combination of mysticism, legend and poetic beauty gives it 'a peculiar atmosphere of spiritual intensity ... which is Welsh' (Hart, 62). As the youngest of the group under scrutiny, Williams is shown in an accompanying photograph aged about twenty-two, dark-haired, with deep-set eyes and distinctively dark eyebrows, looking more like a fresh-faced sixth-former than the Oxford graduate he had recently become.

During early December 1927 Glen Byam Shaw developed appendicitis and as his understudy Williams had the chance to play his first larger role, that of Master Pelham Humphrey. When the long run of *And So to Bed* eventually closed on 21 April 1928 it was on a sour note, after a quarrel with the man whom he almost regarded as his theatrical father, J.B. Fagan. The autobiography mentions nothing of it but there was trouble in the cast as far back as February when Byam Shaw and others, including Mary Robson, left after a dispute. Williams reported that the company had uncovered a hitherto unsuspected dark side to Fagan. He was proving a 'crooked[,] weak minded creature who has vaguely good instincts' undeniably under the thumb of 'an extraordinary wife' (A1 17 February 1928), the actress Mary Grey. Then in March, after three weeks' rehearsal for a new production of *The Cherry Orchard*, Williams was peremptorily informed, on requesting a rise in salary, that he would no longer be required for the play. His professional pride dented and angered by Fagan's attitude that he should content himself with a lower salary out of gratitude to his benefactor for having given him a job in the first place, he sought release from his contract with *And So to Bed*. But Fagan would not let him go, and he was compelled to finish the run. Homesickness prevented him from seeking any further work in the USA and he sailed home immediately to Southampton on the *Aquitania*.

Back in Britain, Williams made his decisive break with the past. Although he still missed his family, home for Williams was now not the borderlands of North Wales but London, and he secured an unfurnished room on the top-floor of

a delightful house overlooking a very green and quiet square,
(A1 21 May 1928)

at 34 Vincent Square, SW1. In contrast, in *Emlyn* his new London home is described having 'fallen on bad times without being evil' with 'a bad-tempered-looking geyser' (E 62), terms rather better fitted to the stereotypical image of struggling actor; but he tried to make it more cheerful by painting the walls yellow and furnishing with bits and pieces from Woolworth's and the Caledonian Market.

Intending now to set up as a professional actor, he wrote round all the London managers, including those responsible for tours, offering himself for work, but making it clear that he was interested only in leading parts, not walk-ons or understudies (which he believed would represent a retrograde step in his career). He also acquired a telephone as an early priority, but spent a dispiriting three months hovering around an obstinately silent instrument, waiting for the call that never came. His first intended commercial play *A Murder has been Arranged* still had no takers, and he began to fill the time by writing another play, again deliberately non-high-brow and specifically tailored for the commercial stage.

The new work, his fourth play, was called *Glamour*, though that was not its original title. Until at least the middle of October it was known as 'Happiness'. At this time it was accepted by C.B. Williams 'a Welshman, and a charming person' (A1 20 October 1928), who chose to direct it himself and persuaded Williams to change the title. A provincial try-out was arranged for the beginning of December at Aldershot immediately prior to a two week run at the Embassy Theatre in Hampstead. There were difficulties over the engagement of a leading lady, since the part required a beautiful actress who at the age of thirty-seven is a trifle *passé*. At least three 'names' of the London theatrical scene turned it down before Mary Dibley, who was familiar to Williams from the flickering silent films at the Connah's Quay Hippodrome, finally accepted. A rainy week in Aldershot just before Christmas did not prove auspicious. Audiences were sparse and neither the weather nor audiences improved. Things were only marginally better at the Embassy a week later. At such a location outside the mainstream, no play could be expected to do big business. Nonetheless the first night went well, its success being assured by the presence of friends, including Megan Lloyd George and a large contingent of London Welsh, all favourably disposed to this newest Welsh recruit into the profession of playwriting. Ena Hughes loyally attended as well and reported back to Miss Cooke on 'George's triumph'. Not least to be admired, she wrote, was his courage in singing an old Welsh love-song

> in duet in front of such a fashionable London crowd. Such a play does more towards raising the prestige of the Welsh than I thought possible (C1 10 December 1928).

Sentiments of that sort betrayed in Ena Hughes a much more intelligent mind than Williams ever gave her credit for.

Personal enthusiasms apart, the critical response was relatively cool. For the *Manchester Guardian* (12 December 1928) it was 'unambitious' and totally predictable in its story of a 'town-struck' couple deciding to abandon the garishness of London for the sunsets of Snowdon; the *Daily Telegraph* found it difficult to take seriously as it was 'all exceedingly sentimental, and nothing in it rings quite true' (12 December). Intentionally he had exploited the two areas of life that he knew best – Wales and the Welsh and the theatre – but it was argued that Williams's subject was only half his. While he was perfectly at home in the Welsh elements of the play – including the folksong 'Y Deryn Pur' ['The pure bird on a black wing / Be my servant, free from care. /Oh hurry to the maiden / That I loved so early'] a staple ingredient of school *eisteddfodau*, a copy of which Miss Cooke secured for him – and the Welshness of the characters, the location of the action in the plush drawing-room of Eve Lone's flat in Leicester Square was less convincing. Its theme of sacrifice, that of the Welsh country girl who, being given the chance of a lifetime to appear in a West End musical (at the price of her honour), eventually determines to throw up her chance of starring in the theatre to return to Wales to look after a penniless blind artist, suggested contrivance rather than verisimilitude. Yet C.B. Williams's confidence in the play, with Betty Hardy as Jill and Williams as Jack (a part which he had written expressly for himself), was sufficiently strong for him to have it transferred to the Court Theatre opening on 31 December. He seemed to think that there was the possibility of a long run. In fact it registered only twenty-four performances, to 19 January 1929. For a first play it was judged as at best worthy and serious in intention, but lacking real backbone as drama.

Interestingly, several critics suggested that Williams's Welsh background had prevented his creating an authentic English setting and that his cocktail-drinking characters were simply stereotypes out of a cheap novelette. If the *Daily Sketch* suggested too dismissively that it was all done at a rather schoolboyish level, Charles Morgan for *The Times* (1 January 1929) was more gracious and came nearer to the essential shortcomings in a play which also had moments of real strength:

> ... we felt always that Mr Emlyn Williams had himself no taste for the gilt on his gingerbread. The impression, together with some happy fragments in the play itself, give hope that, when he chooses to be plain and please himself, he may write for the enjoyment of more than he now supposes.

Williams's weakness was located in the desire to be commercial, to give his audience what he thought they wanted, rather than follow his own dramatic instinct. At a personal level, C.B. Williams thought it a 'nice little play' and Frank Vosper was complimentary about Williams's acting but could scarcely credit the author's denial that he had written it, at least the English elements of it, 'tongue-in-cheek' (E 91). On the face of it, audiences were reasonably happy; but numbers were artificially inflated by the fact, as Williams discovered half way through the first week, that the theatre was being 'papered' on a nightly basis – theatrical jargon for doling out free tickets to make up numbers on unsold seats. His royalties were based on five per cent of the gross takings, but these rarely rose above twenty pounds a night. Of necessity the run terminated after only a fortnight, but a further week was arranged at Richmond.

The experience of *Glamour* underlined certain lessons, personal and professional. It reminded him that, for all his potential success, in family terms nothing would ever really change. Unlike his father (who revelled in every mention of his son in the newspapers) his mother's reaction to the news of the acceptance of *Glamour* for the London stage had been stunningly underwhelming:

> Received your telegram. I hope all this will have no effect on your health. I enclose a muffler as the winter is coming on.

Brother Tom 16 tomorrow (A1 26 October 1928).

For the first time, Williams was brought into direct contact with the powers of censorship exercised by the Lord Chamberlain, whose approval was required for every publicly performed play. In the autobiography he claims to have had no difficulties with the script of *Glamour* since 'I didn't have a Christ or a bloody-hell' (E 78). But in fact the censor (in the earliest of what, with one significant exception in *Night Must Fall*, turned out to be fairly minor interferences with the texts of Williams's plays) attached a caveat to the official licence on that very point. All profane use of the word 'God', which was liberally sprinkled through the first five pages of the typescript, was expressly prohibited. Overall, *Glamour* might have been an artistic and commercial failure but Williams's potential was already evident and he became sought after by theatrical agencies. His sense of professional status and personal worth was almost visibly enlarged when, during the run at the Court Theatre, Walter Peacock (whose firm Golding Bright acted for most of the best-known playwrights including Shaw, Barrie and Maugham) came back-stage and offered his services.

Before the month was out, through John Fernald, a second exposure for *Full Moon* had been arranged at the Arts Theatre for six performances beginning on 30 January, followed by a further week at the Q Theatre, Kew Bridge. The play was most favourably and sympathetically reviewed for the *Era* (6 February) by Richard Clowes, later to become one of Williams's closest friends, who noted its strikingly Chekovian quality. Gradually his circle of theatrical acquaintance widened. Amongst others, his introduction to Mrs J. T. Grein provided him with several opportunities to act in foreign-language productions on Sunday nights at the Arts Theatre Club, beginning with Camille in an adaptation of Zola's grim novel *Thérèse Raquin*. Still only twenty-three, Williams as an actor-playwright with two plays on in London within a month attracted a deal of publicity in the newspapers, and in January he even received a letter from the Urban District Council at Connah's Quay congratulating him on having 'brought distinction' to his home area. The unembroidered reality was, as Williams well knew, quite different.

Financially he was struggling: his plays had made very little money (royalties on *Full Moon* were five pounds in the first week and only three pounds during the second at Kew) and his acting in short-term parts was hardly more lucrative. His exceptional earnings in North America in 1927-8 aside, Williams estimated that during his first two years on the London stage his wages, which averaged two pounds a week, were

> little more than his young brother [Tom] would soon be bringing home as a grocer's assistant (E 100).

The actual figures for April 1927-April 1928 were £291 total, of which £240 had been earned abroad.

For a year that had began so auspiciously, the rest of 1929 – from a professional point of view – was bleak. Williams's longest engagement was in Pirandello's *Enrico IV* (played as *The Mock Emperor*) at the Queen's in March, in which he was Berthold, one of Henry's retinue, and understudied the lead, played by Ernest Milton, who was also the director. This was a hastily arranged revival of a production that had been deliberately halted to allow Mrs Milton to put on a play of her own entitled *Mafro, Darling!*, but which foundered so badly it barely survived the week. A stiff and clumsy piece, the *Daily Mail* (1 March) suggested it 'had the worst Press of any play for a long time'; but its significance in Williams's acting career – he played the part of Beppo – was that it was his first opportunity in the professional theatre to see things through, albeit on an unexpectedly truncated time-scale, from read-through and rehearsal to final production. John Fernald, who was in the replacement cast for *Enrico IV*, reconnected him with his Oxford days and he also met the vivacious Freddie Mell (almost a caricature of the camp actor) in his first part as a walk-on, who was to prove a loyal though entirely platonic friend. The announcement of the play's closure (after just sixteen performances) came so quickly that Williams had not had time to learn his understudy part.

For most of 1929 Williams had no lengthy engagements as an actor, only occasional work: in April the lead in J.T. Grein's Sunday production in French of *Le Pecheur d'ombres* and in July he played in a single matinee revival by William Poel of George Chapman's *The*

Tragedie of Biron for the Elizabethan Stage Circle. It was not the most inspiring continuation of his acting career, and Williams's situation essentially as an out-of-work actor could hardly have impressed Miss Cooke, who came before Easter to stay for one night when passing through London en route to Spain. They tended to avoid discussion of theatrical matters, certainly at a personal level, but they ventured to Somerset Maugham's latest play *The Sacred Flame* at the Playhouse Theatre, starring Gladys Cooper. It was an odd choice for the visit of a maiden schoolteacher: the play deals with euthanasia practised by a mother upon her son, a paralysed pilot, whose wife is pregnant by his younger brother. Denounced as immoral by the Bishop of London, and enjoying a reputation as the most controversial play in London, it did naturally roaring business and was the talk of the town. There is no record of what either Miss Cooke or Williams thought of it.

Miss Cooke was a realist in most things however and she was certainly canny enough to know how hard it was to establish a career in the theatre. Instinctively she understood that what Williams needed as a writer was space. Her advice to quit London temporarily and visit his family at Connah's Quay was timely and it stimulated him into creative action again. Back in the borderland with the family there was a status to be maintained, that of play-wright more than actor. It was in the gloomy parlour of 314a High Street with its redoubtable aspidistra, the haunt of his youth, that he recommenced work on the single remaining copy of the typescript of *A Murder has been Arranged* from two years before and began a process of major structural revision and ruthless cutting. Miss Cooke substantially reinforced her commitment to her protégé in August by paying ninety pounds into a bank account for him at Holywell, indicating that she was prepared, when that was gone, to fund him at the rate of ten to fifteen pounds a month thereafter as required.

With a steady weekly income of twelve pounds guaranteed on news from Walter Peacock that he was wanted for bit parts in Sean O'Casey's new play *The Silver Tassie* opening at the Apollo on 11 October, Williams took a further step into integration in the London theatrical scene by acquiring a flat. With another actor Paul Tanker ('sick of digs and anxious to share till he got married' [E 115-6]), he shared two rooms and a bathroom at 12a Wellington Mansions, right in the theatrical heartland at the top end of Upper St Martin's Lane. It was Williams's home for nearly a year, during which the only substantial domestic change was in January 1930 when Tanker moved out and Williams graduated from the small back room to the large one at the front. The spare room was rented out to an effeminate shop assistant at John Lewis in Oxford Street (christened 'Miss Curtis' by Williams's friends), who uncomplainingly took over the domestic duties of the flat. At some point in November 1929 Williams gave up his bit parts in *The Silver Tassie* when he accepted a secondary role ('four pages ... tightly typed' [E 120]) in another new play which, after excellent notices at its Sunday try-out, seemed destined for a long run. This was Hubert Griffith's *Tunnel Trench*, directed by Reginald Denham (whom Williams knew from Oxford) for the newly opened Duchess Theatre.

War plays had become distinctly fashionable on the London stage and *Tunnel Trench* trailed on the coat tails of R.C. Sherriff's *Journey's End*, an extraordinary success despite its public school boy view of the experience of the trenches. In Griffith's play Williams was to play Private St Aubyn, brother to the leading character, acted by Brian Ahearne. An effectively written cameo role with a single scene set in a shell-hole, it gave Williams the opportunity for authentic death-bed acting in a delirious haze. He believed it might be his big chance as an actor but it turned instead into his biggest humiliation. During rehearsals Denham took him aside to explain that he was to be replaced:

> [i]t's just that you're – well not believable as Brian's brother, you can't help being emotional and ... well, Welsh (E 122).

(His substitute, unnamed in the autobiography, was Leonard Sachs, four years his junior.) After much soul-searching, Williams surrendered to the inevitable. As going back cap-in-hand to *The Silver Tassie* was unthinkable, he swallowed his pride and resigned himself to walk-ons in the Griffith play (as Capt Sandys, Another German Private and An Observer), though increasingly in the conviction that it would be a dismal failure, which it indeed was. It closed on 7 December at the end of its first week.

For Williams, the imputation of his inability to suppress Welshness was no slander on his nationality but a direct attack on his aptitude as an actor and his capacity to articulate accentless English. He never lost his admiration for, nor desire to emulate, Megan Lloyd George's perfect enunciation. To speak the English language

> well and with as pure an accent as possible, neither drawled nor falsely refined (G 130)

was an instinct that went back to his schooldays at Holywell; and at Oxford Williams had done his best to lose any remaining elements of his Welsh accent through stage involvement. But it seemed that his emotionalism, long held, at least by the English, to be a stereotypical quality of the Welsh, could be neither suppressed nor disguised. What rankled more than anything however was that Private St Aubyn was supposed to be a character with a public school background – the very name was sign enough – and at the back of his mind Williams felt that the real reason for his alleged unsuitability was to do with class. In other words, the labourer's son from Flintshire, notwithstanding his Oxford degree and his easy mixing with so many different social ranks at university, ultimately could not shed his past. It was for this reason that Williams felt that his spectacular success eighteen months later as the unhinged aristocrat in the Edgar Wallace thriller *The Case of the Frightened Lady* was nothing less than a triumph and a vindication.

In early 1930 another play set in the Great War provided Williams with an unusually long stretch of eight weeks' work, as M. Jules in Reginald Berkeley's *French Leave*, starring Charles Laughton. This lifted his mood of depression as the engagement, though unchallenging, at least paid well at twelve pounds ten shillings [£12.50] per week. It was interspersed (usually at a guinea a time) with several more intellectually stimulating roles in one-off foreign-language parts in German and Italian for the Greins with the Cosmopolitan Society, and various other minor roles in non-commercial productions mounted by the Venturers Society, the Stage Society and the Three Hundred Club. In one crushingly unsuccessful piece, Lionel Britton's *Brain*, for the Masses Stage and Film Guild, in which

Williams took on two small parts, *The Times* (28 April) commented dryly that

> [n]obody in a very long cast is given any real chance to act, for hardly any of the dialogue is in any sense dramatic.

The only exception to the string of single performances was a short run of fifteen appearances in March at the Everyman Theatre with Sybil Thorndike in a new production of Georg Kaiser's *The Fire in the Opera House*, produced by Mrs J.T. Grein.

Williams's long-awaited breakthrough as an actor came from an unexpected quarter with the offer in the spring of 1930 of what appeared an undistinguished part in a potentially money-spinning Edgar Wallace thriller. His accession to the cast of *On the Spot*, which opened at Wyndham's on 2 April 1930, was momentous from both a professional and personal point of view. Charles Laughton starred as the Italo-American gangster Tony Perelli and after rehearsals had begun Williams was slotted in (at Laughton's suggestion) to play Angelo, his side-kick and right-hand man. He replaced a Canadian actor in the part who was felt to be too tall, too like the other gangsters, and too disposed to overpower the star. Williams's youth and relatively modest stature of about five feet eight (though his passport issued in 1931 optimistically added another inch and a half) was felt to be less threatening. In playing Angelo with an Italian accent to emphasise the bond with his employer's original background he transformed the part and immediately made it his own.

The reviews were universally complimentary, with Williams's Angelo drawing special praise for its clever mix of humour and duplicity. *The Times* (3 April 1930) remarked how he was 'never content with humour alone' but was

> for ever entangling the plot, wheeling in divans to receive corpses, deceiving women, baffling the police and generally, with ... [the] most ingenious mixture of innocence and guile, thrusting forward the adventure.

As James Agate put it in the *Sunday Times* (6 April 1930),

> Mr Williams reminds us, as Angelo, that likeableness and a

naïve, almost cherubic degeneracy may be combined.

Though Williams was eventually to leave the cast early, the total run of the play (which became the talk of the town and was probably Wallace's best thriller) amounted to 342 performances over eleven months to the end of January 1931. As soon as its success was assured, Williams – now making twenty pounds a week – opened a bank account under his own name at the Midland in Shaftesbury Avenue and arranged to send a regular sum home to Connah's Quay. It was a signal to his family and to Miss Cooke that as actor, if not yet as playwright, he had made a name to be reckoned with in the London theatre.

Four:
Emotional Turmoil and Professional Success

Only when Emlyn Williams joined the cast of *On the Spot* in the spring of 1930 did he identify the shadowy figure and fellow inhabitant, often slightly unsteady on his feet, whom he occasionally met and nodded to in the dark entrance-lobby of Wellington Mansions. It was W. Cronin-Wilson, who played the role of the burly policeman DCI John Kelly, which Williams admired for its sensitivity and intelligence. Off-stage he seemed distant and disinclined to talk, and Williams was much taken aback when, after the play had settled down into the routine of a long run, Bill Cronin-Wilson began to take an interest in him. At twenty-four (but looking younger) Williams was the youngest male in the whole cast; and Cronin-Wilson confessed he was drawn by his boyish attractiveness and the residual nuances of a Welsh accent, which reminded him of his batman Gareth, who was killed in the First War (an incident that Williams remembered for use in *The Morning Star*, his war-time drama of 1941). Their intimacy developed quickly and although the relationship was often quite stormy – more so than *Emlyn* suggests – Cronin-Wilson was more or less intimately attached to Williams's personal and sexual life over the next four years until his premature death early in 1934.

Having made his stage debut in 1906 as an extra in *Robin Hood* at the Lyric, Bill Cronin-Wilson toured in North America before the war and in South Africa and Australia after it. But his origins were mysterious. He was illegitimate by birth and there was talk of relationship to a family listed in *Debrett's Peerage*, even of possible distant royal connections, all of which gave him an extra dimension of interest for Williams. That Cronin-Wilson was also a minor playwright – he is credited with three plays, two of them collaborations, between 1910 and 1918 – Williams never mentions in his autobiography and it is conceivable that this side of Wilson's career was unknown to him.

From quite early on Williams harboured suspicions that Cronin-Wilson had a Jekyll and Hyde personality split but he enjoyed uncovering the contradictions in his character and sexuality. On the surface no sexual ambiguity was ever apparent. Homosexuality and bisexuality were fairly common, even fashionable, in certain circles in the 1930s, certainly in the theatre. But the particular generation of which Cronin-Wilson was a part – that grew up in the aftermath of Oscar Wilde's trial and imprisonment – had an inordinate fear of being misunderstood in male friendship and went out of its way to appear straight even when not. He was a devout member of the indigenous drinking set at the Cavour and the Green Room Club, both resolutely and robustly male hang-outs. Any suggestion of effeminacy Cronin-Wilson abhorred; and he later tried unsuccessfully to persuade Williams to drop his acquaintance with the minor actor Freddie Mell, who wore his campness like a badge. The irony here was that Edgar Wallace, their current theatrical employer, was flatly intolerant of what he termed 'pouffery' in any shape or form, as was made clear from his dismissal of his touring manager after discovering his penchant for young men. But he was as oblivious of Bill Cronin-Wilson's or Emlyn Williams's sexual proclivities as those of his star Charles Laughton, who eventually confessed to his wife to having entertained young men on the couch at their home in Dean Street.

No correspondence between Emlyn Williams and Miss Cooke survives for any part of the period when Cronin-Wilson and he were living together: the gap actually begins even earlier, from the first night of *Glamour* at the Embassy, Hampstead, in December 1928 and extends to June 1932, by which time Williams and Wilson, though still friends, had effectively parted company. To the family, as to Miss Cooke, Wilson was simply Williams's flatmate, who happened to share the same profession and who, as his father put it,

> being a gentleman that much older than you judgin by the photos will keep you to the Strait and Narrow (E 173).

Quite as much as Cronin-Wilson, perhaps more so, Williams craved companionship. He reflected that on the whole male friendship was easier to come by and in any case preferable as likely to be less committed than female involvement. This turned out not to be so, for Williams developed a degree of possessiveness that far transcended his feelings for Martin ('Charles Garvenal') at Oxford. At its simplest Cronin-Wilson was the longed-for elder brother, though the relationship was complicated on the former's side because he considered the connection was more like that of father and son, thus playing out the sexual ambiguities implicit in Williams's early play *Full Moon*. Nineteen years separated them: at forty-three Cronin-Wilson was literally old enough to be his father and, somewhat overweight with a jutting lower jaw, he looked his age. Freudian (and indeed Jungian) theories of sexuality gained increasing currency in the 1920s and early 1930s. Williams, while claiming to be only dimly aware of them himself, could give however no surer sign of the physical nature of his relationship than in his admission in the autobiography that

> to me Freud was only a name but I recognized the flavour of incest and it refused to repel me.

In Jungian terms also there was a profound jealousy, a desire as he confessed

> to own another human being, to dominate a man potentially superior to me and who, unflawed, could have dominated me. I craved to rivet the broken pieces together, to coax the rusty watch to tick (E 169).

Their affection for each other gradually deepened as Williams came to appreciate Wilson's special qualities, though too often they became submerged under his need to drink his way to oblivion. And Williams responded to the challenge of reassembling a personality that had been traumatised by war and drink. After 'Miss Curtis' left and soon after the one-hundreth performance of *On the Spot* in July 1930, they took a two bedroom, first-floor flat together above the landlord's butcher's shop at 60 Marchmont Street, Bloomsbury. Most nights from the very beginning they shared the double divan in the living room. Once, in confessional mood, Bill Cronin-Wilson astonished Williams by revealing that he was the father of twins, the result of a one-night stand in Newton Abbot at nineteen years of age. Like many of those who had endured the horror of war, he believed that his sexuality had been turned by the daily experiences of uncertainty and pain and the imminence of indiscriminate death in the French trenches. The Great War turned men in upon themselves and relationships cemented in such circumstances were often homosexual, either temporary or permanent, as in the experiences of such as Robert Graves, Ivor Gurney, Wilfred Owen and particularly Siegfried Sassoon (whose uncertain sexual identity, tested through marriage in the inter-war period, had certain parallels with Williams's own). As Cronin-Wilson put it, after 1918 there was '[n]othing normal any more' (E 176).

Beyond the physical companionship and devotion Cronin-Wilson provided, there was the problem posed by his drinking, which tripped the border into alcoholism. Williams as his self-appointed supervisor tried to wean him off spirits by whatever strategy worked, sometimes simply by hiding the bottle. Within the flat Cronin-Wilson was limited to a single whiskey and soda, though outside he was frequently tempted to considerably more. For a while the strict abstemiousness of Williams's regime, as friends testified, seemed to pay off and Wilson even began to look younger. Yet Williams was always keenly aware how much the experience was a repeat of his mother's with his own father – the chapter describing the Williams-Wilson relationship in *Emlyn* is entitled 'My Father's Keeper' – but the difference was that he felt (unjustifiably, as events transpired) to be in better control of the situation than his mother ever was. On one occasion when Williams was ill and unable to go to the theatre to play Angelo in *On the Spot*, Cronin-Wilson agreed to return home straight after curtain fall but did not arrive until the early hours, having been drinking in the club. In petulant mood, Williams relived by vivid analogy his mother's experience awaiting the return of her drunken husband, his spoilt dinner in the oven, and concluded that he 'could never trust him again' (E 181). Cronin-Wilson was simultaneously sought and rejected, abused yet desired. When he was absent – as every so often when he was on tour with a play – Williams still craved companionship of whatever kind. Loathing sitting at home when there was no play to occupy his attention, he would break the loneliness by visiting favourite haunts like the Long Bar at the Trocadero, in the half-articulated (and if the autobiography is to be credited invariably vain) hope that he might be picked up.

In the early days of their relationship Cronin-Wilson reciprocated Williams's solicitude by seeking out opportunities for his professional advancement as a playwright. He was responsible for *A Murder has been Arranged* finally seeing the light of day. The now dog-eared script (much revised since its first reading aboard the *Carmania*) was offered to the Repertory Players, a group founded by actors in 1921

> to afford those connected with the Theatre an opportunity for furthering themselves in their profession (Marshall, 80).

As one of the several Sunday societies that proliferated in the 1920s and 1930s, it was responsible for 'discovering' one or two worthwhile new plays, such as Patrick Hamilton's *Rope* (1929) and later on Gerald Savory's *George and Margaret* (1937). Williams's play fitted their requirements perfectly and arrangements were immediately put in hand to mount a single performance on 9 November 1930, at the Strand Theatre. The Repertory Players' inviolable rule that no play under their auspices was permitted more than a single performance meant that there was a problem in finding a director, since almost no one of note was normally prepared to invest the necessary effort for a single night. There was also a general difficulty with Sunday productions, namely rehearsing without the set, as in most cases the stages were occupied with other plays during the week. After some persuasion Williams himself agreed to shoulder the entire responsibility of directing, his first excursion into that role but one which he found so challenging and enjoyable that he elected, whenever possible, to direct the majority of his subsequent work as a playwright. The second issue conveniently resolved itself, since Williams's play demanded convergence in place and time between the action and the actual stage on which it is performed.

Emlyn Williams described *A Murder has been Arranged* as 'a ghost story in three acts'. A small family supper, the prelude to a fancy-dress party in celebration of the fortieth birthday of Sir Charles Jasper, whose special interest is in the occult, is about to be held on stage at a theatre reputedly haunted by the ghost of an alchemist and practitioner of black magic murdered almost a century before. The legend of the St James's Theatre (or of whatever theatre the play happens to be staged in) has it that in the event of another murder occurring at the theatre, the ghost of the original victim will walk again precisely ten days afterwards, heralded, as in the historical case, by a dumb woman wandering in off the street. She in turn would fall victim to murder and in doing so facilitate the appearance of the ghost from history. Anxious to test the story's veracity, Sir Charles deliberately holds his party on the tenth night after the fortuitous discovery of a body in an adjacent dressing-room. The event has even more (but unrelated) significance because if Sir Charles survives beyond the hour of his birth at eleven o'clock that very evening, he stands to inherit two million pounds by the will of an eccentric uncle. To add to the anticipation, Maurice Mullins arrives as an uninvited guest. He is a womanizing adventurer, but his kinship with Sir Charles places him next-in-line for the cash inheritance if the former, by some mischance, fails to survive. Not unexpectedly, Sir Charles is poisoned in the middle of Act 2 and Mullins contrives to make the death look like suicide, having tricked his victim into writing his own death note. Remarkably, instead of calling the police, the rest of the party decide to try and trap Mullins into a confession. The atmosphere of menace and fear deepens as a woman with apparently extra-sensory powers walks in off the street – just as in the ghost story – but then dies of fright in response to Sir Charles's death rather than as a murder victim. Deceived into the belief that he has not finished Sir Charles off properly, Mullins concedes defeat over the inheritance; but then, as the church clock in the street strikes the fatal hour, the ghost not of the alchemist but of Sir Charles himself emerges from the black drapes at the back of the set, and Mullins lapses into uncontrollable hysteria. In the flies above the stage, the ponderous mechanism of the safety curtain stirs into action and as it slowly descends, shutting off the stage from the auditorium, he finds himself effectively walled up within his prison: as Williams notes in the text, *'the evening's adventure in the St James's Theatre, London, is over'*.

The innovative aspect of the play lay in its use of setting and simultaneous time. The theatre as its own set was more or less original, although some of the effects are Pirandelloesque. Indeed the play overall is a not altogether easy blend of Pirandello and Edgar Wallace. For the first performances Williams made use of the very latest music, 'a weird blues number I had chosen in a record shop' (E 184). This was 'Zulu Wail', the item marked to be played at the transitional point when the house lights are dimmed and the seven-piece band which, almost unnoticed, has provided continuous background music to the audience's chatter is seamlessly integrated into the world of the play. The entry of Miss Groze (ostensibly Sir Charles's private secretary, but actually in collusion with his murderer), as she suddenly bursts out from behind the main curtain on to the fore-stage to shout 'Stop' in stentorian tones to the band-leader, is chillingly effective. At her insistence the tabs are raised and as the play proper begins a climate of undefined menace takes over. Played out against a set for another play (the one that the theatre is normally occupied by), superimposed on which is the paraphernalia for dinner, a long refectory table lit with a candelabra and laid with places for four, this is a stage set on a stage set. Unusually it has a telephone that communicates to the outside world, connected up at Sir Charles's special request, but the awareness grows that this is a theatre devoid of its everyday presence of actors or indeed any support staff from the doorkeeper upwards. Even the stage lights and tabs are being worked, somewhat inexpertly, not by the theatre's own technicians but by Sir Charles's cook, Mrs Wragg.

Neither the atmosphere nor the potential behind the coincidence of stage and actual time in the play is convincingly exploited. Instead *A Murder has been Arranged* tends to fall back on typically stagy melodramatic effects, blatant exposition (especially in the phone call taken by Miss Groze in the first scene, which could easily have become a perfect source for Stoppardian parody) and occasionally preposterously loaded dialogue. The best element is Mrs Wragg, the fat, middle-aged, down-to-earth cook, in whom Williams created a cameo role with a rich, comic Cockney vocabulary. Fortunately for the play, though she boldly she announces her departure from Sir Charles's service before any shenanigans begin –

> that's what I've got me boa'r on for, and me bag downstairs and me impedimenta packed (1:0)

– she is persuaded to stay on to confront the events of the evening. Impressively created in the first production by Amy Veness, she was first in a line (stretching through Kathleen Harrison to Gladys Henson) of spirited charwomen, cooks and other domestic servants who merrily drop their aitches and sniff their way in gleeful contempt for their employers' opinions through Williams's plays. Caricatures they may be, but Williams had a facility for such cameos. By contrast Williams's villain is surprisingly ineffectual. Mullins begins as a charming if bland young man, but his transition from petty pilferer into swindler, destroyer of women and villain with single-minded determination to be 'the Complete Criminal' (2:0) is glib rather than persuasive because no underpinning psychological conviction or understanding of the criminal mind is revealed. This was an area which Williams tried to make his own dramatically but in this first attempt at the villain he could not see beyond the simple stereotype. On the face of it, Edgar Wallace had no worries over the competition.

At curtain fall after the one-off Strand Theatre performance there was much enthusiasm from the usual back-stage throng, including on this occasion Jack Carus-Wilson and his wife Molly (the future Mrs Emlyn Williams). Nonetheless the process of waiting for the press reviews next day was as nail-biting as ever, though as it turned out critical reactions were overwhelmingly positive. Theatre managers clamoured to negotiate for the play with Williams's agent. The contest was won by the Daniel Mayer Co., who paid royalties as good as Bernard Shaw's (ten per cent at all levels of house receipts) and acceded to Williams's request that the original Repertory Players' cast should have first refusal. After such a rapid rise from obscurity Williams's name as playwright-director appeared across the whole newspaper spectrum, from *The Times* to *News Chronicle*, and was even mentioned in the Welsh religious press, where he was somewhat improbably headlined as the '*Dramodydd Wesleadd Enwog*' [Famous Wesleyan Dramatist]. There were, however, a few reservations. Some critics picked out what was to be a recurrent fault in Williams's writing: his failure to cut out extraneous material. This was behind Agate's judgement (*Sunday Times*, 8 November 1930) that 'the number of ideas involved was confusing'. But the

Manchester Guardian branded the play 'shiversome entertainment' and the *Scotsman* (27 November) declared that Williams's 'profoundly felt sense of the theatre is surprisingly mature'. For the *Observer* (30 November) the special quality of the play was in Williams's insistence

> on his humans behaving more fantastically than the phantasm ...
> It is lunatic stuff, but so frankly, so whole-heartedly lunatic that
> it attracts one the more.

This play and the reaction to it significantly extended his renown on the London theatre scene. Although his Salvationist brother Tom still harboured reservations, his family had long forgiven Williams for his choice of career and his father wrote to him proudly to announce that through his son's fame he had himself become a celebrity at the Summers works on Deeside.

Between the Strand performance of *A Murder has been Arranged* and the start of its run at the St James's on 15 November 1930 Emlyn Williams and Bill Cronin-Wilson left the cast of *On the Spot* – several months before it closed – at the moment of its transfer to the Cambridge from Wyndham's, where Edgar Wallace had a new thriller entitled *The Mouthpiece* all ready to replace it. Possibly as insurance against failure at the St James's with *A Murder has been Arranged*, both actors accepted parts in the Wallace play and Cronin-Wilson (though not Williams) was named in the advertisements as among its stars. Williams explicitly asserts in *Emlyn* that neither actor had anything to do with *The Mouthpiece*: that, as the reviews came out (signalling, unusually for Wallace, a flop) they were merely observers of the author's discomfiture, taking quiet satisfaction in the superiority of Williams's own play. 'Look at the titles', Cronin-Wilson is alleged to have said,

> which play would you book for, *The Mouthpiece* or *A Murder Has
> Been Arranged*?' (E 188).

But the scene is pure contrivance. In *The Times* (21 November 1930) *The Mouthpiece* was described as 'a strangely old-fashioned piece', but Williams was complimented as

> more than equal to the demands made on him by the part of [Commissar Neufeld] a comic foreigner,

as was Cronin-Wilson's performance as 'the good-hearted weakling [Charles Stukeley]'. In pre-production publicity for *The Mouthpiece* Williams even had his photograph as a 'young Welsh playwright' appear in the *News Chronicle* (19 November), so his acting involvement was hardly a secret. And both he and Cronin-Wilson had photo write-ups in the programme. From what motive Williams chose to re-formulate events in such a manner is not clear; but certainly the effect of the distortion is to keep the focus in the auto-biography firmly on Williams's own achievement as a playwright and to emphasise his superiority to Wallace and his play, which was forced to close after only twelve performances.

As usual on first nights, a number of 'good luck' messages arrived for the cast and author of *A Murder has been Arranged* at the St James's before curtain up. Exceptionally, these included telegrams from the headmaster at Holywell County and from the Wesleyan Methodist Church at Connah's Quay. But the notices next day, though generally positive, did not quite live up to expectations raised by the single Strand performance. *The Times* did not bother to re-review, and there was a underlying feeling in other papers that their earlier acclaim might have been overdone. Even so, the play managed a very respectable seventy-seven performances before closing on 31 January 1931; and it later went on provincial tour with Donald Wolfit and Margaret Webster. No further professional production of the play has taken place in London's West End since a brief revival of twelve performances at the Regent Theatre in May 1931 (under Jackson Wilcox), which attracted little attention; but it is still in print in Samuel French's edition and frequently revived in the amateur theatre. Proud of the aptness of his title, Williams was incensed twenty years later in 1950 at Agatha Christie's trading on a similar idea in her fiftieth novel, *A Murder is Announced*.

Within a week or less of the closure of *A Murder has been Arranged* at the St James's, Williams's acting career entered a new phase when he was offered for the first time the title role in a commercial production. This 'miraculous star part' (E 188) as he called it was in *Etienne*, an English version by Gilbert Wakefield of Jacques Duval's recent Parisian success. In a role which recalled Tom Douglas's in *Fata Morgana* (1925), Williams was to play a sixteen-year-old adolescent seduced by an older woman who is his father's mistress. The age of the hero was not a problem, given Williams's boyish figure and youthful looks even at twenty-five. He was actually far more anxious about what was considered at the time the rather torrid scene in Act 2, when his would-be seducer had to slide her hand exploratively underneath his shirt, a piece of business which it was widely believed had only just scraped past the censor along with most of the rest of the scene. In an act of personal censorship, Williams claims he shaved off all his chest hair in case it embarrassed the audience. In fact the official censor objected only to the youth of the boy-hero and insisted as a condition of licence that 'Etienne is represented as being at l[e]ast 18 years of age' and that all references to school lessons should be altered to college work (LCP file). Of the reviews, one of the most intriguing – because it used Williams's Welshness coupled with his working class origins as a somewhat back-handed compliment – was James Agate's in the *Sunday Times* (22 February 1931). While at the start of the play he suggested that Williams had looked

> like an out-of-work Welsh miner [who] gave the visual impression that he would presently doss up to invest his dole in the dogs,

he had nonetheless overcome

> natural disadvantages and generously succeeded where the better-graced juvenile, who relies solely upon his graces, must have failed.

For Agate the Welshness made him foreign, or at least 'gipsy enough to be at least un-English and so possibly French'. Other reviews were less grudging: the *Yorkshire Post* (16 February 1931) for instance thought it 'deeply observed and finely rendered' and the *Evening Standard* believed Williams's portrayal of the hero

> [o]ne of the best feats of acting ... London has seen for many months.

But the play did poor business and after fourteen performances closed on 28 February. Williams was once again unemployed: 'a Star in the Smoke without a part' (E 204).

With Bill Cronin-Wilson comfortably fitted up with a new part in a musical play (*The Land of Smiles* at Drury Lane), Williams, flush with money but depressed at having no work and desperate to write a new play, yielded to his partner's suggestion of a 'cruise' as the opportunity to create space for dramatic composition. The prescription was three weeks out to the Far East on the P. & O. steamship *Ranpura*. Williams began his six thousand mile return voyage on 19 April, sailing from Tilbury via Gibraltar, through the Mediterranean to Port Said, the Suez Canal and across the Indian Ocean to Colombo, in Ceylon (present-day Sri Lanka). He was the only passenger aboard under thirty, but it was his fluency in French rather than his youth which at Marseilles voted him into the job of escorting three older bachelors out on the town. They ended up at one of the city's countless brothels, where Williams found the sexual experience 'agreeably uncomplicated' (E 214), lamenting only that for him fulfilment always seemed limited to such circumstances. The so-called cruise – in fact the ship was simply on her usual scheduled voyage to Australia – was not immediately stimulating: Port Said was dirty and hot, the Suez Canal suffocating and Colombo (where he arrived on 10 May during the monsoon season) was not only insufferably humid but vehemently colonial. There were letters from his father and Miss Cooke, but nothing (though half-expected) from Cronin-Wilson. His host, arranged through a mutual friend, was a prematurely aged ex-patriate Scotsman in the tea trade – 'as alone as an old maid in a Highland croft' (E 220) – who seemed no more inspiriting than the scenery. Nevertheless, during his short stay a new play inspired by the grubby atmosphere of Port Said began to take shape. On the earlier than planned return journey to England six days later aboard the *Maloja* (a sister ship also on the Australia-England express route), it was written into several exercise books, since typing on deck was too awkward. With two-thirds of the script complete by the time the ship docked at Port Said, Williams went ashore briefly to reacquaint himself with its ambience and to correct a few details. By Marseilles in the first half of

June, when the play was virtually finished, Williams decided he had had enough of ships and the sea and opted to cover the final leg home by air (his first ever flight) to Croydon aerodrome.

The news that Edgar Wallace required Cronin-Wilson and Williams for his ponderously titled new melodrama *The Case of the Frightened Lady* came in July 1931, when they were both in St Ives, Cornwall. Wilson was taking a short holiday after the exertions of *The Land of Smiles* and Williams finishing off *Port Said*. For the former there was his usual police role (as DCI Tanner), but for Williams there was the new and exciting prospect of the kind of star role which he had never before attempted: not merely that of a psychopath (excitement enough for one who already evinced a keen interest in such areas) but an aristocratic psychopath. The initial read-through took place down at Chalklands, the Wallaces' country house in Berkshire, where Williams records with undisguised glee how another potential member of the cast (Alfred Drayton, who later dropped out) expressed astonishment at Williams's selection for the part:

> Well, I meanter say, you're a topping little actor but dammit, this chap's a lord (E 227).

Crushingly, Williams retorted that his experience of daily contact with the upper-classes and aristocracy during his studentship at Christ Church could be expected to see him safely through.

Of all parts that Williams played during his long career Lord Lebanon was the one that he enjoyed more than any other, Shakespeare not excluded. It was listed in *Who's Who in the Theatre* as his favourite role. Against a stereotypical English country-house background and supported by a suitably lengthy family lineage, Williams played a seriously deranged mother's-boy of a son, whose madness she has attempted to conceal, finally driven to self-confession as a serial killer. The reviews of the premiere at Wyndham's on 18 August 1931 were outstanding, especially in respect of Williams's own performance. They finally gave the lie to any lingering doubt that he was not up to the mark of public-school or aristocratic characters. The experience of *Tunnel Trench* was now behind him. But what gave him more satisfaction than anything was the comment in one of the notices that, as a peer of the realm, he spoke 'English purely, as it was meant to be spoken' (E 230). He considered that one of the most flattering pronouncements possible on his powers as an actor.

In the following year the American impresario Guthrie McClintic arranged to stage the play on Broadway and, making his second visit to the United States, Williams was invited to continue as Lord Lebanon at the Belasco Theatre in a production for October 1832 reinvented under the title *Criminal at Large*. The outstanding success of *The Case of the Frightened Lady* at home made it also an obvious candidate for filming, in an industry which had only recently developed the technical capacity to produce 'talkies'. Moreover Edgar Wallace had already had several earlier stage plays turned into silent films and was chairman of the film company which held the rights to his works. The screen opened up for Williams an entirely new and challenging area of opportunity in which he rose quickly to the upper ranks. His debut inaugurated a movie career which peaked in the late 1930s but, with its eventual extension into television, spanned more than fifty years to conclude as a cantankerous resident in an old people's home in *Past Caring* in 1985. During November 1931, while the play was still running in London, filming began at the British Lion Studios in Beaconsfield. Williams played his stage role, but the part of DCI Tanner went to Norman McKinnel, a substitution that in Williams's view Cronin-Wilson ought to have more strenuously resisted. The film's director, the American T. Hayes Hunter, was an old-fashioned operator more used to silent movie-making; but the actual process of filming, generally done without rehearsal, Williams considered almost effortless, since he was so familiar with the role. His strategy was merely

> to shrink the stage performance until I was in a real-life room which happened to have a camera in it (E 244).

He was entranced by the degree of reality of the film set (in contrast to the stagy set at Wyndham's), the panelling, pillars and period furniture of Mark's Priory, and took a special proprietorial pleasure in the whole thing:

> I only wished that Dad could be sitting in my canvas chair
> watching his titled son in his ancestral home (E 245).

The movie was released under the title *The Frightened Lady* and Williams's contribution was hailed in *Film Pictorial* (13 August 1932) as

> such an outstanding performance that he can rightly be
> described as one of the biggest 'hopes' in British films.

The same month his proud parents went to see it at Chester in preference to the closer venue of Shotton because, as Richard Williams explained, he had been advised that 'the "machines are better" there' (A1 3 August 1932). An early talkie, it was re-made only eight years later in 1940 with Marius Goring, a fellow Oxbridge graduate, then of more or less equal age to Williams's original Lord Lebanon.

One of the few outlets for new writing in London not hostage to commercial success was the Arts Theatre Club (founded in 1927). Recently it had helped make John Gielgud's name with Gordon Daviot's chronicle drama *Richard of Bordeaux*. For a time in the early 1930s, at a period when it lacked its own management, the club ran a series of Sunday-night performances at Wyndham's under the title 'Mrs Edgar Wallace Presents'. Williams's newest play *Port Said* failed to attract any substantial interest amidst West End managers, but it was an ideal candidate for this series, and 'Jim' Wallace snapped it up, subject to the engagement of a suitable cast. The male lead, an Anglo-Turkish drifter, was a bespoke part for Bill Cronin-Wilson: a tough assignment, a mixture of sophistication and bitterness, but well within his capabilities when sober. The women provided more difficulty, though again Williams had written with certain actresses in mind. This attention to pre-casting while in the act of composition meant that Williams almost always wrote for performers with whom he was professionally familiar, tailoring his writing specifically to their strengths as he knew them. May Agate, of long experience, he decided was perfect for Suzy, the sozzled half-French side of the duo of 'raddled old Toulouse-Lautrec prostitutes' (E 255) who opened the café scene in Act 2; and her companion Edith he envisaged being played by Amy Veness, the Cockney cook of *A Murder has been Arranged*. To Williams's surprise,

1. Emlyn Williams, Oxford freshman, aged 18

2. Mary Williams, aged 20

3. Richard Williams, aged 25

4. Emlyn Williams's birthplace, 1 Jones Terrace, Rhewl Fawr

5. White Lion, Glanrafon, with Emlyn, his father and aunt

6. Miss Cooke

7. Emlyn Williams and Sybil Thorndike in *The Corn is Green*

8. *The Druid's Rest*, St Martin's Theatre, 1944

9. *Night Must Fall* with Kathleen Harrison, Betty Jardine, Matthew Boulton

EMLYN WILLIAMS,
THE ACTOR-AUTHOR, AT HOME.

MR. EMLYN WILLIAMS, who has been making such a big hit in his own thriller, "Night Must Fall," at the Duchess, has a nice home to return to when night does fall! It's in Grosvenor Cottages.

Mr. Emlyn Williams is typing on his knee; while his wife and the dog sit beside him and provide inspiration.

The study in which Mr. Emlyn Williams works. He was born in Wales in 1905, and was intended for a scholastic career. Oxford and the O.U.D.S. made him change his mind.

EMLYN WILLIAMS made his first stage appearance in 1927, and since then has gone on from strength to strength. He is now one of the young men who count in the world of the theatre. His latest success is "Night Must Fall," the psychological thriller at the Duchess, in which he gives one of his wonderful sinister performances, just as brilliant and as frightening as his rendering of Lord Lebanon in "The Frightened Lady," which is his favourite part— or was, until he created Danny! In private life there is nothing sinister about this brilliant young actor and playwright.

MR. EMLYN WILLIAMS and MRS. EMLYN WILLIAMS (formerly Miss Molly O'Shann) in a domestic

Anything less like the sinister "hero" of "Night Must Fall" could hardly be imagined than this study of Mr. Emlyn Williams among his books.

10. Emlyn and Molly Williams at home at 5 Lincoln Street in the _Sketch_

11. & 12. Exterior and garden, 15 Pelham Crescent:
"Love to Miss Cooke from the Williams family 1946"

13. Cecil Beaton's publicity still for *The Wind of Heaven* at St James' Theatre (1945), Emlyn playing Ambrose Ellis

Veness declined – rather grandly – making clear she considered the part not only beneath her as much too risqué, but beneath its author as well. Dorothy Minto was engaged in her place. The female lead, Narouli Kath, went to Maria Burke, who, exceptionally, was not known personally to Williams; but he needed a star name like hers to attract an audience on a Sunday.

Rehearsals were somewhat tense. Bill Cronin-Wilson, unsettled and disconcerted at his first experience of being directed by Williams, could not remember his moves from one day to the next and he was reduced to mumbling apologies. Then a sudden attack of laryngitis gave him a convenient get-out three days before the opening performance and Williams himself was forced to substitute for him. The reviews were unremarkable, most commenting on the unnecessary complexities of the plot. The *Star* (2 November 1931) argued that

> the material would be excellent stuff for a lurid novel that could be laid down at intervals while the bewildered and incredulous reader tried to grasp some of its intricacies;

and *The Times* (2 November) suggested it had 'less originality and, above all, less decision than one hopes to find' in a Williams play. If the notices were disappointing, at least he could take comfort at the implication that his name now conjured up certain expectations. Despite the play's over-complex emotion and above all the typical fault of overbearing local atmosphere, there was still some promise in it. Williams did not cast it aside (as implied by the total absence of further reference to it in *Emlyn*) but returned to the script at intervals over the next two years. Eventually with difficulty, after much cutting and thematic reweaving, a new and radically slimmer version (the product of leisure hours during his American tour in late 1932 to early 1933) took shape under a completely new title, which, he indicated to Miss Cooke, 'expresses the play much better as it is now' (A1 26 January 1933). As *Vessels Departing* it awaited a suitable opportunity for re-staging to present itself.

Bill Cronin-Wilson was difficult to keep under control and Williams was often engaged in slanging matches with him that resolved nothing. Their personal tensions were not dissipated by time and Cronin-Wilson's resumption of serious drinking caused a separation in January 1932 after a dramatic and violent late-night row, the accumulation of months of pent-up resentment of Williams's failure to possess him. Although Williams immediately bitterly regretted his behaviour, it was a big turning-point for both men: Cronin-Wilson in being 'rejected by the only friend he had in the world' (E 243) and Williams in the attempt, as he hints, to grow up emotionally by putting the past behind him. Nevertheless for Williams, having long assumed the role of protective partner in their relationship, his sense of responsibility for Cronin-Wilson remained as strong as ever. Of necessity, the flat in Marchmont Street was given up and Cronin-Wilson took a furnished room in Victoria, while Williams, unable to endure the thought of being alone again, went into independent domestic partnership with Freddie Mell and his former Wellington Mansions flatmate, the ubiquitous 'Miss Curtis' from John Lewis. He secured a three-year lease on a spacious three-storey flat over a shop at 71a Ebury Street, an address that had a mild kudos from its associations with the novelist and playwright George Moore at number 121 and in having been until recently the home of Noël Coward down the road at number 111. To their son's flat in the summer of 1932 Williams's parents came to London for the first time and his father made his first acquaintance with a bathroom.

Williams's principal reputation in the early 1930s was as an actor, not a playwright. Yet after *The Case of the Frightened Lady* closed in February, his stage appearances during the rest of 1932 were few and short-lived: a substantial part in Reginald Berkeley's adaptation *The Man I Killed* (thirteen performances) and Jack in Sutton Vane's fantasy drama *Man Overboard* (his best-paid engagement at £60 a week but the play closed prematurely after only a fortnight). It was his diversification into screen acting on the back of his success with the Wallace thriller that gave him for the first time a settled and substantial financial standing. In mid-1932 he played his second film role in what is entitled 'Young Apollo' in the letters. Based on 'a dreadfully written book' by Anthony Gibbs and directed by Leontine Sagan (the only woman director in Europe at the time), it was released as *Men of Tomorrow*. Williams and Robert Donat (making his film debut) played two Oxford undergraduates in love with two female undergraduates, which at that time at the university was, as Williams put it, 'a formidable improbability' (E 259). They joked about enlivening the film by turning it into a homosexual love story of dons and students. Some sequences were shot at Christ Church and one scene at the Examination Schools, which Williams found rather too realistic. To begin with the work was 'the most delightful engagement possible' (A1 28 June 1932) and Williams reported that he was earning twelve pounds ten per day, or about £400 in total for a month's work. But the actual filming was chaotic. What was 'incredibly boring' in studio work and 'a triumph of mismanagement' (A1 14 July 1932) became, a few weeks later, as the film remained still unfinished, 'the criminal waste of thousands of pounds':

> [e]verybody has a finger in the piece, nobody knows what's happening, everybody bullies everybody else, [and] nobody thinks the film is going to be any good (A1 3 August 1932).

Williams said later that it was hissed off the screen when shown in the West End. Another, but trouble-free, small part in the film *Sally Bishop* (again directed by Hayes Hunter) in mid-August produced a handsome £100 for only five days' work. And indeed Williams was so busy with his film career that he had to turn down a part in the new comedy *Tomorrow will be Friday*, starring Marie Tempest at the Haymarket.

By this time Williams was well-heeled enough to wish to secure his parents' future. He set up an annuity for them in September 1932 (in a legal deed witnessed by Bill Cronin-Wilson) and bought them a brand-new £500 bungalow, complete with bathroom, which was nearing completion a few miles away at Aston Hill, an estate between Queensferry and Hawarden. Double-fronted and severe in the brutalist style of the early 1930s, it was named Glasdir after the Williamses first home together in Wales above Ffynnongroyw. The only striking features of the new house were its three disproportionately tall chimneys, but it also had a bay window on the side, something that his mother had always coveted as evidence of superiority over the neighbours. It had ample room for all their possessions, yet except for a few precious heirlooms, such as the clock and horse-hair sofa, nearly all the household furniture from Connah's Quay was thrown away or burnt and the entire place newly equipped and provisioned at Williams's expense in a day's shopping spree at a Wrexham furniture store. With the help of their son Job, his parents moved in on 5 October 1932 while Williams was in transit across the Atlantic to play Lord Lebanon in New York. The novelty was fascinating. Richard Williams reported that

> [y]our mother is never done with rowling the carpet sweeper. the Mangle and the Electric Ironing and the Cooking stove are in perfect condition we have breakfast ready before you can say Jack Robinson (C1 8 October 1932).

Miss Cooke visited them for tea soon afterwards and recounted to Williams (in contrast to the sentimentalised version of events Williams seems to have invented for *Emlyn*) the slight awkwardness of the occasion on both sides. She found his father

> in great 'fettle' as Yorkshire people say. But my word, y cant say tht [your parents] have a great range of conversatn.
> (A2 13 November 1932)

Williams had begun writing another play back in May 1932, soon after Vane's *Man Overboard* finished its short run. Entitled *Spring, 1600*, it was to be an historical drama, set in the time of Shakespeare, featuring a gender-switching girl who comes to London, secures the part of Viola in *Twelfth Night* and then finds that her emotional entanglement on stage is paralleled off-stage by her love for Richard Burbage. The writing process, including background research at the British Museum, took many months and the script was completed immediately after Christmas 1932, when Williams was well into the New York run of *Criminal at Large*. As there was no possibility of its being accepted in the USA – 'costume plays are anathema here' (A1 5 January 1933) – the completed script was despatched to Miss Cooke for comment and onward transmission to Williams's London agent, Walter Peacock. Both were enthusiastic, with Miss Cooke indicating real pleasure in its quality as an acting play:

> [y]ou've done it this time. Oh I'm so excited ... Perfect for the actors, actresses, perfect – they'll love it (A1 15 January 1933).

Williams's second American experience was shorter at six months but more congenial, because less isolated, than his first. There were some screen tests early on and a couple of tentative offers from Hollywood, though in the end they came to nothing. Humphrey Bogart, then at the outset of his career, came to congratulate him at the opening night of *Criminal at Large*. On his first Sunday he found himself unwittingly at a large gay party, to which he had been invited by two outwardly clean-cut American college-types who called back-stage but subsequently metamorphosed into raging queens. After a martini or two, in the time-honoured way, Williams apparently made his excuses and left. Later in the season (paying his own fare this time) he renewed his friendship with the Hart sisters in Philadelphia and in November Williams attended his first grand theatrical party, for Constance Colier, star of George Kaufman's *Dinner at Eight*. Guests included Irving Berlin, Basil Dean, Gilbert Miller, Edna Ferber and Dodie Smith. The social whirl continued with a party hosted by the American playwright Sidney Howard, whose latest comedy *The Late Christopher Bean* had just received a glitteringly successful premiere at the Henry Miller Theatre, New York. 'So you see', he wrote archly to Miss Cooke, 'I'm just "going places" as they say here'. But his avowal that

> one side of me revels in the superficial gaiety and more than surface wit of it, [while] the other is acutely embarrassed by the shameless artificiality (A1 11 November 1932)

was probably more a caveat introduced for Miss Cooke's benefit than an expression of genuinely divided feeling. For all the American hype and exaggeration, this was exactly the kind of high-powered theatrical scene that Williams delighted in and he made useful contacts. Williams was also privileged to attend the New York premiere of Noël Coward's *Design for Living* in January 1933: 'a riot', he reported slightly enviously to Miss Cooke,

> a wry frothy and completely amoral polite farce most wittily acted (A1 26 January 1933).

Its popularity was such that it was sold out six weeks before-hand. Shortly afterwards Williams reported on an even more 'dazzling excursion into high life' (A1 3 February 1933) when he attended a dinner-party at Mrs Marshall Field's and was placed between Lillian Gish and Mrs Pulitzer. Oddly, given Williams's usual sense of pride in social connections at this level, no hint of this particular New York event is present in the autobiography.

The Late Christopher Bean, the play that was to help change perceptions of Williams from actor to playwright and gave him his first substantial hit, was ironically not an original. During his sojourn in the USA, Sidney Howard's adaptation under that title from René Fauchois's *Prenez garde à la peinture* (Paris, February 1932) came into his hands via Gilbert Miller, who was anxious to mount a production at the St James's in London. Howard's location of the play in New England was considered to depend too heavily on its American idiom and Williams's brief was to reset it for a British audience. The whole revision (for which he received an advance of £70 and a one per cent royalty on production) was completed in February 1933 in record time: four days according to his letter to Miss Cooke, or a week if the authority of the autobiography is preferred. In original form the play, a satire on the wheeling and dealing of art-dealers and critics, drew on incidents in the lives and personalities of Cézanne and Van Gogh; but Williams transferred the setting to a Cheshire village and made the artist English. The crucial part of the maid, whose earnest protection of Christopher Bean's name from the greedy dealers and grubby critics out to exploit the artist's posthumous reputation conceals the fact that she is actually Bean's widow, Williams made into a Welsh servant. He re-christened her Gwenny:

> a picture of my mother and all the Welsh peasant-women of my childhood (E 274).

Cynically he assured Miss Cooke that the play had

> adapted extraordinarily well, and should be God's gift to the Welsh theatre especially amateurs, both in English and Welsh.
> (A1 15 February 1933)

Gwenny was the first Welsh servant part he ever wrote for the theatre, all previous creations in that line having been Cockneys.

Williams met Edith Evans at a small party soon after her arrival in New York to play in *Evensong*. Intrigued by his new play, she was sent a copy of *Christopher Bean* and was so enchanted at the role of Gwenny that she pleaded successfully for first refusal in the London production in May 1933. Having no Welsh connections, indeed nothing Welsh about her except her surname, she had to be coached in the accent by Williams every night for a week in her dressing room at the Queen's, where she was playing an American secretary in *Once in a Lifetime*. On all counts the play was a triumph, with Gwenny hailed by *The Times* as 'an inspiration' and by W.A. Darlington in the *Daily Telegraph* (17 May 1933) as 'voluble, lachrymose, ignorant, generous, and true-hearted', ranking 'as one of the best things [Evans] has ever done – a lovely piece of work'.

In *Emlyn* however Williams records his acute embarrassment at the praise heaped upon *Christopher Bean* on his discovery that the programme and publicity failed (deliberately, so it seems) to mention that the play was adapted from Sidney Howard, implying instead that it was taken directly from the original French. In fact Williams never even glanced at the French text and, apart from some additions necessary for the part of Gwenny, all the admired craftsmanship of the play, its honesty of character depiction and its clarity of line, was Sidney Howard's. It was by far Howard's most substantial achievement in free adaptation. None of the reviewers was remotely aware of the play's provenance: indeed Darlington simply mentioned idly Howard's adaptation having had a completely independent success in New York. For all his alleged discomfiture, Williams did nothing publicly to counter the authorial confusion either at the time or later: it is even listed as adapted direct from Fauchois in the list of his dramatic works in the *Collected Plays* in 1961. In practical terms it meant that in London Williams's name alone was identified with *Christopher Bean* and for the first time he had a substantial hit, but it was one that he could not legitimately claim as all (or even mostly) his own work. When the play eventually closed well over a year later on 21 July 1934 it had completed 487 performances.

After completing his New York engagement, Williams returned home in March 1933 aboard the *Majestic*, to be met at Southampton by Bill Cronin-Wilson, who up to late January that year had been playing in Maugham's *For Services Rendered* and acting as caretaker over the Ebury Street flat. Despite, according to Williams's detailed inventory, Wilson's having broken four tumblers and singed an armchair with his ceaseless cigarettes, the two of them agreed to live together again on a temporary basis, though on the understanding that Williams would not support Wilson financially in any way. As Williams put it, 'I was only half-free' (E 279). On hangover days Wilson was banished to his room above a mews garage in Victoria.

Uppermost in Williams's mind was not *Christopher Bean* but his own two most recent creations: *Vessels Departing* and *Spring, 1600*. John Gielgud was keen to direct the latter and Williams, in some trepidation at meeting the star of *Richard of Bordeaux* (then the sensation of London), called on him to discuss the venture. Gielgud's flat in Upper St Martin's Lane and its occupants – his partner John Perry and other almost permanent fixtures such as Dick Clowes (whom Williams knew as reviewer for the *Era*) and the young and up-coming playwright, recently down from Oxford, Terence Rattigan – became almost as familiar as his own over the ensuing months. Line by line, Williams and Gielgud pored over the script in an attempt to bring it to the point where it could be shown to potential managers and backers. There were special difficulties about the denouement, which was also short on substance, and Gielgud persuaded Williams to reshape it entirely, but in the end with no very evident success. Although Gielgud's triumph in *Richard of Bordeaux* renewed London managers' confidence in the ability of costume drama to draw audiences, interest in Williams's newest play was slow to materialise.

Williams's career in film however advanced hugely in June 1933 when he topped the *Film Weekly* poll (23 May 1933) by more than twenty-six per cent of the vote over his nearest rival (Leslie Howard in *Service for Ladies*) for the best performance in film, as Lord Lebanon. He was immediately put under a three-year graduated contract to Gaumont-British, rising by equal increments from £100 a week in the first year to £300 by the third. By any measure, as

Williams conceded, this was indeed '[b]ig money' (E 292). His first major responsibility was in July 1933 to furnish the dialogue for the film *Friday the Thirteenth* (the drama of a bus crash, in which Williams plays a survivor who turns vicious blackmailer), with Jessie Matthews and Ralph Richardson. At the same time Williams appeared at the Apollo with Ralph Richardson and Diana Wynyard in *Wild Decembers* by Clemence Dane [Winifred Ashton]. He was Brian Aherne's substitute as Branwell Brontë, a crudely written part though one that he endowed with 'abundant colour and liveliness', said *The Times* (27 May 1933). But he could expect no theatrical role to compete financially with film, in which his scripting skills were as much in demand as his acting. In the autumn he was asked to write the entire screen-play of *Evergreen*, a musical with songs by Richard Rodgers. It was principally from his very substantial earnings in film that Williams, on advice, was able to make several canny and extremely lucrative investments in the early 1930s by buying into blue-chip companies such as Shell Oil, F.W. Woolworth and Marks and Spencer, whose shares over time almost literally proved worth their weight in gold.

For some unexplained reason, in his autobiography Williams suppressed all reference to his next substantial achievement in the summer of 1933, the production of the rewrite of *Port Said* as *Vessels Departing*, which opened at the Embassy, Hampstead, on 3 July under the direction of Williams's old Oxford friend John Fernald. Why he should have so distanced himself from the play that there is not so much as a passing allusion to its three-week run, it is difficult to say. One reason may have been that Williams harboured a somewhat condescending attitude to the venue where *Glamour* had first been staged, which he had once described as

> such an out of the way and unadvertised theatre.
>
> (A1 12 December 1928)

He also knew that Embassy productions were not much reviewed in the papers. Nevertheless the *Spectator* (7 July 1933) described *Vessels Departing* as

> a sincere, distinguished, and at times a moving piece of work,

with moments of excellent comedy.

By no means unregarded, the play was actually popular enough to be retained at Hampstead by public demand for an unscheduled third week. It also fielded a strong cast: Flora Robson as the heroine Narouli, May Agate and Dorothy Minto back in their old *Port Said* roles, Edith Sharpe as Mrs Frankiss and a reinstated W. Cronin-Wilson playing Youssef el Tabah.

Despite the extensive revisions, Williams failed to control entirely his old problem of overwriting the local Egyptian colour, which came close to smothering the emotional drama to which it is intended as backdrop. The play showed also how Williams's dramatic talent at this stage in his career focused more intently on the small scene (such as the sleazy café in Act 2 scene 1) rather than the larger unit of the act, and on cameo roles (as in May Agate's disreputable Suzy) rather than the broader sweep of the main characters. Indeed, this was noticed by *The Times* (4 July 1933):

> ... there are times when the Anglo-Turkish café lounger of Mr Cronin-Wilson, with his queer nostalgia for an England to which he can never belong, threatens to entertain us more than the heroine.

It is perhaps to this play that Williams refers in a comment made in an after-dinner speech to the Garrick Club shortly before his death, when he confessed to 'formidable failures' in his career as a professional dramatist, one of which was

> a play over which I lost heart and which I ruined by rewriting, and compromising (K1/15 10 April 1987).

Yet even if *Vessels Departing* disappointed its author in not being transferred to the West End, the fact that he alluded neither to Cronin-Wilson redeeming himself in a part that had defeated him in *Port Said* nor to the reviewer's flattering comment on his friend and lover's powers as an actor is all the more extraordinary, as this was his first and (it was sadly to prove) last appearance in a Williams play.

Emlyn Williams's emotional life faced a critical period during

1933. Bill Cronin-Wilson was still a presence, but their relationship was 'now easy' (E 293), conducted on an amicable, less proprietorial level. Still craving companionship, Williams tended to find his in the pleasant camaraderie of the gatherings of young men at Gielgud's flat; but he also found special delight in socialising with his friends Polly Heseltine and her husband Sonny (with whom he had been friends with since 1929) either in their Chelsea flat or summer bungalow on the river bank down at Thames Ditton, which held a special, almost bohemian attraction. Staying with them one week-end, Williams first set pen to paper on *Spring, 1600*. This was the milieu that he felt most at ease in; and it was here also that his friendship blossomed with Polly's younger sister Molly and husband Cecil Carador Carus-Wilson (known as 'Jack'). He enjoyed their company, even though Jack was somewhat older than both of them; and he found Molly most agreeable to talk to, open, and understanding. To all appearances they were a perfectly matched couple and Williams was utterly unprepared for Molly's shattering news in the spring, upon her return from staying with her sister in Italy, that her seven-year marriage was over. Jack had left her for an walk-on actress in the popular musical comedy *Wild Violets* then running at Drury Lane.

Unused to confessional situations with women, Williams commiserated and out of the need to break the ensuing silence jokingly suggested Molly should have an affair in retaliation, only to find she had already done so with a Russian count in Italy. Williams encouraged her to disclose the sexual details and in exchange told her about his own experiences, at least the heterosexual ones in Rouen, Montreal and Marseilles. He was too uncertain of himself, too inhibited, to ask her to stay for dinner without a third person's presence: 'I was shy of a tête-à-tête with a woman' (E 288). From mid-July onwards however he was invited to spend the summer weekends at Thames Ditton, where Molly was looking after her brother-in-law while Polly remained in Italy. On one occasion when another male visitor unexpectedly needed to stay overnight, the hastily re-arranged sleeping plan involved Williams's giving up his single bed and joining Molly in the large double she had sometimes shared with Jack. By agreement they spent the night in chaste separateness, though by now Williams knew her well enough to tease her about the absence of sex:

> [i]n the middle of the night I did think of waking you up with a thick Russian accent, then thought that would be cheating.
>
> (E 294)

Less than six months after Molly Carus-Wilson's revelation of the breakdown of her marriage and her implied sexual availability, Williams's emotional life was profoundly disturbed again one evening in November 1933, when Bill Cronin-Wilson brought back to the Ebury Street flat for a drink a young man whom he had picked up earlier at a lunch-time drinking session in the Green Room Club. The newcomer rejoiced in the robust Welsh surname of Griffith, coupled with the improbable first-name of Fess (supposedly after the bleak slate-mining village of Blaenau Ffestiniog in Snowdonia where he claimed to have been born).

Williams's life-story contains no more strange, shadowy, or even at times malevolent figure than Fess Griffith. If Williams had wanted to formulate a character for a play, in effect a fictional mate to replace Bill Cronin-Wilson and sexual competitor to Molly, he could hardly have done better. If Fess had not existed, he might well have felt disposed to invent him almost as a composite male lover. As it is, the name is almost certainly not authentic and the few personal details revealed about him are mostly not independently verifiable. Unlike Bill Cronin-Wilson, no picture of him is to be found in any of the family scrapbooks. Fess is shrouded in a seemingly colourful and mysterious past, much like his stage incarnation as Dan in *Night Must Fall*. His early childhood was said to have been spent in north Wales until the age of ten, when his parents moved to Gloucester, where he became a member of the cathedral choir. Later he joined the Navy for a short time but then appears simply to have become a sexually promiscuous drifter, with no long-term relationships or feeling for anyone of either sex until at the age of twenty he met Emlyn Williams. Fess shared characteristics which had first attracted Cronin-Wilson to Williams, while Williams himself was taken by Fess's good looks, his mixed Welsh accent and his air of casual indifference. But Fess was an altogether more worldly proposition and Williams made him into a character in his own emotional drama:

> what made him sexual in his own way was ... a transparent pallor which spelt smoky saloon bars, and – when he smiled lazily – a top tooth missing, just far enough from the centre not to be unsightly (E 304).

In the manner of Dylan Thomas's 'conscious Woodbine' in *Return Journey*, Fess had a cigarette more or less permanently attached to his lower lip.

Undoubtedly Fess made a deep first impression, but for the immediate future Williams's attention was entirely directed elsewhere to the preparations for *Spring, 1600*, which after a difficult gestation period seemed – finally – close to fruition. Nearly everyone who read the script was captivated by its charm, but financial backing was not forthcoming and no commercial manager would risk production without it. In the absence of other offers a syndicate was established in late November, capitalised at £2,500 from investments by Lady Ashstead (a millionairess friend of Dick Clowes's father) who was principal backer, Richard Clowes senior, John Gielgud, Victor Saville, Michael Balcon and Emlyn Williams. This was the first play in which Williams directly invested his own money. It had a great deal of promise, not least in Gielgud in his first ever role as director and a cast which included Isabel Jeans as Lady Coperario and Joyce Bland (a last minute substitute for Edna Best) as Ann Byrd, the young heroine. There was also a small part for Molly Carus-Wilson under her maiden name of O'Shann. Gielgud and Williams worked well together and spent many hours closeted in the former's flat working over the script. Even so, Gielgud kept demanding new scenes and revisions of others right through the rehearsal period.

In *Early Stages* Gielgud acknowledged that he misjudged the value of the play and the amount of production ornamentation which could be loaded on to an already weakish script. Under the elaboration of the set design by Motley, a party of madrigal singers and the live monkey which was brought in to sit on Lady Coperario's shoulders, the 'slender plot sank gradually deeper and deeper into a morass of atmosphere and detail'. By the opening, on a total spend of £4,000, the play was way over budget.

At the first night on 31 January Sarah Grace Cooke, whose enthusiasm for the play had never diminished, was present (in a long dress) for the first time ever at a Williams' premiere. Given her critical acumen, it was surprising that she had failed to perceive that the trouble with the play was its desultory ending. Ann Byrd's love for Burbage proves fruitless and she has to return to her mother and her Essex home. Williams it seemed was unable to make up his mind whether it was a love story or not and, if so, how to be true to its inevitably tragic disappointment. What it lacked in conclusiveness was to some extent mitigated by the splendour of its setting, including a breathtakingly delightful opening scene with William Byrd at the virginals in his Essex garden and a later one when a Shakespeare rehearsal is in progress around Richard Burbage's great bed. Gielgud attempted to compensate for lack of material in Act 3 by raising the pace of the action, but still in performance it was a very long play, over three hours.

Critical interest was sharpened by the presence of Gielgud in the unfamiliar role of director, yet his closeness to the play and its author blinded him to its inordinate length and by extension to Williams's recurrent problem of overwriting the background. Writing film scenarios had not yet cured Williams of his fatal attraction to luxuriance in dialogue. Substantial cuts were vital and these were effected at a stage call the following day, saving a full forty-five minutes' running time on the second night. Remarkably in view of the severe problems over timing, none of the dailies was especially critical. On the contrary, they noted several excellent performances, such as Ian Hunter's Burbage, Isabel Jeans's cameo as Lady Coperario and the continuous liveliness in Joyce Bland's Ann Byrd, even though the character as written was pronounced by *The Times* (1 February 1934) to be 'not a very solid one', indeed rather chill and unrealistic. Williams's attempt to do something fresh and interesting with a costume drama was rightly acknowledged: 'loveliness and laughter in plenty', proclaimed the *Morning Post* (1 February). But although James Agate spoke of 'this unusual and charming play' (*Sunday Times*, 4 February) he had a deadly sting in his tail. Rejecting the whole of the first act as unnecessary, he described the Motley set as 'all too new and sterilized' and suggested that the play was best regarded only as a *'divertissement.'* Audience numbers for *Spring, 1600* were never particularly large, but its fate was sealed when a London smog (a typical 'pea-souper') descended for days on end. The play was taken off after twenty-one performances on 17 February.

Nevertheless it was one of those pet pieces that Williams could not let go. He tinkered with the script on and off for years thereafter and eventually, in a much revised version (performed by the Company of Four, a branch of the impresario Binkie Beaumont's empire of H. M. Tennant Ltd), the play was premiered as a Sunday members-only night at the Lyric, Hammersmith, on 6 December 1945. Andrew Cruikshank took on Gielgud's old role. It had a nominal success by virtue of its longer run (until 13 January 1946) but in truth Williams's revisions did not lift the play sufficiently to attract either critical attention or to sustain audience numbers.

About the beginning of February 1934, while *Spring, 1600* was in the early days of its short run, Williams (apparently quite by chance) met up with Fess Griffith again, drinking in the Long Bar at the Trocadero. There was, it seems, exploitation on both sides. Fess spun a story about difficulty in paying his rent and Williams immediately seized this as the excuse to invite Fess to move in with him until he found a job. Events in the micro-drama moved rapidly as Fess's few possessions were installed at Ebury Street next day. That night, at Fess's instigation, they shared the double bed in Williams's room; and early next morning Bill Cronin-Wilson, calling round unexpectedly, found them together. On recognising the identity of the sleeping figure beside Williams, he reddened, turned on his heels and stalked off with the words: 'I see ... I certainly did start something' (E 320). Cronin-Wilson could not have known exactly what he did start. For a year or more Williams was seemingly obsessed by this man, eight years his junior, who rapidly became a fixture in his life. He was fascinated by the ease with which Fess wore his sexuality and his awareness of the spell he could almost at will cast over both women and men. What capacity Fess had for feeling, or what scruples, if any, is difficult to judge: but what became clear was his adeptness at using others' weaknesses for his own sexual and material gratification. On his side, Williams never seemed able to make up his mind exactly where Fess fitted within a triangle bounded by the roles of companion, chauffeur and sexual partner.

Reluctant to attend any more performances of his play and temporarily free of new work for Gaumont-British, in early February, on a sudden impulse (like the holiday to Hanover or the cruise on the *Ranjura*) and within hardly more than a week of Fess's move into the Ebury Street flat, Williams decided on a continental excursion. Relying on Fess's automotive knowledge, he bought a second-hand Morris Oxford (registration number OF 4357) for £40. Without saying farewell either to the cast at the Shaftesbury or to Bill Cronin-Wilson at the Apollo (where he was appearing in *Escape Me Never*) Williams was driven down to Southampton for the overnight ferry to Le Havre. Williams claimed that there was no suggestion of his play finishing when he left; but this could not have been so, since the continental trip began either on or shortly after 13 February – the date the Automobile Association issued the International Fiscal permit allowing Williams's car to be re-imported tax-free on return. This was just four days before *Spring, 1600* closed.

Apart from requiring Williams to light him a constant supply of cigarettes, Fess was an undemanding, unintellectual driver-companion. The pair had no detailed plans but they drove via Rouen, where Fess apparently enjoyed the services of a prostitute, allegedly in the self-same premises where Williams had lost his virginity a decade earlier. They then continued south-west to Bordeaux, across the Spanish frontier and on down to Gibraltar and the Rock Hotel, his contact address for messages from Gaumont-British. Over several days on the long journey south the details of Fess's chequered personal and sexual history slowly emerged. His short spell in the Royal Navy had introduced him to the nocturnal gay pick-up scene at the Alameda Gardens in Gibraltar. Despite sometimes pleading naivety in such matters, Williams confessed to have heard about it also and resolved to savour the experience for himself. The episode was simply humiliating: the Spanish male prostitutes resented his presence and took to stoning him out of the area.

From Gibraltar, Williams was summoned home by telephone to begin work on additional dialogue for Hitchcock's thriller *The Man Who Knew Too Much*. After making arrangements for the car to be repatriated by sea, he and Fess took the train and cross-channel ferry home, arriving at London Victoria two days later at the beginning of March. They were confronted by the devastating news of Cronin-Wilson's death. Aged forty-six, he had died from double pneumonia on the evening of 16 February, just days after Williams and Fess had landed in France at the start of their tour.

Williams's guilt was immeasurable. Bill Cronin-Wilson had died a lonely death in Charing Cross Hospital, unaware (because no one dared tell him) that the man he cared for most deeply and for whom he asked on his death-bed was not only absent from the country but reinforcing his betrayal by being driven through France and Spain by a new companion who was Cronin-Wilson's substitute. He had also suffered the ultimate and ironic indignity of a pauper's burial, no help being possible from his friend and erstwhile lover who was one of the richest men in the London theatre. To Ben Lamb, an old mate of Cronin-Wilson's from way back, who had arranged the funeral, Williams slipped a cheque for £50 and asked him to forward any outstanding bills: 'I was not being generous, it was conscience money' (E 334). When Molly Carus-Wilson came round to commiserate, she met Fess on the stairs, going out for the evening to see if he could score at the Fitzroy pub. Williams lied by introducing him as 'my cousin, Fess Griffith' (E 335), on the totally spurious grounds that his grandmother had been a Griffith. Fess was represented in similar terms to Dick Clowes when he came to visit. Like Molly, he was not taken in, but Williams almost came to believe it himself as the battle in him between what he described as the good (Molly) and the bad ('in the shape of a harmless Welsh cousin about the house') became 'more insistent than before' (E 354).

It was Molly, not Fess, who was Williams's greatest comfort in the days that followed Cronin-Wilson's death and to whom he opened up emotionally. She too found help in him for her depression over her marital break-up. The bond of shared confidences brought them closer, but the circumstance and speed of Williams's proposal of marriage, probably sometime in late March, was as bizarre as it was unexpected. According to the dramatised account in *Emlyn*, it took place out of sheer impulse at the Ebury Street flat, with Fess hovering in the background dispensing drinks and in the presence of Molly's friend and landlady. This was no ordinary proposal. Made in the aftermath of the most unsettling and traumatic event in Williams's emotional life and in earshot of the man who had supplanted Cronin-Wilson in Williams's life and consciousness, it was literally a whim of the moment, made from an instinct to chivvy Molly out of her mood of despondency. Perhaps equally impulsively Molly accepted. Next morning she gave Williams the opportunity to withdraw his offer, but he declined.

It is evident that Williams certainly did have serious doubts about marriage, not least in the restrictions it would impose upon his occasional homosexual roamings, these mysterious 'sallies' as they are termed in the autobiography (E 340). He managed however to convince himself that all his sexual encounters with men had in no sense been either physically or emotionally satisfying. Nevertheless it was a difficult and troubling area: after all Williams might have said much the same about his previous relationships with women. But instead of articulating his emotional and psychological doubts to his future wife he proceeded to demonstrate at least his material suitability for Molly in a way redolent with the puritan-inspired ethics of his Welsh background. His defence against doubt was to show the measure of his feeling in terms of money. He escorted her to the Midland Bank in Shaftesbury Avenue, where she was shown a statement of his personal worth, including his top-class share portfolio. Everything proclaimed the message that 'the man who had asked her to marry him was rich' (E 341), indeed so rich that she would never have to worry about money ever again. With such an unlikely introduction, so began the long process of Williams's acclimatisation to marriage, Molly on one side, eager and committed, and on the other Williams, fearing unequivocal commitment and deeply troubled by his uncertain sexual orientation.

Essentially there were two specific obstacles to be overcome, both very different in character: the practical difficulties attached to Molly's divorce (including the willingness or not of her estranged husband to agree to one) and Fess Griffith. The first issue was a matter of discussion and persuasion, while the second Williams saw, somewhat naively, as in essence a simple gender choice between Molly and Fess. But what was equally at stake was quality of feeling: the difference between the warmly protective and protecting monogamy he would enjoy with Molly over a rough-edged sexual alliance with a sometimes glacially uncommitted Fess. Molly Carus-Wilson was aware of Williams's erstwhile relationship with Cronin-Wilson and she was not long in discovering the extent of his feeling for Fess. Her commitment to Williams was genuine and deep, but over the next few months the magnetic attraction between Williams and Fess more than once placed large question-marks over the wisdom of her pledge. It seems likely that Williams was not disinclined to be bounced into a permanent heterosexual relationship, but Molly had an even stronger determination, and that was to see off her rival in Fess by the risky strategy of inducing Williams to confront his own ambivalent sexuality.

In *Emlyn*, Williams presents himself as bisexual and in a loose sense he was probably right; but his sexual experience with women was at best limited to a few one-night stands, almost always in brothels, whereas all his committed relationships were homosexual. On balance it is the latter description which seems to suit more accurately his sexual behaviour up to 1935. This made marriage even more of a gamble. Examples of women who married in awareness of the predominantly homosexual proclivities of their partners were not encouraging. The potentially distressing nature of the experience is well illustrated in the case of Syrie Maugham's ten years of unhappy alliance with her playwright husband. Somerset Maugham's homosexuality was carefully hidden from public knowledge, but his private relationships with successive male secretaries continued unhindered. Nevertheless Molly might have found comfort in the retrospective comment by Freida Lawrence (*Memoirs and Correspondence*) to Middleton Murry on one period of her marriage to D.H. Lawrence:

> I think the homosexuality in him was a short phase out of misery
> – I fought him and won.

In May 1934, soon after the engagement, Molly took an annual lease on a wooden property called the Holme Bungalow at Wymondisbury, on a small island in a backwater of the Thames, near Staines. She was perfectly aware how much Williams enjoyed such a sanctuary belonging to her sister and brother-in-law, just far enough away from the frenzied life of London, for rest and relaxation. With neither mains water nor electricity (just Aladdin oil lamps), 'The Bung' as it was always known was a kind of 'gypsy river-retreat' (E 342). The self-same environment and even period Williams was nostalgically to recreate fifty years later in 1986 for his very last play *Cuckoo* (a revision of *Beth*), set in

> [a] bungalow on a small island in the Thames, near Hampton Court. The time is 1935, a fine morning in May.

Perhaps Molly thought she might manage Williams better away from Ebury Street, where Fess was a constant object of attention. But in fact, as Williams makes clear, he considered Fess as much a part of the household there as he was in the London flat. Molly however soon regarded him as the cuckoo in the nest. She was in contest with a psychological deep-seated fixation on Williams's part. Fess was not only sexually enticing in his own right but he was Williams's link with the guilt of the immediate past: he was, as it were, Cronin-Wilson's last gift. Especially in the London flat, where nothing of Wilson's remained, the erotic presence of Fess was a living memorial to him: his 'lithe, smooth body and the amiable smile, was my bond with a dead man' (E 346).

Williams's professional life as far as the stage was concerned was stagnant for six months from the early spring to autumn 1934. After the closure of *Spring, 1600* he was not to appear on stage again until early September. As Piers Gaveston in Hugh Ross Williams's *The Rose and the Glove*, a drama about Edward II, the experience was so dispiriting for him he hardly counted it as stage work at all. This was followed shortly afterwards on 25 September by *Josephine*, a drama about Napoleon. Williams, on commission from Alexander Korda, adapted from the German and played a small part. Starring Mary Ellis and Frank Vosper, with Molly O'Shann as an extra in the crowd, it was hissed on the first night at Her Majesty's Theatre and closed after six performances, having received notices which

Donald Wolfit (who had a bit part), only half-jokingly described as 'the worst since the turn of the century' (E 378).

On the credit side, there was the new distinction of playing Shakespeare on radio in Clemence Dane's *Will Shakespeare*, produced by Val Gielgud for the BBC Home Service and broadcast on Shakespeare's birthday on 23 April. And from mid to late summer film work, most of which could be done at 'The Bung' with Molly and Fess in attendance, came fairly regularly. There were additional dialogue commissions for *Chu Chin Chow* and for Hitchcock, 'homework' which Williams sensed was 'checked and passed [at the studio], like laundry' (E 345). This was supplemented by roles in *My Song for You* and *The Iron Duke* ('a small part in a big film' [E 367], starring George Arliss as Wellington), neither of which was very successful. At a different level, he played the role of the mad eighteenth-century Danish monarch Christian VII in the film *The Dictator*. Of his work on this film made at the ATP Studios in Ealing during 1934 there is for some reason no mention in *Emlyn*, but *Today's Cinema* (8 February 1935) described Williams's achievement as

> a brilliantly clever and subtly satirical portrait that is among the most notably individual screen performances we have seen.

Earlier rather than later in the summer of 1934 the relationship between Williams and Molly Carus-Wilson advanced to a sexual level for the first time. Significantly, they first slept together off Williams's own territory in Molly's rented room in Draycott Avenue, South Kensington. Despite all the sexual peccadilloes of her husband, Molly was by this point fully reconciled to the fact that divorce would only come about from his side rather than hers. And she was aware that to satisfy the court proper evidence of her adultery would be required. For best results Molly would need to become pregnant. Meantime, for appearances' sake, to Williams's cleaning woman at Ebury Street Molly Carus-Wilson suddenly became Mrs Williams – Williams told her that they had been secretly married – and Fess was banished to the top floor flat, a demotion which he accepted with apparently perfect equanimity as if in belief that it was only temporary and that his superior position in Williams's emotional hierarchy was effectively unchallenged.

Most of Williams's writing was done at 'The Bung', which was occupied virtually every weekend. Here Fess tended to flaunt his sexuality as if in temptation, whether dressed in his white swimming shorts – Williams, more primly attired in his strapped one-piece bathing suit, envied to the point of jealousy his graceful diving abilities – on lazy days down on the river, or in goggles and heavily overcoated astride his new Rudge motorcycle which, on an impulse he was later to regret, Williams agreed to buy for him. Ostensibly in gratitude for his willing assistance in the household, the bike was in reality Fess's coming-of-age present. More than that, it was a reckless surrender to Williams's wilder obsessiveness with Fess. And Fess, for his part, simultaneously teased and titillated him with stories of his sexual conquests, whether easy lays over nubile shop girls from Woolworth's or equally willing male partners encountered in neighbouring pubs. He was strong in sexual appeal but ultimately resistible because Williams sensed in him cold detachment and exploitation rather than security. In Fess there was none of the shared confidences or companionship that he had enjoyed with Bill Cronin-Wilson. Molly recognised the obsessiveness of his love for Fess and Williams eventually confessed as much, glad to be free of the secrecy; but he denied any pleasure from the feeling. Fess had a kind of intimidating presence which both Molly and Williams, in their different ways, found deeply uncomfortable.

When it came to the point, the confrontation with Fess was made easier because it was on grounds not of emotional feeling but of financial dishonesty, which Williams found easier to justify. According to the details of the episode in *Emlyn*, Williams discovered quite by chance that he had falsified the dealer's invoice for the motorcycle by £30 on a total bill of £81. 3s 9d. With Molly in support he tackled him with the intention of exposing him as a cheat. His arrogance undented by the accusation, but inwardly enraged – he wore 'a look as primitive as I had ever seen on a human being' – by being deprived of the bike, Fess accepted his fate, gave up the keys to the bungalow and to Ebury Street and left with no word of protest. As he sauntered nonchalantly off the premises to return home to Gloucester, Williams saw him as 'empty of affection, of conscience, of humanity' (E 366).

While regretting the separation almost as soon as it was effected, Williams was determined to persevere without him. Molly had already acquired a modest car of her own, but Williams attempted to show how his reliance on Fess in practical terms at least as chauffeur for his Morris Oxford was now ended by employing a Staines garage attendant to teach him how to drive. Driving never came easily to Williams through his lack of co-ordination – he terrified passengers witless with his frequent failure to distinguish brake and accelerator – and at the first excuse, an accident in 1935 when he rammed the back of Molly's Austin Seven, he was to give it up permanently. From then on Molly was the sole driver in the family.

The trouble was that Fess was not easily dismissed like a disgraced servant caught with his hand in the till, and Williams's emotions took some considerable time to adjust to his absence. Molly realised as much, yet sympathetic as she generally was as a listener and confidante, her belief that Williams just needed to get him out of his system was at the very least naïve. She was aware that her recommendation of a re-establishment of relations as a test of mutual feelings was a high risk make-or-break strategy. What she did not know was that Williams had already made a fetish out of Fess's former possessions, the fiercely masculine motorbike (even more intimidating than a car) which thrilled with untried power and even his discarded shoes, still smelling of their original owner, which he secretly tried on.

Williams's new-found, if unrefined, ability to drive a car was an important element in his attempt to deal with his fixation, even if it proclaimed an independence of Fess which he did not properly feel. His journey was marred by a slight accident, caused by misjudging clearances in Cheltenham's crowded main street, but his confident arrival shortly afterwards at Fess's Gloucester home, having driven himself the seventy-odd miles from Staines, was a triumph and Fess was properly impressed. It helped Williams stay in charge of the relationship. This was reinforced when Fess (accepting with hardly a change of expression Williams's invitation to re-occupy the top flat at Ebury Street) was calculatingly humiliated by Williams's insistence on doing the driving back to London: 'in front of his parents it was a double emasculation' (E 372). In succumbing to what he had

earlier described in conversation with Molly as the madness of inviting Fess back to 71a, Williams was testing himself to the emotional
limits. After Williams garaged the car, they went out to dinner and
on return occupied separate rooms at the flat. The following day
Williams left to drive down to the bungalow, suggesting that Fess
come by train twenty-four hours later. He did not do so and shortly
afterwards a letter arrived, indicating Fess's intention to return
home to Gloucester. Enclosed was the five pound note Fess had
been given before Williams's departure.

Fess understood that he had lost the initiative in the relationship
and that consequently the likelihood of his being able to exploit
Williams any further, either sexually or materially, was now remote.
Molly commented that it was 'not a bad exit' (E 373), but it was not
a final one. Fess was exorcised neither by this event nor (as Williams
insists) the selling of the Morris after the accident in 1935. He was
eliminated from his consciousness, as far as this was ever possible,
only when he put him into a play and gave substance to his character on stage by playing the Fess-inspired role himself.

Five: From Night to Morning

The genesis of *Night Must Fall*, the first big success that Emlyn Williams could call expressly his own, was more complex than anything in his work to date. The germ of the play seems to have come from newspaper reports in October 1934 of the imminence of Mancini's much-publicised trial for the body-in-a-trunk murder at Brighton, which helped trigger some basic details. But more important stimuli were the high-profile murderers from the past who now flooded into his imagination and began to give some shape to Williams's conception of Dan, the baby-face killer who carries his first victim's head around in a hatbox. There was the otherwise charming Patrick Mahon, a decade previously, whose girl victim was left in a trunk in a bungalow; and a bit closer to home Sidney Fox, an erstwhile pick-up of one of Williams's acquaintances from the Long Bar at the Trocadero, who five years earlier murdered his invalid mother at a Margate hotel for the insurance money. (The alternative account of the play's origin in the introduction to the *Collected Plays*, Williams's chance meeting on a train with a woman who had had tea with 'nice and ordinary' Fox at her aunt's house in Surbiton only weeks before the crime [CP, xvii], is presumably either a complete fiction or a very small part of the truth.) Significantly, the original idea was for Mrs Bramson, Dan's third-act victim in the play, to be his real mother rather than a surrogate, but Williams rejected the idea on the grounds that though truth was indeed stranger than fiction no one would ever find it credible.

More powerfully present than anything else in the provenance of *Night Must Fall* were elements of deep-seated fantasies and obsessions out of Williams's personal experience. None was more curious than his German adventure four years previously, when on an impromptu solo holiday he found himself embarked on a 'macabre excursion, of the mind' (E 192), following directly in the footsteps of a serial killer of the recent past. On one of the several occasions in his life when Williams's innate restlessness urged him to relax abroad – this one directly after the closure of *On the Spot* after 342 performances in January 1931 – he travelled to Berlin in search of excitement, having been assured by Freddie Mell that it was '[t]he wickedest city in Europe ducks' (E 191). In the 1930s, as presented by Christopher Isherwood in *Goodbye to Berlin* (1938), it was indeed notorious for its sexual diversity and homosexual promiscuity; in its night-clubs, brothels and drinking dens rent boys, female prostitutes and transsexuals were common sights. What gave it a special allurement was that, unlike in England, homosexuality was not illegal. Berlin offered sexual freedom, but whatever Williams expected or wanted from Berlin he claimed not to have found. His guide to the sexual hot-spots of the city, the Berlin reporter for the *Morning Post*, under injunction to show him 'everything', failed to deliver; the drag queens of the El Dorado club did not impress.

After a visit out of duty more than enthusiasm to the Deutsches Theater, there was nothing to detain him further and next day Williams took the train to Hanover, where his real adventure began. Stimulated by his compulsive reading of William Bolitho's *Murder for Profit* (1926), a compendium of real-life crime, he set out to tour sites associated with the vicious crimes perpetrated in the winter of 1923-4. This was in line with a curiosity that Williams had already succumbed to at home, notably in the Robinson case of 1927, when the dismembered remains of the street-walker victim, picked up in Chelsea and murdered in an office in Rochester Row, turned up in a left-luggage locker at Charing Cross. It was an episode which Williams identified as having 'aroused an interest to be permanently tangled with my professional life' (E 17).

To judge from the ease with which he entered into the Hanover tour it was probably planned in some detail well before Williams's arrival. He began much more than a physical venture: it was a journey into the self. In the foggy, darkened streets the elements of theatre were evoked as he set out on his ghoulish pilgrimage, beginning in the dimly lit waiting-room at the Hauptbahnhof. This was the location where forty-five-year-old Fritz Haarman, by day a burly, jovial family butcher, used to befriend young male victims (ultimately twenty-seven in number), who were then lured back to his bed-sitter and murdered during sexual gratification. Bones from their dismembered corpses on sale in the shop were turned into soup by unsuspecting customers. In precisely the same way that he later became fixated by the Moors murderers, Williams was keen to obtain firsthand evidence from police files. He fabricated a story about writing a thesis on criminal psychology and claims to have fooled the Hanover authorities into allowing him to see all the witnesses' depositions and many photographs. Among the latter were the murderer's shabby bed-sitter ('pitted with poverty and cluttered with the details of monotonous daily life, each spelling reality more clearly than the last' [E 196]), pathetic family album pictures of the victims and two of Haarman himself, one of which was posed naked in profile for the police camera. Williams 'half expected' the man's penis 'to bear some weird mark of the horror' (E 197) of his crimes; but it did not and the ordinariness of his genitalia served to intensify both the horror and the fascination. Once again he found himself at that compelling border-line between the ordinariness of everyday life and the profoundest evil and depravity.

The experience sparked in Williams's imagination the idea of 'sexual licence in relation to murder' (E 198) as possible material for a play, even to the extent of envisaging Charles Laughton playing the lead. But once again it was only an academic exercise since Williams was perfectly well aware that none of the details could be directly employed without involving irreconcilable problems with censorship. Bizarrely, however, the Hanover adventure also made him consider more deeply the parallels between Haarman and Bill Cronin-Wilson, in whom he had already detected elements of a Jekyll and Hyde personality. There were correspondences that went beyond their merely sharing a similar physical build. Haarman at the time of his crimes was much the same age as Wilson was in 1931 and, like him, attributed his homosexuality to experiences in the trenches during the Great War. Fortuitously, Williams and Cronin-Wilson also happened to live together over a butcher's shop. But by the time that *Night Must Fall* began to take shape three years later during the autumn of 1934, these events from the past were overlaid by the increasingly disturbing presence of Cronin-Wilson's successor in Fess Griffith. Williams had been especially struck by his seeming indifference to the former's death and recognised with increasing distaste his capacity for deceit and calculation. In his imagination Fess was slotted easily into the cold, dispassionate role of a potential murderer, yet ironically that only intensified for Williams the chilling charisma of Fess's physical presence. The peak of his baleful influence was in the mid to late summer of 1934, in the months following the marriage proposal to Molly:

> I was getting no ounce of pleasure from a presence which was essential to me (E 348).

Even when Fess had been banished from the bungalow after cheating over the motorbike, Williams sought to get him back and it was Fess who left Williams in the end, not the other way round. This magnetic hold over those who seemed to have every reason to shun him he built into the character of Dan in *Night Must Fall*. It was the play, not his marriage, which seems to have brought him some measure of freedom from the obsession.

After well over a month trying to establish the outlines of plot and character, Williams set to work on *Night Must Fall* on 25 November 1934, the eve of his twenty-ninth birthday, and was soon committed to the same writing routine he had established in New York: 'midnight till four, then the whisky nightcap' (E 353). The script, after all its revisions, rewritings and repeated cutting – Williams tried to remember that overwriting was his gravest fault and lopped fully twenty lines off one of Mrs Bramson's speeches on her nightmares – was completed by late January 1935. Walter Peacock then successfully interested the Cockney manager J.P. Mitchelhill (principally associated with Priestley's productions at the Duchess), who branded it 'very 'orrible but it grips yer all right' (E 389). Later on Noël Coward, who saw the play twice and was sent a personal copy, made something of the same point in his own self-consciously camp fashion:

> I say, Williams, that was no end spiffing of you to send me your little play. As one chap to another don't you think its just the teensiest, weensiest bit unpleasant here & there? but I suppose you writer fellows use everything as grist to your mill. / Love to you & the little woman / Coward' (C2 5 July 1935).

Since Williams had written the part of Dan with the intention of playing it himself – upon the success of which the whole play would turn – it was decided that, contrary to the now usual practice, he should not also direct. Instead the job went to Miles Malleson, an author-director with a sound reputation, whose most recent work had been at the Shaftesbury with his own adaptation of Hauptmann's *Before Sunset* (1933). As was often the case, much of the casting had been done already in Williams's mind: Kathleen Harrison for the comic cook and Angela Baddeley (now married to Glen Byam Shaw) as Olivia, the niece who becomes fixated by and drawn to the murderous Dan. For the crotchety, wheel-chair bound invalid, Mrs Bramson, all the actresses considered suitable – Edith Evans, Sybil Thorndike, and even the almost legendary septuagenarian Mrs Patrick Campbell (who had not acted in London for close on twenty years) – were not available. The choice eventually fell, at Malleson's insistence but with reluctance on Williams's side, on another septuagenarian, Dame May Whitty, who in private at least, as her daughter Margaret Webster records, was dismissive both of the part ('an old beast in a wheelchair') and the play ('just a thriller', which had no chance of a long run).

Advertised with triple exclamation marks as the 'world premiere' of Emlyn Williams 'in his own play', the first performance of *Night Must Fall* took place at the King's Theatre, Edinburgh, on Monday 29 April 1935. The three weeks' try-out took the play on to Newcastle and concluded at Glasgow. This period gave the production time to settle down before exposure to London audiences. It was also a test of quality and popularity, though provincial success was no cast-iron guarantee of a London run because of the difficulty finding a theatre vacant at the right time. First indications for Williams were not promising. While the Edinburgh reviews were not unkind, audiences were noticeably sparse: in fact box-office returns for the whole first week amounted to only £437. At Newcastle, business was even worse and just before commencement of the final try-out week in Glasgow, Williams convinced himself that the play was finished and even sent his parents their train fare so that they could see it before it closed permanently. The fate of Williams's play remained in doubt until the very last Glasgow performance, when news came that the Duchess Theatre would become free on the early closure of Priestley's *Cornelius* (which even Ralph Richardson as star could not save). On 31 May, *Night Must Fall* would succeed it for an indefinite season.

The main setting of the play, a 'tawdry but cheerful' wooden bungalow in Essex belonging to the cantankerous wheelchair-bound invalid Mrs Bramson, bears more than a passing resemblance to the riverside summer retreat that Williams and Molly had on the Thames. Here the river is replaced by a dark conifer forest surrounding the property; but like 'The Bung' there is no electric light, only Aladdin oil lamps. Olivia, Mrs Bramson's niece, not pretty and already past normal marriageable age, is currently considering a proposal from Hubert Laurie, a thirty-five-year-old *Telegraph* reader ('moustached, hearty, and pompous'), who describes himself as 'not what you'd call a terribly brainy chap, but I am straight' (1:0). Trapped by her lack of money into remaining with her aunt, Olivia is tempted by his offer but declines because Laurie, though amiable enough, is such 'an unmitigated bore'. Nonetheless she resents her enslavement and even confesses in an unguarded moment to Dan her murderous feelings towards her aunt. Dan suggests that this is a fantasy, since few people actually have the capacity to do such things, though he underlines the fact in an unnecessarily obvious way (he studies his hands and chuckles to himself) that such acts are perfectly within his capabilities.

Dan, who first appears half way through Act 1 after the police have come to give notice of a missing female from the Tallboys Hotel, is 'sort of Welsh, I think' (1:0) according to the maid Dora Parkoe, and he later reveals to Olivia (2:2) that one of his earliest memories is of Cardiff docklands. (Presumably he means Tiger Bay, now no more, but once the toughest area of the city and a notorious red-light district.) Like Fess Griffith his accent is somewhat indeterminate, a bit rough and ready but, as Williams's stage directions insist, *'more Welsh than anything else'*. In further direct imitation of the original he wears *'the stub of a cigarette dangl[ing] between his lips'*, has also been to sea with the Navy and exudes an air of vanity coupled with a subdued confidence in his ability to ingratiate himself, as he does almost immediately with Mrs Bramson by solicitude for her health. By the opening of Act 2 she regards him as the son she never had and he is calling her 'mother'. Dora has already succumbed to his dangerous charm and is two or three months pregnant by him. As she observes, there is something subversive about his manner, something unexplained behind his baby-faced looks: 'I never seem to get 'old of what 'e's thinking, somehow'. Similarly, Olivia is perfectly aware that '[h]e's acting ... every minute of the time. I know he is' (2:1).

It is Olivia who introduces a principal theme of the play, that of the evil and the macabre invading the common concerns of everyday. If, as the police believe, there is a body out there in the woods beyond the immediate confines of the bungalow garden, then it transforms an ordinary October morning into an extraordinary one bordering on daytime nightmare. Dan elaborates the point later on by invoking the idea of church-goers sitting piously in their Sunday-best clothes being about to find their daylight metaphorically compromised by the knowledge of night and the wickedness that surrounds them in this spot: the holy is squeezed out by the evil because however bright the day night must eventually come:

> to-day will be the same as all the other days, and come to an end, and it'll be night (2:2).

Significantly Dan, who claims to have been brought up on the Bible, teases Mrs Bramson by suggesting reading out of the dusty family sized copy languishing on top of the desk, knowing that her real interest is in the stories about her in the *News of the World*, a copy of which he carries under his arm. The religious cynicism comes directly from Fess and his mockery of his experience as a choirboy at Gloucester Cathedral with what Williams feelingly described in *Emlyn* as 'a derision beyond atheism' (E 380).

Of Dan's responsibility for the murder of the hotel guest whose decapitated body is eventually discovered in the ash-pit at the bottom of the garden, the audience is of course never in doubt: the play open with the judge pronouncing Dan's death sentence after his trial. The effectiveness as a device of removing the main element of mystery Williams already knew from Edgar Wallace's *On the Spot*. For this reason the heavy hints of further crimes to come – such as

Hubert Laurie's (of Mrs Bramson) 'She'll be found murdered one of these days' (1:0) and Mrs Bramson's own kittenish comment on Dan's being a 'caution! You'll be the death of me!' (2:2) – work better on the level of comedy than dramatic irony. Laurie and Mrs Terence the cook dismiss the possibility of Dan's being the murderer as preposterous because to them he is so ordinary. But at the end of Act 1, when Dan is heard singing 'I'm mighty lak a rose', the self-same song the gamekeeper in Shepperley woods reported hearing on the afternoon of the murder victim's disappearance, Olivia begins to perceive the truth. Williams's strategy is to divert his play away from the conventional 'who-dunnit' to 'why-dunnit' and to turn the spotlight instead on the psychology of the murderer and those like Olivia who suspect the truth yet choose not to reveal it. His other innovatory scheme was to employ 'weirdly dramatic background music' (CP, xvii) in order to underline the state of Dan's mind. This device was to have been modelled on the lines of the panatropes already common in film, but more because the technology was not yet advanced enough for use in the theatre than that it was too 'filmish', he was forced against his better judgment into making the words alone carry much of the atmospheric weight of the play.

There is no special dramatic subtlety in their execution, but the darkening events of the *Night Must Fall* parallel the movement from morning to evening, light to dark, innocence to corruption. Much of the threatening atmosphere is dependent in production upon a well thought-out and executed lighting plot. This is because the dialogue supporting these transitions (which in other contexts might have had perhaps a Chekovian ring) tends to sound hackneyed, even meretricious. Olivia abruptly remarks in Act 1 '[h]ow bright the sun is to-day' and confides to Hubert her train of thought:

> I often wonder on a very fine morning what it'll be like ... for night to come. And I never can. And yet it's got to ...'.

Sensitivity to atmosphere is supposed to be a part of her literariness. As the action naturally progresses over a double time-scale of morning through afternoon to night over a period of fourteen days, the morning sunshine of Act 1 is replaced by duller afternoon weather and a darkening sky. As the denouement approaches the oil lamps are lit and Dan (not usually given to profundity) observes,

> [t]he light's going .... The daytime's as if it's never been; it's dead
> ... (*Seeing the others stare, with a laugh*) Daft, isn't it' (3:1).

In ways never intended by the author, a modern audience might be forced to agree.

Williams was fascinated, not to say obsessed, by the psychology of murder and the pathology of death. In Dan he attempts to investigate the phenomenon by reference to his experience: the men whom he had known whose personalities hinted at the double life, his avid reading and personal investigation in and around the lives of prominent murderers of his own time, and a morbid curiosity about dead bodies going all the way back to his childhood in Glanrafon and the ritual viewing of the coffined corpse of young Kate Edwards, daughter of the Gyrn Castle gamekeeper, who had 'died of something called pew-monia' (G 53). Given the background, the degree of personal involvement over Fess and the amount of thinking and research (in Hanover and elsewhere) that went into his obsession, Dan in *Night Must Fall* is a less complex figure than might be expected. Williams is not here imbued with any special insight into the criminal mind. Dan's characteristics are evidently intended as diluted versions of ones which Williams found in his model: Fess was just as perplexing, lacking in feeling and sexually magnetic to Williams as Dan is meant to be to Olivia in the play. In the stage character it is as difficult to find sexual as psychological depth: Dan's hold on Olivia tends to be no more than inferentially suppressed sexuality. Given that the play more or less as it stands originally attracted some attention from the censor, Williams was almost certainly prudent in playing down the issue, even though the idea of a woman in love with a murderer is traceable back to Shakespeare's time.

Out of all Williams's plays, the censor evinced greatest interest in *Night Must Fall*. In his Reader's Report (9 February 1935), Assistant Examiner Henry Game commented on its 'above the average' quality as '[a]n almost too successful essay in the macabre'. Olivia was seen as 'a Strindbergian figure' and Dan as 'a horrible but clever creation of criminal psychology'. He recognised that there might be some qualms raised over Dan's reading from the New Testament just before the murder of Mrs Bramson in Act 3 but concluded that this was

> very effective dramatically and quite sound criminal psychology and personally I see nothing to offend even the Fundamentalist in this (LCP file 935).

On the express permission of the Chief Examiner, the Bible readings were allowed to remain in the script. However Mrs Terence's reference to Mrs Bramson as a 'bitch' (1:0) (even though done under her breath) was not permitted: 'devil' was produced as an alternative on the official side, but at Williams's own suggestion 'sour-faced old hag' was finally adopted for the licensed text.

Potentially more problematic were the references to Dan's exploitative attitude to women and sex and to Mrs Chalfont's supposed nymphomania. Olivia's inquiry (2:1) whether there were prospects of Dora and Dan getting married is met with Dora's response that she has almost never talked to him. The succeeding lines in the licensing copy are cut completely and no alternative was substituted:

> [Dora] Except o'course for you-know-what.
> [Olivia] And that's all it meant?
> [Dora] You'd be surprised 'ow little it can mean, miss. The fuss they make. It beats me.

The other problem was to do with Mrs Chalfont, where Dan makes out that she had had a string of sexual partners and was on the look-out for more (2:2). In Dan's long speech to Inspector Belsize admitting to an affair with her, the line 'and all the fellows she'd had, and was having' was replaced by the much weaker 'an' all the other fellers she'd been after' (again Williams's suggestion). Certainly all such deletions and substitutions were irksome rather than seriously damaging to the play, but they underline how impossible it would have been for Williams to have written any more explicitly sexual elements into the relationship between Dan and Olivia. *Night Must Fall* was finally licensed for public performance on 21 March 1935, after an abnormally protracted detention at St James's Palace of around six weeks from submission of the initial typescript.

The mood of the play is notoriously difficult to judge, and the ease with which the lead actor can fall into mere melodramatic gesturing has been proved by recent London revivals, none of which has been able to recapture the play's original success. There is a developing air of menace and inscrutability merged with a degree of black comedy. At times this dissolves into a more mundane level of humour that gains Dan easy acceptance in Mrs Bramson's household. He is so ordinary, yet is both angel in appearance and devil in conduct and morality. Olivia has two scenes with Dan which attempt to explore motivation. She ascribes to him an 'incredible vanity', which she holds up as a characteristic of a murderer (which may well be the case for some, if not for all, but quite how she would know is not clear). Her insistence that Dan is acting all the time, something he will not deny, is part of her analysis of the criminal in general: her theory is that 'it's the criminals who can look you in the eyes, and honest people who blush and look away' (2:1). Like so many villains from Richard III and Iago onwards, Dan certainly is a supreme actor, but the one self-revealing moment comes in dialogue with Olivia (2:2), with whom he plays a cat-and-mouse game, knowing she has guessed the truth. He stops short however of giving her the satisfaction of his confession, even though Olivia is an exception to his general lack of respect for women. His main rancour is against a society that requires him to serve others for whom he has nothing but contempt. He needs to be somebody, however that status can be achieved: if by no other, then by being a celebrated murderer. Olivia finds that unswerving commitment to self-aggrandisement totally compelling. It is why she never reveals to the police, as she might have done at the end of Act 2, the contents of Dan's hatbox and why she is drawn back to the bungalow in the dead of night in the knowledge of Dan's crime and the danger posed to her as a potential third victim. Her enslavement to Mrs Bramson is replaced by the irresistible allure of Dan: she will lie to protect him, even to the point of implicating herself. But Dan cannot accept that, not from any wish to save Olivia from herself, but because he refuses to share the glory of his crime with anyone else. The full-mouth kiss that he plants 'suddenly and violently' on Olivia at the close of the play (before immediately resuming his trademark of the dangling cigarette) is a mixture of victory and defiance. It is also the only sexual gesture in a play which implies sexual chemistry on Olivia's part without ever actually exploring it. Olivia's reaction to Dan underplays the sexual element, but it sublimates Williams's former relationship with Fess. Both are excited by the dangerous in the ordinary, the unfathomed depths behind the facade. Olivia abandons herself to that feeling of excitement in Dan because of, not in spite of, his crime, just as Williams abandoned himself to another man to whom he was simultaneously attracted and repelled. Given the issues raised, the play's conclusion as Dan is delivered into the hands of the law is, however, disappointingly conventional.

The production of *Night Must Fall* was, within its genre, one of the sensations of 1935. It had an especially strong cast of experienced players, from the comic servants upwards. Amongst the cluster of domestics, the presence of at least one who speaks their mind and intimidates their employers had become virtually a standard ingredient of Williams's playwriting: he enjoyed the stereotype and found comedy in their toughness and in the sharpness of their tongues. Kathleen Harrison as Mrs Terence made a special mark, but splendid as she was there was some truth in the assertion (*The Times*, 1 June 1935) that, as a character, she was not really necessary. Indeed both she and Nurse Libby were mere 'tricks of the theatre'. As the morally disgraced Dora, Betty Jardine was suitably submissive in a role that was later taken over and played to brilliant effect, though it was somewhat against her usual grain, by Patricia Hayes. May Whitty as Mrs Bramson, manipulating her wheel-chair about the stage with the grace and precision of an experienced skater, was reported to have given 'a rare authenticity to the old woman's doting vanity' and discovered 'a natural terror in her end', with the last scene between her and Dan. Williams's own performance was widely praised because it never became sensationalist. As *The Times* put it,

> [a]s dramatist and as actor he has chosen to live inside the murderer's mind and to communicate his experience in a play that combines suspense of plot with genuine imaginative tension.

Without exception the other notices were equally positive: 'a brilliant success' (*Daily Telegraph*), 'a thriller of brilliance and imagination' (*Morning Post*) and 'the hit of the season for those playgoers who want their spines chilled' (*Daily Express*).

Night Must Fall had an uninterrupted life on the London stage of 436 performances covering nearly thirteen months until 20 June 1936. For the period it was an extraordinary success, no doubt aided by its appearance in print as one of the six best plays of the year in Victor Gollancz's *Famous Plays of 1935* (all the rest of which are now long forgotten). From London the show immediately went on a prearranged tour to the USA with all of the original cast. To Williams's surprise its reception across the Atlantic was much cooler than at home. Reporting to Miss Cooke on his and Molly's socialising at the 'most exquisite [country] house I've ever seen', belonging to the Marshall Fields on Long Island, he added that *Night Must Fall* was 'not setting the New York River on fire' (A1 27 October 1936). In July after a break of three weeks – not the immediate single week-end transfer that Williams claimed (CP, xviii) – it re-opened at the Cambridge Theatre, London. Under Glen Byam Shaw's direction, with Esmond Knight as Dan supported by a completely new cast (except for Patricia Hayes), it clocked up another 205 performances before closing in January 1937 after a total of twenty months. It was filmed twice. In the 1937 version Robert Montgomery's Dan diluted the menace of Williams's reading, but while in 1964 the MGM remake, starring Albert Finney (with Mona Washbourne and Susan Hampshire), gave Dan somewhat more credibility critics were convinced that nothing in the performance matched the quality of Williams's original. On neither occasion did Williams have any part in production or screenplay and he was not entirely satisfied with the results of either film version. However John Van Druten's addition to the 1937 script of a couple of kitchen interviews between Olivia and Dan did gain Williams's general approval: fifty years later he recalled them as 'frightfully good' (Berry, 521).

Though perfectly traditional in structure, *Night Must Fall* was regarded in its day as innovatory in attempting to bring an analytical quality to the study of the criminal. This was recognised by contemporary reviewers as making it different from other plays in the genre of the crime-thriller like Edgar Wallace's and even superior to Anthony Armstrong's clever but never repeated success in *Ten Minute Alibi* (1933). Williams minimised the role of the detective and focused attention on the revelations that naturally emerged in discussion between the murderer and a woman of intelligence, fascinated, almost mesmerised by his power. But to modern audiences and critics *Night Must Fall* has been seen as past its time. It was revived briefly at the Theatre Royal, Stratford East, at the end of April 1947 (for sixteen performances only), but the play was then, as far as the mainstream professional theatre in London was concerned, ignored until 1986. Modern-day responses tend to underline just how much the success of the original relied on Williams's own performance as Dan, with its magnetism charged by his personal involvement in the character.

When the Greenwich Theatre staged a revival to celebrate Williams's association with the theatre for over fifty years, the choice of the 1935 thriller was a risky one, given how much it had been overshadowed by Williams's other big successes in a more distinctive Welsh vein in *The Corn is Green* and *The Wind of Heaven*. The production was handled in consultation with Williams, who perhaps unwisely added a few new period touches to the script (even though the original is supposed to take place in the present) and made some structural alterations in order to tailor it around a single interval. Taking advantage of the new opportunities available in a theatre now freed from censorship, he also attempted to give the language more spirit and to invest it with a measure of explicitness that the Lord Chamberlain could not have permitted in 1935. In Williams's final version of 1986 Dan's closing lines read: 'Well, I'll be strung up at the end, but ... I'll give 'em their money's worth at the fuckin' trial!' and the play ended with the stage 'dominated by a huge graphic image of the scaffold, and of the dangling noose' (D7/4).

Though Williams meant the play to remain in its period, there was an uncertainty in production whether the play actually was to be seen as period or contemporary. This was ultimately self-defeating and even the fairly extensive tinkering with the 1935 text could not disguise the fact that the play lacked psychological credibility in the less innocent final decades of the twentieth century. In the

FROM NIGHT TO MORNING

Guardian (18 December 1986) Nicholas de Jongh sneered at

> this musty old theatrical corpse which has been exhumed from
> the theatrical mausoleum as if it still had the power to thrill.

Indeed this was not the worst of it, for a decade later in October 1996 the critical reception of another revival of the same play delivered an even severer blow to Williams's reputation. Directed at the Haymarket by John Tydeman and starring Jason Donovan, formerly of *Neighbours* (the Australian soap-opera), it attracted such universal opprobrium that it is doubtful whether any commercial producer in London could gamble on mounting the play again. Donovan, whose strangely wayward accent provoked much adverse comment, failed to generate any degree of menace. For Michael Darvell in *What's On* (16 October), he was 'about as threatening as being pelted with marshmallows'; the *Sunday Times* (20 October) suggested that Donovan was 'acting in a different play' from the rest of the cast; and *Time Out* (16 October) hinted mischievously that the play re-created for real Stoppard's 'hilarious Cluedo parody', *The Real Inspector Hound*. Even setting Donovan's performance aside, the truth was that the play failed to make any convincing psychological headway into the nature of the psychopath. And it did not work as a period piece, because, as the *Daily Telegraph* (12 October) commenting on the badly dated nature of the dialogue said, it 'made Agatha Christie sound like Anton Chekov'. Even the *Sunday Times*'s novel deconstructionist view that the play might have a value in representing something of Britain's uncertain attitudes to Fascism in the mid 1930s failed to help it gain an audience. Faced by a virtually unanimous hostile onslaught, disastrous box office returns and minimal advance bookings its premature closure was inevitable and took place on 2 November, a full six weeks early.

*

Emlyn Williams's second – and what was to be his last – volume of autobiography begins in April 1927 at the commencement of his career as actor-playwright in London and concludes with the tabs poised to rise on the Essex bungalow set at the Duchess Theatre on the opening night of *Night Must Fall* on 31 May 1935. All is breathless anticipation. Williams implies a new beginning as a married man and as an established playwright, for the success of *Night Must Fall* was in no doubt. That Fess had apparently disappeared for good and his mythologised self as the baby-faced page-boy from the Tallboys Hotel, having had a reasonably successful outing in the provinces, was about to be recreated in a London theatre, made marriage not only possible but desirable against future lapses. There were four photographs on Williams's make-up table at the theatre on the first night: his father, his mother, Miss Cooke and Molly. Fess was not amongst them: his face was reflected in the mirror, made up as Dan. On stage Williams even wore Fess's own cast-off shoes.

That in retrospect Williams saw 1935 as a kind of golden year, a fulfilment both professionally and emotionally, is suggested not only by its being the narrative culmination of the autobiography but by the fact he recurred to it nostalgically as the time-setting for at least two late works, the novel *Headlong* and *Cuckoo* (the rewritten version of *Beth*). The order of events that year however was different from that presented in the autobiography. Williams makes out in *Emlyn* that he was already married by the time the curtain rose on the first night of *Night Must Fall*. It evidently suited him to draw together the two events as an appropriate and telling climax. Carus-Wilson, after a little financial persuasion, initiated divorce proceedings in December 1934 and the petition against his wife was heard in early May 1935, citing as co-respondent, George (rather than Emlyn) Williams. Luckily this reduced the possibility of publicity. Shortly afterwards, with Williams engaged on the final preparations at the Duchess for *Night Must Fall*, Molly arranged a tenancy on a three-storied house, 5 Lincoln Street, Chelsea, which was to be their London home for the first thirty months of married life. Williams says that he was married on a Friday in the window between the end of the provincial try-out of the play and the first night on 31 May. But this was not so. What caused the delay is not known – Moll's pregnancy was already far advanced – but it was in fact another six weeks before they were married, just over seven weeks before the birth of their first child.

The ceremony took place on a Monday at the Register Office in the registration district of Eton on 8 July 1935. Best man was fellow author and actor Rodney Ackland. He is never mentioned in *Emlyn* but the friendship with Williams had begun when he was a member of J.B. Fagan's repertory company at Oxford in the 1920s, and increasingly they shared many common interests in film and theatre. His adaptation of Hugh Walpole's novel *The Old Ladies*, directed by John Gielgud, had recently closed after a run at the St Martin's Theatre. The other witness was Dorothy Langley, then playing Nurse Libby in *Night Must Fall* (who went on to play Sarah Pugh in *The Corn is Green*). Under his full name of George Emlyn Williams (of 5 Lincoln Street, Chelsea) the bridegroom is shown in the official register as 'Author', but the corresponding column for Molly (Mary Marjorie Carus-Wilson, formerly O'Shann, who gave her address as The Holme Bungalow, Wymondisbury) was left blank. Williams maintains in *Emlyn* that he made the registrar's eyebrows rise by representing his father's profession as a labourer (as on his own birth certificate). It made a good story but in fact he is described as 'of Independent Means', which, given that Williams had been supporting his parents financially for the past three years, was a good deal more accurate, if less striking. Molly gave her father's profession as 'Chartered Accountant'. The ceremony was a very private affair; almost no one outside a very small circle knew about it, even within the cast of *Night Must Fall*. Indeed the popular press did not learn about it until nearly a week later, when the *Sunday Express* (14 July 1935) was one of the first to report that 'the brilliant actor-dramatist' had married 'secretly some time ago', his bride being 'an Irish brunette who was formerly on the stage in musical comedy'. There was no possibility of a honeymoon, and Williams went on playing Dan eight times a week (six nights and two matinees) in *Night Must Fall* for more than eleven months, before taking the play on a North American tour in the summer of 1936.

If *Night Must Fall* had a less enthusiastic reception in New York than might have been expected, the play nevertheless seemed to confirm Williams's principal strength as a writer rather than performer in his having successfully negotiated the barrier between actor and playwright. It also made him an international writer as it was translated into French (not by Williams) for performance in

Paris under the peculiar title *L'Homme qui se donnait la comédie.*

Williams's marriage and career seemed made, but, on the professional front at least, Williams was soon to suffer a stinging reverse. His next play was not just a misjudgement but an abject and miserable failure. Written at the suggestion of and specifically for John Gielgud, *He was Born Gay* was begun in 1935-6 during the run of *Night Must Fall*, ready for his return from an arduous six-month American tour as Hamlet. As they knew from *Spring, 1600* both men worked well together despite their very different backgrounds. Born of professional parents, Gielgud was raised in a large house in Kensington, with nursery, hot baths and servants and boarded at Westminster School. Almost an exact contemporary of Williams, he never went to university, but his performances at Oxford Playhouse with Fagan's company coincided with Williams's time as an undergraduate at Christ Church. Gielgud recalled him tucked up, reading, in an armchair in the corner of OUDS clubhouse. Later when they came to know each other as friends and fellow professionals, Williams respected his discrimination and Gielgud found Williams a witty and amusing presence in the otherwise serious job of rehearsal. But Gielgud's judgement was not quite as sound as he liked to think, and Williams would have been wise to take notice of the former's past failure to curb his stylistic excesses in costume drama. After playing Hamlet for so long, Gielgud's instinct was not to take another romantic lead, arguing the necessity of appearing as soon as possible in a play which allowed him to wear trousers otherwise people would think of him as permanently encased in tights. But Gielgud fell under the spell of Williams's new play so much that he agreed not only to undertake the youthful hero, the disguised Louis XVII, but to direct jointly with the author. As with *Spring, 1600* their partnership was close and productive. Williams assured Miss Cooke that

> John & I have been through the script with magnifying glasses, and I think it's pretty final now – he is delightful to work with, so quick and nimble, and yet so fair (A1 14 March 1937).

The new play had an unusually long five weeks' exposure to provincial audiences before facing the London critics. Beginning at

Glasgow on 12 April (where exceptionally the notices were bad), it continued to Manchester, Birmingham, Edinburgh and Oxford during Eights' Week, before finally arriving in London at the Queen's Theatre. The family went to see the performance at Birmingham, sitting 'in state' in a box. Richard Williams was 'in the seventh heaven', but 'which heaven my mother was in', Williams told Miss Cooke, 'it's always difficult to tell'. Afterwards when his parents went back-stage to meet the cast, his father behaved like Edward VII and assured Gielgud that 'the play was "nicely mixed together" and that Lady Atkyns [played by Sydney Fairbrother] was "a caution". Altogether their visit was a great success' (A1 [May 1937]). Audiences at the try-out venues, even including Glasgow, were mostly enthusiastic and Manchester was a sell-out, but the frustrating exception (in a repeat of the experience with *Night Must Fall*) was Edinburgh. At the King's Theatre numbers were sparse and everyone seemed 'determined not to laugh' (A1 7 May 1937).

The play's somewhat awkward (and nowadays thoroughly misleading) title is a direct translation of Marie Antoinette's valedictory remark (*'il est né gai'*) on her son Louis XVII, king in name only for two years, who was guillotined in 1795. Williams builds on one of the many stories which surfaced later to suggest that he was not executed but hidden abroad, where he survived in disguise. *He was Born Gay* is set in the year 1815 in the Dell household at Dover, where the so-called 'lost dauphin' is employed as a music master under the unlikely pseudonym of Mason. His safety is the concern of his sister 'Miss Mason' (Gwen Ffrangcon-Davies); but compromised by his love for a woman and his ambitious nature the agents of the restored King Louis XVIII eventually catch up with him. Rather than face arrest he drinks the poison that his would-be captors provide.

With costumes and set designed by Motley, the play opened at the Queen's on 26 May 1937 to reveal an exquisitely crafted Georgian drawing-room, breathtaking in its verisimilitude. This was about the only aspect of the play that the critics admired. Otherwise they were merciless. Especially trenchant was Charles Morgan in *The Times* (27 May), who wondered what could have possibly induced Gielgud and his co-star Ffrangcon-Davies to have appeared in the play or Williams to have written it, for this was one of the occasions when

> criticism ... rubs its eyes and withdraws hastily with an embar-
> rassed, incredulous, and uncomprehending blush.

An ill-matched mixture of farce and nostalgic reflection, the play failed because Williams was unable to determine its focus or nature, a fatal flaw which it shared with his previous historical piece, *Spring, 1600*. Gielgud was given all the grave and reflective passages, but it was impossible to take them seriously. Morgan argued it was only respect for him as an actor that prevented the audience collapsing into embarrassed laughter:

> when for long, long passages of rhetoric Mr Gielgud whimpers
> childish memories of prison, or, in flowing periods, spreads
> emotional tremors over the beloved scenery of France, or, while
> reading aloud a proclamation of one of the impostors, droops
> into dreaming retrospect of the glories and the flunkeys of
> Versailles, one holds fast to the arms of an astonished stall and
> prays that no one will laugh out loud before it is over.

The only reason no one actually did, Morgan declared, was because the audience must have imagined they were in a church listening to a sermon. Critical hostility was so strong that the play survived only two weeks, a total of thirteen performances. Its dismal failure, all the more shocking after its generally successful provincial try-out, gave Gielgud his shortest ever run in any play as either director or actor. In truth Gielgud was too close to the play in both roles: he failed to curb its author's more poetic effusions and was flattered by a part for which he was also disastrously miscast. As Williams noted in retrospect, his leading man's 'innate nobility' (CP, xx) announced his royal lineage at his first entrance as surely as if he had been wearing the French crown itself and in that sense the play was over before it had begun. It was never revived professionally in London, though it was occasionally taken up by amateur groups.

Williams was at this time as much preoccupied with film as he was with theatre. From 1935 to 1938 he was associated in several ways with nearly a dozen motion-pictures: as writer of screenplay, contributor of additional dialogue, or as actor. Most of his acting roles involved murderers or madmen, often in combination, of which his appearance as the headmaster of a prep school leading a double life in *Dead Men Tell No Tales* (1938), a film based on Francis Beeding's novel *The Norwich Victims*, was one of his most successful. Williams was often dismissive of this kind of film work but the real attraction for him was that it was extremely lucrative. His role in this 'preposterous' film ('they're paying me £1000 for 3 weeks work, so I can't ignore it' [A1 24 November 1937]), as described to Miss Cooke, involved having a set of teeth made to produce the change in his appearance required by the script. But the trivialising and the pretentiousness of the movie world was nowhere more evident for Williams than in his experience as a camp, sybaritic Caligula early in 1937 in *I, Claudius*, starring Charles Laughton, Merle Oberon and Flora Robson, a film famously never finished. In a report of its progress to Miss Cooke he described it being 'in complete chaos', mainly because of the 'quite impossible' Laughton's inability to find his character: he 'has mad ideas [and] never stops talking nonsense about psychology'. Irritatingly, he needed the abdication speech of Edward VIII played 'over and over again', simply to get the feeling for a Roman emperor addressing the Senate (A1 14 March 1937). But at £50 a day (even when he was not used) Williams could not complain, especially as there were often opportunities for real achievement in film-making.

In Arthur Wood's thriller *They Drive by Night* (1938), which vies with the best of Hitchcock, Williams gave a perfectly judged performance as the gritty, embittered, Swansea-born ex-convict Albert ('Shorty') Matthews. Immediately on release from Pentonville, he unluckily finds himself at the murder-scene of his former girl-friend and is wrongly suspected of the crime. The camaraderie of the world of the long-distance lorry drivers on the Great North Road is robustly evoked, against which Williams gives a compelling depiction of a man on the run. Even finer was his appearance as Joe Gowan, the ex-miner now bookmaker, intent on revenge for being wronged in love, in Carol Reed's *The Stars Look Down* (December 1939). Its graphic treatment of A.J. Cronin's tough northern mining world, its poverty, unemployment and street violence, was in stark contrast to the romanticised imagery of *The Corn is Green*, especially as the activity of filming and Willliams's nightly performance in the play continued in parallel for a time. Glowering, sinister and unfeeling, Williams as Joe Gowan gave a brilliant portrait of single-minded veniality and social-climbing, which has been described as '[t]he most riveting and repellent study of working-class evil' in British cinema of the period (Berry, 201). Something of Fess's ruthless sexuality too seems to have briefly re-surfaced in this film characterisation, as well as that mesmeric quality which was remarked on by critics of Williams's stage performances.

It was no accident that in Williams's Shakespearean debut at the Old Vic, beginning with Angelo in *Measure for Measure* (12 October 1937), the roles he played were allied to the obsessional interest in perversions and twisted psychological mind-states that he so much exploited and enjoyed in film and stage work from *The Case of the Frightened Lady* to *Night Must Fall*. His creation of Richard III in Tyrone Guthrie's Old Vic production (2 November), which, like *Measure for Measure*, was also seen at the Buxton Festival, fascinated A. E. Wilson of the *Star* (4 November). He saw

> some unusual quality about Williams. He compels attention ... [and] the eye never wonders from him when he is on the stage.

For Miss Cooke, Shakespeare was the ultimate test for her protégé and she was glad to grant him at last his full credentials as an actor:

> [t]o me, you are realising full stature as an actor. I can make no comparison of Angelo & Rich III, but in both, to me y were the character, no longer you (A2 25 November 1937).

After Williams's success there was some talk of his playing Shylock in the joint Gielgud-Byam Shaw production at the Queen's in the following spring (March 1938). But the part was taken by Gielgud himself and Miss Cooke, believing that it was a perfect role for Williams, felt '*furious* that John is dng' it. Apart from a single matinee appearance in Bud Flanagan's *Some More Shakespeare* (Palladium, January 1942), a similar opportunity, with the RSC, was not to present itself for almost another twenty years.

During the high summer of 1937 the Williamses quit their

Lincoln Street home for a much smarter address, but still within the SW3 postal district, at 15 Pelham Crescent: such a grand house that before long Richard Williams in his letters began to refer to it as 'the estate'. It was indeed of ample size to accommodate a growing family. News of the birth of Alan on 28 August 1935, their first child, arrived during a matinee performance of *Night Must Fall*. Noël Coward came to the evening performance and brought a bottle of champagne to celebrate with the cast after the show onstage in Mrs Bramson's bungalow. To Miss Cooke next day Williams confided:

> I would have been terribly disappointed if it had been a girl –
> but don't say so – even to Molly (A1 29 August 1935).

Coward was invited to become one of the baby's godfathers (and Miss Cooke a godmother) at the christening at Chelsea Old Church later in the year. When a second son, Brook, arrived in January 1938, the Williamses became to all appearances a perfect model family.

Emlyn Williams was now an actor and playwright of some distinction, mixing with quite a smart set. Inevitably the style magazines of the day took a considerable interest in the minutiae of Williams's life. Complete with photographers, they came to report on and record their taste in furniture and interior decoration. In *Homes and Gardens* (June 1938) the Pelham household was held up as an example of how a Regency townhouse could be comfortably adapted to modern living: restrained, uncluttered and retaining a classic simplicity. In contrast to almost universal practice in establishments of this quality and distinction, the Williamses did not employ an interior designer and most of the furniture was bought by Molly at auction. In the dining room a Regency table and chairs stood beneath a five-branched candelabra and in the window was an 'Empire' sideboard. On the same floor was Molly's bedroom: 'a symphony in pink'. Williams also had a separate single bed in an adjacent book-lined study-bedroom. Upstairs, occupying much of the top floor, was the nursery. Somehow the house needed Miss Cooke's stamp of approval before it could fully feel like home, and three months after the move she was invited to stay for two days in November 1937. Neither Williams nor his family dwelt on the incongruities between Pelham Crescent and his upbringing in relative poverty on the Welsh border. He simply regarded it as a proper expression of his status, achieved through hard work in theatre and film. He lived stylishly and the house itself, tasteful yet unostentatious, was an affirmation of his ability to compete on equal terms with the English upper middle-class. Just before the war the Williams family also acquired a new out of London retreat in rural Berkshire. In contrast to the wooden 'Bung' (which had been disposed of because of danger to the children in being so close to the river), this was a four-hundred-year-old farmhouse called Park End, in the village of North Moreton, not far from Didcot, which over time they extended and improved. Williams disliked some forms of showiness: when alone he always travelled Third Class on the train and preferred buses to taxis; but most weekends after the war Molly drove the family down to Berkshire in their Daimler, which in the early 1950s was replaced by a Rolls-Royce. Here they played tennis (Williams's favourite sport) and entertained theatrical friends in a manner which recalled the erstwhile house-parties of Mr and Mrs Edgar Wallace, at Bourne End.

After the experiments of his Oxford days, from 1930 onwards Williams was seduced, on the one hand, into populist dramas like *A Murder has been Arranged* and *Night Must Fall* or, on the other, visually stunning costume plays with insubstantial story-lines as in the two pieces directed by Gielgud. Williams was determined that his next piece should be very different by combining commercial appeal and period setting but principally drawing on his greatest strength: his sense of Welsh life and community and the romance of his own experience. Williams's imagery of Welsh life, in some ways a mythologised version, was defined less by his own border home at Connah's Quay, which was diluted by Englishness, than the Welshness of households in the heartland, such as the William George's at Criccieth. They had a quality of coherence absent from Welsh-English border life. Yet quite as important was the image of rural Welsh life that he had seen occasionally created in the theatre, as in *The Dark Little People* (1924) by J.O. Francis or *A Comedy of Good and Evil* by fellow graduate and compatriot Richard Hughes. The former he acted in as an amateur and the latter he saw under the Fagan regime at Oxford Playhouse in 1925, when it impressed him greatly. To Miss Cooke he described it as

> a curious metaphysical play of Welsh cottage life, extremely well
> played with some charming accents and an admirable set – a
> cottage room with mangle, settee, sofa, harmonium, photo-
> graphs, tracts and every conceivable brickbrack [*sic*].

His verdict was 'how faithful it was to Welsh life' (A1 15 March
1925). On that reality, defined in a sense by its homely clutter,
Williams imposed a version of his own story. There was a ready-
made element of drama in his sudden translation through a very
special education – a kind of cross between the fairy godmother in
Cinderella and Professor Higgins in *Pygmalion* – from the poverty of
Welsh-English border life to the glittering prizes offered by a scholarship to the University of Oxford.

Work on *The Corn is Green*, Emlyn Williams's greatest dramatic
achievement, began in the winter of 1937-8. Ironically for a piece
which was so close to home, much of the writing was done abroad.
The first act was finished by early February 1938 at Kitzbühel
(where he won £30 on the roulette wheel at the casino), and the rest
he expected to complete in the south of France at Monte Carlo,
though some of the third act was actually written by the seaside at
Dymchurch and other parts during filming for *They Drive by Night*.
Before the end of March it was complete in a long version that
Williams acknowledged needed cutting. A copy went directly to
Miss Cooke and Williams awaited her verdict with trepidation.

It was he confessed 'useless to pretend that the character of Miss
Moffat is not based very largely on yourself', though with 'a great
deal of dramatic license'. As this was drama not life (in contrast to
her portrait in *George*, to which she was invited to contribute and
then to comment on before publication), Williams stressed that there
were two main areas of dramatic conflict, neither of them based on
the real-life situation: Morgan Evans and the girl, and Morgan
Evans and Miss Moffat. The denouement of the play was described
as 'completely away from the original' in real life and he was keen
to assure her that there was in the piece as a whole 'nothing to
offend or annoy' (A1 23 March 1938). There was however a contra-
diction between his expressed willingness to remove such material

if Miss Cooke so desired, while at the same time asserting that anything of that nature was present it was because it was necessary to the dramatic structure and resolution. In any case, he argued, the likelihood of anyone making the assumption that the illegitimate child and Miss Moffat's adoption of it was based on truth was remote, but in that event it would be his reputation that would suffer rather than hers.

Wales in the 1930s experienced in common with many other parts of Britain severe economic depression, but conditions were particularly severe in the South Wales coalfield, where the high levels of unemployment brought abject poverty and social deprivation. Welsh politics in consequence acquired before the end of the decade an extreme radical edge which alarmed certain middle-class elements in the more comfortable areas of England. But *The Corn is Green* was not a contributor to the political debate, except perhaps by default. Its location in the historical past – somewhere in the last half of the previous century (that is, at least fifty years before the date of production) was part of a strategy which fulfilled two aims. First, it established a proper distance from the past relationship between Williams and his school-mistress mentor, and secondly, it quite deliberately detached the play both from the immediate political context of south Wales and more general issues of national identity. This made it unlikely that it would be viewed as a comment on social and educational conditions in the mining valleys or as confronting such issues as language and the survival of an indigenous culture under threat of domination from a powerful neighbour. To an extent, it has been argued, the play

> is designed to allay those fears [of the English middle class] – fears with which Emlyn Williams could himself, perhaps, sympathize, at least in part (Thomas, 70).

Whether indeed anything quite as premeditated actually played any part in the conception of *The Corn is Green* is debatable; but what is certainly true is that Williams, while claiming to be indifferent to political issues, was keen to mute the possibility of anything in his work being seen as critical of England and the English, a position that was even more carefully articulated in his film *The Last Days of*

Dolwyn in 1949.

Miss Cooke found it extremely difficult to put her immediate reactions to *The Corn is Green* into words. She tried at least twice in letters during March 1938, but the locutions did not come and on each occasion she had to concede defeat. While there was for her a sense of exhilaration in the quality of the play, the profoundly close personal element made objective judgement almost impossible. Casting about for a handle on which to base her critique, she wondered whether the portrait of Miss Moffat was 'too flattering' and whether the theme was 'too slight', only to dismiss these queries as not what she meant at all (A1 March 1938). Her more considered reaction was delayed until Miss Cooke saw the play in performance, which she did in August 1938, during its provincial try-out at Manchester Opera House. Naturally the prime focus of attention was in her own portrait and the views on education which Miss Moffat expressed:

> I was interested to see myself, for much of myself is there – do you realise how much? Do you realise that Higher Education for girls has never thrilled me!!

As she perceived, there was little enough in Miss Moffat's establishment or her views which suggested sympathy with education for girls, despite her own achievements, certainly at the upper level. 'Will any critic makes a note of it?', she wondered (A1 25 August 1938). (Interestingly they did not, perhaps because Miss Moffat does gesture once to her own achievement as breaking two thousand years of female suppression and there are girls in her class, though they have no speaking roles.) Miss Cooke however was no feminist; she was proud of her Victorian attitudes and at Holywell County actively sustained the gender divisions in education. Not one of her several special pupils was a girl. Her real fear about the critics' reaction to the play was to do with its possible sexual element: 'Im so afraid, so afraid, of a lot of talk abt "repressed sex"', she confided, even though Williams had attempted to reassure her on that point. Indeed she put her finger on an issue that in the play Williams delicately refused to address.

Williams's relationship with his mentor, Sarah Grace Cooke,

senior teacher at Holywell County, at school not close (as in the play), gradually became established on a warmer footing. But it was long after school and indeed after Oxford before they began to exchange thoughts about the nature of their relationship. Even then the talk was very tentative and restrained. On her side, with some embarrassment, she surmised that their continuing friendship had brought advantages to both of them: not only had she 'got much pleasure & happiness' from it but Williams had 'taught [her] a great deal' (A2 18 June 1928). Yet right to the end of their correspondence over forty years she was never anything other than 'Miss Cooke' to Williams and Miss Cooke never called her protégé by any name other than George. When she came to London in 1930 and saw Williams in *On the Spot* they kissed each other on first meeting; but Williams reveals in his autobiography that all through school the relationship was business-like rather than affectionate. Indeed, as he progressed through the school the space between them never seemed to narrow. She provided him with new boots, a weekly copy of the *Observer*, financed his trip to France, and dosed him daily with cod liver oil. But it was a seemingly unemotional and at times disconcertingly distanced relationship. Miss Cooke was disposed to wonder if Williams was aware how much of the real Miss Cooke there was in Miss Moffat, but she might have been surprised to know how much of him was actually in Morgan Evans's smouldering animosity over his treatment as a Pavlovian dog.

Although he claimed not to have written the role specifically for her, Williams had long had Sybil Thorndike in mind for the part of Miss Moffat. Not only would she would be a good draw for the play but she had strong affinities of character with the real-life Miss Cooke. Having made her stage debut a year before Williams was born, she was by 1938 a much travelled and respected star. Recently returned from playing Mrs Conway in Priestley's *Time and the Conways* in New York and having just finished playing Volumnia in the Old Vic's production of *Coriolanus*, she was already a valued friend and fellow professional. Their association went back to Williams's student days at Christ Church, when he carried a spear in her open-air production of *Medea* (1925), and they met again in the cast of the Everyman Theatre production of Kaiser's *The Fire in the Opera House* (1930). She had a soft spot for things Welsh and readily agreed to take on the role of the social worker turned schoolmistress. Thorndike was actually rather old for the part at fifty-six; reviewers tended to refer to her Miss Moffat as an elderly spinster, whereas Williams is quite clear in the play that she is 'about forty', that is not much older than Grace Cooke was when he first came in contact with her. During rehearsals Thorndike was introduced to the latter, whom she credited with helping her get into the part, to the extent of loaning her Williams's old exercise books. Over time Sybil Thorndike came to embody for her the very essence of her own identity.

Williams's other instinct to persuade Marius Goring, whom he knew from film work, to play Morgan Evans ('if he can look young enough' [he was twenty-six]) was not carried through – Goring was in any case to be otherwise occupied from October with a modestly successful Bulgakov adaptation, *The White Guard* at the Phoenix – and Williams, now in his thirty-third year, decided to play the part of the fifteen-year-old miner himself. That decision, which may have been in the back of his mind all along given Williams's predilection for creating parts for himself in his plays, mutated the drama into an even more marked sublimation of his own biography. Indeed, it seems inconceivable that Williams even considered an English actor for such a thoroughly Welsh role. The considerable use of the Welsh language would have made heavy demands on anyone unfamiliar with its accent and rhythms. Also, the action is punctuated several times by Welsh songs, sung in choric voice, which play an essential part of the atmosphere of the drama. The practical difficulties generated by these features called for special care in the final casting, which in the event reinforced the authenticity of the English-Welsh divide in the play. The incomers into the Welsh community were all experienced English actors versed in the traditions of London theatre. Apart from Thorndike herself, there was London-born, privately educated Freddie Lloyd (who had recently completed a classical season at the Queen's with Gielgud) as the Squire, Christine Silver (Miss Ronberry) who played a spinster role for two years in Dorothy L. Sayers's detective play *Busman's Honeymoon*; and Kathleen Harrison (Mrs Watty) and Betty Jardine (her daughter) had both acted in Williams's plays before. With the exception of Dorothy Langley (from *Night Must Fall*) as Sarah Pugh, all the Welsh roles were played by Welsh actors. Williams and John Glyn-Jones (whose performance as Goronwy Jones got several creditable mentions in the reviews) apart, few of the rest had much professional theatrical experience and in the case of Morgan Evans's two mates, none at all. William John Davies as Idwal Morris and Glan Williams as John Owen were young miners from Blaenrhondda working at Fernhill Colliery and had been recruited by Williams himself, on advice from the local headmaster and producer of Treherbert Amateur Dramatic Society, during a talent-spotting visit to south Wales in the early summer of 1938. Prospects for continued employment at home were bleak and they hoped to make careers in the theatre, but beyond the association with the original production and first revival of *The Corn is Green* it seems they never succeeded.

The action, which occupies three years, takes place in 'a small village in a remote Welsh countryside' called Glansarno, which (with its 'o' ending) sounds like some bastardised Welsh form with echoes of Williams's childhood Glanrafon. There is just one set, the living room of a substantial house named 'Pengarth'. Perhaps resulting from the influence of Michael Weight as designer the house, architecturally speaking, seems less Welsh than middle-class south-east English with its two porches (one stone, one trellised), flagged floor, and bay window enclosing a window seat. The interior however is stocked with traditional Welsh items: the clutter which Williams had enjoyed in other Welsh plays he had seen, like a long-case clock, dresser, settle, and spinning-wheel, the kind of furniture which the husband-seeking spinster Miss Ronberry believes is 'so virile'. Besides Williams's careful specification of degrees of Welsh accent, the use of the Welsh language (which in places gives the play a bilingual quality), the folksongs and the mining valley background, the essential atmosphere of the play is formed by the continual clash of two quite separate yet to some extent at least stereotypical idioms of English and Welsh. This controlling feature made it impossible to translate the play into Welsh without making nonsense of its whole *raison d'être*.

Because Lilly Christabel Moffat, M.A. (Aberdeen) exhibits some of the characteristics, in handwriting and style of correspondence, of a military man she is, prior to her delayed arrival halfway through the first scene in Act 1, assumed by the local community to be L[ieutenant] C[olonel] Moffat, M.A. She has come to take possession of her inherited property. In the flesh, her self-confidence, her education, her manner, her dress (a collar and tie, matched with 'a dark unexaggerated skirt'), and perhaps most of all her bicycle called Priscilla, seem to mark her out as a representative New Woman of the end of the nineteenth century. Miss Moffat's principal characteristic (shared with Miss Cooke) is 'her complete unsentimentality'. She is also fiercely independent, very businesslike. Her ex-thief cook, Mrs Watty, calls her a 'clinker'; she has given up on the idea of marriage and advises the fluttery Miss Ronberry to do the same.

Apart from the broad linguistic distinctions between English and Welsh, the secondary class divisions of this play are heavily marked by accent and idiom. Miss Moffat's accompanying servant, Mrs Watty, is a thorough Cockney, while her daughter Bessie, the temptress in curls and tarty earrings to whom the hero of the play succumbs, is desperately trying to surrender her identity by losing her accent so that she can pass for a lady.

These two apart, the incomers are militantly English. Squire Treverby, owner of the local mine, is invested with all the worst kind of stereotypical characteristics of the English country gentleman: blustering, moustachioed, gaitered, and red-faced through drinking too much. His clipped language, liberally sprinkled with 'by Jingo', 'deuced' and 'fellow', might have come out of P. G. Wodehouse, and belongs by descent to a tradition stretching back at least to Restoration theatre. Miss Ronberry is also an unremarkable stereotype of the resident spinster; she has no individualising characteristics, apart from her wimpishness. Her provenance is also rather unclear. From Williams's clumsy expository device of mutual friends (the London-based Wingroves), who have told Miss Moffat all about her, it is evident that she has some money and some education, but her presence in Glansarno is unexplained. She knows no Welsh. Indeed she shares with the Squire a disparagement of the language. To the latter, a somewhat unconvincing product of Cambridge University, the natives babbling away in Welsh is 'as bad as being abroad' (1:1), a gag which later appears in *George* as an echo of what Williams allegedly once overheard from one of the guests at a Gyrn Castle shoot.

Miss Ronberry and especially Miss Moffat are identified as educated gentlewomen, while most of the Welsh characters are simple peasant types, essentially monoglot with smatterings of English; they tend to retain the strength of their accents. The exception on the Welsh side of the linguistic divide is the hymn-singing bachelor John Goronwy Jones, who went to grammar school and is significantly described as having a 'marked, but not exaggerated' accent. As Miss Moffat unkindly recognises, he has been 'educated beyond [his] sphere' (1:1) to become a solicitor's clerk with no prospects either in employment or his emotional life. Like Mrs Watty he is 'saved', but in his case it is to fill in the yawning emotional gap in his life. Morgan Evans has more English than the other young miners, which he learned from his now deceased 'mongrel' father, who 'had a dash of English' (1:2), but he speaks it strongly accented.

This community also distinguishes people on the basis of their attendance at church (essentially Tory and English) or chapel (essentially Liberal and Welsh). Miss Moffat doesn't know which she is: she doesn't have to make a denominational choice since she is above such matters of dogma. Her religion lies in her mission as an educationalist: this missionary work in Wales is for her as necessary as any mission to Africa:

> When I heard that this part of the world was a disgrace to a Christian country, I knew this house was a godsend; I am going to start a school, immediately.

She recognises the exploitation that goes on in the coal mines by the owners, but cannot perceive the exploitation in her own agenda in bringing civilisation to those 'born penniless in an uncivilized countryside' (1:1).

In two years Miss Moffat's star pupil is transformed from being barely articulate in English to studying Greek (as Williams did for the London Matriculation). His status is defined by Bessie Watty as '[s]tuck-up teacher's pet' and by his own acknowledgement that in the village he is '[c]i bach yr ysgol' [*lit.* 'the school's little dog'] (2:1).

Education for Morgan emasculates him, as well as drawing him away inexorably from his own kind and cultural environment. Miss Moffat seems fired by a vision which is as much a fulfilment of her own needs as those she presses upon Morgan Evans. She has no thought of the cultural dislocation she imposes on the Welsh community by her aggressively English educational regime. She has personally benefited from an university system in Scotland – there were a few opportunities in England as well – which had only just begun to allow women to be initiated into the mysteries of higher education. Indeed Aberdeen was one of the pioneers in this regard, but significantly Wales had no university of its own, even for men, until 1872. Whatever the effect of her missionary zeal, she is fiercely independent and totally at ease in her spinsterhood. But events conspire to force her to relinquish her own identity in order to save the new one she has created for Morgan Evans. In taking over responsibility for bringing up the child whom Evans fathers, she reverts to the conventional female role of motherhood. Miss Moffat's sacrifice is to do women's work, bringing up baby (perhaps ultimately a new protégé?), while men do men's work, which in this case manifestly excludes Evans having to face up to paternal responsibilities.

Miss Moffat's vision is that Morgan Evans may one day become a great political leader of 'our country'. But as he goes forward into a bright new dawn at Oxford it is plain that the country that Miss Moffat's expects him to serve is certainly not Wales as such but Britain or, rather more particularly, England. Yet this is hardly a convincing future. There is no indication that Morgan Evans has any abilities in this regard. Indeed here Williams was probably reflecting an aspect of the relationship with Miss Cooke that he could never quite figure out: whenever they met, after his schooldays, she insisted on introducing what was for Williams the alien subject of politics.

The ending tends to sentimentalise and conventionalise the play. In one sense it was necessary to divert any sexual element in the play away from Miss Moffat (and hence away from Miss Cooke): but Mrs Watty's comment as the baby, almost forgotten, is sent over like a parcel from the inn ('I only hope nobody'll put two and two together, ma'am, 'e's the spit of 'is father' [3:0]) actually suggests the

185

possibility of what Williams and Miss Cooke wanted most to avoid.

The Corn is Green – the title comes from Morgan Evans's essay on the coal-mine, which stuns Miss Moffat with its limpid, poetical beauty – raises issues of importance on education, language and cultural identity; but none is fully explored. Wales is throughout given a stereotypical imagery of simple innocence, linguistic backwardness, and folk-singing; and Morgan Evans's outstanding academic achievement does nothing to relieve it, because he replaces his old identity by one that is determined by English notions of success. To that extent the play reinforces the notorious mid-nineteenth-century 'Blue Book' argument that equated the Welsh language with a backward peasantry, for whom the only hope of a new life was English and English education. Literateness in this play means very specifically literacy in the English language. Moreover, as she implies by her cruel commentary on Goronwy Jones's being over-educated for his sphere, Miss Moffat believes that there is no point in education within Wales for Wales: education was necessary simply because it provided the means to escape. By implication Miss Moffat's school carefully preserves the system of the 'Welsh Not' (no speaking of Welsh in school-time). As Old Tom, who has adopted Queen Elizabeth I, Shakespeare and Wordsworth as his icons, remarks: there's '[p]lenty Welsh at home, not in the class please by request scoundrels and notty boys!'; and he is '*furious*' at his daughter Sarah's addressing him in Welsh during lessons (3:0). The only voice raised in defence of the language comes from Goronwy Jones who before exposure to Miss Moffat's evangelising influence observes sarcastically to Miss Ronberry:

> It is wicked, isn't it the Welsh children not bein' born knowing English, isn't it. Good heavens, God bless my soul, by Jove, this that and the other! (1:1).

Three days at Oxford sitting his scholarship examinations including a viva voce turn Morgan Evans completely. He glimpses a new world outside:

> I have been a prisoner behind a stone wall, and now somebody has given me a leg-up to have a look at the other side (3:0).

Evans literally finds his voice at Oxford. As he repudiates his native culture by loss of his original accent, so his English expression and vocabulary has 'immensely improved, and he expresses himself with ease'; and he immediately employs his old Welsh accent to mock the narrowness of his old life. Outside, the village is dressed in its best and the miners are singing in expectant celebration of Morgan Evans's gaining his Oxford place, unmindful that his success also entails his abandoning his homeland. Multiple ironies accumulate but the triumph of Miss Moffat's mission is presented uncritically; and the undercurrents of Evans's situation go unremarked. Williams's best-known and finest play is also his most colonialist.

Rehearsals in London for *The Corn is Green* extended over a lengthy period, beginning for Sybil Thorndike as early as March. For Williams, she was 'simply perfect' and became more like Miss Cooke as every day passed. After the final dress rehearsal at Manchester on the Sunday before opening night, Williams remarked on Michael Weight's 'superlatively good' set: how 'tiny and forlorn' it looked in the midst of the Opera House stage, 'but very cosy and inhabited all the same'. Thorndike had 'never been so good' but Betty Jardine as Bessie Watty 'had not yet found her feet' (A1 14 August 1938). Provincial reviews were complimentary on the whole, especially those in the Liverpool papers, where Williams was more or less seen as a local playwright, but the *Daily Dispatch* (16 August 1938) was disappointed that what promised to be 'a drama of social conflict' ended as 'a more or less conventional comedy'. On 20 September the play opened in London at the intimate Duchess Theatre in Catherine Street, just off the Aldwych. Within a month, with box office returns and advance bookings exceptionally healthy, Williams could regale Miss Cooke with the news that the play was expected to run at least a year, 'if Hitler is kind to us – isn't it unbelievable?' (A1 5 October 1939).

London was on the whole kinder to the play than were the provincial critics. The evasions of the political and cultural issues of the play were not generally matters of special comment, and there was more or less unanimous agreement that Williams had shown that he had overcome his perennial problem of overwriting. Spare and economical, its setting, in which the use of Welsh folk songs was consistently remarked on as an especially moving feature, was perfectly evoked. The reviewer for *The Times* suggested that the village world was presented with a 'rare feeling of humanity', fully sufficient 'to cloak its minor improbabilities' (21 Sept 1938), a strength of the play which resonates through the decades. (Of the revival at the Old Vic the *Financial Times* [24 May 1985] commented on its sense of community which is 'articulated with almost more poetry and more vigour than in any play since written and that includes David Mercer and Trevor Griffiths'.) With the single exception of the Squire, whose presentation Freddie Lloyd struggled (with precious little help from Williams's text) to endow with at least some veracity, even where the lesser characters verged on stereotypical exaggeration, the play delivered what *The Times* described as 'the quality of truth that belongs to unextreme caricature'. Williams as Morgan Evans earned much praise for his conviction and progression from 'sullen fire' to 'brilliant liveliness', while Sybil Thorndike's Moffat was seen to employ 'intelligent common sense' and to have allowed the right balance to come through between humour and emotion.

Amidst a generally congratulatory set of reviews only the *TLS* (5 November 1938), reviewing the published Heinemann text, struck out on a somewhat different tack by suggesting that the London theatre seemed to have recently fallen victim to a 'Welsh invasion'. Perversely, it concluded that Williams's play, although a 'powerful success', ultimately had to surrender first place on originality to Charles Morgan's debut drama *The Flashing Stream*. In general, the press reaction might be described as positive and earnest in its praise without being impassioned. Audiences, on the other hand, showed tremendous enthusiasm for the play, and as early as mid-October *The Corn is Green* had broken the box-office record at the Duchess Theatre. The big draw was Sybil Thorndike rather than Williams. At matinees, he reported, the play

> goes even better than at night – rows and rows and rows of middle-aged women – I told you! (A1 19 October 1938).

The adulation extended even to the royal family, and in due time there came a summons to an audience of Queen Mary, who attended a performance in November. Though a loyal supporter of the monarchy, Williams seems to have been somewhat disconcerted by the experience. His strategy, he explained to Miss Cooke, had been to behave 'like a respectful servant'. Queen Mary, he insisted, was

> kind but not gracious ... the impersonal reticence of many years highly perfected (A1 11 November 1938).

He was considerably more impressed and more at ease with the unassuming natures of George VI and Queen Elizabeth, who called for him at the end of the second act of the play in the following February: they were

> simply charming – she is so pretty and natural, the fresh complexion of a very young girl, and one completely forgot who they were after the first minute (A1 16 February 1939).

On 20 October 1938 *The Corn is Green* became the first of Williams's plays, albeit in short excerpt, to be broadcast from London. In their bungalow at Aston Hill in the Welsh borderland his parents listened in and his mother reported that

> the Quickest 20 minutes that went by was last night lissoning to your Play we did enjoy it it is new every time we hear it the weather is very nice these days hoping it will last (C3).

In all the play ran for a total of 394 performances, very nearly a year, up to the outbreak of the war. On Monday 4 September 1939 all theatres were closed forthwith on orders of the Home Secretary until the impact of the anticipated air raids was known. At a stroke huge numbers of theatrical professionals nation-wide were suddenly thrown out of work. George Bernard Shaw in a letter to *The Times* (5 September 1939) protested against this 'masterstroke of unimagina-tive stupidity'; and managers like Basil Dean warned of the crisis in the drama brought about by the absurdity of London's theatres being 'turned on and off like a tap'. Lifted for most provincial music halls and theatres in mid-September, the ban remained in force in London for over a month, thus forcing West End managements to take refuge in out-of-town venues like Golders Green (where

Gielgud got his production of *The Importance of Being Ernest* going within a few days), Streatham Hill and the Mercury at Notting Hill. *Design for Living* and *The Corn is Green* each had a week's run from 25 September at the two first named; and then the latter had a further week at the Golders Green Hippodrome from 2 October. Even when the West End was allowed to reopen on a rota basis in late October, chaos reigned as there were so many productions vying for the limited number of available theatres. Williams's play did not find an immediate home and the intervening months were filled as far as possible by touring. In November, when *The Corn is Green* visited Cardiff, Williams made his first ever appearance in Wales as a professional actor, more than twelve years after his London debut. When a theatre finally became free in London at Christmas the 'Entire Original Cast' opened on 19 December at the Piccadilly. To maximise the run everyone took a voluntary pay cut and by June 1940, when the play went out on another national tour, it had completed a further 208 performances.

The London theatre in wartime was an uncertain business, liable to disruption at any moment. But when the initial panic was over audiences gradually returned and accepted the risk of air-raids. There was encouragement from the government for theatres and cinemas to continue to provide entertainment as a means of boosting morale. Some theatres were obliged to run early performances and to close by eight o'clock, while others were permitted the usual time of eleven. Over Christmas and New Year 1939-40 *The Corn is Green* was allowed twice daily performances.

At the outbreak of hostilities Williams was almost thirty-four and thus not included in the initial call-up procedures, but during 1940 ('working hard at his German') he applied for intelligence work with the RAF (A6 24 July 1940). By this time he was much involved in writing and occasionally acting in propaganda films for the Ministry of Information and the authorities believed that he would contribute best to the British war effort by continuing in the same line. He was also used in propaganda work on radio and his voice became well-known for the 'Postscript' series of talks. Some of these were broadcast beyond the United Kingdom, occasionally even to North America, where Molly (who was with the children and also supervising the tour of *The Corn is Green*) heard him from time to time on the wireless. Williams endeavoured to reassure her against his possible conscription into the armed services for by continuing to write propaganda films he was likely to have his occupation classed as 'reserved' (A6 28 August 1940). He was involved in the film *Mr Borland Thinks Again* (August 1940), which was intended to encourage silage production, and in May 1941 he acted in the 85-minute *This England, Our Heritage* (sensitively re-titled *This Scotland* for showings north of the border), which in a flagrant attempt to deconstruct class barriers showed landowner and labourer fighting side by side in harmony through the centuries from the Norman Conquest and the Spanish Armada down to the two world wars. Williams was recruited into the Wallingford Home Guard for North Moreton. Park End, his weekend Berkshire retreat (part of which was used for evacuees), became an ever more important refuge from the London bombings as much for all the family valuables from Pelham Crescent as for Williams himself.

Emlyn Williams enjoyed a remarkably high profile in 1940 in having two plays running at the same time, at the Duchess and Apollo theatres, while writing a third, *The Morning Star*, for production the following year. Evidence of Williams's penetration into the very highest circles of the theatrical establishment came on 6 June, when his election into membership of the Garrick Club made him a kind of honorary Englishman. Across the Atlantic *The Corn is Green* opened to great acclaim in New York with Ethel Barrymore as Miss Moffat at the National Theatre in November (477 performances) and went on to win the New York Drama Critics' Circle award for 'the best play of foreign authorship presented in New York during the season of 1940-41'.

The huge success of *The Corn is Green* gave Emlyn Williams a new credibility in the London theatre. Now with the backing for the first time of H. M. Tennant Ltd through the powerful impresario Binkie Beaumont (a fellow Welshman, who had a finger in most theatrical pies and bitterly regretted turning down the earlier play), *The Light of Heart* opened on 21 February 1940 at the Apollo. For four months until 8 June, when both plays closed on government orders as part of further war-time restrictions, it overlapped with the second run of *The Corn is Green*.

For this new play Williams reverted to a theatrical scenario some-what reminiscent of *Glamour,* and with something of the emotional dependency infused into the relationships in *Full Moon*. But it had a stronger plot, and its central character Maddoc Thomas, played with power and insight by Godfrey Tearle (for whom it was written), was more securely focused. The part combined the strength of a once great Shakespearean actor (whose origins in Rhoslan, Flintshire, more or less amount to a private joke) with the pathos of a man run to seed by alcoholism and memories of the trenches. Ironically he is utterly dependent for emotional support on his crippled daughter Cattrin, whose 'lightness of heart' gives the play its title. Professedly, Maddoc now collects Welsh folksongs but he is reduced to occasional jobs like announcer at the Ideal Homes Exhibition or playing Santa Claus in Selfridges' Christmas grotto. He is persuaded to seize the chance of a spectacular comeback playing Lear in a C.B. Cochran production, but relapses into his old habits before the opening night, which is cancelled owing to the star's 'laryngitis'. The shattering news that Cattrin (who discovers her disability was caused when as a baby she was dropped by her drunken father) is to live a life of her own for the first time through marriage, unhinges him. Feeling betrayed he then overhears Cattrin rescind her decision in order to continue to look after him; but unable to bear responsibility for ruining her life a second time, he commits suicide by jumping from an upper-floor window.

In some ways the bond between the girl and her father echoes elements of Emlyn Williams's relationship with Bill Cronin-Wilson, not least in the latter's debilitation through alcoholism and Williams's sense of entrapment into the role of the elder man's keeper. In Act 2 Maddoc is even referred to as drinking in the Green Room Club, Cronin-Wilson's old drinking haunt. On a more public front, the recognition of Williams's sureness of touch in evoking the theatrical context led *The Times* (22 February 1940) to comment that

> [n]one but an author who was also an actor, could have written this distinguished play, for in its background there is a more authentic rendering of the magic of the stage than can be found in hundreds of plays which have dealt directly with theatrical life.

As he acknowledged, Williams 'wanted to write a play about the theatre as I know it', from the inside' (CP, xxiii); and indeed one unusual feature was the display of professional name-dropping, not just of Cochran but several other prominent members of the London theatre scene. The Covent Garden production of *King Lear* is supposedly to be directed by John Gielgud and there are references to the possibility of Maddoc's acting with Edith Evans. In the licensing copy these latter were attached to Marie Tempest, but the censor (presumably after seeking the views of the individuals concerned) ordered the name change. (For some reason too the censor required Maddoc's casual reference to Lords cricket ground in Act 2 scene 1 to be altered to the Oval.)

Williams was comfortable within his theatrical circle and liked to work with people he knew. As director of most of his own plays, including this one, Williams tended to gather round himself a kind of personal repertory. Michael Weight was again responsible for the set design, Angela Baddeley from *Night Must Fall* played the heroine and Williams's favourite actress Gladys Henson (in a shabby old cardigan, sporting '*a bird's nest*' hair-style, '*tender feet and a permanently toneless voice*') as the charwoman Mrs Banner made her first of five appearances in first runs of Williams's plays. For *The Times*, Tearle proved fully up to 'all his author's claim for the mimic actor' and Baddeley played the selfless Cattrin with 'delicate precision', yet to Williams's surprise all the principals were in the end overshadowed by the minor character Fan, the stage-struck gallery girl, performed with enormous vitality and comic verve by Megs Jenkins, who added yet another triumph to her growing list of successes in theatre and film. It was one of those brilliant cameo roles for which Williams continued to demonstrate his special facility: '[a] joint creation by author and actress which touches greatness', said Darlington in the *Daily Telegraph* (22 February 1940). James Agate in the *Sunday Times* (25 February 1940) provided his usual back-handed compliment by describing the play, generally thought to be one of the best that had so far surfaced in war-time London, as

> one of the oddest concoctions ever set before an audience – a
> rag-bag of a play which, because its author has a spark of some-

thing like genius, is infinitely more entertaining than some more aristocratic reticules.

After its enforced closure in June 1940 *The Light of Heart* went on provincial tour; but as Godfrey Tearle was unable to continue Williams took over the leading male role himself. Of necessity this required a remarkably dextrous piece of editing – 'a delicate but impudent piece of surgery the like of which I shall never do again' (CP, xxiii) – whereby Williams transformed Maddoc Thomas from ageing father to dissolute thirty-five-year-old brother of the stricken Cattrin. Returning to Oxford to test out the revised script at the Playhouse, Williams was prompted into nostalgic reflections on how fortunate his generation had been in the 1920s:

> we had all that fun with no clouds on the horizon beyond those of our own making (A6 23 November 1940).

On tour to Cardiff in the following week Williams advised Miss Cooke that the new version was 'going wonderfully' and that the reworking had actually improved the play: it

> is in many ways more effective – (the brother, I mean) less senti-mental in some ways and more sympathy for the girl at the end (A6 28 November 1940).

Not so convinced was James Agate, who saw the play at Oxford and felt that Williams's presence in it had ruined the whole piece. Agate reportedly argued, as Williams informed Molly, that he

> should stop acting it <u>at once</u> and let (who do you think) Edmund Willard [then in his late fifties] play it and so (I suppose) let the tour die a thousand deaths. Can you believe the conceit ... ?
> (A6 28 November 1940).

In this revamped guise the play eventually returned to London in 1941. It re-opened at the Globe on 4 June and ran for 180 perfor-mances until 1 November, but as Williams was later forced to acknowledge he was indeed miscast and the play had lost its edge. In 1942 it also had an outing on Broadway, but being too much attuned to a specifically London experience proved one of

Williams's rare American failures. By contrast it had some success as a film under the title *Every Night at 8.30*, with Monty Woolley and Ida Lupino. One of the contributors to the screenplay, Williams discovered many years later, was Scott Fitzgerald.

On countrywide tour, Williams was made aware of the effects of aerial bombardment in 1940-41 on cities such as Liverpool. In November 1940 he snatched a weekend at Glasdir, notable for a row with his mother over the blackout arrangements: apparently she insisted on using black paper to cover the electric light-bulbs rather than the windows. When his parents went to see *The Light of Heart* at Southport, Mary Williams was dismayed by the devastation seen from the train as they passed through Liverpool. At Swansea early in 1941 Williams recorded (coincidentally in terms later echoed by Dylan Thomas in *Return Journey*) what was probably the last eyewitness impression of the old town whose commercial centre, about three weeks later, was razed to the ground in a three nights' *blitzkrieg*, which lit up the sky for forty miles westward to Pembrokeshire. '[I]t isn't as pretty as when I was here before', he wrote to Molly, 'but not as ugly as one expected, places never are' (A6 2 February 1941).

For *The Morning Star*, the London bombings were the main inspiration. Things were particularly grisly about the time the play was completed in October 1940. There was the constant threat of air-raids and when three bombs fell in the vicinity of Pelham Crescent (one of them being a direct hit nearby on number 22) the inhabitants were evacuated to the Savoy Hotel for the night. The worst incident concerned the Pelham Restaurant on the Fulham Road, where Williams was a regular diner when Molly was absent from home. It was more or less completely destroyed and fatalities occurred when the structure collapsed on the air-raid shelter beneath, which was flooded by a burst water-main. Williams kept from Molly the probability that but for the delay to his train he would have been there at the time. Such were the events which underpinned Williams's evocation of this period of the war, though by the time the play actually appeared in London late in 1941 the grimmest realities of the dark days of the air-raids had begun to fade.

Williams's most abiding memory of this period was of what he describes as his 'first macabre experience' in seeing the corpse of an air-raid victim. It occurred on the night of the Pelham Restaurant tragedy, when he had returned after the weekend to Paddington on the train from Didcot ready for an early morning start at Elstree studios. Never one to take a taxi when public transport was available, Williams enquired if the buses were still running from two ARP wardens and a policeman who were arguing whether the air-raid damage in the area was 'bad enough' for the road to be closed to traffic next day. Told he might be lucky further on, Williams began to walk away but then noticed two booted feet protruding from underneath a tarpaulin. 'I just couldn't describe how I felt', he explained to Molly,

> ... everything, fright, awe, sickness, excitement, even elation, at having at last seen what I'd been waiting for 5 weeks to see (at the back of my mind) and glad I had been able to stand up reasonably to it. You know I've never seen anything remotely resembling a car smash. The next minute I was in the bus ... it's so unreal (A6 13 October 1940).

Some of the feeling of general incongruity produced by the wartime emergency Williams incorporated into *The Morning Star*, but that same borderline between the ordinary and macabre also fed directly into his obsession with murder and the criminal mind.

During the war there was little opportunity for the extended provincial try-outs of the 1930s. *The Morning Star* was premiered at Liverpool (1 December 1941) and in London immediately afterwards at the Globe (10 December). Its realistic evocation of an air-raid, the first ever onstage, warranted a programme note indicating that the siren would sound faintly during the early part of the play and that in the event of a real emergency evacuation signs would be illuminated both sides of the proscenium. Much depended on its atmosphere but *The Times* (11 December 1941) wondered

> how many care to be reminded of what it was like to lie on a divan in a London drawing-room listening to the droning immediately overhead and the somewhat more distant explosions until some woman said: 'It's no good, I'm going to make some tea'.

Williams, who also directed, played Cliff Parrilow, the doctor-cum-novelist, who after making a brilliant discovery in medicine is cold-shouldered by the medical establishment and (like his creator) is tempted by script-writing in Hollywood. Both his performance and Angela Baddeley's as the wife, who finds she is playing second fiddle to the doctor's mistress, were regarded as sincere and in their way affecting; but more than one reviewer suggested that owing to the lack of substance in the text, they were in truth not far removed from cardboard cut-outs. Too often in his search for effect Williams resorted to staginess and melodrama. His main characters seemed to be sacrificed to give prominence to his primary theme: that of the need for moral values to survive even in exceptional conditions of war. The *TLS* (28 March 1942) in reviewing the published text went further and declared that

> any old story would have done for *The Morning Star* so long as it served to bring a sufficiently demoralized hero to the fiery test of bombs over Chelsea

to demonstrate that

> love and trust are things we can be sure of so long as we do not lack the courage to fight for them.

But Williams's real strength was on more familiar ground: less in moral platitudes than in the affectionate reincarnation from plays stretching back to *A Murder has been Arranged* of the worldly-wise, mind-speaking, comic servant (played by Gladys Henson): 'a portrait lifted straight from life – the true-born Cockney to the core', W. A. Darlington commented in the *Daily Telegraph* (11 December 1941). Despite its limitations and unashamed status as a *pièce de circonstance*, *The Morning Star* was one of the most popular plays of its time, unaccountably so in the opinion of several critics. For the *Daily Mail*

> this play ... about houses being smashed to rubble, corpses, blood, operations, and other grim horrors is surely much too grim.

Yet in the peculiar circumstances of the war there was perhaps a need to see such things on the stage as part of the strategy to cope with them, and Williams simply responded to the public mood. Eight months later, to the amazement of the critic of the *Evening News* (26 August 1942), audiences were still flocking to the Globe. Although the weakest of Williams's mature plays to date, it caught the mood of the time. It even had some success in New York in the autumn of 1942, where the production by Guthrie McClintic, starring Gladys Cooper and Gregory Peck (just at the outset of his career), was described as

> a sincere and gallant tribute to the courage of the English [*sic*] people under fire (*Mirror*, 15 September 1942).

In London the play finally closed on 12 December 1942 after an unprecedented run for Williams of 474 nights, a record unmatched by anything in his later career.

An entirely new departure for Emlyn Williams during the early years of the war was to direct plays other than his own. The controversial American playwright Lillian Hellman (whose early play *The Children's Hour* was banned in Britain until 1960, owing to its lesbian theme) brought her latest pieces *The Little Foxes* (1939) and *The Watch on the Rhine* (1941) to London in 1942. Attracted by their confrontational nature, Williams agreed, at the invitation of Binkie Beaumont, to direct them both. At the Piccadilly Theatre in October the former realized only thirty-seven performances; but there was compensation in the phenomenal success, especially for a foreign play, of *The Watch on the Rhine*, which occupied the Globe stage for no fewer than twenty months from April 1942 to December 1943, making a total of 673 performances.

Again during this period, and at Beaumont's request, Williams adapted (using the translation by Elisaveta Fenn) *A Month in the Country* (St James's, February 1943), starring Michael Redgrave as Rakitin. Since Turgenev's play relies so much on creation of mood, the possible pitfalls were legion, especially given Williams's lack of experience in Russian drama, but the link with Chekov in some of his earliest dramatic writing undoubtedly helped. Overall it was a production, according to *The Times* (12 February 1943) in which

FROM NIGHT TO MORNING

Mr Emlyn Williams has succeeded more nearly than any other producer for the English theatre in satisfying its difficult requirements.

It was a handsome compliment on Williams's first venture into the classical Russian repertoire, underlined by well-filled houses for nearly seven months until the end of October, totalling 313 performances. Once the initial doubts of working with texts not his own had dissipated, Williams enjoyed the discipline of directing other writers' plays – over a decade later he also directed, and as Hjalmar Ekdal starred in, Ibsen's *The Wild Duck* at the Saville in 1955 – but although it was an important extension of his experience it was in the end not a development of his career that he went on to pursue. Partly because events conspired differently, he discovered areas of renewed interest and concern much nearer home that gave essential shape to the course of his professional life as a writer over the rest of the decade and on towards its effective closure in the 1950s.

Six: Coming Home

Knowing the misery and loneliness of cheerless New York hotel rooms or squalid bed-sitters in north London, Emlyn Williams valued home and the kind of homeliness associated with a coal fire blazing in the snug of the White Lion or at the humble cottage in urbanised Connah's Quay, where the combination oven-grate shone 'immaculate with black-lead and gleaming irons' (G 149). Yet long before the Second World War home for Emlyn Williams had come to mean not Flintshire but fashionable South Kensington or, during the war, the rural idyll of his four-hundred-year-old cottage in the Home Counties as refuge from the London bombs. Indeed in June 1944 their house in Pelham Crescent was damaged in an air-raid and the Williamses were exiled for almost two years until it was repaired to their satisfaction in May 1946. This was yet another displacement to add to an already unsettled period from 1940. For two years at the beginning of the war Williams had been separated from his wife and children while they were in the USA and he was at home in London. From 1943 onwards there was a quickening sense of loss through the death of his father, then of his mother, coupled with the retirement of Sarah Cooke from teaching and her return to her native Yorkshire. Although Williams retained a foothold in Flintshire because his brother Job continued to live there, these changes effectively deprived him of the last direct links with his native Welsh border. Severance tended to heighten rather than dilute the Welsh elements in Williams's work. Most of the pieces of the 1940s from about 1943 sublimate aspects of his own experience, bringing him back into contact with areas of his identity, those elements of his Welshness which had become diffused by his long professional association with the London theatre or with which he had simply lost touch.

Effectively between the closure of *The Morning Star* in December 1942 and the London premiere of the comedy *The Druid's Rest* in January 1944 – a period spent mostly in provincial touring as Dan in *Night Must Fall* – Williams's name as playwright, except as an adapter, was absent from the London stage for the first time since 1932. This year-long respite from metropolitan theatre with its pressing demands on playwright and actor may be seen in retrospect as having provided Williams with an opportunity for significant re-ordering of priorities, personal and professional. For his next play, gestated itinerantly in dressing-rooms and anonymous hotel bedrooms around Britain, Williams returned to the kind of historical Welsh setting which had been such a successful formula in *The Corn is Green* and it remained his central focus for the rest of the decade. Set in the idealised Edwardian summer of his early childhood, *The Druid's Rest* (dedicated in Welsh and English to his father, who died six months before its first production) was heavily steeped in Williams's memories and to a large degree created out of remembered details of life at the White Lion at Glanrafon, with some elements added from Berthengam (and the Traveller's Rest opposite their cottage) and the cramped but homely domestic enclave of 314a High Street, Connah's Quay. His set specification for '*[t]he back-parlour of a small public-house in the Welsh village of Tan-y-Maes*' requires a 'spench' (a cupboard built into an awkward corner), open fireplace adjoined by seating, Welsh dresser, horsehair sofa and long-case clock, while about the faded walls are engravings and framed religious texts incongruously flanking a mirror engraved with 'Bass is Best'. The village name mimics the Welsh identity of the White Lion: Pen-y-Maes (*lit.* 'top [of the] field') simply becomes Tan-y-Maes (*lit.* 'under [the] field'). A framed photograph of the simple whitewashed building at Glanrafon, with his father standing outside under a signboard proclaiming Richard Williams as licensee, invariably stood on Williams's table in his dressing-room at whatever theatre he happened to be playing.

Although Job Edwards, the fifty-year-old landlord of the Druid's Rest ('*rubicund*', '*moustached, simple, vain and emotional*'), shared his first name with Williams's maternal grandfather and his middle brother, the character was largely modelled on the positive qualities of his father. But because Williams chose to make Job married to a Londoner (he was mindful of Gladys Henson's comic talents as a Cockney), his mother was barely recognisable in the characterisation of Kate. Formerly a dresser at the Alhambra Theatre, she first met Job in the 'Chamber of 'Orrors' at Madame Tussaud's on 'one o'them Licensed Victuallers Outin's' to London' (1:1). She is in fact one of only two English characters in the whole play. Apart from Kate and Lord Ffynnon, an English peer with a local title and estate at Ffynnon Castle, who spends the play resident at the inn pretending to be a commercial traveller known simply as 'Mr Smith' only to be mistaken for a wife-murderer on the run, the other characters form a motley collection of Welsh eccentrics, few of whom are actually necessary to the plot. There is the bicycling Suffragette Sarah Jane Jehovah, who is also one of the *'Morwynion Jehovah'* [Handmaidens of Jehovah], possibly echoing Williams's brother Tom's involvement with the Salvation Army; Zachariah, the village bobby, slow-witted and unimaginative; and sometime chapel deacon Isshmal Hughes, removed from office after taking to drink and now a poet-tramp living under a haystack, who speaks no word of English in the play but cons Dante's *Inferno* in the original. Amongst these colourful individuals Glan, the family's elder son, is by comparison bland and uninteresting. His thirteen-year-old brother Tommos is the imaginative one, an insatiable reader of anything from the serial in *Woman's Weekly* or one of 'them blood an' thunders' to *Jane Eyre* and *Adam Bede*. He stands for the exaggerated stimulation of Williams's own childhood. As he warns his mother when she temporarily prohibits further reading to prevent him from purveying any more fabrications, 'I'm not a liar, I got a terrible imagination' (1:1).

In the closed community of Tan-y-Maes there is no telephone and the outside world intrudes only by way of newspapers or visiting delivery men and commercial travellers. Its passion is singing and all its energies are dedicated to winning the village choir competition at the National Eisteddfod, an event that has been brought at the local landowner's invitation almost to their very doorstep after a fire devastated the original venue in Caernarfon. Lord Ffynnon's connection with the competition empowers him to apply unusual conditions. In between the four cantatas or sections of the musical test piece – fittingly, in echo of the murder sub-theme, this is 'Cain and Abel' – a member of the choir is to recite four original sonnets. But in their desperate anxiety to win the villagers fail to notice, until it is almost too late, that they must be in English and designed 'to promote friendship between the two cultures' (2:2). Even though the mysterious 'Mr Smith' is a suspected murderer, once it is established that he can write poetry he is happily subsumed into the community to assist its frantic attempt to meet the competition deadline. He trails a hat-box around with him, his only luggage, in a burlesque allusion to *Night Must Fall*; and like Dan he seems to be 'one o' them double natures' (3:1), as Zachariah puts it. The bizarreness of the idea recalls Synge and the hero-worshipping of Christy Mahon, supposed parricide and 'Playboy of the Western World'. Yet although there is amused exploration of the wilder reaches of the Celtic imagination – which Kate Edwards in her sober way does her best to resist and discourage – Williams's play is not on the same level as Synge. Much of the comedy arises out of simple cross-purposed dialogue, notably from the supposed penetration by the villagers of Smith's disguise as a murderer when his real *persona* (known only to Tommos and the audience) is a peer of the realm who has come to Tan-y-Maes to try and live, at least for a while, the simple life of poems and pints.

The Druid's Rest opened at the St Martin's Theatre on 26 January 1944. To some extent it was carried by its charm and novelty, partly through the unusually free use of the Welsh language (even more extensive than in *The Corn is Green*). But its lack of plot placed a huge burden on what was in essence little more than a group of well-observed village characters or, as Agate put it, 'amusing sketches' (*Sunday Times*, 3 January 1944), muddling their way to a truth which the audience is in possession of from the opening of Act 2. Privately, Agate confessed that 'Welsh idiocy does not amuse me as the Irish does' (*Ego-7*, 17); but on the whole Emlyn Williams succeeded in impressing the critics. Recognising the precarious hold which 'a farcical comedy which disdains the element of surprise' may be said to have on its audience, *The Times* (27 January 1944) praised the contrasted comic value supplied by the redoubtable Roddy Hughes as Job and Gladys Henson as Kate. There was a sharpness too about the 'consistently droll' performance of Tommos ('*a sturdy solemn boy ... in knickerbockers and Eton collar*'). Unfortunately the reviewer confused the actors: the part was actually played by Brynmor

Thomas, not the eighteen-year-old newcomer Richard Burton whom *The Times* credited. Burton, specially recruited after a casting session in Cardiff, was indeed making his theatrical debut but as Glan the elder brother, not Tommos. As the former Burton received no mention at all.

While *The Druid's Rest* continued its run in London, Williams became attached to the Allied forces' entertainment service (ENSA) and in February 1944 was despatched on tours of France, Belgium, Italy and the Middle East with productions of his own *Night Must Fall* – travelling out to the Royal Opera House, Cairo, by mid-year – together with two other rather more recent hits of the London stage. He acted as Charles Condamine in Coward's *Blithe Spirit*, which at home ran throughout the war and into peace-time from July 1941 to March 1946 (then an unprecedented total of 1998 performances), and in Rattigan's war play *Flare Path*, which was also a big draw at the Apollo between August 1942 and January 1944 (680 performances). By such standards the original pre-war run of *Night Must Fall* looked very modest. In early May, at the start of a tour which took in Capua, Salerno and Barri, he arrived in Naples. He was now in uniform since 'you can't move a step in civilian clothes without being challenged' (A1 8 May 1944). Conditions were not easy generally but the company enjoyed a cut above usual army austerity by being billeted on the sixth floor of an apartment block in a dormitory of camp beds. At home, towards midsummer 1944, the gallery of Welsh eccentrics in *The Druid's Rest* began to lose their charm for London audiences and the play closed on 17 June after a creditable but unspectacular run of 180 performances.

It was nearly a year, close to the end of the war, before Williams had another play on the London stage. His mood in the middle to late war years was more deeply affected by events in north Wales than perhaps he cared to admit. Within a period of about fifteen months during 1943-4, Williams was faced with the severance in quick succession of those links which, despite his establishment as a leading London playwright, still bound him in several important ways to his native Flintshire. In July 1943 his father died at home at Glasdir, Aston Hill, thus depriving him of his most-loved parent and most faithful family correspondent. Just a few weeks later, at the end of the summer term, Miss Cooke retired after twenty-seven years' service from Holywell County School to make her permanent home back in her native Leeds; and the following year while he was in Amiens with ENSA, he received news that his mother had died after a three weeks' illness on 18 October 1944. Mary had not adjusted well to widowhood and Williams regarded the death as a release from her fifteen months of 'solitary confinement'. Glasdir he offered to Job; but the prospect of returning there to sort out his mother's things Williams knew would be painful: 'I dread going into it', he told Grace Cooke, 'it will be so full of her' (A1 27 October 1944). Although the link with Miss Cooke continued unbroken to her death almost twenty years later – her last letter to Williams is dated 20 April 1964 – it was nevertheless the end of an era. With both his parents gone and Miss Cooke established in Yorkshire, the regular, weekly exchange of letters dating back to his first excursion to France in 1921 between Williams and his principal correspondents in the Welsh border country finally came to a close.

In Williams's next play *Trespass* (staged in London from mid-July to the end of November 1947), an over-plotted drama described, like *A Murder has been Arranged*, as a 'Ghost Story', the Welsh element, which is mainly located in the discovery that the main character, supposedly a fake Italian medium, is really a Cardiff shopkeeper who can genuinely trespass into the world of the supernatural, is not central. With the exception of the substantially revamped version of *Spring, 1600* (which had a brief success in a production by the Company of Four, directed by Williams with Andrew Cruickshank as Burbage, at the Lyric, Hammersmith, in December 1945), all the major works for stage and cinema which occupied the remainder of the decade were inspired by Celtic myth or versions of Welsh life: *Pen Don* (1943), *The Wind of Heaven* (1945) and the film *The Last Days of Dolwyn* (1949).

Of the three Welsh pieces *Pen Don* is the least known and the most obviously Welsh; but its setting in Celtic mythology at the time of the *Mabinogion* and King Arthur gave it a preciousness that

Williams had not attempted since *Full Moon*. This belated exercise in the application of the mythic has led at least one earlier biographer to claim that this play is one of Williams's greatest achievements: Richard Findlater wrote of its resemblance, in quality of language, to Synge. Dale-Jones subsequently regarded *Pen Don* as Williams's 'farthest departure from naturalism' (*Emlyn Williams*, 61). This is certainly true; but although it is tempting to suppose that Williams was a frustrated mythic or lyric playwright seduced into writing commercial drama, the reality is that he was more secure in the naturalistic sphere, writing in the well-tried, three-act formula. Whatever strengths he had were best demonstrated there.

Although different in kind from almost anything he wrote – the closest affinities are to the early symbolist work – *Pen Don* is unhappily impregnated with the persistent fault of overwriting that Williams had striven so hard to eliminate from his art. Its setting is a castle on the fringes of Snowdonia, the embattled retreat of a tribe who have escaped the clutches of the foreigner English and now in Pen Don (home of the mother goddess of the earth) await their acceptance into Avalon. A strange mix of symbol, lyricism and humour, its premiere in the war-time obscurity of the Grand Theatre, Blackpool, where it ran for ten performances from 22 December 1943, was auspicious neither in location nor time of year. Williams played the part of Bran Calon Lan, one of the twin sons of the heroine, Lowri Can Mlynedd [Lowri of the Hundred Years]. Though it was politely received by a predominantly non-Celtic audience, it attracted almost no critical attention. If there were any plans for a London performance, they were quickly put aside. A decade later however Tyrone Guthrie, who had long admired its ambient qualities – he is said to have regarded it as the best play of the last thirty years – prevailed on Williams to make a 'drastic revision' of it with a view to a revival. Both author and director agreed that the play's interests would

> perhaps be better served by an amateur cast in Wales than by a professional cast in London.

Williams himself bore the entire cost of the production over three successive nights at the Royal Institution, Swansea, from 4 May

1954. The cramped venue – not a theatre but a lecture-room seating about one hundred people – provided little more than a bare rostrum to which there was only limited access from a corridor running immediately behind: there was also no curtain and lighting was minimal. Indeed it was just as well that, according to Guthrie's programme note,

> illusion was not to be our aim so much as ritual. The method of staging is therefore of the simplest. All is left to the actors.

There was only one professional in a cast otherwise drawn exclusively from members of Swansea Little Theatre, among whom the outstanding performance came from Eileen Llewellyn-Jones as Lowri the mother figure. According to the *South Wales Evening Post* (5 May 1954), she 'would make some of our best character actresses look like amateurs'. After the conclusion of the short run at Swansea (which included a fourth night at the Arts Hall, University College of Swansea) the play was restaged at Cardiff High School and won the praise of Dennis Griffiths, critic of the *South Wales Leader* (26 May 1954), for its epic and poetic qualities. In reviving the play with a Welsh cast before Welsh audiences and critics honour was perhaps satisfied, yet even with Guthrie's name attached to it as director the play failed to generate more general enthusiasm either from the public or from insiders in the theatre. The revised version of *Pen Don* was never staged professionally and Williams never managed to interest a publisher in it. That he had conflicting emotions about this play as much as his early dramatic writing at Oxford is evident. It is absent from the listing of fifteen plays and three adaptations facing the title-page of the *Collected Plays: Volume One*, as are also *Glamour* and *Full Moon*. Twelve years later, opposite the title-page of *Emlyn*, *Pen Don* appears for the first time properly inserted in the list of Williams's works between *The Druid's Rest* and *The Wind of Heaven*, but at the same time all three of the earliest plays, that is including *Vigil*, were dropped entirely.

Williams's most familiar dramatic ground was nineteenth-century Welsh life, the setting for *The Wind of Heaven* and *The Last Days of Dolwyn*. Although they have very different, indeed contrary, outcomes, they also share at least one significant element in common: the return of an exile to his Welsh homeland. The origin of the former apparently went back to Williams's visit, during the latter part of the war on tour with ENSA, to Palestine. Recalling the event nearly a decade later, he described walking into Bethlehem as a return to one special and vividly memorialised moment of his childhood in Glanrafon a moonlit Christmas Eve. He stayed up late and heard the distant sounds of a group of miners from Point of Air colliery assembled on Pen-y-Maes, the field above the inn,

> singing in a way that no other choir has sung for me since, even at the Eisteddfod.

He maintained at the Rhyl National Eisteddfod in 1953 that this special moment of connection with his early memories, 'half Wales, half Holy Land', produced 'a strange and powerful emotion' which determined him to set a version of the fulfilment of the Messianic prophesy in a village setting in Wales in the middle of the previous century (translation of 'Yn ôl i Gatre', Rhyl, 1953). A rather more prosaic account is at least implied in *George* when the message of the Christmas story adapted to Welsh village life comes in a brief moment of connection at a summer *Gymanfa* [hymn-singing festival], as the guest preacher's rhetoric moves Williams to see Nazareth in pastoral Flintshire, with the farm boys of Glanrafon as the Bethlehem shepherds. There is no mention here of *The Wind of Heaven*, but recollected experience of spiritual revelation seems designed to echo that presented through Ambrose Ellis's regeneration in the play.

The play opens in the summer of 1856, weeks after the conclusion of the Crimean War, in the village of 'Blestin'. As a name it reassembles elements of Blaenau Ffestiniog (the slate village supposed to have been once the home of Fess[tiniog] Griffith) while at the same time suggesting overtones of 'blest', 'blessing' and perhaps even 'wounded' (from the French *blessé*). It is presented literally as a dead-end community in the sense that it has no future. No child has been born there since the day eleven years before in 1845 when the flower of its youth was drowned in a sudden squall that overtook a sailing party off nearby Port Blestin. In bitteress at the calamity, sexual relations within the village have ceased, as has the spontaneous singing which used to animate the streets. Dilys Parry, a recent incomer, suffers from an Ibsenite deadness at the beginning of the play, paralysed by her premature widowhood (her young husband having fallen victim to cholera on his way home from the Crimea), which only serves to confirm her rejection in adulthood of what she considers the specious palliatives of religious faith. But *The Wind of Heaven* is about coming back as much for its principal character Ambrose Ellis, played by Williams himself, as for Gwyn, the supposed incarnation of Christ as the boy-Messiah. And Dilys Parry, half Welsh on her mother's side, who has inherited the old manor house of Blestin from her maternal uncle, has also come back to her origins. In Blestin she recovers enough of the language to use Welsh terms of endearment (*'ymechani'*, *'annwyl'* and *'fanwylyd'*) to her servant Bet and to communicate on simple conversational terms with the old village shepherd, Evan Howell, for whom the English language (learned out of the King James version of the Bible) is very much a foreign tongue. Her coming back, like Ambrose Ellis's, though in a much less ostentatious way, puts her back into touch not only with her buried native roots but readmits her into the language and religious faith she lost twenty years before, coincidentally about the same time as Ambrose disowned Wales and its language.

Ambrose Ellis, born illegitimate thirty miles away and now a circus owner living in Birmingham, has returned to try to confirm the reported existence in Blestin of a phenomenon, potentially valuable as a circus curiosity, of a small man or dwarf possessed of magical powers to conjure music out of the air. Originally christened Emrys (the Welsh form of his name), Ambrose Ellis left Wales twenty years earlier to become a school teacher in England, where he changed his name and 'repudiated' his native language. Then he fell in love with the circus and by dint of ruthless ambition and hard work eventually came to own one. His manager Pitter (who prides himself on being 'before all else a student of human nature' [scene 1], a latter-day dissector of motivation, like La Bruyère) senses that underlying the brash confidence smoulders a volcanic fire that will burst into life when Ellis's 'true Celtic self', now concealed beneath the flashy waistcoat and oily hair of 'the cynical braggart' (scene 2), finally emerges. Yet the unbelieving, callous exploiter of human cravenness at his Birmingham circus turns out to be the one chosen to carry the message to the world of the returned Christ, apparently incarnated in thirteen-year-old Gwyn, bastard son of Dilys Parry's servant Bet. Having in his unassuming presence brought music back into the village, he has over the past seven years had a tranquillising effect on the whole community, which, quietly and unsensationally, appears to have made up its own mind on the authenticity of the boy-Messiah. The message is slow in reaching the cultivated isolation of Dilys Parry. Aloof in her manor house, she takes 'no interest in the village' and 'expect[s] the same courtesy in return' (scene 1). Rejecting the fiercely uncompromising label of atheist, Dilys is presented as an educated woman with 'an open mind' (scene 2) on the existence of God. She needs to regain her reverence for wonder first. Ellis's enquiries are the catalyst and Dilys's faith – she has not been inside a church since she was fifteen – is restored as a result of Evan Howell's moving narrative on the music or wind which occasionally blows through the village, reinforced by Bet's story of her son's rescue of a maimed lamb. In the battle between her rational mind and natural resistance to superstition on one side and the strength of the emotion of the moment on the other, Dilys surrenders to the belief that nearly two thousand years of waiting have ended in Blestin in fulfilment of the prophecy in John 5:24 ('The hour is coming, and is here, when the dead shall hear the voice of the Son of God. And they that hear, shall live'). As the outsider Pitter puts it,

> I would say that you are over the border into a country for which
> we materialists have no passport, and no desire (scene 4).

Even at the end, after Gwyn has apparently raised from the dead twenty soldiers who lay stricken with cholera in the local hospital, Pitter clings to the notion that there may be some rational explanation for everything that has occurred.

Ambrose Ellis's faith is severely tested by the arrival from Birmingham of the materialist Mrs Lake. Her fears of Dilys Parry as rival for the affections of her man are quickly dispelled but she brings news of a business opportunity as chairman of a prestigious company which will release Ellis from provincial entrapment and give him the 'mantle of social dignity' (scene 5). As he succumbs for the moment to the temptation to return to Birmingham with her, a cock crows three times in the distance. At this heavily underlined signal of his betrayal Gwyn as Christ-figure is immediately consigned to bed, mortally ill. The doctor procured from over the border in Shropshire (because the local man is too frightened of infection to attend) arrives too late to save Gwyn, who in his final message before death reiterates Ellis's status as the chosen one. In his resolution to become an itinerant preacher to the people of Wales, Ellis's native language begins to return after twenty years' lack of use. Slowly, hesitantly, under tutelage from Evan Howell, he picks his way through the words of the Lord's Prayer.

Williams's abandonment of the conventional three-act formula of earlier plays here in favour of a six-scene structure was no more than a cosmetic attempt to suggest a new form. In fact Williams's unwavering instinct throughout his career was to defer to the terms and structure of the well-made play. What was new at least for him in *The Wind of Heaven* was not form but theme: that of spiritual regeneration, in this case that of a whole Welsh community. Ivor Brown referred to it wittily if slightingly as 'The Passing of the Third Floor *bach*' (in Agate, *Ego-9*, 82); and indeed there is a thematic resemblance to Jerome K. Jerome's *The Passing of the Third Floor Back* (1909), in which a stranger renting a room in a Bloomsbury lodging-house has a strong and positive moral effect on every other resident. Identification of the stranger with Christ, though hinted at, is never made directly. Indeed it was not possible to do so since under the rules of government censorship no personation of God or Christ was permitted on the stage, a ban which operated until as late as 1966. While *The Wind of Heaven* makes very clear by implication and allusion Gwyn's status as the boy-Messiah in the play, the Lord Chamberlain's official licence was endorsed with a warning that no explicit identification could be made.

For Williams there was possibly a certain Celtic bravado in tackling such a difficult and sensitive area, yet the motif of the country boy as Messiah, in the historically removed mid-Victorian setting of a century earlier, is actually the least successful element in the play. The theme was indeed another manifestation of his interest in what might lie beyond the boundaries of the everyday; but in this case instead of evil and the macabre Williams chose to engage with the possibility of divine revelation. Part of the problem is that the setting is not particularly convincing at the historical level (a remote Welsh village thronged with sightseers, police vainly trying to control the crowds and reporters from the *London Times* [*sic*], somehow seems too modern for 1856), with the result that the characters and their motivations tend to invite judgement as if they belonged to a contemporaneous rather than period play. Williams is uncomfortable with the language of the spirit: its attempted poetic idiom make it sound stilted, unnatural and even sentimental, as when Ambrose has to speak about 'spanning the world with one healing step' or the wind (of heaven) that blew through the village at the moment of Gwyn's death which 'rose up, into the loving sky' (scene 6). Bet is much more credible in her simple thankfulness at her son's release from pain. It seems likely that Williams at least partly invested Dilys Parry with some of his own experience of religion and endorsed her acceptance of the need to fill the spiritual void: there are parallels between her rejection of the church at fifteen and Williams's spiritually withdrawn presence in the chapel of his childhood. As Dilys is transfigured by her Blestin experience, so Williams seems to have been genuinely moved by his experience in Palestine in 1944 and made some attempt through this play to re-establish contact with his spiritual side, which also involved redefining himself as a Welshman in a world in which Wales has become the chosen land for the Second Coming. Significantly what is variously described by the sceptics in the play as 'religious mania', an 'evangelical bout', 'the five days' wonder of Blestin' takes place quite outside the confines of conventional religious institutions. Indeed, oddly for Wales, the village seems to have been effectively abandoned by religion for the past one hundred years: there is no chapel and the church has long been converted into a shop. Blestin's particular form of spiritual revival seems to require no aid from the religious establishment, perhaps because Williams's own spiritual return journey (like Cliff Parrilow's intimation of something spiritual 'very high up, very far away ...' in *The Morning Star*) was too personal to involve traditional institutions. The quite proper possibility in these circumstances that the whole experience is mere hysteria or fantasy is left to the sceptic Pitter to articulate, but even he seems mesmerised at the final curtain by the power of Dilys Parry's transcendent faith: '[h]is eyes quail before hers, and his head is slowly bowed' (scene 6). The gesture implies that the sceptic's line is in the end only tokenism. That seems to be reinforced by the judgement of *The Times* (13 April 1945) that *The Wind of Heaven*

> has the quality of a moving Welsh sermon [but] ... is apt to value an emotion not for its continuing power over the mind but for its intensity.

It is arguable that the more effective and more genuinely accessible motif in the play is that of the returning exile, who in re-crossing the geographical border between England and Wales finds himself on the boundary of a new life: he rediscovers both spirituality and his language. Ambrose Ellis, outwardly the showman (a debased form of the actor-director), subconsciously carries the guilt of the man who has turned his back on his native land. He has changed his name, lost his Welsh mother tongue, speaks perfect English but with an indeterminate accent that suggests some 'vague effect of the Continent' (scene 1). He has returned to exploit its resources in the shape of the boy phenomenon whom he hopes to be able to lure into circus employment at the lowest possible wage. Dilys too has compromised her roots, speaks English with little or no intrusion of a Welsh accent; her arrival at Blestin is not selfish or motivated by greed but therapeutic. At first uncertain whether she will stay and continue her lease on the manor house, she joins Ambrose in his spiritual re-education of the nation. His mission fired by a simple, unquestioning faith puts him back in contact with his childhood innocence. Alone before the forces of nature on the mountainside above Blestin, he describes a feeling of almost Wordsworthian intensity – integrating earth, sky and sea in 'the adoration of the moment' (scene 3) – in an epiphany of spiritual redefinition.

Following its successful provincial try-out, the London premiere of *The Wind of Heaven* took place at the St James's Theatre on 12 April 1945. It was one of the most nerve-wracking of first nights Emlyn Williams ever attended, because of the special, almost fragile, nature of the play and the possibility of a fundamentally unsympathetic reception. Williams knew very well, apart from the inevitable posse of newspaper critics, what first-night audiences were like: 'terrify-ing, hard glittering faces' who demand to be entertained. He described the experience as a

> battle between the play and a typical hardboiled London first
> night audience (A1 14 April 1945).

Williams's fear was that the theme of spiritual regeneration and recovery of faith might be too much for them in this play, 'which can only blossom under a certain amount of "suspension of disbelief"'. Indeed that was the very level on which J. C. Trewin concluded it did not work: 'we may admire but we suspend belief' (*English Theatre*, 70). Williams was not sanguine about his chances. Philip Page for the *Daily Mail* appeared to be drunk and kept nodding off; and from James Agate, whom he noted sternly as arriving thirty-five minutes late and missing the first scene and a half, Williams held out no hope of a fair hearing: 'Whatever he says tomorrow one can have nothing but contempt for', he wrote to Miss Cooke. Yet Agate's review was in fact one of the better ones, unusually complimentary. He was genuinely moved by the play and impressed not only by Williams's representation of a 'man in spiritual travail – a beauti-fully thought-out piece of acting' but the 'miracle' combination of Diana Wynyard and Meg Jenkins as mistress and servant and 'a soul-shaking performance by Herbert Lomas as the shepherd [Evan Howell]' (*First Nights*, 173).

Of all of Williams's plays, *The Wind of Heaven* was the only one which was formally translated into Welsh (by J. Ellis Williams as *Awel Gref*). In English it remained a popular piece for amateurs and in 1956 was adapted for a showing on television. As the most promi-nent Anglo-Welsh playwright then writing, Williams was well aware of the responsibility that lay with him in the promotion of the image of Wales. Traditionally in the theatre the foreigner is a figure either of curiosity or fun. This is acknowledged in Evan Howell's naïve assumption that Ambrose Ellis will give him a job in his circus simply because he is Welsh, for

> when the English behold somebody not English, they laugh very
> hearty. Lo, I would shew myself as a Welshman (scene 2).

The irony is, Ambrose Ellis assures him, that the English public is 'a trifle too jaded' for that to work any more. But throughout his work Williams takes refuge in history. The Wales that he shows is always filtered through the past, a more distanced form of Williams's own past. Blestin is a throwback to a more superstitious age. There is a self-conscious attempt to create an ideal of Welsh community life which relies on the stereotypical imagery of a Welsh peasantry barely articulate in English, living out a simple life close to the soil and enlivened by singing Welsh hymns and folksongs. In that sense Williams perpetuates a mythic world of simple Celtic innocence on the borders of rationality. Ambrose is taken back, readmitted into the community he rejected because he recovers his childhood innocence, just as Williams's own sense of the essence of the Welsh village – not that of border life in Connah's Quay but represented by Glanrafon – was also bound up in his re-creation and to an extent reinvention of his childhood, that prelapsarian world from which he was abstracted by school and Miss Cooke. Flawed though it may be, it is *The Wind of Heaven*, not *The Corn is Green,* which represents Williams's least equivocal commitment to his homeland.

The contrasting faces of Williams's attitudes to his own Welshness are present in the links and oppositions between *The Wind of Heaven* and *The Last Days of Dolwyn*, the only movie he both wrote and directed. It was made for Alexander Korda under the British Lion label and was Williams's first excursion into film-making sitting in the director's chair. Owing to his inexperience in the role, his assistant director, Swansea-born Russell Lloyd, was essential to the whole project. It was he who taught Williams the technical vocabulary of film-making and directing, though in fact Williams spent less time behind the camera than in front of it, dealing with interpretation. Essentially Williams saw filming as an extension of the stage, not a separate medium with its discrete resources and qualities; and as he explained in an HTV interview, 'I was really concerned with myself and the acting' (Berry, 523). All the studio work was done at Isleworth, Middlesex, but for authenticity Williams required a large part of the film to be shot directly on location in north Wales. More than sixty possible sites were visited by the film crew before Rhydymain, a grey village typical of the area, built in stone and slate, just to the north-east of Dolgellau, was finally selected. Even here there were certain inherent disadvantages to be overcome. Apparently the chapel was too monolithic (as 'enormous and formal as those nonconformist mausoleums we all know in the suburbs of great cities') and there was no pub, yet both were essential institutions for the purposes of the film. But while a simple coat of green paint and softening of the chapel outline with artificial ivy solved the first problem, the conversion of one of the village houses into a pub was delayed until Rhydymain's acquisition of 'licensed premises' had been aired and approved in public debate in chapel. Further to mollify local sensibilities, the base unit of 'the pagan film world' was billeted five miles off in Dolgellau itself. Rhydymain's name in the film as Dolwyn, Williams invented on the model of Colwyn Bay, having rejected his original choice of Glanrafon as 'too difficult for English tongues to get around' (*Listener*, 23 June 1949).

Williams followed his usual stage practice in recruiting a cast of principals the majority of whom had worked with him previously on stage. Under Williams's patronage Richard Burton, now twenty-four, made his screen debut (with fellow Welshman, a very youthful Stanley Baker as understudy). Having picked Burton out for *The Druid's Rest*, and recognised several parallels between his early life-story and his own, Williams was keen not only to advance Burton's professional career but manipulate his personal life (which he persisted in doing through Burton's successive marriages). In pursuit of the latter goal and in a largely vain attempt to keep his hard-drinking, womanizing protégé on the straight and narrow, he introduced him on set to Sybil Williams, who would soon become his first wife. Above all however the film was to be a vehicle for Edith Evans, whose performance as Gwenny, the Welsh maidservant in *The Late Christopher Bean*, had so much impressed Williams fifteen years before. In her part as Merri (which sounds like Mary with a North Wales accent), the caretaker at the village church, Williams said he intended to capture the humble peasant type represented by his late mother. In reality the portrait was invigorated with rather more native wit and resourcefulness than Mary Williams was capable of and imbued with more genuine affection than Williams ever felt for his mother in life. Burton played Merri's adopted son Gareth, recently returned home from Liverpool. One of Williams's stalwart character actors, Roddy Hughes, played Caradoc, landlord of the village inn, and the octogenarian Allan Aynesforth (creator of the original Algernon Moncrieff in Wilde's *The Importance of Being Ernest* in 1895, who specialised in aristocratic parts) was plucked from retirement to play the English landowner Lord Lancashire. Williams himself took the male lead as the returned exile, the embittered, conscienceless Rob Davies, who comes to Dolwyn intent on what seems a preposterously disproportionate form of revenge.

As in *The Wind of Heaven*, Williams insisted on historical distance. The film is set in 1892 with the village of Dolwyn under threat of inundation over creation of a reservoir to supply water to Lancashire. Dolwyn itself is portrayed with considerable affection – the imagery of church and pub is grafted intimately into village life – in this idealised vision of turn-of-the-century Glanrafon. The camera lingers on both institutions, especially the bar and its *bonhommie* (where landlord and local bobby collude in a little poaching), and the spire of the church symbolises the last defiant stand against the betrayer. A shepherd boy sings a haunting Welsh folksong. The effect that Williams was intent on portraying was essentially that Celtic paradise that he had known as a child.

The issue of drowning Welsh valleys to provide water for England was not in 1949 the highly sensitive one it became in Welsh politics after the decision to flood Treweryn in the early 1960s, though it was still political in nature. But this was no nationalist drama. Williams deliberately shied away from confronting the politics. Betrayal in this Welsh village comes not as perhaps might be expected from some rapacious English landowner who tramples recklessly on local feelings, but from one of its own. To have made Lord Lancashire the villain would have been seen as an attack on the English, Williams confessed in his HTV interview, and that was not his intention. The role of destroyer falls instead to Lancashire's agent, the Welshman Rob Davies, who bears a grudge against Dolwyn for its harsh treatment of him as a boy when he was caught thieving. Returning in adulthood after twenty years' absence, he is determined to make his native village pay; but the price strains credulity as it is nothing less than total obliteration.

The official film premiere took place in London at the Empire, Leicester Square, on 21 April 1949. Because this was a film with a special significance for Wales there was a separate Welsh premiere at the Plaza in Bangor six days later, followed by a south Wales showing in Cardiff on 4 July, when Williams's 'eloquent tribute by a Welshman to his native land' was reported by the *Western Mail* (5 July 1949) as the city's 'biggest film event of the post-war years'. While the film had only a brief run in London because of low audiences, several high points both in the atmosphere of the film and the quality of the acting won critical praise, though even by the standards of film-making in 1949 the storyline and development of the plot were rightly seen as absurdly melodramatic. Williams's own portrayal of the villainous Rob Davies created powerful tensions and Dame Edith Evans, best known for Millamant in *The Way of the World*, demonstrated in her creation of the very different nature of Merri, according to *The Times* (22 April 1949), several qualities inspired by the Restoration character, notably

> the same sense of style ... [and] the same capacity to find loveliness and significance in each casual line.

Emlyn Williams directing Edith Evans was a stunning combination. Nowhere is this more apparent than in the key scene in which Merri confronts Lady Dolwyn – who represents faded local aristocracy forced through financial embarrassment to sell out to Lord Lancashire – to plead with her to do her duty by the village and save it from inundation. Merri begins as petitioner and Lady Dolwyn as the petitioned, but gradually the traditional stations are inverted as Merri asserts her own kind of authority. With only a limited vocabulary in English in which to express herself, her few words, a mixture of guile, pretended innocence and irony, are deployed with great subtlety. She transcends the class barrier with such indiscriminate ease that at one point she is found ministering to Lord Lancashire's rheumatism, for which she prescribes a homespun cure. Williams wrote himself into the subtext of this film as much as into the plays. He here inhabits both Lady Dolwyn and Merri, torn between two conflicting roles, two classes and two cultures; and on the male side he is both Lord Lancashire as benevolent English gentleman and Rob Davies, returned exile cast as betrayer. They contribute to the complex set of responses Williams has to class deference (and difference), to Wales as homeland and England as adopted land. There are tensions that are not resolved in the film because they involved crises of identity and commitment that were unreconciled in Williams's own life.

In some sense perhaps an over-compensation for Williams's relative neglect of Wales, the film was open to the charge of Celtic exaggeration, of being what the *Illustrated London News* (14 May 1949) considered 'more Welsh than Wales itself'. Several reviewers who were themselves Welsh or had Welsh connections were critical of its sugary atmosphere. For Dilys Powell there were too many harps harping, shepherd-boys singing and girls hopping: in short too much very obvious filmic bustle for it to be taken too seriously. John Ormond Thomas drew attention to another aspect of Williams's tonal overplay by suggesting that had he as critic the power to remove any one thing from the soundtrack it would be the singing of the Welsh national anthem as the villagers trekked in forced exile over the hill away from the flooded village. Although Ormond's overall responses were 'mixed', he conceded nonetheless that it was 'a better film about Wales than I've seen before' (*Picture Post*, 30 April 1949). During August 1949 a shortened version of the sound track, adapted by P.H. Burton, was broadcast on the BBC Home Service.

In the same year as *The Last Days of Dolwyn* was released Williams was recognised by the University of Wales by the award for services to Welsh culture of an honorary LLD. It was conferred by the newly installed Chancellor, the Duke of Edinburgh, at the University College of North Wales, Bangor, during the same ceremony at which Williams's old friend Lady Megan Lloyd George received a similar honour. At lunch they were seated opposite one another. In the citation for the degree Williams was described as

> one of those who have carried their native gifts abroad yet without severing his old ties or forgetting the rock from which he was hewn.

But there was perhaps a hint of wryness in the Vice-Chancellor's recognition that Williams's corn had ripened 'in the congenial climate of the English theatre' (as opposed to the Welsh). That congeniality indeed quickly took him back to London to complete *Accolade*, his final play of the decade.

Accolade was premiered at Liverpool's Royal Court on 31 July 1950, prior to opening in London at the Aldwych on 7 September. There were unusual features about the production. First, in choosing Glen Byam Shaw as director rather than direct the play himself, Williams was going against a practice he had adopted ever since *He Was Born Gay* in 1937, and secondly, the cast included no one that had acted in any of Willliams's earlier plays, which flew in the face of the unofficial repertory company that he had built up over the years since 1935. As Williams himself was to play Will Trenting, the difficult nature of the part is sufficient explanation for his not wanting to direct (the same reasoning as had been used over *Night Must Fall*); but the unfamiliarity of the casting seems to indicate how much of a new departure, a clean slate, this drama was intended to be. In addressing new thematic territory *Accolade* confronted tensions and ambiguities deep within Williams's own psychology, a process that brought him into conflict with Grace Cooke, who failed to appreciate the significance. For more than twenty years Miss Cooke had been to varying degrees positive in her reaction to all of Williams's dramatic work. With this piece it was different. Retirement had not dulled her critical faculties; she was horrified at both theme and treatment. She loathed the play and wrote, white hot, to tell him so, suggesting that he might be best advised to burn her letter before reading it. Williams always insisted that *Accolade* took longer in gestation and in the writing than any of his other plays, so he was especially shocked at this first ever major disagreement with Miss Cooke, as well as stung by the force of her uncompromising – and to a degree uncomprehending – hostility.

Williams's hero is a Jekyll and Hyde personality. Will Trenting's homely name and respectable family life with wife and public-school boy son belie his other life as 'Bill Trent', a frequenter of low life in Rotherhithe pubs, which provides material for his novels while at the same time presenting opportunities for drunkenness and illicit sex.

This Wildean 'Bunburying' with sexual intent shocks his publisher, but his wife Rona is tolerant of his weaknesses from long acceptance of his unusual needs. A Nobel Prize winner, Trenting is plunged into personal crisis on accepting a knighthood in recognition of his further services to literature at the precise moment that his black-mailer (who has photographic evidence of his debauchery) comes in for the kill. A failed writer, the blackmailer turns out to be the father of the girl. Trenting's worst moment, which is also the most power-ful scene in the play, comes when he has to confess his folly to his offspring. For Miss Cooke perhaps the severest criticism possible was that the play combined strong Ibsenite and Shavian elements, both utterly abhorrent to her. She detested plays with theses:

> it's an argument. Great Scott! I never tht that you wld do an argument. However in the world <u>are y gng to end it</u>!

In defence of his hero to Miss Cooke, Williams denied that the play was an 'argument' at all:

> it is a picture of what (in the author's opinion) happens when a famous man gets into a scandal and realizes he can't have it both ways (A1 17 July 1949).

There is certainly some strength in the confessional scenes and power in the blackmailer's exultant triumph as he forgoes money for the satisfaction of bringing his victim before the law. Williams seems to make a plea for tolerance of the impossible demands for sexual probity put upon public figures. But the outcome is incon-clusive and that was what Williams intended. Out on bail awaiting trial for interference with an under-age girl, Trenting is threatened by an angry crowd assembling outside his home. As their hostility mounts one of the mob suddenly lobs a brick through Trenting's window. For *The Times* (8 September 1950) it was 'a difficult story' which at times stretched credibility, but there was praise for Williams's skill in suggesting the double-sided nature of the hero, whose needs are shown early on to be dangerously damaging to his reputation, by laying 'much stress in the later scenes on what is child-like and innocent in the great man'. Although there was some disquiet at the idea of a thirteen-year-old actor having to listen to the sordid details of Trenting's confession, there was admiration for the frankness with which Williams had addressed the issues. Evidently the degree of tolerance for sexual issues had expanded at St James's Palace – where Henry Game, original reader of *Night Must Fall*, was now the Lord Chamberlain's Chief Examiner, an office he had held since 1936 – because to everyone's surprise *Accolade* progressed through the licensing process in record time and emerged unscathed. For *Theatre World* (September 1950) it was gratifying

> to know that the Censor permits healthy discussion on the stage of problems which would have shocked our grandfathers to the point of speechlessness.

The motif of the double life surfaces time and again in Williams's work. That Williams should have chosen at this stage in 1949-50 to treat that motif in terms of sexual promiscuity may be said to reflect his need to write his story through drama. Williams had frequently toyed with, and immediately abandoned on grounds of practicality, the idea of writing a play with a homosexual background in the 1930s; but even in the somewhat more liberal climate of the early post-war period he was realistic enough to accept that the censor would never have allowed Will Trenting's sexual leanings to have been for a young boy rather than a pubescent girl, though indeed that is the way he first conceived the plot. (Terence Rattigan originally intended in *Table Number Seven*, the second play in *Separate Tables* [1954], to make the lead character Major Pollock homosexual but was forced by fear of censorship into writing a more conventional drama.) But if Williams's handling of his sharp-edged theme was decorous enough to avoid intervention by the censor, ironically what was permitted on stage was not also necessarily acceptable for the young medium of television. When in 1957 *Accolade* was adapted by Elspeth Cochrane for a ninety-minute showing as 'Play of the Week' on Granada TV, with Isabel Dean and James Donald, it carried in *TV Times* (10 May) the warning 'unsuitable for children'. Another commentator, Robert Cannel (C6, unidentified newsclipping), previewed it 'one of the most uninhibited and potentially unpleasant plays ever presented to a TV audience'.

It is impossible to ignore correspondences between certain

features of *Accolade* and Williams's own personal history. Williams's marriage, though basically a very happy one, had been contracted fifteen years before in full knowledge of the respective sexual narratives on both sides, including in Williams's case bisexuality. Trenting observes that marriage has been good for him because it offered a steadying influence on his wayward existence but not an absolute impediment to it. The degree of trust and understanding on both sides ensures that he will always come back to the security of his marriage. Williams's own marriage was important to him but not without its difficulties of temperament, not least during the war years when Williams and his wife had to endure long periods of separation. Between June 1940 and June 1942 for instance they were parted by three thousand miles of Atlantic Ocean. He insisted, against Molly's plan for return, that for safety's sake the children remain in New York at least for the time being and that preferably Molly should stay with them. Molly found this difficult to understand, yet Williams argued that they were not 'an ordinary married couple' and that if Molly returned without the children they would argue too much and say

> all sorts of things neither of us mean – you know what we're like
> sometimes (not often thank God) like the day before you left and
> I really couldn't bear that again (A6 26 December 1940).

However these long periods of loneliness through separation were (as any kind of loneliness always was for Williams) unbearable and he longed for companionship, including sexual. There were lapses at this period and again probably later (though Williams always insisted that the intervals between needs were constantly lengthening). Mostly they were casual encounters and mostly with men, though not exclusively so.

At the time of his marriage Emlyn Williams's real fear, directly expressed in *Emlyn,* was that his occasional impulses to homosexual foraging would be curtailed or stopped altogether. Indeed Williams in the sexual sense mirrors the split personality of his hero. Trenting is magnetically drawn to the low life, to the covert existence of Rotherhithe, partly by its very contrast with the respectability of his other life as a famous writer, but more insistently because of

Trenting's need for indulgence in a heterosexual version of 'la boue', that homosexual twilight world which Williams hinted at finding so attractive in the 1930s. In *Accolade* Williams was inspired by the recognition of the need for alternatives, the acceptance that marriage did not 'resolve' his own divided sexuality. Rona Trenting stands for the tolerance and acceptance needed from time to time in a Molly Williams who had already shown such qualities in marrying a confessed bisexual. Miss Cooke, who had not the remotest conception of Williams's complex sexual life, least of all his occasional liking for rougher trade, could not have been more wrong when she implied that the theme was purely academic for him, that it was a play which 'reeks of the ink-pot, but not of the streets':

> I said I knew nothing abt sexual incontinence, but it strikes me that you know less! (A2 [July 1949]).

Maybe there is something of the pasteboard in Williams's conception of his hero but it was not from want of knowledge. Friends who knew him well were astonished at the closeness to Williams's own situation. Yet if there are evasions too in the issues raised and in the ending, certainly *Accolade* is Williams's most adult play and his most direct confrontation with his double nature. At the first night, John Gielgud coyly remarked on the play's being 'rather too autobiographical' (Harding, 152) for his taste, little suspecting how three years later - in the very year of conferment of his knighthood – he personally was to know the anguish of exposure of the discrepancy between public image and private sexual behaviour.

For Williams as actor and playwright, the double life continued to fascinate. In his portrait of Fenn in the thriller *Someone Waiting* (1953), the wronged father metamorphosed into an obsessive avenger against those responsible for the false conviction and hanging of his son for murder – a case which bore a distinct resemblance to the Christie- Timothy Evans controversy of the time, though Williams claimed the likeness was pure coincidence – challenged the genre stereotype by its narrative ingenuity and tension. Fenn's righteous obsession with justice makes the real interest of the play psychological. This turns, as *The Times* put it (26 November 1953), mainly on the spectacle of an ineffectual little man who has never been good at anything but chess turned by the conviction that his son was innocent into a icily calculating villain.

Williams played the part himself in a shabby raincoat, his relatively small stature intensifying the character's increasingly sinister nature. It proved a taut and chilling psychological thriller, derived from templates which Williams had begun to create as far back as *Vigil* in Oxford in 1926.

There was a similar common denominator of obsession in the villains created in Williams's three acting roles in the late 1950s for the Shakespeare Memorial Theatre, during the directorial reign of Glen Byam Shaw. At Stratford in 1956 he played in repertoire Shylock, Angelo (the role Gielgud had played in the previous Stratford production in 1950) and Iago, but all to good rather than outstanding notices in a season which was littered with big name stars. The choice of roles was significant: his acting repertory of this period is all of a piece with his fascination with psychologically perplexing and obsessive individuals.

In a related but different way, it is not difficult to see what he was attracted to in Dickens, in whose novels in the 1950s he developed a consuming passion and perfected a solo reading performance to rival Dickens's own. Although he would then have known relatively little of Dickens's own sexual history with wife and mistress, Williams's interest in him was first of all in a fellow professional as artist and performer but whose sense of the contrasts between the macabre and the everyday, ordinariness and otherness, were equally close to his own, as in some ways were his methods of work. Dickens investigated obsessively, wrote from personal observation, walked the streets at night simply to experience their special quality of mystery and even danger. Drawing on what he knew of Dickens's own practice and the evidence of the scripts, Williams dramatised a number of extended readings from the novels, the first of which dated back to a version of Lady Dedlock's revenge on Mr Tulkinghorn 'shot through the heart', broadcast on the wireless in May 1942. However the first series proper for stage performance was tried out at Drury Lane in February 1951 (when *Accolade* was nearing the end of its run) and, after an acclaimed provincial tour beginning at Cambridge Arts Theatre in July, opened in London in October of the same year. Its tremendous success led to an American tour in January 1952 and a second series in London from the following September. To a large extent these readings reflected his interest in the criminal underworld – as did his recreation of Dickens's famous reading of the murder of Nancy in *Oliver Twist* – and in the large-scale contrasts of Lady Dedlock's double-life in a panoramic novel like *Bleak House*. The drama in Dickens's narratives was naturally present, but Williams sought to enhance the effects by accumulating props which reflected Dickens's life or which actually belonged to him. In essence he cultivated a physical resemblance to Dickens and attempted to recreate his immediate environment.

Williams was always slightly apprehensive about his reception as a professsional actor in his home territory. But performance of the Charles Dickens readings was only part of the reason why Williams returned to north Wales for a visit in the summer of 1953. Primarily it was in response to an official invitation to be president of the day at the Rhyl National Eisteddfod in August at the ceremony of welcome for returning exiles, many of them from far-flung corners of the world. Under the auspices of the eisteddfod committee he was also asked to present, for the first time to a Welsh audience, his by now celebrated readings from England's national novelist. At the same time, in recognition of his contribution to Welsh literary and dramatic life, Williams was initiated into the Druidic mysteries of the *Gorsedd* [bardic circle] by 'Cynan', the Archdruid (otherwise Albert Evans-Jones, a teacher and Methodist minister). What Williams may not have known (relatively few did) was that Cynan had another role as dramatic censor, having since 1931 served on the Lord Chamberlain's committee as reader of plays in the Welsh language. If Williams was aware of this connection, it was in such an environment probably an irony on which he, who had never attempted a Welsh-language play, might not have been keen to dwell. And there was the further irony that Cynan himself might have been aware: that if Williams actually had committed himself to Welsh language writing he could not have expected, nor would he have achieved, either the status or success that he did. There were pitifully few outlets for an aspiring Welsh-language dramatist, even at the National Eisteddfod. As Williams was aware from personal experience, even at the major competitions the standard of entry was in some years too low to warrant the award of the prize. At Aberystwyth in 1952 W. J. Gruffydd (who had rejected Williams's play at Mold in 1923) withheld the bardic crown for a poem on 'The Created' after a disappointing competition which he said 'marked the nadir of a gradual deterioration during the past 15 years' (*The Times* 6 August 1952). And the drama was in trouble quite regularly as very much the poor relation in terms of its low standards. Since Williams's milieu as an embryonic and developing playwright was Oxford and London not Wales, the decision to write in English was not in the end the result of a choice between two competing languages. Even if circumstances had been different, in his desire to make a name for himself in the theatrical world, Williams had never really had a choice because there was no professional Welsh-language theatre either for him to act in or to write for.

From the platform in the Pavilion at Rhyl Williams delivered the speech of welcome to the unusually large number of Welsh exiles attracted back to Wales for the largest cultural event in its calendar. It was lauded as one of the most 'elegant' [*ceinach*] and effective addresses ever given at an eisteddfod. He came as an exile speaking to exiles with a speech entitled 'Yn ôl i gatre' [Coming Home]. There were several snippets in the course of the speech of the two other languages with which he was most familiar (English and French) but it was essentially a Welsh speech through and through, spoken strongly in an idiom which impressed those who harboured suspicions that his long sojourn in England might have enfeebled his capabilities in his native tongue. He evoked movingly childhood memories of life in the village of Glanrafon and of his return visit a year previously, after an absence of nearly forty years, when he walked up through the fields to a vantage point where he could look down on the village chimneys, the horses grazing in the fields, the White Lion, externally little changed since his own day, and in his imagination compose a still vivid picture of his mother emerging from the back door of the inn to feed the chickens in the yard. He told of the bleak contrast with life at the border with England at Connah's Quay and of the way that his native language was made a matter of fun and of his consciousness of the special nature of his Welsh heritage. Williams spoke to an audience the large majority of whom were passionately concerned for the fate of the Welsh language; and the personal testimony of one who, as reported by *Y Cymro* (14 August 1953) had been 'steeped' [*trwytho*] in the language – its resilience having survived not only Connah's Quay but Oxford, London, New York and Hollywood – generated in them a feeling that was not far removed from religious experience. The twenty-minute speech was greeted with huge applause and became one of the main talking points of the week. Archdruid Cynan remarked on the sense of pride there was in Wales for the 'great work' he had done, and especially how in making plain his reverence for his origins Williams had done much service in 'proclaiming the name of Wales wherever he went' [*Mae'n chyoeddi enw Cymru lle bynnag yr â*]. The Welsh-language press reported it as 'a gem of a speech', and Goronwy O. Roberts, a local M.P., summed up the exhilaration felt that one of 'the masters of spoken English' had acknowledged publicly to the Welsh in 'true Welsh' [*Cymraeg gwirioneddol*] his debt to the language and cultural ethos of Wales [*y Gymraeg*]. As Williams explained, he had spent 'the greater part of my life among strangers; [but] to-day I have come home' (*The Times*, 6 August 1953). If anyone thought it, no one dared spoil the mood of celebration by suggesting Williams's homecoming might not unfairly have been described as the return of the prodigal son.

In Williams's readings three days later from Dickens he was recreating the practice not just of Dickens himself but coincidentally that of the Flintshire tailor-novelist Daniel Owen, who raised the consciousness of his work-mates by reading to them excerpts from the novels of the period, not only Dickens but Thackeray and George Eliot. At the National Eisteddfod the readings took place off the official field. On Friday 7 August Williams was booked to appear at the Assembly Hall in Holywell reading from *Bleak House* and a piece in Welsh from *A Tale of Two Cities* in what the programme announced as 'a special translation by Cynan'. The main Dickens reading took on the following night at the Queen's Theatre, the last full day of the Eisteddfod, when the official English playbill announced two performances with separate programmes: a reading of *Bleak House*, followed by 'Scenes from Famous [Dickens] Novels'. The evening event was notable for a rather extraordinary incident (as reported in *The Times*, 10 August 1953), though whether it was rehearsed or spontaneous is difficult to be sure. During Williams's reading in English of passages from *A Tale of Two Cities*, he was interrupted by two little girls, dressed in traditional Welsh costume of red plaid skirt, white apron, shawl and bonnet, who mounted the stage and presented him with a copy of 'Y Ddawns Wagedd', Cynan's translation (which he had used the previous evening) of 'The Fancy Ball'. They solemnly removed the (English) red rose which Williams wore in his buttonhole in imitation of Dickens and substituted a (Welsh) daffodil. Seemingly more delighted than offended at the interruption, Williams then found his place in the Cynan translation and resumed his reading in Welsh. The incident almost certainly had political ramifications reflecting divisions at this time within the Eisteddfod Committee itself on imposition of an all-Welsh rule (meaning of course no English), which militant defenders of the language argued was the logical step for a festival dedicated to the celebration and upholding of Welsh. Yet equally it might be understood as a pointed comment on what some might have regarded as Williams's insensitivity in reading in English England's favourite novelist to a predominantly Welsh-speaking audience at Wales's most Welsh festival.

Williams's 'coming home', introduced to his eisteddfod audience somewhat inaccurately as '*y hogyn o Drelogan*' [the boy from Trelogan] (*Y Cymro*, 14 August 1953), was as double-edged as his leaving. On stage in Rhyl all the ambivalence and complexity of Williams's attitudes to Wales and the Welsh, to England and Englishness and above all to the two languages seemed to meet. The actor as returned exile reads Dickens's *Tale of Two Cities*, significantly a tale of exiles living between two cultures, and meets face to face his pre- lapsarian Welsh self. Whatever feelings he may have had he is an actor adept and professional enough to absorb them into the seamlessness of the performance. Williams was splendidly capable of doing what actors are supposed to be good at. He created *persona*. And Williams did render a good performance as a Welshman (Morgan Evans, Maddoc Thomas, Ambrose Ellis and Rob Davies are all Williams, each in different ways) just as he gave a good performance as an Englishman (the urbane Sir Robert Morton of Rattigan's *The Winslow Boy* or his favourite part as the demented aristocratic psychopath Lord Lebanon in *The Case of the Frightened Lady*). These examples, as with many others, are parts he came to believe in. Williams knew how to give his audiences exactly what they wanted. He adapted according to whether he was meant to be the cosmopolitan London actor-dramatist, or 'the boy from Trelogan'. But Williams was interested most of all in bridging the two cultures not dichotomising them, because (like his sexuality) his aspiration was to be at home in both. 'Coming home' for Williams meant sloughing off the Londoner and theatre professional in Emlyn Williams for a necessarily reinvented border identity as George Williams. In a late speech that was exactly how he imaged himself for a Flintshire audience in 1987 six months before his death:

> I settle into the train at Euston as <u>EMLYN WILLIAMS</u> in indelible ink: but by Chester, that ink has slowly faded, to become a name in faint pencil, while another name is taking its place, in ink just as indelible. The word <u>GEORGE</u>.

At home with his brother Job, who still lived at Hawarden, he is plain George 'and it is only at Euston that EMLYN turns up again – that sophisticated Londoner' (K1/14). That admission from one who was continually constructing and reconstructing self-images reinforce how much George Emlyn Williams truly was a border man on the frontiers of two existences and two self-contradictory identities. In the linguistic, cultural and sexual tensions thus created he found his authentic voice as a dramatist.

Series Afterword

The Border country is that region between England and Wales which is upland and lowland, both and neither. Centuries ago kings and barons fought over these Marches without their national allegiance ever being settled. It is beautiful, gentle, intriguing and often suprising. It displays majestic landscapes, which show a lot, and hide some more. People now walk it, poke into its cathedrals and bookshops, and fly over or hang-glide from its mountains, yet its mystery remains.

The subjects covered in the present series seem united by a particular kind of vision. Writers as diverse as Mary Webb, Dennis Potter and Thomas Traherne, painters and composers such as David Jones and Edward Elgar, and writers on the Welsh side such as Henry Vaughan and Arthur Machen, bear one imprint of the border woods, rivers, villages and hills. This vision is set in a special light, a cloudy, golden twilight so characteristic of the region. As you approach the border you feel it. Suddenly you are in that finally elusive terrain, looking from a bare height down onto a plain, or from the lower land up to a gap in the hills, and you want to explore it, maybe not to return.

There are more earthly aspects. From England the border meant romantic escape or colonial appropriation; from Wales it was roads to London, education or employment. Boundaries are necessarily political. Much is shared, yet different languages are spoken, in more than one sense. The series authors reflect the diversity of their subjects. They are specialists or academics; critics or biographers; poets or musicians themselves; or ordinary people with however an established reputation for writing imaginatively and directly about what moves them. They are of various ages, both sexes, Welsh and English, border people themselves or from further afield.

John Russel Stephens's earlier books already reveal his perceptive grasp of the foibles that permeate the theatre and its playwrights, and there must be few more fascinating topics in that area than the life and work of Emlyn Williams. He equals Somerset

Maugham's record of five plays on the London stage concurrently, but himself also starred in one of them; he illustrated his obsession with evil with a book about the Moors murders – which still preoccupy us – but speaks endearingly to us too through the extraordinary attachment to his early mentor Sarah Cooke, whose story pervades this account as it did Emlyn's life. Doubtless greasepaint and footlights were his real home, but he tried and tried to write a play for Wales, and more than once came close, as again Stephens's account indicates.

Abbreviations

MSS

For full details of items cited, see Bibliography. There are well over a thousand letters and a very large number of other papers and miscellaneous items in the Emlyn Williams collection at the National Library of Wales, Aberystwyth. The abbreviations below correspond to the scheduling of correspondence and other papers as listed in the catalogue of Emlyn Williams Papers. For convenience, letters in the text are referred to by date rather than the number assigned by NLW.

A   Letters, in Emlyn Williams Papers, National Library of Wales

C   Scrapbooks, in Emlyn Williams Papers, National Library of Wales

E   Talks and Speeches, in Emlyn Williams Papers, National Library of Wales

L   Notes for Autobiography, in Emlyn Williams Papers, National Library of Wales

K   Miscellaneous Speeches, in Emlyn Williams Papers, National Library of Wales

*

LCP   Lord Chamberlain's Papers and Correspondence, British Library

Published Works

CP   *The Collected Plays of Emlyn Williams* (1961)

E   *Emlyn: an early autobiography 1927-1935* (1973)

G   *George: an early autobiography [1905-1927]* (1961)

Bibliography

MSS sources

Emlyn Williams Papers (National Library of Wales, Aberystwyth, Ceridigion)
Letters of Emlyn Williams to Sarah Grace Cooke
Letters of Sarah Grace Cooke to Emlyn Williams
Letters of Emlyn Williams to Molly Williams
Miscellaneous letters from various correspondents to Emlyn Williams
Scrapbooks of Emlyn Williams
Typescripts of *Full Moon, Glamour, Pen Don* etc; definitive text of *Night Must Fall* (October 1986)
Speeches, including 'Yn ôl i gatre' [Coming Home] (Eisteddfod Genedlaethol Cymru, Rhyl, 1953)
Preliminary notes, letters, discarded sections, reviews etc for *George* and *Emlyn*

Lord Chamberlain's Papers and Correspondence (British Library, London)
Correspondence files on Emlyn Williams's plays
Licensing copies of Emlyn Williams's plays

Primary printed sources

The Collected Plays of Emlyn Williams. Volume One (London: Heinemann, 1961) [contains *Night Must Fall, He was Born Gay, The Corn is Green, The Light of Heart*]
George: an early autobiography (London: Hamish Hamilton, 1961)
Emlyn: an early autobiography 1927-1935, (a sequel to *George 1905-1927*) (London: Bodley Head, 1973)
Accolade: a play in six scenes (London: Heinemann, 1951)
Cuckoo: a play (London: Samuel French, 1986)
The Druid's Rest: a comedy in three acts (London: Heinemann, 1944)
The Late Christopher Bean, in *Famous Plays of 1933* (London: Victor Gollancz, 1933)
The Morning Star: a play in three acts (London: Heinemann, 1942)
A Murder has been Arranged: a ghost story in three acts (London: Samuel French Ltd, n.d)
Spring, 1600: a comedy (London: Heinemann, 1946)
Trespass: a ghost story in six scenes (London: Heinemann, 1947)
Vigil, in *The Second Book of One-Act Plays* (London: Heinemann, 1954)
The Wind of Heaven: a play in six scenes (London: Heinemann, 1945)

BIBLIOGRAPHY

Secondary sources

Agate, James, *Contemporary Theatre, 1926* (London: Chapman & Hall, 1927)

The Contemporary Theatre 1944 and 1945 (London: Harrap & Co, 1946)

Ego -7: even more of the autobiography of James Agate (London: Harrap & Co., 1945)

Ego -9: concluding the autobiography of James Agate (London: Harrap & Co., 1948)

First Nights (London: Nicholson and Watson, 1934)

More First Nights (London: Victor Gollancz, 1937)

Berry, David, *Wales and Cinema: the first hundred years.* (Cardiff: University of Wales Press, 1994)

Brown, Ivor, *Theatre 1955-6* (London: Max Reinhardt, 1956)

Carpenter, Humphrey, *OUDS: a centenary history of the Oxford University Dramatic Society 1885-1985* (Oxford: Oxford University Press, 1985)

Dale-Jones, Don, *Emlyn Williams* [Writers of Wales] (Cardiff: University of Wales Press, 1979)

Findlater, Richard, *Emlyn Williams: an illustrated study of his work* (London: Rockliff, 1956)

George, Siwsann, and Stuart Brown, comps., *Mabsant: casgliad o hoff ganeuon gwerin Cymru. A collection of popular Welsh folk songs* (Talybont, Ceredigion: Y Lolfa, 1991)

Gielgud, John, *Early Stages* (London: Macmillan, 1939)

Harding, James, *Emlyn Williams: a life* (London: Weidenfeld & Nicholson, 1993)

Hart, Olive Ely, *The Drama in Modern Wales: a brief history of Welsh playwriting from 1900 to the present day. A thesis* (Philadelphia: [privately published], 1928)

Hunt, Hugh, et alia, *The Revels History of Drama in English. Vol VII 1880 to the present day* (London: Methuen, 1978)

Johnston, John, *The Lord Chamberlain's Blue Pencil* (London: Hodder & Stoughton, 1990)

Lane, Margaret, *Edgar Wallace: the biography of a phenomenon* (London: Heinemann Ltd, [1939])

Lawrence, Freida, *Memoirs and Correspondence*, ed. E. W. Tedlock (London: Heinemann, 1961)

Low, Rachel, *The History of the British Film [1906-1929]*, [2 vols.] (London: Allen & Unwin, 1949, 1971)

Marshall, Norman, *The Other Theatre* (London: John Lehmann, 1947)

Osborne, John, *Almost a Gentleman: an autobiography. Vol. II 1955-1966* (London: Faber and Faber, 1991)

Owain, O. Llew, *Hanes y ddrama yng Nghymru* [A history of the drama in Wales] *1850-1943* (Liverpool: Cyngor yr Eisteddfod Genedlaethol, 1948)

Reynolds, Ernest, *Modern English Drama: a survey of the theatre from 1900* (London: Harrap & Co, 1950)

BIBLIOGRAPHY

Rowse, A. L., *A Cornishman at Oxford* (London: Jonathan Cape, 1965)

Short, Ernest, *Theatrical Cavalcade* (London: Eyre & Spottiswoode, 1942)

Thomas, M. Wynn, *Internal Difference: twentieth-century writing in Wales* (Cardiff: University of Wales Press, 1992)

Trewin, J. C., *Dramatists of Today* (London & New York: Staples Press, 1953)

The English Theatre (London: Elek, 1948)

A Play To-night (London: Elek, 1952)

Trewin, Wendy, and J. C., *The Arts Theatre, London 1927-1981* (London: Society for Theatre Research, 1986)

Waugh, Evelyn, *A Little Learning: the first volume of an autobiography* (London: Chapman & Hall, 1964)

Wearing, J. P., *The London Stage: a calendar of plays and players [1890-1959]* [14 vols] (Metuchen, N.J. & London: Scarecrow Press, 1980-1993)

Webster, Margaret, *The same only different: five generations of a great theatre family* (London: Victor Gollancz, 1969)

Periodicals

Cherwell, Daily Express, Daily Mail, Daily Mirror, Daily Sketch, Daily Telegraph, Daily News, Era, Evening Standard, Film Pictorial, Film Weekly, Financial Times, Glasgow Herald, Homes and Gardens, Illustrated London News, Isis, Listener, Liverpool Daily Post, Manchester Guardian, Mirror [New York], *Morning Post, News Chronicle, Observer, Oxford Outlook, Oxford University Review, Scotsman, South Wales Echo, South Wales Evening Post, Star, Theatre World, Time Out, To-day's Cinema, Sunday Times, The Times, Times Literary Supplement, TV Times, Western Mail, What's On, Y Cymro, Yorkshire Post*

Acknowledgements

In writing this book I have incurred debts of gratitude to the staffs of the National Library of Wales, Aberystwyth (especially Ceridwen Lloyd-Morgan and Lona Jones), the Manuscript Room of the British Library, the Royal Institution of South Wales, Swansea, and the Library of University of Wales Swansea. Amongst individuals to be thanked for help of various kinds are my colleagues Dr James A. Davies, Professor M. Wynn Thomas and Dr John Turner; and my father-in-law Mr I.T. Jones, who helped me locate some Welsh folk songs. I am also grateful to John Powell Ward for the invitation to write for the Border Lines series. He read my typescript with an eagle eye and suggested many detailed improvements, though naturally I am responsible for whatever errors remain. My greatest debt is to my wife Ann, who supported and encouraged me throughout and also translated where necessary from Welsh into English. I dedicate this book to my two children, who in speaking both the languages of Wales possess what Emlyn Williams referred to in his speech to the National Eisteddfod at Rhyl in 1953 as 'a valuable and free gift'.

Quotations from Emlyn Williams's letters and from other related MS. materials in the National Library of Wales are by kind permission of the Literary Executors and Trustees of the Emlyn Williams Estate; and those from *George* and *Emlyn* are by courtesy of Hamish Hamilton and The Bodley Head respectively. The Lord Chamberlain's papers, correspondence and licensed play scripts at the British Library are Crown copyright. Every effort has been made to obtain relevant copyright clearance. Photographs in the plate section are reproduced by permission of the National Library of Wales.

Index

About the Author

John Russell Stephens is a Senior Lecturer in English at University of Wales Swansea. His main interests are in theatre and drama and he has contributed to several works of reference, including the *Cambridge Guide to Theatre* (Cambridge, 1988, 1992, 1995) and the forthcoming *New Dictionary of National Biography* (Oxford). He is author of *The Censorship of English Drama 1824-1901* (Cambridge, 1980) and *The Profession of the Playwright* (Cambridge, 1992).

The Border Lines Series

Elizabeth Barrett Browning Barbara Dennis

Bruce Chatwin Nicholas Murray

W.H. Davies Lawrence Normand

The Dymock Poets Sean Street

Edward Elgar: Sacred Music John Allison

Margiad Evans: Ceridwen Lloyd-Morgan

Eric Gill & David Jones at Capel-y-Ffin Jonathan Miles

Gerard Manley Hopkins in Wales Norman White

A.E. Housman Keith Jebb

Herbert Howells Paul Spicer

Francis Kilvert David Lockwood

Arthur Machen Mark Valentine

Wilfred Owen Merryn Williams

Edith Pargeter: Ellis Peters Margaret Lewis

Dennis Potter Peter Stead

John Cowper Powys Herbert Williams

Philip Wilson Steer Ysanne Holt

Henry Vaughan Stevie Davies

Mary Webb Gladys Mary Coles

Samuel Sebastian Wesley Donald Hunt

Raymond Williams Tony Pinkney

Francis Brett Young Michael Hall